NIGHTSCAPE

DOUBLE FEATURE Nº1

The
Thousand-Eyed Fear

Derrick Ferguson and
David W. Edwards

The
Q for Damnation

Arlen M. Todd

IMPERIAD
ENTERTAINMENT

Portland, Oregon USA

Imperiad Entertainment
Portland, Oregon USA

The editor gratefully acknowledges the help of Sarah and Jean-Claude Marin in crafting the passages in French. Any mistakes, of course, are entirely those of the editor.

First Imperiad Entertainment trade paperback edition December 2016

For information about special discounts for bulk purchases, please contact Imperiad Entertainment at info@imperiad.com.

Cover art by Simon Fowler (www.cataract-operation.com)
Designed by Ryan Peinhardt

Printed in the United States of America
ISBN 978-0692787373

For more on the Nightscape universe, visit www.nightscapeseries.com.

The Tomb of Winged Devils

Nolin positioned himself on one side of the rock obstructing the underground tunnel and embraced it in a bear hug. The slab was ungainly large at the bottom and tapered to a wedge. Moving it a serious degree would take his utmost. He closed his eyes and pitched forward as if to surprise it. His thighs strained against the weight. The rock trembled in its groove then shifted and yawed toward the wall. Paul beamed his light into the uncovered top half of the passage.

"Like a giant outten the Ol Testament," Dixie whispered to Babette. She struggled to find her voice, astonished at Nolin's strength, until an oily-black something glinted in the light. Membranous wings flitted in and out of view. She muttered a French vulgarity and drew her weapon.

"Back! Put it back!" Paul yelled.

Nolin worried he'd already pushed the boulder past its tipping point. He felt the rock's momentum taking him with it. The muscles in his shoulders and arms bunched in agony. His heels started off the ground and he wrenched himself backward. The rock seesawed a bit—enough for a couple of pygmy-sized imps to pass through. Another scurried to do the same and was crushed between the settling rock and the tunnel's edge. Its oversized jaw spewed broken teeth and driblets of gum.

The creatures flapped to the limits of the domed ceiling, gleaming against the greater darkness like fresh tar. They scrabbled the air with sickle-shaped claws and long, thin tails. Paul waved his flashlight in a hectic effort to keep both creatures in view. The imps shrieked their displeasure at the stabbing brightness and stooped to attack, tucking their tails behind them.

From *The Thousand-Eyed Fear*

Other Works in the Nightscape Series

Main Series Books
Cynopolis
The Dreams of Devils
Early Darkness

Double Feature Books
No. 1: The Thousand-Eyed Fear | The Q for Damnation

Short Fiction
Spawn of Cloud & Sword

Comic Books
Entombed .

Plays
The Barren Cross

Films
Nightscape (or, Road without End)

Albums
Project Nightscape, *To Sin Against Our Mercies*

NIGHTSCAPE DOUBLE FEATURE NO. 1

The
Thousand-Eyed Fear

Derrick Ferguson and
David W. Edwards

Contents

"Is there a logic of history? Is there, beyond all the casual and incalculable elements of the separate events, something that we may call a metaphysical structure of historic humanity, something that is essentially independent of the outward forms—social, spiritual and political—which we see so clearly?"

Oswald Spengler, *The Decline of the West*

Chapter 1
The Moving Fortresses

28 November 1917
Outside Cambrai, France

The German A7V tanks rolled over the British defensive fortifications, mechanized landslides indifferent to the screams of the dying under their treads. The vanguard of *sturmpanzerwagen* numbered a dozen strong and was spread out enough to prevent easy targeting. Geysers of wet earth havocked the air around the armored vehicles as exhausted British gunners scrambled to find their range.

Since the beginning of the battle eight days ago, the British had managed a series of hard-won victories, pushing the Germans back from Havrincourt and crossing the Hindenburg Line. The British had then commandeered and fortified the trenches dug by their enemies. The Germans, stung by their humiliating eviction, had launched this sweeping tank assault.

Tanks were a relatively new addition to the battlefield. The British had first made use of its Mark I tanks at the Battle of Flers-Courcelette about two years ago. Although those early models had been slow moving and given to frequent breakdowns, leaders on both sides were quick to recognize the strategic advantages of the concept. Design advances in the interim had borne out their expectations. British Mark IV tanks had made surprisingly short work of the formidable defenses here at Cambrai, driving the enemy into a frenzy. The Germans had retaliated by deploying their own tanks in a desperate but disciplined bid to outflank and outmaneuver their foes. The British had met them straight-on in the southwest corner of the wood, determined to bully the Germans into submission with their larger, more heavily armored vehicles.

Both strategies had proved hideously effective in racking up the dead.

British howitzers zeroed in and began taking their toll on the iron behemoths. One shell struck a tank squarely in the side. The force of the explosion kicked it over. Frantic voices leaked from the hull. The soldiers bottled up inside clawed at each other to escape the rush of flames. None did. The fuel and ammunition sparked and burst, leaving a smoking crater nearly a hundred feet in diameter. Charred remains scattered piecemeal over the entrenched British. Most of the defending soldiers ignored the gore. They'd seen much worse, here and elsewhere.

Several, however, broke ranks, scrambling away, screaming for God, their mothers, *anybody*, to save them. They splashed through the black, calf-deep trench water.

Staff Sergeant Quincy McNeil cursed and shouted, "Hold the bloody line by damn! Come back! That's a direct order!"

The soldiers pretended not to hear. They continued their mad flight, tripping and stumbling over the bodies of their dead comrades. McNeil pointed his revolver at the nearest retreating back.

A strong hand pushed his arm down. McNeil choked back his anger when he realized his immediate superior, Captain William Davenport, had been the one to intervene. The captain thrust his chest forward and said, "The hell, Staff?"

"They're deserting, sir!"

"And you'd waste precious ammo shooting them in the arse? Best save your ammo for the coming infantry! Look, man!" He waved toward the line of implacable A7Vs without risking a look above the parapet. "Those tanks are holding their positions! They know they've got us pinned with their machine guns!"

McNeil cursed again, wishing he knew how to swear in more than one language. This was a situation where cursing in the Queen's English alone struck him as woefully inadequate.

Following that first tank hit, the remaining German tanks retreated just out of artillery range and, from positions of relative safety, raked the trenches with lethal gunfire. Any British soldier foolish enough to make a run for safety was cut down within a pitiful few yards.

To McNeil's mind, it was a just punishment. "Why the hell wasn't our artillery brought up to support this position, sir?"

The captain raised his voice in order to be heard over the yelling, gunfire and fitful explosions. "Because our esteemed Colonel Breen is more concerned about securing his command post. I sent word days ago for at least two dozen tanks. It was clear the Germans were going to make a push to retake this position."

"Well, of course they were, sir!" McNeil said. His broad face was hectic with color and beaded in sweat. He hefted a perisher or trench periscope above the sandbags to survey the field. His small mouth twisted into a rictus of horror. "Blast and damn!"

"What is it, Staff?"

Lowering the perisher, McNeil said, "Infantry, sir. Those Huns are bringing up mortars, getting them in position, storm troops with machine guns and flamethrowers right behind them. Another five-ten minutes and we'll be overrun." He sleeved sweat from his low forehead.

"Maybe those scarpers figured the odds right, eh, Staff?"

"No better way to die than up against it, sir. Six generations of Mc-Neils have served in Her Majesty's army and I'll be damned before I turn."

Davenport grinned and clapped his staff sergeant on the shoulder. "You're a good man, McNeil. I'll be sure to put you in for promotion when we're drafted into God's army."

"Can't we pull back, sir?"

"To where? It's a hundred yards to the next line and the way those tanks are firing, every man jack of us will be plugged straightaway." Davenport checked his revolver to make sure it was fully loaded. His face was naturally pale so he couldn't be accused of blanching in the face of duty. He had chipped plaster cheeks and a crooked nose with large black nostrils. A prim school teacher sort. "Afraid there's nothing for it but to go down faces front and the Lord's Prayer on our lips." He brought his weapon chest-high and opened his mouth to order a suicidal charge over the bags.

McNeil caught the captain's elbow.

Davenport frowned. "What, Staff?"

McNeil cocked his head like a foxhound on point. "Something's coming, sir... planes, yeah."

"Then they must be Richthofen's. His damned squadron owns the skies over Cambrai."

McNeil pointed and said, "Well, there's some of our flyboys don't know that, sir!"

Davenport trembled at the sight of three gunmetal gray Bristol Fighters streaking out from behind the clouds. The two-seater bi-planes were fast, agile and deadly effective.

"My sweet Lord," Davenport murmured. "They must be either total madmen or the luckiest fliers alive. How the bloody hell did they get past Richthofen?"

The two men watched the planes pass over the array of tanks and German infantry beyond. A few Germans took potshots at the planes but it was an empty gesture. None of the rounds came anywhere near the screaming fighters. The planes were famously powered by Rolls Royce Falcon engines. The British marooned in the trenches relaxed their trigger fingers and allowed a measure of hope.

The Bristol Fighters broke formation and peeled off in divergent loops to join again over the enemy. The first plane opened up with its forward Vickers machine gun, strafing the infantry. A swath of Germans convulsed under the unforgiving barrage. Blood misted the air. Those on their feet after the initial salvo weren't upright for long. The gunner engaged the rear-facing Lewis: *vip-vip-vip*. Hot lead ripped into flesh and shattered bone. The dead and wounded turned the mud carmine.

The second plane went pell-mell for the tanks. As it zoomed in low, the gunner didn't use his Lewis; instead, he tossed stubby, tear-shaped bombs. The plane came in so fast the gunner had time to drop only two. But his aim was spot on. Both struck home in successive flashes. The

British broke into cautious cheers. The remaining tanks started back into the trees but were unable to get the necessary speed to avoid the plane's second pass. Two more A7Vs were blasted to trifling scrap.

The third Bristol Fighter circled high above the mayhem, presumably on the lookout for enemy fighters. The German air ace Baron von Richthofen and his squadron of ravening killers had driven off the Royal Flying Corps days ago. If McNeil had told Davenport this morning that three British planes would come to his aid by afternoon, he would have thought the man barmy.

The cowed Germans scattered and ran for safety. Soldiers weighed down with flamethrowers abandoned their weapons to speed their retreat. The first Bristol Fighter dived at the fleeing men like a hawk stooping after choice field mice. The Vickers roared bullets. The rounds perforated a couple of discarded petrol tanks. Eight men disappeared in the ensuing fireballs so quickly they had no chance to scream or cry for relief. One took a full ten steps mantled in flames before finally, mercifully, collapsing.

The last of the tank crews abandoned their vehicles, clambering from their hatches to join the mass withdrawal. The second Bristol Fighter hurried them along with bursts of strafing fire and a couple of precision-thrown bombs. Another pair of tanks went up in plumes of fire.

The British, astonished and reassured, cheered with more and more confidence. Some isolated groups even assayed a celebratory song. And why not? A few short minutes ago they'd faced certain destruction and now here they stood, alive, wonderfully alive. Perhaps they would die tomorrow or the day after, but for now it was enough to live amid the receding battlenoise.

The Bristol Fighters formed up and came in for a joint landing on the denuded plot between the forward and support trenches. Captain Davenport and Staff Sergeant McNeil climbed up to full sunlight. Once the stout McNeil caught his breath, he gave out orders to his men: "Remain where you are and see to the wounded. The Captain and I will have a word with the lads, yeah. You'll have plenty of time to thank em. Just hold your positions and keep your eyes peeled."

The pilots and gunners shimmied out of the cockpits, flushed from the heat of their weapons. Davenport noted they hadn't gone unchallenged. There were constellations of bullet holes across the wings and fuselages. The planes carried seven men in total. "The extra man must have crammed in with one of the gunners, Captain," McNeil grunted. "Ballsy bastards."

The lead pilot removed his leather aviator's cap and goggles to reveal black hair trimmed to military standards and light blue eyes made small from effort. He was a wiry six foot three and moved with an easy, vigorous stride. He acknowledged Davenport with a smart salute. "Lieutenant Quigg reporting, sir."

Davenport returned the salute while trying to hide his shock at the pilot's youth. Despite his size, Quigg looked scarcely old enough to have graduated Sixth Form. "At ease, son. Which squadron are you with?"

"Begging the captain's pardon, sir, you would be...?"

McNeil jumped forward, his face darkening. "Cheeky little bugger! The captain was killing Huns before you was breeched and you—"

The captain placed a stern hand on McNeil's shoulder. "That'll do, Staff. It's well to be reminded of protocol now and again, and he's more than earned the right." He turned to Quigg and said, "Captain Davenport, Third Army, Eighth Eastern Division. And this fellow with the Chesterfield manners is Staff Sergeant McNeil."

The staff sergeant barely registered his name. "Blast and damn!" McNeil blurted, staring at the pilot's team. Now that they also had removed their caps and goggles one thing was clear: they were as young, if not younger, than their squad leader. "I got tinned meats older'n these lads."

"Lads that fight and fly like men," Davenport said. "Lieutenant, I take it you were looking for us?"

"Aye, sir. You should've received orders to assist my squad on a matter of great urgency." He spoke in a firm but cordial Irish brogue.

Davenport was instantly impressed with the lieutenant's demeanor. The youth didn't so much as wrinkle his nose at the pervasive reek of piss and shit and rotting death. He might be a boy, but he had the self-possession of a canny old sweat. "I'm not aware of any such orders. But we've been out of touch with HQ for some time. Your arrival was just the hammer. I thought Richthofen had the air war decided."

Quigg's disconcertingly blue eyes shadowed over. "We left Duxford with a three plane escort but ran across the enemy some thirty miles west. Our escorts—they..." He shook his head then, recovering his voice, quoted from a popular Irish poem, "Our skies have many a new gold star."

"Amen, son." Davenport grimaced at the sentiment. He was inured to the larger carnage by necessity, but individual deaths still had the power to evoke raw emotions. The war hadn't bled the feeling out of him yet. He started to lead the way to his command dugout. "Come along then. We'll contact HQ and get this sorted." He gave the pilot a sidelong glance. There was something familiar about the lieutenant's name. Hold on, he thought. He recalled a *Daily Herald* story from a year or so past about an Irish lad with peculiar qualities nicknamed Strong-boy...The realization forced a grin. "You wouldn't happen to be...?"

"Aye, sir. That I am." The pilot worked his jaw to suppress a shy smile. "Lieutenant Nolin Quigg of the Fifth Royal Irish Lancers. And these," he said, gesturing to the youths flanking him on either side, "are the so-called Lost Boys." He met the captain's eye with a sobering look. "At the risk of sounding immodest, sir, we're here to end this ruddy war."

Chapter 2
The Dreamer Sleeps at Last

Circa 1351
Yuriev Monastery
Novgorod the Great, Russia

Although hieromonk Mixail had gone without sleep for days (how many, exactly, he couldn't say), he continued to dream. It seemed as if the waking dreams would never end and he was glad of that prospect. He had come to live into the promise of his dreams as he had once lived into the promise of God. His dreams, in fact, were of a new god— mercurial, amorphous and visceral at once. At least he hoped it was a god. It would be a grave disappointment to have given up his soul and sanity for less.

He would gladly have suffered the dream-god's chastisement to settle this uncertainty. If you must, he thought, say as Jesus Christ did to St. Thomas on the eighth day of the Resurrection: *Because thou hast seen me, Thomas, thou hast believed; blessed are they that have not seen, and have believed.* He wanted only to know the god's presence: its word, its will, its law. Because he had witnessed miracles that violated the Holy Spirit. He had felt the heat of heresies come alive. He had known the dark between the stars.

Mixail stepped over fresh bloodpuddles as he made his way back to the library. He had been compelled to leave it and the final, unfinished pages of his manuscript to retrieve more ink from his quarters. His dagger had tasted blood three times running this errand.

All of his brother monks had degenerated into bestial dreamshapes. They stirred about, driven by blind instinct or vestigial habit, pursuing the swimmy visions in their heads. Mixail believed these terrible changes were the consequence of fighting the dreams. At first, he'd considered the dreams a tolerable misfortune but now they were as much a part of him as the air he breathed. His fellow monks apparently struggled with separating dream from reality. The two overlapped like thin sheets of vellum held crosswise to the sun. The trick, Mixhail found, was to regard the dreams as gauzy projections from a *lanterne vivre*. It was the only way he could discharge his new duties.

The dream-plague was Brother Rampeuse's fault. Rampeuse was a math-obsessed hieromonk and former *Imyaslavtsy* (Name-glorifier) trained at Mt. Athos. He'd dedicated himself to discovering a new system of geometry capable of penetrating the black mysteries of the infinite. Mixail wasn't an overly-educated man. He'd been a modest farmer and goatherd when he lost his wife and daughter to the *mor zol* (evil plague). The loss had sent him on a dispiriting journey of nearly two years that ended at the monastery But he'd heard enough from Rampeuse about the geometric elegance at the center of the universe to grasp the dangers inherent in his fellow monk's abstractions. Somehow, Rampeuse's mathematical pursuits, combined with his radical spiritualism—intended to divine the one true name of God—had unleashed the dream-god and its terrible doubling of reality.

Hearing a lumbering stride ahead, Mixail hid in the shadow of an alcove. One of the transfigured brothers hove into view, legs like a stone colossus, gibbering in unrelieved sorrow. Mixail breathed into his unclean robe to keep from choking on the vile odor, dagger at the ready. What had once been the monk's hands were now scaled nubs, yellowish and oozing a clear pus.

Mixail waited for the abomination to round a corner before continuing to the library. The occasional shriek of agony or wail of despair assailed him from behind closed doors. These sounds of suffering moved him to pray, and because he knew of no appeal his new god might accept, Mixail recited the Jesus prayer Rampeuse had taught him: *Gospodi Iisuse Khriste, Syne Bozhe, pomiluj mja, greshnago* (Lord Jesus Christ, Son of God, have mercy on me, the sinner). He repeated it meditatively, breathing in while calling to the dream-god and breathing out while seeking its mercy.

Just inside the door to the library lay the naked bodies of Brother Jonero and Brother Vidas locked in an obscene embrace. Mixail bolted the great wooden door behind him and stepped over the hideously mutated forms without another glance. One look had more than satisfied his curiosity. Brother Jonero's formerly mahogany skin was the mottled green-black of alligator hide and Brother Vidas was covered in bestial fur. The textures mingled in disquieting patterns Mixail was afraid to trace.

He hurried through the cavernous library that occupied almost the entire east wing of the monastery. Shelves running from floor to ceiling teemed with volumes written or transcribed by generations of Yuriev monks over the last three hundred-odd years, many, if not most, filled with recent manuscripts cataloging the manifold names of God.

In the center of the library was the scriptorium, a semi-circular space appointed with a dozen desks of oak and wrought iron. Mixail took up a seat at a centermost desk, unstoppered his bottle of iron gall ink, and breathed an uneasy sigh. Almost immediately, the dreams in his head resolved into images sharper, more vivid and tangible, than any reality he had ever known. Images he now had to translate into words fit for common understanding. Words that made plain Rampeuse's sacred geometry, revealed the essential symmetries of existence and correlated the worlds of the seen and the unseen.

He dipped his reed pen into the ink and began to set down his dreams on the smoothed calfskin parchment. He wrote in the Latin of Ovid as fast as his pen and dexterity permitted. There was a formulaic economy to the language. It consisted largely of nouns, adjectives and verbs. He dispensed with prepositions, conjunctions and particles; subordinated conjunctions to after the beginning of their associated clauses; separated adjectives from nouns—all at a frenzied tempo. The dreams suggested he had little time. The concepts he translated now were not meant to be contemplated for long. At least not by a human intelligence. Mixail worked into the small hours of the night. He did not eat. He did not sleep. Once he heard a shuffling something that sobbed like a baby. It was a distant noise then a breath on his neck and nothing, gone. He voided his bladder where he sat. He was indifferent to the stink. He alternated between states of hysteria, laughing then weeping into his chest.

The new god lurked behind his mind's eye, watching, waiting... for what, exactly, Mixail had no idea. He was resigned to merely sensing its presence, worried that putting questions to it or doubting its purpose would prompt it to forsake him. It's possible Rampeuse would have known how to discern the dream-god's motives. But Rampeuse was no more. He had departed this earthly plane—willingly—to join with the dream-god body and soul. Their merger had resulted in a prolonged headache of mathematical gibberish. That feeling had passed after a day or so, superseded by patchwork visions of sublime horror.

Mixail's fingers cramped and stiffened into claws but he couldn't stop writing. Just as the wind might fill and change the shape of a tower from the inside, the dream-god fleshed him out. When morning broke at last, the manuscript was complete. He didn't dare wonder what the new god needed or wanted from it. The volume would—

Mixail jerked upright at a cold and lasting thought... His delirious labors were over. The dream-god had vanished. Or more accurately, withdrawn to a higher realm, leaving only an acute sense of absence behind. Like a blindspot in his brain.

He placed his sore and swollen fingers in his mouth and sucked on them. It helped bring saliva back into his mouth and ease the pain. All he had to do now was bind the stack of parchment and arrange for the manuscript's preservation. He would have to carry out these tasks posthaste. Sanity was gradually returning, and with it, the mounting urge to hang himself.

Chapter 3
Seasons of Fear

28 November 1917
Outside Cambrai, France

Nolin Quigg had to give the Germans credit for knowing how to design and build fortifications. The dugout was not only well-ventilated but reinforced with concrete and solid spruce beams. There was even room for him to stand upright. He'd been forced to crouch in lesser dugouts for hours at a time.

Captain Davenport sat himself in a camp chair, grateful to be out of the trenches and off his feet. He waved for Nolin and his squaddies to crowd around. "Staff, we need to reach Colonel Breen and now. Send two, no, three runners. Brief them fully on the situation with Lieutenant Quigg here. They're to get through to the Colonel no matter what and return with definite orders on how to proceed. They're also to reiterate my request for tank support. Make sure they're explicit on this point: we can't hold this position without those land creepers. Otherwise, we'll have no choice but to retreat the next time the Huns launch a serious offensive. Clear?"

"Crystal, sir."

"Off with you then. And come back straightaway you've done that."

"Captain Davenport, sir?" Nolin interposed himself between the captain and the staff sergeant. "May I ask a favor?"

"What is it, Lieutenant?"

"Could the sergeant see to it our planes are covered over? There's camouflage netting in the compartment between the cockpits."

"Of course. Staff?"

McNeil confirmed the order with a curt nod, miffed at the notion of taking direction from Nolin, then set off.

"Coffee, Lieutenant?" Davenport asked, indicating a wood stove in the corner. "I can't vouch for the quality but at least it's hot."

"Lemme take care a that, Cap'n," offered one of the only two Lost Boys with stubble on his cheeks and chin. "You and the Lieutenant got a lot to jaw-jack bout." He finger combed neck-length hair as he walked to the stove then picked up the blackened coffee pot and shook it.

"American, are you?" Davenport asked.

"Yessir. Born 'n' bred in the hills a Tennessee."

"You're a long way from home, son."

The young man winked and said, "Got a sleight for waywardness. They don't call us the Lost Boys for nuthin." He waggled a hand at the plank shelves adjacent to the stove. "Where c'n I find the coffee?"

"There's a stack of small tins on the top shelf there—to the left in the white paper sleeves. It's what the French stock in their reserve packs. Godawful ersatz coffee tablets, I'm afraid. One should do."

"That's Private John Hodge," Nolin said by way of introduction. "We call him Dixie—not after the cooking pot, mind." He then proceeded to acquaint the captain with the rest of his squad, starting with a fire-plug of a Dutchman by the name of Eric Cedarstrom. "He's my demolition expert. I wouldn't advise messing with his haversack."

Eric gave the captain a lazy salute. Despite his stocky build, his hands were slim verging on the feminine.

Nolin gripped the shoulder of the thin black youth to his left. "My sniper, Private Joseph Jenkins," Nolin said.

The private doffed his souvenir *hechtgrau* cap in Davenport's direction. His mischievous grin couldn't help but compel the captain to return it.

"Do not let smile fool, Captain," said a squaddie of Japanese descent. He leaned forward in a camp chair. Small eyes in a wide face gave him an abstracted, backcountry look. He came from a long line of fisher-folk—turtle-backed and mutely defiant before the vagaries of nature. "He big time rifle. Prince Joey kill, *anð*, more all us together. But I try catch up, honor emperor." He stopped running an oiled rag over his carbine long enough to give a short bow. "Private Katsuo Fukai, sir. *Dozo yoroshiku.*"

Nolin turned to the dark-haired youth to his right. He was the shortest of the group and the most intense. His gray, deep-set eyes were fixed on Davenport as if to divine the captain's innermost thoughts. His curly hair was cut in a close Roman style. "Sergeant Lucca Nicastro, my second-in-command," Nolin said. Unlike the others, the sergeant didn't salute, bow, nod or otherwise acknowledge his introduction.

The final member of the Lost Boys lurched forward and extended a hand as if to compensate for Lucca's disregard. At a gangly six and a half feet tall, he had to stoop to keep from cracking his head on the ceiling. Receptive blue eyes flashed from behind horn-rimmed glasses. "Pleased to meet you, Captain," he said with a soft Irish lilt. "Corporal Paul Weygand."

"Paul's my auxiliary brain," Nolin said. "On civvy street he was buck-ing to be a first-rate mechanical engineer. If there's a machine he can't figure, repair or improve then it hasn't been invented yet." He con-sidered his squad with unconcealed pride. "Believe me, sir, this is one steady go up gang."

"You've no need to convince me on that score, Lieutenant, flying in like bats out of hell..."

The staff sergeant returned in a fresh sweat. He brushed through the Lost Boys to stand before the captain and give a clipped salute. "The runners are off, sir. They estimate three hours roundtrip, God willing."

"Very good," the captain said. "We were just getting to the lads' mission."

"So that's what it's come to, yeah? Us depending on this motley lot of beer boys—"

"See here, Staff. I won't have you insulting—"

Nolin held up a hand. "It's quite alright, Captain. I think Staff Sergeant McNeil's just having a poke at us to see if we'll jump. I bet he was just getting around to calling me a dirty Mick."

McNeil threw back his head and guffawed. "Sure an you're okay, Lieutenant. You want to swing on me, I won't kick."

There was a shocked silence at McNeil's proposal. It was clear he had no idea who Nolin was—a mystery of science and self-discipline, not yet mature in his special talents, but already a potential type—something historic. To a man, the Lost Boys imagined the staff sergeant laid up in the hospital in various attitudes. "That's a certain ticket," Paul said to himself.

Nolin held out his hand for McNeil. "It was all in fun, right?" The staff sergeant didn't hesitate to shake, though it put his yellowing teeth on edge.

"Now that we've dispensed with the pleasantries, Lieutenant…?"

"Of course, sir. Intelligence says there's a weapons research base in this region, likely underground. The base houses a prototype tank codenamed *Kettenblitz*. According to our spy, this prototype combines the best of our Mark IV and the German A7V. It's well-nigh impregnable and outfitted with a .75 caliber cannonade. Like a land-based *Dreadnought*."

"The devil you say," McNeil muttered.

"If I faced the devil in his den, Staff Sergeant, I'd say the same." Nolin shot him a grim look. "Word has it the weapon will be operational any time now. After today's flare up, I don't need to tell you what will happen if the Huns get it in the field."

"Coffee's up, anybody innerested," Dixie announced. He handed out canteen cups of the hot liquid. The men forgave the bitter taste, grateful for the opportunity to warm their hands and insides. The coffee brought the impromptu briefing to a halt for several minutes. Prince Joey took advantage of the break to determine how well his sniper rifle had traveled. Dixie and Eric resumed their long-running game of Crown and Anchor over a camp chair. Eric always kept the special dice and felt playing surface on his person. The others drank their coffee and worried after their mission. Time was fast running out. McNeil made a double time trip to the forward trench and returned, wisps of hair ruffled, to report no enemy movement.

"Plot next move," Katsuo offered.

"They've only one, Private," Davenport said, "and that's to roll right over us with everything they've got, including this bloody... *Katzenblitz* of yours."

Lucca almost choked on his coffee at the captain's mispronunciation. *Katzenblitz* meant 'cat attack.' "*Kettenblitz*—'chain lighting.'" When he saw Davenport's reddened face, he added a perfunctory "sir."

The captain said, "Lieutenant, what's so special about Cambrai the Huns would set up here?"

"We don't know exactly but we have a damn good hypothesis," Nolin said. He gestured at Paul with his cup. "You want to walk the captain through it?"

The lanky youth stepped forward and adjusted his glasses higher on his nose, a bit unnerved at the prospect of detailing his theory to the captain. It had been met with derisive laughter from the top brass. He ran a hand through his flyaway hair, cleared his throat and said, "It's this way, Captain: Sometime around the start of thee-uh thee-uh French Revolution, pockets of unrest erupted across the country. Peasants took up arms and, for no apparent reason, attacked the local gentry or in some cases even those in neighboring villages. Thee-uh the rationales for these assaults remain vague to this day. But records from the time agree on one thing: The peasants were seized by an unreasoning fear that they, thee-uh themselves, would soon be under siege. They considered their rampages preemptive strikes."

"Was it a food shortage?" Davenport asked. "That was a leading cause of the revolution, after all."

"I wish it were that simple, but no; in fact, many of those gripped with this irrational fear burned their own crops and slaughtered their own stock. They preferred to destroy their livelihoods rather than allow some invisible enemy to do it. Thee-uh these incidents spread until almost the entirety of France was swept up in violence."

Paul removed his glasses and wiped a distracting smudge from the right lens with his shirt cuff. Though he stammered from a surfeit of thoughts rather than nervousness, it was embarrassing all the same. "Thee-uh these weren't organized revolts with political aims, either. In most cases, the peasantry regarded their taxes as fair enough, ate relatively well, harbored no serious grievances with the government…"

"But you said this was at the start of the French Revolution," McNeil said. "Mebbe it was just a warm-up for the main action." His voice was laced with sarcasm.

Paul went on with his argument for the sake of completeness though he had the feeling it was already lost. "Ah, but the Revolution had distinct political goals. Thee-uh thee-uh motive force in this instance was this irrational fear of attack—mass hysteria, which in earlier, less sophisticated times, was associated with witchcraft and malingering." Paul replaced his glasses on his nose. "It lasted for only three months or thee-uh thereabouts before petering out. Except here."

"Here? You mean Cambrai?"

Paul nodded. "Every nineteen years like clockwork the people of Cambrai fall victim to this fear-plague. Ever wonder why it's such a heavily fortified town?"

"Now that you mention it … ," Davenport said.

Paul ticked off the years on his fingers: "1808, 1827, 1846 on up to the latest wave—1903. June to August in each of those years has seen a return of this monomania and still, none can pinpoint its origin or why it comes on." He tried a scholarly angle. "Thee-uh the ancient Greeks would've called it a form of Dionysian madness—intoxicating and transient. It invites people to lose themselves in a larger whole. Like music and dancing—sometimes dismissed as folk-diseases—only more psychologically damaging. Aristotle theorized that most crimes and other bad actions could be traced to an imbalance between desire and reason, desire in this case, meaning fear. Perhaps his—"

McNeil, visibly impatient with all this gabble said, "So what are you saying? What's this silly-sallie theory of yours have to do with the supertank?"

"What it suggests is that thee-uh this research facility might have existed long before the war—to investigate the fear-plague—and further, that this entire war may be a terrible extension of it. Think about it: no one claims responsibility for this conflict. There are plenty of official factors, naturally thee-uh the assassination of the archduke, various obligating alliances, growing militarism, imperial ambitions, et cetera, et cetera, but to me thee-uh thee-uh simplest is this: a mass hysteria that set those mutual alliances tumbling like the interior mechanism of a lock. *Non vi, sed mente.*"

McNeil looked first at his superior officer then at Paul in disbelief. "And you expect us to buy this *Boy's Own* yarn?" No doubt he was one of those presumptuous boors who see themselves as brave realists.

Nolin's voice was as calm as McNeil's was strident. "I assure you of our seriousness. Paul, Lucca and I... well, we have a certain expertise in these matters."

"And those matters would be what, xactly?"

"Let's just say, arcane phenomena beyond your ken."

"I believe we've heard enough, eh, Staff?" Davenport said, rising from his seat. He gave Nolin a hard look. "We owe you our lives, son, I grant you... But I'm a God-fearing Anglican. I won't brook any talk of the supernatural outside His powers to control. There's no good Christian purpose in it. You're welcome to get some shut-eye here while I wait for Colonel Breen's orders. If you've a legitimate cause, we'll take it up; if not, I expect you'll be on your way."

"Aye, sir," Nolin said.

The Lost Boys cleared a path for Davenport. The captain's face was gaunt with disappointment. He marched from the dugout, followed by a smug McNeil.

"*Sto cazzo!*" Lucca snorted as soon as their hosts were out of hearing range. "I told you there's no use trying to enlighten these know-nothings."

"Softly, Mouse, softly," Nolin said as he held out his cup for a refill. "Davenport seems trustworthy. I thought he deserved an explanation." Dixie obliged with more coffee. Nolin had a much easier time downing the bitter liquid than the rest of his men. The childhood training regime that had rendered him immune to all but the most virulent poisons had, at the same time, blunted his sense of taste.

"I'm with Mouse on this one," Eric said. His amphibious features gave him a chronically dour look. He had thick, bulging eyelids and a mouth turned down like a chub's. "We have worries enough without aggravating the man in charge." He crossed to the opening of the dugout and brushed a hand against his cheek stubble. "Be dark in another two-three hours. What say we strike out on our own, to hell with waiting on those duckboard harriers? We know the orders."

"Question is: you know this country? Cause this Brooklyn boy sure as hell don't." Prince Joey sat with his MI903 Springfield rifle in his lap. Saying that he ate, slept and went to the latrine with his weapon was no exaggeration. The gun's stock was imprinted on his dimpled right cheek like a scar. "We gotta have a guide or a damn good map. Or we gon fall in a trench full a Huns."

"Prince J's right," Nolin said. "We can't negotiate this part of the country without the captain's help, especially at night. If we're forced to try it, that's something else, but for now, let's wait on the runners. No harm in catching a few winks."

"Too smell to sleep," Katsuo said, wrinkling his nose. "*Yare yare.*"

The squad understood his meaning. Trenches were home to all manner of nauseating odors: bilge water, unwashed bodies, feces, trench foot and other fungal infections, the sweet decay of rats and human flesh. To breathe in this mix was a terrible intimacy. It wasn't uncommon for newly-arrived troops to vomit at the first bracing whiff.

"Wrap a scarf round your face," Dixie suggested. "Works for me. Course yours ain't been perfumigated by one a them Parisian beauties." Dixie was always going on about girls of high polish none of them had ever seen.

The Lost Boys made themselves as comfortable as their makeshift accommodations permitted. A couple of louse-ridden cots against a timbered wall led to a minor squabble among the privates. But it was soon settled by a few rounds of Rochambeau. Dixie and Katsuo walked away with the cots (paper over rock in the last round), and the others, grumbling for show more than out of any real emotion, resigned themselves to woolen blankets on the plank floor.

Nolin took Paul and Lucca aside. "You lads go on and get some shut-eye too. I'll cover first shift and tap you in a couple of hours, Paul."

"We should work up a plan in case we have to go it alone," Lucca said. "Those damned *Crucchi* could come back at us at any time. Whether we get the word from Davenport or not, we have to be ready to go up the line."

"I know," Nolin said. "If you'd like, give me this shift to weigh the options and I'll wake you first instead."

Paul gave Lucca's shoulder a friendly shake. "Besides, I'm s'posed to be thee-uh the one to worry."

"More like the one who runs off at the mouth—through his hat."

"What're you going on about? I was the very model of restraint. Didn't even mention thee-hu, thee-uh aurora over Germany cited in Virgil's first Georgick or thee-uh—"

"See? You're like a yarn ball of nonsense."

"Mouse," Nolin sighed. "It was my decision and the longer you stand there fuming, the less sack time you'll get."

"Not to mention keepin the rest of us awake," Prince Joey said.

Lucca felt the argument had been settled from the get-go. Nolin and Paul had grown up together. How was he ever supposed to get a fair shake?

Paul shot Lucca a knowing look and quoted from *Peter Pan*: "So come with me where dreams are born and time is never planned. Just think of happy things and—something something—in Never Never Land."

"Ever think that's exactly where the *Crucchi* want to put us?" Lucca asked.

Paul arranged his woolen blankets on the floor. "You're free to think up a new squad name come your watch." He was liable to drop out momentarily. The tension inherent in his mental life wore him down to the point he could nap under almost any conditions.

Eric chimed in: "If it means a mess-tin of proof spirit for inspiration, I will do it."

"The Dublin papers gave us the bloody name, blowing the whole orphans of war ruse," Nolin said. "No need to be loud about it."

"With that kind of cheering on, no wonder we had a revolution," Lucca said, retiring to a corner of the dugout. He pulled a tattered Pall Mall copy of *Dr. Nikola's Experiment* from his haversack and settled against the wall, knees drawn toward his chest. A tin of dubbin on the map table served as a candle. Lucca squinted to make out the book's print in the eerie green light. *When, nowadays, I look back upon the period I spent in Nikoka's company, one significant fact always strikes me…* The title character was a Venice-born master of deduction, science and the occult. Lucca was drawn to the anti-hero's courage to make a destiny for himself. The doctor allowed his talents to lead, not worrying about the boggle of human interests.

Nolin let the Italian-American runaway brood. Sometimes, Lucca just needed a little time with his books to regain his composure. Nolin smiled to himself at Lucca's outspokenness. The sixteen year old was shrewd, imaginative and unafraid to do the dirty work the squad occasionally required. He was also the stealthiest soldier Nolan had ever seen. Lucca used his circus training in acrobatics and escape artistry to full advantage in the field. He could monkey down a twenty-meter ash tree onto an unsuspecting foe and take out an enemy agent with garroting wire as silently as a spider scissoring its immobilized prey.

Too restless yet to engage in the serene force exercises that conditioned his reflexes and sense of focus, Nolin crossed to the dugout opening. The hazy sky was like a frosted glass setting for the westering sun. Without a view of the blasted topside, the scene was almost tranquil. Something his mother Fianna often said came to mind: *Find moments of peace whenever and wherever you can.* This counsel had seemed trivial during his sometimes painful growing up when he'd been subjected to rigorous physical and mental training. But it had come to sustain him more and more during his time at war. The conflict was disorientating all the way around. The difficult emotions it prompted begged detachment. He had to remind himself occasionally that this earth was its own gift and to experience it was a privilege.

The memory of leaving home against his mother's wishes still pained him. He'd rationalized his decision as one in keeping with his late father's ideals; however, he'd joined the Fifth Royal Irish Lancers for his own reasons, most notably, to put his abilities to the test in a historic cause. While he had no interest in worldly fame, he considered the idea of hiding his talents while other, lesser men suffered, humiliating. He worried humanity was on the brink of a crucial flashpoint, and whatever it might be—a revelation or a harrowing—he was determined to try for progress. Even at the risk of exposing himself to his father's old enemies, or more accurately, enemies of his father's mentor, Captain Nemo. What choice did he have? The war was where the action was, where the course of mass man and perhaps, the soul of democracy would be decided.

He reached inside his sheepskin aviator's jacket for his writing paper and O'Donnell fountain pen. He would write his mother a letter assuring her of his safety and abiding love. His family began and ended with her now, and she pined for him, he knew, like a fading hope. The longer he was at war, the more dangerous his missions, the less likely a reunion seemed. He tried to picture the two of them on a stroll through the forested grounds of his family's Kilkeel estate, talking, joking, laughing, as if he'd merely been away at university. The picture refused to come together. He was too preoccupied with the here and now, with the powers and mysteries attending this conflict. The mission was off to an inauspicious start and he recognized that, despite Paul's clever suppositions, the real threat to their cause had yet to be revealed.

Chapter 4

Things Seen and Unseen

3 April 1899
Aachen, Germany

Black clouds swifted over Germany's westernmost town, Aachen, and released an angry deluge. The rain came down with such force that it blurred the vision and stung the skin. The downpour soon cleared the cobblestone streets and squares of pedestrians. Once the place where the Kings of Germany were coronated, the town was now known mainly for the technical institute RWTH Aachen University. The school was distinguished by its breakthrough research in the fields of chemistry, electricity, mechanical engineering and, less publicly, in what might be termed 'spiritual science.'

The university's esteemed professor of physics, Wilhelm Wien, observed the storm through one of the four huge windows in his den. Situated on the gentle crest of a hill, his manor house normally afforded an expansive view of the town. He could see nothing at present, however, except storm-roiled blackness and the rain slurring on the glass. The weather mirrored Wien's mood. He'd cancelled his scheduled lectures and appointments for the last three days, too anxious to do much but wait on the return of his field operative, Mr. Gumm. Not even the research for his paper on the electromagnetic basis for mechanics held his attention for long.

Wien had waited nearly six months for evidence either for or against his latest hypothesis regarding blackbody radiation. He expected the answer at any moment. The wait dated back to his secret consultation with Dr. Karl Fairongu at the College of Technology in Vienna. He'd arranged for the eccentric Dr. Fairongu to build the spectroscopic devices needed to test his theory and then hired Gumm to deploy them. Wien understood there would be grave dangers involved in field testing the devices. Getting a reliable reading at some sites presented serious physical hazards—crossing remote snowscapes, negotiating unstable mountain passes, trekking through pathless forests. Others entailed trespassing, destroying property, and maybe, if discovered by agents of rival interests, murder. The professor was no man of action. He had no illusions on that score. So he'd directed his aged manservant, Mayfair, a veteran of mid-century campaigns in the Cape Colony and British India, to find a suitable field operative. Mayfair had returned in short order with an imposing but surprisingly dignified Englishman, Boris Gumm.

The introductory interview confirmed the astuteness of Mayfair's choice. Gumm was over six feet tall and wolfish in aspect. His short black hair stuck up like an animal pelt brushed the wrong direction. Dark amber eyes looked out from under brows as thick as his mustache. The box pleats on his tweed Norfolk jacket were ended and inverted to allow for his powerful build. Even at ease on the den's central divan with a brandy in his hand, Gumm radiated the energy of two men. "Mayfair says you need some risky work done," he said without preamble. "Bit of traveling involved."

"Yes, the job will require visiting twenty-three separate sites throughout western Europe. I've identified the exact coordinates for each. There can be no deviation from these coordinates, regardless of any obstacles—topographical or otherwise."

"And what would I be doing at each site?"

"Operating a scientific instrument called a radio spectrometer. It's been designed for ease-of-use, but you would need to recalibrate it at each site."

"Yes, *sicher.*" Gumm took a draught of brandy. "But as the expert, why not do it yourself?"

"Some of the sites on my list are bound to pose... difficulties that go beyond the locales themselves. I'm out to prove or disprove a theory that could change not only our understanding of the physical universe, but Man's relation to God. I must needs be honest on this point: you are bound to encounter other interested parties—scientific and religious—out to steal or suppress the data you'd be collecting."

"You mean secret societies?"

Wien nodded.

"La Société Voudon Gnostique, the Palladistes, the Hermetic Order of the Golden Dawn, the Society of the Black Sun...I've had little truck with their like but that doesn't mean they're unknown to me. The circles we travel have sometimes overlapped. I can't be frighted by folktales and rumor." He gave the doctor a sharp look. "What would you have me do if I encounter these...rivals?"

For the first time, Wien looked uncomfortable. He toyed with the brandy snifter between his hands. "Whatever you see fit. I don't care to know the details. This complication doesn't..."

Gumm leaned forward and fixed the professor with narrowed eyes. He gave off an aroma of horse sweat and brisk winter air. "*Viel Feind, viel Ehr* (The greater the danger, the greater the honor)." His German was better than passing fair. He downed the remainder of his brandy. "This device, tell me more. What does it do?"

"Have you any scientific training, Mr. Gumm?"

"None but what I've gleaned in the course of my adventures."

"Well, my investigations likely go beyond what you've come across. Not to imply you're unintelligent or incapable of grasping—"

Gumm waved the doctor's concerns away. "Not at all, not at all. It's just that in my line of work, I don't have the privilege of dealing with many well-educated men. My employers aren't usually your sort, if you take my meaning."

Wein regarded Gumm with new eyes. "You're more refined than I expected, sir."

"Given your status at university and the nature of this job, I'm prepared to be on a level with you, doctor. Boris Gumm is an assumed name. I come from a once-prominent family. Sadly, father rather liked gambling and drink more than was good for him. Or us—his family. He died owing large sums to various business partners and creditors. Mother ran off with a Prussian banker and my older sisters immigrated to America. I changed my name to hide my disgrace and joined Her Majesty's army. I served over ten years, most of those in an elite unit, and then went into the soldiering business for myself." Gumm smiled and held up his empty glass. "A decision I've never regretted."

Wein rose to summon Mayfair with a bell pull hidden by a tapestry ribbon. "I appreciate your openness Mr. Gumm. I had my own father troubles after a fashion. When he took ill, I was compelled to delay my university studies for several years in order to manage his land. Not quite so permanent a change, but…" He thought to say more on the topic then decided against it. "My research concerns a peculiar type of electromagnetic radiation. It's my intention to prove the existence of this radiation and more importantly, to discover its mysterious source."

Mayfair entered the den and Wein gestured to the empty glasses. "I call this phenomenon blackbody radiation. It has a unique and continuous frequency signature which only my radio spectrometer can detect. This device represents a singular means of penetrating the invisible world around us and measuring its hidden influences."

Mayfair finished freshening up the drinks and took his leave. Gumm had the politeness to hold his breathy laughter until the servant had gone. "You sound like you're talking ghosts, man!"

Dr. Wein shrugged. "No, not ghosts. That would actually be a relief. No, I suspect something else—something with far more destructive power."

That interview had taken place some three months ago, and shortly thereafter, Gumm had departed for the Netherlands. The Englishman had sent periodic updates on his progress. Wien had received the last such letter—postmarked Bruges—twelve days ago. The letter indicated Gumm was on his way to the first of three French locales and gave his anticipated return date as 31 March. When Gumm didn't show, Wien was seized by a fitful paralysis. His mood pendulumed between black despair and chary optimism. He paced the den in a gray, unbuttoned morning coat and matching trousers. Events appeared to have spun out of control. He might never know what happened to Gumm, or more importantly, to the spectroscopic gauntlet he'd designed. His anxiety refused to let up.

An urgent knock made his heart skitter. "Yes, come in."

Mayfair opened the door but remained in the hall. He was a servant out of livery. His jacket was something a game keeper would wear. "Quickly, sir. It's him."

Wein fell in behind Mayfair. The manservant led him downstairs at a troubling pace. "I've no idea how long he's been here, sir. Mrs. Lavery heard a scratching or bumping at the scullery door and asked me to investigate. And there was Mr. Gumm sprawled on the back steps, chilled and wet. I lugged him into the kitchen and then called for you."

"Why didn't he come to the front door, I wonder?" Wein muttered. "You don't suppose he was followed?"

"Do you want me to check the grounds, sir?"

"Help me with him first. We'll get him to bed then arm ourselves."

When they reached the kitchen, they found the head cook, Mrs. Lavery, leaning over Gumm, wringing her apron in silent distress. Gumm was flat on his back, one chalk-white hand across his forehead, the other tucked into his hunting jacket.

"*Heidewitzka!*" Wein dropped to a knee next to him. "Gumm. Gumm, can you hear me?"

Gumm's eyelids fluttered open. Some of the life had gone out of his eyes. "Professor...," he wheezed. "Got here... soonest." He smiled weakly at his own dark humor before lapsing into a daze.

Wein gestured for Mayfair to take Gumm's head and shoulders while he took up the man's feet, and together, they hustled Gumm into a spare room. As they lay Gumm on the bed, his left arm swung free of his jacket. Wien gasped.

Gumm's exposed forearm was encased in the gauntlet spectrometer of studded leather and brass. The device consisted of a central instrument for measuring magnetic field strength and two smaller, adjoining meters for gauging amplitude and frequency. The hand poking from the gauntlet was red and swollen. Mayfair regarded it with dismay. "Sir?"

Wein waved him off. "Food, dry clothes and yes, brandy. *Beeil dich.*" Turning to Gumm, he asked, "How much pain are you in?"

Gumm stirred, eyes half-open. "Pain? The arm's... bout paralyzed." He strained to raise the gauntlet.

Wien came to his aid and placed the gauntlet across Gumm's chest. "In a moment, *mein freund.*" He hurried into the adjacent office and returned with a brass sphere roughly the size of a human head. The sphere was topped by a large circular gauge. Three electronic leads trailed from an indented section of the device. Wien placed the sphere on the bed next to Gumm and began to attach its leads to the underside of the gauntlet. Gumm's ashen face pointed up the blood price of the doctor's investigations. The man trembled into unconsciousness. Wien felt for Gumm's pulse at the neck and was relieved to find it, however irregular. That was enough. The doctor couldn't bring himself to stop his preparations. The studs that encircled the elbow-end of the gauntlet glowed a headachy blue. The sphere emitted a low crackle.

Wien put a hand on the device to feel its energizing hum. Did the needle waver? He bent over the main gauge. The hairs on the nape of his neck stirred with static electricity. The needle gave a little bounce, flatlined then jumped to its uppermost limit. *Donnerwetter!* It was undeniable. The device worked, it actually *worked*. The hum oscillating through him was like a song in his heart. Now the earth's secrets were as good as his. Now he would know the unseen light behind the world.

Boris Gumm woke the following morning in a well-appointed bedroom. The room's mix of handpainted wood and Persian rugs reminded him of his early growing up days—when his familiy was still together and happy in their ignorance. He sat up in the spindled French bed. His left arm was bandaged from the elbow down and the swelling in his hand had lessened. His knee-length nightshirt gathered up around his thighs as he straightened his back. His stomach grumbled something fierce. He was about to lay the covers aside when there was a gentle knock at the door. Without waiting for a response, Dr. Wien poked his head in. "Good, you're up, yes." The doctor swept into the room dressed in a single-breasted morning jacket. "Feeling better?"

"A bit rummy but with a decent cut of steak and a good stiff drink I'll be on the mend." He ran a hand along the uneven growth of beard along his jaw.

"Is that a common English breakfast?" Wien asked, looking toward the open door. Mrs. Lavery entered the room bearing a pushcart loaded with covered trays. She parked the cart at the edge of the bed and began lifting covers. "I'd say not, doctor," she answered for Gumm. "But this will do, no doubt." She shifted her gaze to the field operative. "Plenty of cold meats and cheeses, soft-boiled eggs, these crusty rolls here, Brötchen, to be eaten with marmalade or honey as you like. And to drink, goat's milk, apple juice and—"

Gumm was quick to reach for the brandy decanter on the far corner of the cart.

The head cook gave his hand a gentle slap. "Tut-tut, Mr. Gumm. This is a fine German repast and you'll eat every bite first, I'll be bound. Once that's done you can drink yourself dizzy for all the care a'me! Now, let me fix these trays and we'll get some food into you."

Wein stood back, grinning widely. "Best do as she says, Mr. Gumm. I'll be back shortly."

Gumm scarcely acknowledged the doctor's exit. He was more mouth than mind at the moment. He bent to his food with alacrity, using utensils only when admonished by the cook. She reminded him in her country English that manners were as important in the fields as at the Queen's tea. The cold cuts proved to be first-rate, especially the sausages.

He was into his first generous glass of brandy when Wien returned with several rolled-up maps tucked under his arms. Mrs. Lavery took that as her cue to leave and, with the exception of the brandy, rolled the pushcart and its contents away. "*Sehr gut, danke,*" Gumm said to her departing figure.

The doctor spread the maps on a square mahogany table Mayfair had manhandled into the room during the night. He secured the corners of the maps with silver chess pieces. "Are you fit enough to…?"

"Oh, yes, of course," Gumm pronounced. But when his feet hit the floor, the aches accrued by nearly six days of foot travel came back to him.

"Allow me," the doctor said. He helped Gumm for several paces to the table and into an armchair of tufted velvet. As shaky as he was, however, Gumm held fast to his brandy. He belted back another two fingers' worth. "Good God, did I need that."

"You had me worried, Mr. Gumm—before and after your arrival."

"It was a rough business all round, doctor." He gestured for the decanter left on the nightstand. Wien obliged him. "This is just the medicine, *danke schön*," Gumm said.

"What can you tell me about your journey? Where did you meet with success?"

"Was it then?"

"Absolutely," Wien said. His eyes gleamed with open pride. "A thousand times yes."

"I'm glad for you, doctor, I am. But I can't help feeling—I know—there must be…" He shook his head. "There's more to this than your science can explain." He poured another brandy then, rethinking it, doubled the amount.

"How so?"

"I'm, well, I got the first indications in Ireland." His eyes roved over the maps until he found what he was looking for and pointed. "There—outside of Kilderry—the fifth site on the list. It was two-three days before I found a willing guide."

"The conditions…?"

"It has a history. It's known as a place for criminals and madmen, atrocities of all sorts—thieving, rape, suicide, murder, what-have-you. A few days before I arrived, a newcomer to the area—a charwoman—got lost there and died in the night, supposedly out of sheer fright." He tossed back his drink. "Fortunately, your gold pieces were persuasive enough to secure the guide."

"So what happened?"

"Nothing. Not a blessed thing. I adjusted the gauntlet as instructed and waited. The needles barely moved. A weak signal? False read? No bloody idea. But the legend of the place—that's the important part."

"From there, you went to Scotland, yes?"

Gumm nodded, tracing his route on the closest map with a finger. "I followed the list in a roundabout way: Isle of Man, England, Spain to the heel of Italy, Austria, Poland, Germany, Belgium and then, well, I had to detour through Great Britain."

"Rival interests?"

"I guess I attracted their attention in Poggiorsini, a small Italian village that goes back to the first crusades. There's a farm there open to weary travelers. I suspect the proprietor tipped them to me." Gumm leaned back in his chair.

"Tipped whom?"

"Never knew for sure. Some sodding witch cult or other. They wore animal masks of different sorts. I found these carved-horn trinkets— amulets?—on one of the bodies, beads, feathers, other trumpery. They pursued me through the Apennines and into Austria. I thought I'd lost them at one point outside of Trento, but... I don't know. It could've been another group that picked me up in Günzburg. After that..." He broke off, unwilling to revisit his haywire memories. "But you said you didn't want the details."

Wien looked put out. His broad forehead creased in irritation. "I didn't mean—"

"No, you're right not to. They don't matter now. I'm here and alive." He set his glass on the table. "I worried about losing the gauntlet so I kept it on day and night. It grew to weigh on me—the thought of it."

"I didn't find any logs on your person."

"I sure as hell wasn't going to let those daft bastards get their hands on them." Gumm put a finger to his temple. "Don't worry. I memorized each and every reading."

Wien could hardly contain himself for want of details. "I trust you did, Mr. Gumm. But your last letter indicated little to no activity through Belgium. Following your detour, did you make it to France?"

"I completed the list, yes, though not without difficulties. Starting in Liège, I was compelled to make my way on foot, using the Meuse River to my advantage." Gumm scowled. "Actually, I couldn't walk for a day, almost two. I managed a bloody slow crawl. My muscles cramped on me. Poison, I figure. Nothing overt." He remembered feeling his blood thicken, the anxious heartbeats between pulls across the cold dirt. He'd never been so alone and vulnerable. "I take it the pages of their witch-bible were toxic, absorbed by the skin. I noticed too late all of the bastards wore gloves. Couldn't even read the damn thing—some kind of cipher. Destroyed it in the river soon as I was up to it."

The doctor felt a pang of regret at the loss, but didn't let it show on his face. "When Mayfair found you at the backdoor, I worried you might have been followed. We searched the grounds but found nothing out of the ordinary."

"No, I lost them for certain. I made damn sure of that. Wasn't about to spend the rest of my days in a sleepless funk. They would've hunted me down to my origins."

"It was France then—where you found the signal?"

Gumm's eyes darted over the maps. He tilted his head to match the skew of the one he was looking for. "Yes, here," he said, tapping the spot. "Near the town of Cambrai."

"We must go at once."

"We? No, my friend, not me."

"If it's a matter of payment—"

"You misunderstand. It would put my soul at risk. Never gave it much credence before, frankly, but this place... It prompts such feelings." He had approached the town on the verge of dusk, wary for reasons other than the witch cult, making his way through the woods instead of taking the road. Near the town walls he found a dying bat he'd initially mistaken for something edible like a water vole or marmot. The bat snuffled in distress. Its nasal folds oozed blood. The bat was commonly believed to be a witch's familiar. He should've known then he would never escape them. "There was an atmosphere of apprehension over the town I've sensed before only in battle. You hold yourself in a constant state of readiness, expecting the bombs to fall or the shooting to start at any moment. Your nerves tighten, you clench and unclench your fists... But this—this was supposedly a peaceful hamlet.

"The coordinates weren't far from the Escault River. I donned your gauntlet, made the adjustments and waited. For a short time, I felt relaxed—the darkening sky, the gentle trill of the river... Ever since I was a boy I've loved the outdoors, the water. The river ran black, a gully of reflected stars. Then my calm was shattered at once..." He fell silent and gazed into his empty glass.

"The witch cult again?"

Gumm shook his head, eyes downcast. "Fear—everlasting fear. The emotion paralyzed me almost as much as the poison did later." A tremulous quality crept into his voice. "I've been scared before, of course. Any soldier who says he's never had the shakes is either a liar or a fool. But this was different: pure, undiluted fear. It shook me to the pith of my soul. I could do nothing but drop to my knees." Gumm had come to believe that every wild place had a defining sound, an undertone. The undertone there was squallish—all tension and disruption. His breath stopped short with the memory.

He gathered himself and went on: "Then your damnable gauntlet went about its mischief. The needles jerked to and fro and my arm raised itself of its own accord as if the gauntlet had been magnetized. My fingers stretched out toward the night sky without me willing it." Gumm turned his head slightly so he could look Wein directly in the eyes. "And by God there *was* something there..."

"What?" The intervening silence was a torment. The doctor never imagined the source could manifest on a physical level. Maybe it was a case of what Dr. Freud called conversion hysteria—a psychological condition that produced physical symptoms. "*What?*"

"I don't know. An energy? A spiritual force? I have no qualms in saying it was too much for my poor brain to hold. I could hear myself raving in a language I didn't know. The voice was both my own and strange. I made sounds the human throat was never made to utter. This sound filled me up until I had no more words of my own. And then... I don't know. I must have blacked out. I woke the following morning with a terrible thirst, drained." Gumm thrust his bandaged arm across the table. "To my horror, I also discovered your gauntlet had fused to my skin. No amount of force could dislodge it. How did you...?"

"Once I siphoned its collected energy, it came off easily. I apologize for any undue alarm you suffered."

Gumm shrugged off the apology. "You explained the risks as you knew them. Where is it now? The gauntlet *and* the sphere?"

"My study—just a few doors down."

"A shame you didn't destroy them."

Wien was taken aback by the vehemence in Gumm's voice. "Whatever for? It's essential for my researches. Without it, I could never prove the existence of blackbody radiation, much less discover its source."

Grumm wobbled to his feet, steadying himself against the table. "But what if the source was no simple quality of nature? What if you knew it to be... intelligent?" He snatched up the decanter and seemed about to pour another shot when he reversed his grip on the crystal and smashed its base against the doctor's forehead. Blood and brandy spattered his nightshirt. The doctor collapsed to the floor and twitched his last, eyes open but unseeing. Grumm tottered to the window, satisfied in the knowledge that he had spared the doctor the exquisite tortures he'd endured at the hands of La Fratellanza di Bestie—days in a drugged stupor, alternating between needling pains and numbing herbal balms. The fateful lunacy of the Cambrai incident had destroyed his former certainties. The undertone was an insistent reality now, a pressure that only the cultists' wild religion could possibly relieve. He knew his ailment—his curse?—was beyond the help of science. It was a sickness of the soul. Even the doctor's fine brandy couldn't dull the sense that the rawest parts of him were exposed to open air.

He would hobble upstairs to the den and draw the curtains across its expanse of windows. That was the agreed-upon signal for the animal-headed cultists hiding in the woods to advance on the manor. But first, for reasons he couldn't fully explain, he would return the chess pieces scattered across the table to their proper positions on the board.

Chapter 5
Welcome to the Suicide Club

29 *November 1917*
Outside Cambrai, France

Nolin awoke several heartbeats before Lucca's hand touched his shoulder. One of the many tutors his father had engaged for him was The Immortal Broz. The Tibetan had taught Nolin to develop what accomplished mystics and martial artists call a 'proximity sense.' On most occasions, nobody could approach Nolin without alerting him—even while asleep. But Nolin didn't sit up right away. He continued to feign sleep until Lucca gently shook his shoulder then made a show of waking up.

Lucca grinned at Nolin's pretended surprise. The lieutenant routinely hid the full extent of his abilities where strangers might notice. Nolin sat up and asked, "What is it?"

"One of the captain's runners is ready to brief you."

"Just the one?"

Lucca nodded. His eyes were dark from more than fatigue.

Nolin jumped to his feet. The other Lost Boys were starting to yawn awake and work out the stiffness in their backs and limbs. Lucca left Nolin to escort the captain and his men inside. By the quality of the slanted light outside the dugout, Nolin figured it was just a few minutes shy of dawn. The soldiers in the trenches were doubtless climbing onto their firesteps in preparation for the ritual exchange of gunfire known as the 'morning hate.'

Captain Davenport, Staff Sergeant McNeil and the runner, a corporal encrusted in mud, took seats at the table. "This is Corporal Hitch-cock," Davenport said without preliminaries. "He's one of the three I sent to confirm your bona fides with Colonel Breen."

Nolin gathered the other runners had failed to return.

"My condolences, sir."

"Not necessary but appreciated. It appears Colonel Breen had orders concerning you that he somehow never passed on." Though his face was tight with forced calm, his voice trembled. Nolin suspected Colonel Breen's superiors would soon receive a detailed report on the matter.

Davenport continued: "I'm to provide you and your squad with all due assistance to get you into Cambrai. If you make it back, I'm to provide an escort for your report to the colonel. All of this, of course, assumes we're alive when your business is done. Indications are the Germans plan to make a bold push in the next day or two. And we've plans of our own that have implications for your mission—for both good and ill. But I'll get into that shortly." He motioned the runner closer while keeping his eyes on Nolin. "There was a coded message included in the orders the Colonel received from MII. Hitchcock was instructed to relay it only to you, personally." Davenport turned to Hitchcock. "Go on, lad, then you can rest up."

The corporal swallowed the jink in his throat. "I hope you can understand it, sir. I don't know the language. I had to guess at how to say it from the spelling. Here goes," he said and swallowed again. "*Cenhadaeth cod Arwan…gwariadwy sgwad.* That make sense?"

Nolin glanced to ensure Paul was out of earshot. He was the only other squad member who understood Welsh. To his relief, Paul was busy feeding the wood stove. "*Gwariadwy* with a 'gw,' right?"

"Yes, sir."

Nolin smiled with his mouth but not with his eyes. "Splendid job, corporal." He was determined to resist the message's grim meaning. He cared too much for his men to dwell on it. They'd volunteered for this mission, no questions asked. Because of him. They deserved better.

Davenport added, "Yes, splendid, lad. Go on. You've more than earned a rest." To McNeil, he said, "Get Bascomb and Hartley in here on the double."

"Right, sir." McNeil departed on his errand, leading the corporal out.

"These men know the region as well as any eagle owl," Davenport said. "You'll need their help in getting to Cambrai, starting in the trenches. Trying to go overland is asking for a bullet. Too risky. Look here ..." Davenport beckoned for Nolin and his men to examine the map spread out on the table.

"These trenches we took from the Germans are extensive. They go all the way to the west here where they end at a bridge crossing. We're fortifying our position there now. But here's your best shot, I think. To the right, the trenches stop at the edge of a forest. If I were you, I'd use that forest for cover to get into the town proper." Davenport looked up at Nolin. "It won't be easy, to say the least. There's a ridge between the forest and the town walls. No cover whatever. Bald as an egg. You'll have to cross it best you can but I'm betting the Germans will have a gun emplacement there to greet you."

"One thing at a time ... sir," Nolin said with feeling. "Let's get there before we start worrying about what's waiting for us".

"We can help you out by laying down artillery fire," McNeil suggested. "A heavy three and a bit minutes might be enough for you to get from the forest to the walls, yeah."

Katsuo asked, "Why go daylight? Night travel big time safer."

Davenport shook his head. "I've got men stationed throughout the trenches from here to the forest. You try navigating them at night and you're liable to get shot before you've had a chance to identify yourself. I suggest you push through the trenches during the day then wait for nightfall." Davenport's face darkened as he continued: "And if that wasn't challenge enough, here's the kicker: there's going to be a major offensive during your operation. Thirty tanks are coming up to make sure we can hold this position. These tanks, along with some heavy caliber artillery, are supposed to shell the town about where you'll be. I'm speaking of the big guns, not what you've seen here so far. I'm afraid it's going to get chancy."

"Are you serious?" Eric asked in a voice full of vinegar. "We have to get past the German army and into the city, infiltrate the base, destroy this *Kettenblitz* and get back out, all while our own troops are shelling the hell out of the area? *Geen centje pijn.*"

Prince Joey slapped him on the back. "What's a matter, buddy? War ain't the party you thought it was?"

Eric gave him a withering look. "Just one day with fair odds and a shot of Damrak at the end of it, that is all I ask."

"Keep dreamin big…"

"Shame we're not on bank holiday," Nolin said. "Give the map a proper study now. Mission security prevents us from taking it along." He started to walk away from the table when Davenport intercepted him.

"Don't you want a look-see yourself?" Davenport asked.

"After my men," Nolin fibbed. He'd already committed the map to memory. He was well-versed in various mnemonic techniques and other memory tricks. His father used to play a game with him in which he would randomly call out a book title and page number. Nolin was expected to recite one or more lines from the selected page. If he succeeded then he was allowed to spend a day as he wished, which usually involved riding his prized Arabian stallion, Aldebaran. But if he failed then that meant a day of sparring against his close combat instructor or a coterie of wild animals.

McNeil re-entered the dugout along with two soldiers, both of whom snapped to and saluted.

"At ease," Davenport said. "Lieutenant Quigg, Privates Bascomb and Hartley. Privates, you'll be under the lieutenant's command while you guide the squad through the trenches." Davenport turned to Nolin. "Will you need them after that?"

"I don't expect so."

Bascomb looked at Nolin with something akin to wonderment. "Lieutenant Quigg? Blimey!" He saluted again. "Sure an it'll be a pleasure to be servin with you, sir!"

"There's one thing I'd like to see, if you please, Lieutenant," McNeil said. He produced a scrap of tank metal from behind his back. "We've heard the stories about why they call you Strongboy. Would you mind?" He gave a devilish smile.

Davenport snapped, "Staff, the lieutenant isn't some circus sideshow."

"That's quite alright, Captain," Nolin said, not wholly disguising his annoyance. He accepted the fragment and hefted it in one hand. It was about the size of a dinner plate and as thick as his thumb. He frowned at the prospect of bending it. The Lost Boys grinned widely. They'd seen variations on this act before.

"German, I take it?"

"I don't mean to embarrass you," McNeil said. "But you know, you hear the stories and think…"

Without preamble or even much effort, Nolin crumpled the scrap into a ball and returned it to McNeil. "You'll let me know if you need a pair, right?"

The staff sergeant looked on in heated disbelief.

Davenport burst out with a contagious belly laugh. Wiping away tears of mirth, he said, "Staff, you'd best get with Corporal Nicastro to co-ordinate the timing of the bombardment."

"Yes, sir." McNeil was glad for the excuse to turn away.

"We move out in ten," Nolin informed the squad.

As the Lost Boys gathered their supplies, Nolin offered his hand to Davenport. "Thank you for everything, sir. I'm grateful."

"God bless you, son," Davenport said, a bit wary of Nolin's grip. "You and your lads do your best to come back."

"I *am* a Royal Irish Lancer, sir." Nolin said with feeling. He sized up Bascomb and Hartley at a glance. "You two on point with me. Paul, right behind, then Dixie, Eric, Katsuo and Lucca. Prince J, you take the flank, gun ready. Let's move with purpose."

Davenport and McNeil watched them go, trepidation in their hearts. "Think they'll make it?" the captain asked.

McNeil regarded the hunk of metal in his hand. "Either way, the lad's one for the next *Britannica*."

Although the trench was wide enough for the Lost Boys to walk side by side, they advanced single file in case of attack. The mud sucked at their boots and spattered their worn-out uniforms. Corpses dissolving in the slime revealed themselves as random limbs and shreds of clothing. The men tried not to imagine the last moments of these anonymous dead, how they suffered, wounded and drowning in the muck, the world above unknowing. At least a fresh streak of creosol dulled the stench.

Eric shied from a gray, protruding hand. "This is no trench. It is— what you say?—a catacomb."

Lucca shook the loose-skinned ring finger. "*Buon pomeriggio.*"

"The silent type," Prince Joey said.

"Good match for our nattering Paul then, thee-uh thee-uh."

"E'en he can do better'n a Hun," Dixie said.

"Hold it down back there," Nolin chided. He turned his attention back to what Bascomb had been saying about the trenches.

"One of the first things we discovered when we took em over was the Jerries dig a lot farther down than us. Can you believe we found what looked like an officer's club? Barracks? Even a barber shop?"

Nolin slowed the line as he approached a blind turn where the trench veered toward their destination. "Hence, the regular patrols—to uncover any hidden dugouts."

Bascomb nodded. "Every once in a while we'll come across three or four of the buggers and—"

They rounded the corner to find a British officer and a half-dozen soldiers crowding the passage. The soldiers immediately readied their weapons. The Lost Boys responded in kind. The officer's sleeves bore the rank insignia of a lieutenant.

"Identify yourselves," the lieutenant said with gruff authority.

Before Bascomb or Hartley could reply, Nolin stepped forward and saluted. "Staff Sergeant Damrak, Third Army Eighth Eastern Division. We're heading out to various listening posts, sir."

The Lost Boys said nothing and held their ground, trusting Nolin had good reason to misrepresent himself. Bascomb and Hartley followed their lead.

The lieutenant gave Nolin a derisive once-over. "Awfully young for a staff sergeant."

"Field promotion, sir. We've taken heavy losses these past few weeks."

The lieutenant remained aloof. He reached into a bag slung around his shoulders and pulled out a timeworn map. "You can prove yourself then by pointing out our positions and briefing me on your losses." He beckoned for Nolin to approach.

Nolin drew nearer. As soon as the lieutenant bent to the map, Nolin shoulder-charged him and shouted, "They're Huns, lads! It's an ambush!"

Chapter 6
The Gauntlet

Excepting Prince Joey, the Lost Boys charged past their stunned guides and into the fray. Prince Joey raised his Springfield with practiced alacrity, targeted an imposter lunging at Nolin from the left, and fired. The bullet creased the German's neck, tumbling the man into the ever-present mud. Prince Joey was sure his mentor, one of the New York Police Department's first Negro officers, would've been coolly impressed.

Nolin lifted the fake lieutenant by the collar with his left hand and drove his right fist into the man's jaw with stunning force. "Resist the urge to kill him," Nolin said, tossing the dazed German to Bascomb and Hartley. "We'll need some answers after this." He turned back to the scrum of arms and elbows. Curses in several languages issued from the scuffle. "Chivvy along, lads," Nolin said. "This is no time to have a wrestle. There could be more in the area."

Lucca hoisted himself on the shoulders of one German to boot another smack in the face. "They're so good at pretending… If only they'd lie down and play dead." He followed the kick by spinning around and dropping on the prone man's chest knees-first. His victim gave a pneumatic wheeze and went limp.

Paul leapt onto his chosen man's head and shoulders as if on the top of a pine tree. The German toppled backward into the mud with Paul straddling his chest. Paul quickly pinned the soldier's arms with his bony knees. "*Eho dum!*" he yelled and pulled his helmet off by the chin strap to crack the German's skull, rendering him unconscious.

Lucca bent to retrieve a dropped enemy weapon. "*Eho dum?*"

"What? I'm just trying to class things up a bit." Paul scrambled to his feet to find the other Germans had been likewise dispatched.

"No trouble," Eric said mock-seriously and spouted a Dutch insult that sounded like gargled glass.

"Prob'ly better with gunfire mixed in," Dixie said.

Hartley was in open-mouthed awe. "How—you—you—"

"We ain't all bluff and jokes, cousin," Dixie said. "But the jokes—they're good, yeah?" He motioned for Katsuo to lend a hand trussing up the prisoners with hanks of rope.

"How did you know they weren't real Brits?" Bascomb asked.

Nolin pointed to the groggy lieutenant Bascomb and Hartley supported by the arms. "His sleeves. No officer in the field wears his rank insignia. That's asking for a sniper's bullet."

"Blimey!" Bascomb gave the man a shake. "Here now! Come round, you. A *proper* lieutenant has some questions."

Nolin gripped the prisoner's neck in both hands, not to throttle him, as the guides expected, but to massage vital arteries. The fake lieutenant jerked to full consciousness, though his legs proved too fickle for him to stand unaided.

"What the devil?" Hartley blurted.

Nolin stepped back to take his measure of the captive. "I induced a rush of blood to the brain." He snapped his fingers to get the German's attention. "Up here, *mein freund*. Focus now. We're on a timetable so I expect to have to ask these questions only once. Who are you and what are you doing here?"

The prisoner felt his split lip with his tongue. "Leaving."

"You mean deserting?"

"No, it is for honor, what we do, to protect our eternal souls."

Behind Nolin, squad members traded puzzled looks. Nolin continued his interrogation: "What are you carrying on about?"

The German withdrew into himself. "Nothing. I surrender. Take me in, *bitte*."

Lucca brandished the stiletto he used to trim his nails. "Come on,

Crucchi, that's just asking for it." He indicated Nolin with a nod. "He's the reasonable one. I suggest you give him what he wants *so schnell wie Sie reden.*" In *The Lust of Hate*, Dr. Nikola's personal servant Ah-Win is sentenced to *ling-chi*—the infamous "death of a thousand cuts"—for attempting to poison the Viceroy of Kweichow. What the sentence entailed is never described in detail, but Lucca was sure he could improvise a suitably grim version.

"He must be from the research facility," Paul said to Nolin. "You heard what Bascomb said about these trenches, the network of dugouts. It's possible there are hidden tunnels about, even a direct line to the base."

"That would speed things along," Lucca said.

"Alright, he comes with us," Nolin said. "Bascomb, Hartley, take charge of the others and march them back to the captain when they're able."

"Where are you taking me?" the fake lieutenant asked. A note of trepidation had crept into his voice.

Nolin advanced on him. "The base where you're hiding the *Kettenblitz.*"

At this, the imposter recovered his footing and, straightening to his full height, wrested Hartley's pistol from its holster. He waved the gun in a spasm of desperation, shaking free of Bascomb's grip.

"Now, now. No one needs to get hurt," Nolin said. "More than they already are…"

The German leveled the gun at Nolin's chest and pulled the trigger. The report echoed through the receding mist and into the pale morning sky.

Nolin collapsed hard on his back.

The Lost Boys shouldered their weapons en masse.

"Don't," Nolin croaked. His chest seethed with pain. He pushed himself onto his elbows. "We need him alive."

The fake lieutenant trembled in disbelief. The point of impact was clear from the powdered hole in Nolin's uniform. His gun hand shook with indecision.

"Aye, I'm bulletproof," Nolin announced as he struggled to his feet. "The question now is: are you?"

The German's eyes turned a pensive black. He snarled something in his native language then thrust the Webley in his mouth and sprayed the trench with his brains. The needlessness of the act unsettled the squad as much as the violence of it.

"Damn it all," Nolin muttered.

"Did you catch what he said?" Lucca asked. "*Rette mich*... Save me— save me from the fear with a thousand eyes."

Dixie's acne-blotched face twisted into a frown. "Say again?"

"He was off his chump," Prince Joey said. "Crazy as a old Tenderloin pimp."

Katsuo shook his head. "He not crazy. I explain you good: he big time scare."

"Katsuo's right," Nolin said. "I read it in his body language."

"Maybe he's got men out after him?" Dixie offered.

"That's a sound notion... But I think it was something else."

"Why did I know you were gonna say that?"

"Let's move out," Nolin said. "Bascomb, Hartley, my orders still stand. Give a full report of what's happened. We're continuing with the mission. The covering bombardment should begin as scheduled."

"You sure about this, Nolin?" Paul asked quietly.

The lieutenant looked down at the dead man leaking his lifeblood into the mire. The upturned face was like a *Bauta* mask with stringy pulp and nothingness beneath it. "Now more than ever."

Once Nolin and his men climbed out of the squalid mud and into the forest of elm and poplar, they made much better time. They had their own pace that ate up ground without exhausting them. It was a relief to breathe aromatic loam on the wind instead of boggy remains. The plan was for them to burn daylight then make the final run at dusk. They paused in a closely wooded area to catch forty winks and chow down in shifts. After a time, however, the monotonous terrain—the almost bare trees, the ashen leaves on the ground—took on the dismaying qualities of a limbo. The forest's cathedral quiet became a disturbing presence. It was as if they'd stumbled into a stilled and altogether separate world—one free from war, but teeming with its own as-yet unseen dangers. They filled the unnatural silence with the battlenoise in their heads.

Eric endured the minor agonies of his oversized haversack, wondering if he would get a chance to make use of its contents. There were no planned demolitions this time but Nolin wanted to be prepared for any eventuality. He didn't grudge Nolin the idea. Military life was much like being part of the railway workers' union or the *Sociaal Democratische Arbeiders Partij*. Decisions were made on principle and you did your best to make them work. He could handle the labor. That wasn't the issue. It was a matter of speed. He wanted to charge through the enemy as fast as possible so he could get home. The Netherlands' neutrality hadn't protected it from terrible food shortages. His father put a brave spin on the family's situation in his letters but Eric understood they were suffering. Their pain spurred him on more than his own. He was young with ages to live. His parents deserved more in their final days.

Close to the forest's edge, Nolin gestured for the squad to stop. As a body, the Lost Boys dropped to one knee and readied their weapons. Nolin signed for the men to stay put while he scouted head. Moving as soundlessly as smoke, Nolin vanished into the ranks of gray-barked trees.

The squad remained in formation, alert but unworried. If Nolin had suspected enemy troops nearby, he would have signaled it. "You got the best eyes, Prince J," Dixie whispered. "See anythin'?"

Prince Joey tensed every time Dixie addressed him outside of a firefight. He couldn't help detecting a sarcastic drawl. He somehow associated Dixie's voice with a heinous *New York Times* editorial he'd read on the voyage to Britain. The editorial by "an esteemed physician" argued that the South was threatened by "cocaine-crazed negroes" to whom the drug imparted expert marksmanship and an immunity to bullets "large enough to kill any game in America." Prince Joey had the impression Dixie considered his rifle skills similarly unearned, a kind of racial trick. Then again, maybe the recent spate of race riots back in the States and the prospect of returning to Brooklyn a second-class citizen had made him unduly cynical. He took his eyes from his scope. "Here he comes now."

Nolin emerged from the distant underbrush and made his way back to them at speed. "We're almost through. About a hundred and fifty meters of forest then a dirt-bald slope and the walls of Cambrai. Lucca, how long before that covering bombardment?"

Lucca held his watch to his face in the softening light. "Twenty-two minutes."

"Enough time to catch our breath," Nolin said for the benefit of the squad. He could have gone for hours yet. His stamina was as impressive as his prodigious strength. He motioned for the others to follow and they reached the last of the buffering trees in short order. There was a deceptively gentle slope between them and the imposing town walls. They knew how summits mysteriously retreated as you climbed.

"There it is, lads," Nolin said. "We'll have to double-time it. What do you think?"

Dixie checked the webbing on his haversack to make sure his gear was fully secured. "Goin to war is like goin to church, boss—you get rebuked for your doubts. Best not study too much on it."

"That's what you're good at, eh?" Eric said.

Dixie laughed reflexively with the others. He was open about his impatience with planning. He was content to be a man of material action and let others do the thinking.

"See the emplacement?" Lucca asked Nolin.

"Only just. The fog is stealing back in."

"Hey, Lucca," Prince Joey asked. "We got time for a cigarette?"

"You have any left?"

Prince Joey patted the cigarette case in his chest pocket. "Just the one."

"That's all I can smoke at one go."

"Don't even think it, man."

After securing his haversack, Katsuo took one knee and surveyed the featureless expanse of hill. The space between his shoulder blades was tight and clammy with sweat. He regarded survival during wartime as a matter of divine luck and wished he knew how to win it. His uncle— a midshipman aboard the destroyer *Ikazuchi*—had lost his leg in the Russo-Japanese War. The crippling shot had occurred amid a minor skirmish in the Japan Sea. His upper thigh ruined, the uncle took cover behind a bulkhead and sang the National Hymn to calm his nerves: "May the reign of the Emperor continue thousands of years..." His uncle often joked that one advantage of a wooden leg was the ability to pick up a sock with a tin-tack. But he always said it with downcast eyes. His patriotic heart alone had not satisfied the *sai no kami* (deity of luck). Katsuo wondered what ritual he might fulfill to appease the deity. Before he could do more than mouth the beginnings of a prayer, however, a faraway tempest rent the sky. Lucca's hand came down and he was off with the others, released to his own humble luck.

The ground erupted in geysers of dirt. The Lost Boys ran flat out, weapons hugged to their chests, hearts straining. Their haversacks assumed new weight. Katsuo stumbled at a close-by detonation, fell, and scrabbled on all fours, ears ringing and ringing. The ground quaked under his feet without pattern or proportion. Stinging clods of earth darkened the air. The atmosphere thickened, grew pungent, choking. In mere moments, he'd fallen a fair distance behind. His squadmates became faint drop-shapes that passed for people. He imagined his spirit exploding upward like so much dust.

Nolin waited until the squad was halfway up the hill before starting his run. With his speed and stamina, he could easily have beaten everyone to the summit. But he'd stayed back in case of any injury. The barrage made for a mad continuum of thunder. He shielded his eyes from the showers of pulverized clay with a forearm. Through narrowed vision, he saw Katsuo pitch onto his back. Nolin hurried to intercept him. Katsuo was fussing with the straps to his pack when Nolin seized him by the elbow and yanked him upright. "You clear to run?" Nolin shouted in his ear. Katsuo nodded, his eyes fierce slits, and wib-wob-bled forward. Each detonation echoed inside him, threatening to lift his head off. Nolin worried after the lad. Katsuo was the least experienced among them and, given his rough English, the least knowable. Prior to meeting Katsuo, Nolin's exposure to Japanese culture had been limited to a taciturn *bujitsu* tutor and Müller's *Sacred Books of the East*. Nolin sped to catch him and offered a steadying hand. Katsuo had been noth-ing but dutiful and fearless. It hurt sometimes how much Nolin cared for his men.

The shelling ceased as the pair neared the stone wall encircling Cambrai. The others were bent over double or slumped against their haversacks, chests hammering.

"Don't tell me you were scared," Lucca said.

"And you weren't?" Paul asked between gasps.

Lucca shrugged. He enjoyed making Paul twitch and stammer.

"Only because you lack thee-uh the sense to be."

Katsuo shed his haversack and sagged to the ground next to Prince Joey. He was bone-tired but thankful for the feeling.

Prince Joey fingered his last cigarette, waiting on Nolin to call for a break. He was leery of wasting it. "Tough going, huh, Katsuo?"

Katsuo was too winded to do more than whistle in reply.

"They was hateful loud, those bombs, that's for sure," Dixie said. His voice had been rendered toneless by the blasts. He tugged an earlobe experimentally.

Nolin joined Eric in examining the machine gun emplacement at the base of the rough-hewn wall. It was an empty, makeshift structure, long abandoned or perhaps, never used.

"Looks like the bombardment was for nothing," Eric said.

"In this instance," Nolin said, "nothing means something. What, I don't know. But the sooner we get over that wall and make our rendez-vous, the sooner we'll find out."

"Want me to blow a hole in it?"

Nolin smiled and gestured to the haze lingering over the cratered hillside. "That wasn't enough for you?"

There was a dark flash in Eric's gray-blue eyes. "Blame boredom and dangerous thoughts."

"That's likely what got us into this bloody mess. But keep those thoughts to hand. No telling what we're up against this time."

Chapter 7
They Bleed Electric

Unlike the outlying woods, Cambrai offered no respite from the ravages of war. Damage from bullets or shells marked every building. Some, including a medieval church, had been reduced to rubble. Elms that once lined idyllic avenues lay broken and scattered across the cobblestones. Much to the surprise of the Lost Boys, the devastation was thrown into high relief by the surviving streetlights. Towns typically extinguished their streetlights to avoid becoming aerial targets. The squad made its way to the rendezvous point by scurrying from one misshapen shadow to the next.

Ducking under the eaves of a half-wrecked chateau, Dixie said, "I don't get it—the lights. Fer why?"

"Maybe this is a trap and the lights will make it easier for them to hunt us," Eric whispered.

"And where are the townfolk?" Prince Joey asked.

Katsuo pointed out a bloated corpse twisted across a loose pile of bricks. A throng of blue flies obscured the man's face.

"Hope you know Lucca's sense of humor is weird even in America," Prince Joey said.

After about an hour of tense skittering along the edges of deserted streets, the squad came to a bullet-scarred tavern. A tattered French flag dangling from a lamppost identified it as the rendezvous point. Nolin approached the front door and the others closed around him, quieting their footsteps on the wooden porch. With a hand on his rifle, Nolin rapped out the Morse code password: L-A-D-A-G-U-E. A few moments passed. He registered a light scuffling behind the door and renewed the grip on his weapon. A muffled voice said, "*Le mot de passe à nouveau.*"

Nolin signaled his men to create a wider berth around the door and stepped to one side to repeat the code on the doorframe. The muscles at the back of his neck tensed.

The door flung open, revealing a bearded, gap-toothed man. He raised a kerosene barn lantern to Nolin's dirtied face and waved the squad inside with a .32 caliber Browning Short. "*Dépêcher intérieur. Nous vous attendions à la porte dérobée.*"

"*Nos instructions étaient pas spécifiques sur ce point,*" Nolin said.

As soon as the squad hurried into the darkened interior, the greeter shut and bolted the door.

"*Es-tu*—" Nolin began.

"*Par ici,*" the man said and turned his back on the team to lead it behind the bar and into a dusty storeroom. The low-ceilinged room was occupied by eight armed French—seven men and one woman. They followed Nolin and his men with their guns. An older man wearing a sheepskin jacket over a loose linen shirt stepped forward. He was bald except for a few wisps of gray around his ears. He furrowed his wild brows. "*Mais enfin! Un tas de garçons de gras.* I expect true war-men."

"What was that?" Nolin said. "Can't hear on account of the bombardment we dodged to get here." He wouldn't stand for repeated insults from a ragged band of farmers and laborers. "This your rebel group? All of them?"

The leader slapped the barrel of his rifle. "Also the sixteen here."

"Then the disappointment's mutual." Nolin offered his hand. "Lieutenant Nolin Quigg."

"You may name me Labrecque," he said, waving away Nolin's hand. "It seem we must take a decision. Perhaps I lead the group. I know Cambrai, the ah *espion.*" A slight whistle accompanied each breath.

"I am indeed young, Monsieur Labrecque, but ideally suited for this mission. My men also have experience and proven skills. That's why MII tasked us with it." He gestured to the conspicuous bullet hole in his uniform. "I can't take responsibility for the lives of your fighters. I daresay they look a scraggy bunch and—"

"*Quelle insulte.* We have been together since two years against the *Boche.*" He gave a derisive snort.

The slim brunette stepped in front of the old man. She wore a gray dress-trousers hybrid known as a *jupe-culotte.* The trousers sported narrow military-style stripes along the outer seams. "*Zut alors, Papa!*" she said. "Enough senseless man-talk." Labrecque started to say something but cut it short when she thrust a palm in his face. "I am no older than him. Would you call me unfit?" Lebrecque looked away, chagrined, like a rude drunk who suddenly realizes how he sounds.

Despite the well-meaning tortures inflicted by his father, Nolin could never have spoken to him in such a manner, not even to his ghost.

The woman's expression softened on turning to Nolin. "I apologize. We have suffered much, these last months, Papa more than most. *Goutte à goutte, l'eau creuse la pierre.*" She slipped her Luger into a trouser pocket and extended her hand. Her styled lashes gave her hazel eyes the look of a cat. "Babette."

"Nolin." Her hand was rough but warm. It made him self-conscious about his sweat and stink. "My men, they're called the Lost Boys but will respond to almost anything in the thick of it."

Babette gave the men a humble nod then glared at her comrades until they grudgingly lowered their weapons.

"I'm grateful for your help, Mademoiselle." Nolin said. "What now?"

"We rendezvous with our spy. He will guide you to the base. Where we go, you can rest and have refreshment." She removed a woolen cap from a trouser pocket and pulled it over her short, curly hair. "*Au revoir, papa.*" She pecked his stubbled cheek.

Lebrecque returned the kiss with an impulsive hug that lifted her boots off the ground. "*Être prudent fille.*"

"As you want," she said in a low tone and made to leave. At the threshold to the kitchen she turned to say, "And try to keep the men out of the rum."

"Wait." Eric put a hand on Nolin's arm. "They have rum?"

Nolin gently shouldered him aside to follow Babette. "You heard her. This party's breaking up."

Falling into line, Paul whispered to Eric, "*Drinkus interruptus.*"

"Even I know that is not real Latin," Eric said and hurried to catch up with the rest of the squad.

By the light of a pale moon, Babette led the Lost Boys through the outskirts of town to a blasted and falling-down train yard. "We cross the tracks here. Watch your footing. Some of the rails are twisted out of place." Her breath roiled the crisp night air.

"Is there a curfew? Is that why the streets are empty?" Nolin asked.

"The entire town is empty."

Nolin skirted a tangle of rail. "What do you mean? The Germans drove them out? Are troops bivouacked here?"

She swallowed the stubborn catch in her throat. "Most fled, but some—several hundreds who stayed behind—they are gone, taken by the *Boche* about five weeks ago. For prisoners or no, I cannot say. I try not to think on it too hard, the possibilities. My sick mother was among them. She has pain or—how do you say?—*picotements.*"

"Tingling."

"*Oui*, tingling, along one side of her body. It makes me despair to think what has happened."

"*Je vous prie de bien vouloir accepter mes sincères condoléances.*"

"I appreciate your sympathy. But I would rather you promise to take me along."

The thought set Nolin's heart churning. "We face long odds against the Huns with no reinforcements or chances for rescue. You can't be that reckless, Babette."

She gave a sly smile. "Do not underestimate me too."

The backside of the train yard opened out on a marshy pasture. The squad kept to the fence line, alert to every distant bark or automobile roar. Presently they came to a two-story farmhouse sagging in its field. Babette gave a coded knock on the door. A tall, hard-featured man with a military intensity but a full beard answered. He held the door for Nolin and his men, nodding in greeting, then secured the bolt. A signal lantern in the front room provided dim illumination. The Lost Boys dropped their haversacks and rubbed their hands to restore a measure of warmth. Leaning on the mantle, Dixie said, "Sure wish we could have a fire."

"Better a tot of brandy," Eric said.

"Brandy?" The lantern light accentuated the age lines under the stranger's eyes. "Ah, a man after my own heart. You'll find a half-bottle in the kitchen if you've a mind."

"Belay that task," Nolin said. "Let's first secure the house."

"Young mister—"

"*Lieutenant* Quigg."

"Lieutenant ," the stranger noted wryly. "The house is as secure as it can be under the circumstances." He gave Nolin's hand a curt shake. "Boris Gumm." He was curiously dressed in German military fatigues sans rank insignia and an ebony skullcap.

Nolin glanced at Prince Joey. "How about a position at the window?"

"Yessir."

"You're not German," Nolin said to Gumm.

"Whatever made you think I was?"

"Babette referred to you as a spy. I thought you'd be an army turncoat."

Gumm took up a *bergere* upholstered in faded blue velvet. "I *am* a turncoat. Just not the sort you expected." Whether standing or sitting, his imposing manner gave the impression he occupied more space than a typical man his size.

The Lost Boys arranged themselves around the signal light on the wooden pallet coffee table. Eric remained on the outer circle of light near the fireplace and downed the last of the gin from his pocket flask, figuring he could soon refill it with brandy.

Nolin said, "You're the one who provided MII the intelligence on the *Kettenblitz*?"

Gumm nodded. "I served as an advisor to Oberst Böll and his chief scientist Dr. Geiszler for a period—nine, nearly ten months. I assure you, however, I never had any intentions of betraying my country or the Allied cause. It was a matter of scientific and ah, personal interest. Nothing partisan."

"You're a uh an engineer then?" Paul asked. He was anxious for details on the design of the experimental tank.

"Not in the least."

"Then what would the—"

Prince Joey let out a low whistle. Katsuo threw himself over the signal lantern until he could put it out for good. The room plunged into darkness.

"What is it?" Nolin asked.

From his kneeling position at the bay window, Prince Joey said, "Not sure xactly. Men lit up with strange headlamps."

"How many?"

"Six-eight. Hard to tell. They got blending cover or something. Look about thirty yards, I mean—what? twenty-six?—meters out and closing."

"Twenty-seven point four meters," Paul said.

Babette snicked the safety off her Luger. "Infernal creatures of the *Boche*. They can sense fear."

"Well, it wasn't me," Eric said, pocketing his flask. "I just washed mine down with gin.

"*Puppen Shatten*—Puppet Shadows," Gumm said. "That's what Geiszler christened them. Resurrected corpses, fire-blackened and infused with etheric energy."

Lucca gave Nolin a nudge. "When's that Irish heritage kick in? With this kind of luck, I'd hate to know what we'd face if you were, say, Italian."

Nolin put a hand on Babette's elbow. "This would've been worth a mention."

"Would you have believed me?"

"You've no idea." Nolin raised his rifle. "Standard five-point defense, lads, flashlights out. Mr. Gumm, if you'd be kind enough to show Prince J to the roof..."

"Aim for the head and don't stop shooting until they're down good and proper," Gumm advised. "They don't die like men." He headed for the entryway stairs now illuminated by Prince Joey's flashlight. Lucca and Dixie followed to take positions on the second floor. The others dispersed to the doors and windows closest to their predetermined compass points.

"We're a bit chin-strapped but these are some fine lads," Nolin assured Babette as he confirmed that his weapon was fully loaded. The supernatural had preyed on him since birth. In his head, arcane evils kept multiplying until the heap of them succeeded the whole of reality. Was it possible his generation was doom-haunted? The weird war the Lost Boys had been fighting lent some credence to the idea.

"Three in back," Katsuo announced from the kitchen.

"I'll help cover the front door," Babette said. She posted up behind the settee to complement Eric's line of fire from the stairs.

Nolin crouched under the bay window. His heart skipped at the sharp crack of Prince Joey's rifle—three shots in quick succession. Another controlled barrage came from the second-floor. *Lucca*. He thought he heard one, maybe two bodies fall to the soggy ground. But there were no distinguishing cries or curses. Nor any return fire. Against his better judgment, he ducked under the curtains to gauge the threat. His chest gave an involuntary surge. The *Puppen Shatten* advanced at a steady, unhurried pace. In the weak moonglow, they appeared to be living shadows. Their eye sockets and gaping, toothless mouths glowed with white, otherworldly energy. One of the creatures was down on its back, its skull shattered, venting radiation into the night. "They're vulnerable at a distance!" Nolin shouted. "Let em have it!"

Bodies thudded against the backdoor, shaking loose the dining room furniture piled against it. Katsuo and Paul shouldered their weapons and fired through the door. Splinters of wood clouded the room. The lead attacker stumbled back, but the others came on, unperturbed. Paul recoiled at the sight. They were still recognizably human through their alien facial features and carbonized skin. "Reminds me of that castle on Lake Oberholtzer."

"The Storm, ē *to* ...," Katsuo said.

"The Storm Warden, aye. Those armored minions?"

Katsuo severed a grasping arm with a concentrated salvo. "Ah, big time fun."

Paul shook his head in consternation. As he recalled, Katsuo had almost died on that mission—twice.

Nolin smashed the glass from the corner of the bay window to combine his fire with Prince Joey's and Lucca's. The enemy's ranks had grown considerably beyond the original handful, suggesting a hive mind or coordinating intelligence. The vanguard was closing on the front door. "Eric, we need Mills grenades out front!"

Eric scuttled to his haversack near the fireplace. "Second floor window?"

Before Nolin could respond, a whoosh of obscuring soot from the fireplace signaled the arrival of a *Puppen Shatten*. The creature emerged in a crouch, its optic energies writhing like serpents. Up close, the naked creature assumed horrible definition. Its body was grossly thin and distended; its skin was a hard, puckered char; and its eyes and mouth burst with uncanny light. Eric spun away from the monster, trying to blink the soot from his eyes. The creature yoked him around the waist, its grip hot to the touch. Babette recovered from the billowing ash enough to retaliate. The bullet dislodged a jagged chunk of the creature's shoulder. She squeezed the trigger again, but to no effect. The gun was jammed.

Nolin covered the distance in an eyeblink and swung his fist, knocking the creature backwards. Eric tumbled to the floor, along with bits of the monster's jaw. The creature quickly regained its balance and thrust its head in Nolin's direction. Its optic tendrils whipped forward. Nolin ducked the attack and snatched up an armchair as a shield. The tendrils crackled with etheric current. The creature rocked back on its heels, pounded by a volley of bullets. Babette pressed her assault with Eric's rifle until the creature disintegrated into a cindery jumble. Eric got to his feet, dispersing a drift of residual energy with a wave. "Mu- much appreciated," he rasped.

Another *Puppen Shatten* spidered down the chimney. Nolin's left arm pistoned out to shove Babette out of harm's way. The undead menace came at Nolin, jaws wide, and the lieutenant sunk a leg of the armchair through its mouth and out the back of its throat. Reflexively, the creature clamped down on the chair leg, snapping it free. Nolin kicked the creature in the chest, throwing it against the mantle and blocking the emergence of yet another menace. "The door!" Nolin shouted.

Eric and Babette rushed toward the door when a pair of creatures burst through the window. Cascading glass caught in the diffused beam of a flashlight. Babette laid out the attackers with a staccato rifle burst, fogging the room with fetid dust.

Nolin drew his Webley, plugged his opponent's head several times, then stuffed its crumbling carcass into the fireplace. The other creature lurking there struggled to clamber out. Nolin exhausted his magazine on it, shearing it to pieces. "Sod off back to hell!" The house was pandemonium. He registered sounds of fighting on every side. "Paul! You and Katsuo alright?"

"I don't thee-uh think so!" Paul answered between howls of gunfire. "I thought God loved me!"

"Eric," Nolin said, "we still need those grenades. Call Dixie down from upstairs to help here. I'll be in the kitchen." He ran to the rear of the house where a half-dozen *Puppen Shatten* stumbled amid a mess of furniture and undead remains. "We're nearly out of ammo!" Paul yelled.

"Best pick your shots then," Nolin said, putting a creature down with a bullet to the forehead.

Nolin helped slow the onslaught, allowing Katsuo to focus on accuracy. Katsuo racked up one kill after another in a steady rhythm, all the while tamping down the impulse to look for Nolin's approval. His magazine emptied just as a wave of reinforcements breached the crashed-in backdoor. Nolin was out of ammo, too, with no time to reload. Katsuo choked down on his rifle and charged, adopting as his battlecry the traditional Japanese expression of delight at a rush of fireworks: *"Kagiyaaa!"* He swung his weapon with an enthusiasm and power Bingo DeMoss would have envied. The lead creature's head exploded into useless black shards. Katsuo dove into the mob, cratering torsos and whacking off limbs. Nolin ripped what remained of the kitchen door from its hinges and deployed it as a battering ram, forcing the few intact creatures outside. A backward-tottering creature took a headshot from Dixie's position at an upstairs window. Katsuo used the break in the action to draw his revolver. He had the measure of these creatures now. Paul sidled up to him with his last full magazine and together, they resolved to finish things.

A gobby scream returned Nolin to the front room. He found Babette loading her Luger with a new magazine in an effort to clear it and, closer to the stairs, Eric, feet scrabbling against the lowest steps, overpowered by a *Puppen Shatten*. The creature's optic tendrils bored into Eric's temples. The hapless soldier bucked and heaved. But the creature held fast, merciless, its energies burrowing into his brain. Eric arched his back in an agonizing whipsaw motion. His unmanly shriek ended only when Babette jammed her reloaded Luger into the base of the monster's neck and beheaded it point-blank.

Nolin booted the creature's remains against the wall and bent to his stricken friend. He smelled the bitter ozone of a lightning strike. There was no pulse, no sign of life. Even the color had gone from Eric's eyes. They'd been reduced to orbs of jellied white.

Babette guarded the entryway, unleashing a strobe of rounds at the last two *Puppen Shatten* on the threshold. The creatures ruptured and ruptured again. Their animating essences dissipated like gouts of lake mist.

A single bloodtear stained Eric's cheek. Nolin wiped it away with his cuff and thumbed Eric's mutated eyes closed. His heart thundered in his throat.

"That seems to be the last of them," Lucca said from the top of the stairs. He pulled up short when he spied Eric's body. "Is he …?"

Nolin could barely nod. He felt the sting of angry tears behind his eyes.

Lucca put a warning hand out to Dixie as his comrade emerged from a back bedroom. Dixie caught a glimpse of Nolin cradling Eric. Time stuttered to a halt.

Babette held one of Eric's hands in both of hers as Nolin arranged him on the tufted settee. Guilt made a hollow of her insides. If only she'd been faster at loading her Luger … If only she'd thought to use a grenade when the door was first breached … The ifs would never end no matter how long she lived. She choked back a hitching sob.

Paul and Katsuo entered from the kitchen. Paul grasped the situation instantly. "G'd blind me," he muttered.

"Where's Gumm?" Nolin asked. His voice had the hoarse authority of the bereaved. "Dixie, get them down—"

"I'm here, Lieutenant," Gumm said, strolling down the stairs. "I have to admit you impressed me here."

Nolin took a calming breath before saying, "That's all well and good, but I'm not after your favor, just your cooperation. We need to leave—now—for the base."

Gumm held up a prevaricating hand. "I'm afraid you misunderstand the situation. I don't take orders from you. If you want to live through this, you'll let me determine when and under what conditions we infiltrate the base."

Frustrated anger spread from Nolin's chest to his shoulders and neck. Gumm couldn't know what a mercy he showed him by keeping his composure. He remembered his training in the stoic philosophy of Marcus Aurelius: *You have power over your mind—not outside events. Realize this and you will find strength.* If Nolin allowed his blood to fire, there's no telling what might happen.

Gumm came within kissing-distance, smug and careless in his tone. "I'm an independent party, not subject to—"

The prick of a stiletto in the small of his back compelled Gumm to reconsider his words. "Another insult and I'll sever your spine," Lucca said. He dimpled Gumm's lower back with the tip of his blade. "That will leave me at least an hour to make the last moments of your life more miserable than you can imagine."

"This isn't necessary," Gumm balked. "We've a mutual cause."

"Then prove it," Nolin said. "Spill everything you know about this base and its defenses, starting with these *Puppen Shatten.*"

Gumm indulged in a self-satisfied grin. "Those are the least of your worries, Lieutenant. Trifling experiments. No, the true threat is something on an altogether grander scale: a force that will either glorify us as gods or condemn us to animal corruption and chaos."

Chapter 8
The Brotherhood of Beasts

Oberst Dietrich Böll walked around the experimental tank, gesturing to the several mechanics readying the vehicle to go about their duties. He'd worn his field uniform, complete with medals, to signal the seriousness of his inspection. But the unbearable heat generated by the welding torches and gas generators in the underground bay had soon obliged him to unbutton his jacket. Sweat pooling under his protective skullcap had started to trickle down his temples and forehead. He dabbed at the perspiration with a handkerchief before it ran into his small, dark eyes. "A redoubtable weapon, eh, Dr. Geiszler?"

The doctor quirked an eyebrow. "It is a marvel of human engineering, surely, but insignificant compared to the Mimirodat. If we are remembered at all after this conflict, Oberst, it will be for that discovery and little else." He spoke through gritted teeth as if pained by the effort.

Böll gave his chief scientist a liberal berth. Dr. Geiszler stank of feverish sweat. His obsessive study of the Mimirodat and of the fourteenth century grimoire, the *Ater Opus*, clearly took precedence over hygiene. The doctor sported an unkempt beard and unconscionably long hair. In his black skullcap and high-collared lab coat, he had the look of a pale, latter-day Confucius.

"I meant only that the machine is impressive on its own," Böll said. He supposed it was foolish to expect Geiszler to praise his contribution to the project. "Obviously, the Mimirodat is the crucial element." Ten meters long and four meters high, the tank had been designed expressly for transporting the Mimirodat into Allied territory. The hull consisted of armor plating a record eight centimeters thick. Each side boasted three swivel-mounted machine guns with another two at the rear. A fearsome .75 caliber cannon protruded from the angled nose. The *Kettenblitz* easily weighed a thousand metric tons. No less than four sets of caterpillar tracks driven by an equal number of Daimler engines could put it in motion.

"Will it be ready for the transfer as scheduled?" Böll asked. "The Allies are fortifying their positions, calling up their tank battalions. It's crucial we strike within the next twenty-four hours." He inclined toward the one hundred and twenty meter ramp that sloped to the surface.

"We have worked out how to move the dais as a unit. But I'm concerned the transfer will disturb the *beleuchtet Organellen*—those floating cell organs in the crystals. We could give them the equivalent of vertigo, weakening our hold on the Mimirodat." He thrust a hand inside his coat to emphasize his point.

"You understand the timetable is fixed, *ja*?"

"No question."

"The creature has proven resilient so far. I'm more concerned about you—your health. I need you fit and ready for this operation," Böll said. He could no longer ignore the sweaty itch under his skullcap. He removed the cover and ran a hand through his graying hair. "You're the only one who can control the creature now that Herr Gumm..." He grimaced.

"I had no choice but to...dismiss him. He would have been our undoing." Geiszler flashed on his last argument with Gumm, how the mercenary had threatened to "steal away" the Mimirodat in dreams. He despised Gumm for thinking the creature was here for Man's benefit, like a gateway angel. What hopeful weakness! The Mimirodat was nothing less than a god of primal chaos. "I only regret failing to put a permanent end to the matter."

Böll glanced at the ancient sigils inscribed on the inside of the skullcap. He had the peripheral impression of undulating movement and quickly returned the cap to his head. It was enough that Geiszler's symbolic magick insulated him and his troops from the influence of the Mimirodat. Investigating further seemed an unnecessary risk to his normality. Böll prided himself on his stolid common sense.

"Ready, Oberst?" Every moment apart from the Mimirodat set him further on edge.

"*In einem Moment, bitte.*" Böll approached a scattering of blueprints on a nearby workbench. He scanned the drawings until he found the plans for the redesigned mount. As discussed with Geiszler weeks ago, the Mimirodat's dais was to be installed slant-on like a parabolic reflector. He wanted to confirm the design on paper to avoid having to climb up the tank. The design appeared to be as he remembered except for one detail: a funnel-like structure over the dais. "Doctor?" he called. "I take it this is your amendment?" He pointed out the new structure.

"Ah, a minor change. I thought, perhaps, in the open air, it might be necessary to constrain the Mimirodat's energies more tightly. That tubular cavity," he said, tracing it with a fingertip, "can hold a sizeable chunk of crystal."

"It looks more like a rifle scope than anything else. Or a frame for a magnifying lens."

"It can serve more than one purpose," Geiszler said. "I have run tests over the past eight days with the focal point aimed harmlessly at the stars. You are, of course, welcome to see it for yourself." His tone was mocking. He knew how much Böll dreaded the creature.

The Oberst stiffened and said, "That would be best." He'd be damned before he'd let Geiszler make a burlesque of military discipline.

Following Gumm's self-aggrandizing story, Nolin gathered Paul and Lucca in an upstairs bedroom to debrief while the others prepped for an early-morning departure. Those not at rest were expected to keep watch over Gumm. Eric's body remained on the settee, a stark reminder of what they had to lose. In Dixie's sorrowful words, it looked as "white as a sulfured apple." Nolin planned to retrieve it on their return to the front.

Paul shifted on the edge of the child's bed uneasily, knowing that its usual occupant was likely a prisoner of the Germans or lying somewhere in an open grave. Gumm had only squatted here for the evening. He sheltered in a different place each night in an effort to avoid German patrols. The air had a tinge of attic mustiness. Paul summoned as much sympathy for Nolin as his wearied heart could take. "You know thee-uh lads, Lieutenant. They're knackered and shaken, but you won't hear any whinging."

"Eric's death was a hard blow, no doubt," Lucca said. "But they know the dangers, or at least, accept them. The mission hasn't changed." He sat on the end of the bed while Nolin took up a position against the mirrored bureau.

"He's not thee-uh first…," Paul said.

Nolin said, "I know. It's the unfairness of it. So much future wasted…He was only twenty."

"You can't hold yourself responsible. You've taken more risks than thee-uh the rest of us combined. No one begrudges you your, uh…"

"Unique abilities," Lucca said.

"Sure," Nolin said in a clipped voice. He wondered what they'd say if they knew the corrupting secret to his strength. The need to cover it up, the shame and the fear of being found out was a constant strain. "Thinking ahead now, what's your take on Gumm's creature?"

"Thee-uh thee-uh Mimirodat? I don't know." Paul threw up his hands. "I've never run across its like in the literature. But Gumm's rather daft on the topic. Could be known under another name…"

Nolin asked, "Could it be the source of the fear-plague? The nineteen year cycle? Maybe even the whole bloody war?"

"That would be my theory. Gumm said the Huns intend to use it to uh…"

"Confuse our emotions, get us to fight ourselves." A sly grin crossed Lucca's face on finishing another of Paul's sentences.

"Must you do that?"

"What?" Lucca said, feigning innocence. "You sound better that way."

Nolin leaned forward. "Is this the Mimirodat at work or…?"

"Sorry," Paul said.

Lucca cast his eyes to the ground but remained tight-lipped.

Nolin pressed on: "Based on Gumm's description, I think it's too dangerous for us to leave it intact. We should agree at the outset on destroying it."

"If we could turn it to our advantage," Lucca said.

"*If*...That's not a risk I'm willing to take. I've said it before, but I'm more sure than ever that this is a moral-spiritual crisis. The patchwork and damnable nature of this war, the way killing is treated as a mere engineering problem—better planes, better tanks...We've lost the center, lads. I don't trust either side with something like the Mimirodat. We aren't above falling prey to the same kind of overreaching that doomed the Greco-Romans."

Paul said, "There is thee-uh the theory that history isn't just cause and effect, but an unfolding of some larger uh metaphysical reality. Maybe we're simply poxed by fate."

Lucca said, "I can't believe Man is only a pawn of history."

"Balls up your sense of self, eh? The small man always aiming for something larger."

"Don't forget that a pawn that makes it to the end of the board gets promoted." Lucca's smile turned serious. "It can become a rook, a knight, a bishop, even a queen."

The spectre of Nolin's hideous duplicity raised its head again. He squelched it, promising himself to perform some serene force exercises once the meeting concluded. "All I meant to say is that the stakes are higher than this mission and the Allied cause. But we agree, right? We destroy the Mimirodat."

Lucca shrugged. "If we can..."

"Aye," Paul said. "Not that we can trust Gumm to help."

"Absolutely not," Nolin said. "But what's the alternative? For the nonce, we've no choice but to follow him." He thumbed the stubble on his chin. "The more pressing matter is Babette."

"I heard you talking in thee-uh kitchen," Paul said.

"She insists on coming along."

"Bit conspicuous, don't you think? Not too many Hun soldiers with her..." Lucca fumbled for a decorous word.

"*Curvarum?*" Paul offered.

Lucca returned Paul's grin.

"Short of lashing her to the cylinder stove, I'm afraid there's not much we can do." Nolin got to his feet. "She's not afraid to fight outside her weight class, I'll give her that. It's...after Eric..."

Paul hated seeing his childhood friend struggle with burdens beyond his control. He had enough worries as it was. "She'll do, Nolin."

"Alright then," Nolin said. "Grab some bully beef and rest up." He clapped to signal the end of the meeting. Paul slipped out with an encouraging nod and Lucca made to follow. Nolin put a staying hand on his shoulder. "A word, mate?"

Lucca watched Paul go with a pang of envy. It made him angry to think of how much he wanted Nolin to extend to him the same easy trust. "What is it?"

"I have to ask...About Gumm...Would you have gone through with it?"

"If he'd pressed me, yeah, probably..." He sounded more defensive to his own ears than he meant to be. Nolin had a habit of bringing out the unwanted family feelings that had driven him to run away: obligation, constraint, a distorting insularity. Sometimes he felt like he'd left his immigrant circus family in America for another in Europe.

"Not that I don't appreciate your loyalty. But this war..." Nolin was reluctant to probe too deeply, sensitive to how they were only a scant few years removed from childhood. "Don't let it blight your conscience."

"The war hasn't changed me, Nolin. I've always been this way. I've always believed death was final. Despite the mysteries we've seen over the last three years—the daimons and spirits, the God-Kings of Avalon—I still believe it. That's the only thing that scares me. And that's why, sometimes, we have to be as merciless as death itself."

Nolin was struck by how cold Lucca sounded. It was as though he'd lost his parents in the war rather than deserted them for it. "Sometimes." He gave Lucca's arm a gentle squeeze. "But only sometimes."

Approaching the control room for the Mimirodat's holding chamber, Böll and Geiszler were intercepted by an anxious corporal. "Oberst," the corporal called at a sprint. "Oberst..." He slowed before Böll and saluted, chest heaving.

"Out with it, Corporal."

"We have a...report, sir. From the west entrance." The corporal took another deep breath before continuing. "The *Puppen Shatten*...are late in returning, sir."

"How late?"

"Nearly two hours, sir."

"Doctor? Were they on routine patrol or...?"

"Nothing out of the ordinary." Geiszler fondled the ends of his greasy beard. "Perhaps Gumm. As you know, he has a rapport with the...entity. He might have managed to subvert my influence over them."

Böll put a hand on the corporal's shoulder. "Double the entrance guard and put all security personnel on alert. Quickly now: pass the word."

"Sir." The corporal saluted and took off down the corridor.

"Any other possibilities?" Böll asked.

Geiszler lifted his beard to reveal an iron passkey on a simple chain around his neck. The control room's lock had been wall-mounted at about chest height. He inserted the key without removing it from the chain. "No, none." The door slid back on deep-set rails with a resounding *clunk*. "Unless...unless they have given out entirely. Undead is not always the same as immortal." He ushered Böll inside.

The Oberst was shocked at the room's state of disarray. Classified folders and their attendant documents, essential grimoires and unfiled project notes were scattered across the instrument panels bordering the observation glass. Böll made to push aside one of Geiszler's notebooks when he noticed that the doctor had not only filled the margins of the open page with barely legible scrawls, but had continued his last entry on the instrument panel itself. "Doctor," he said evenly.

Geiszler showed no sign of hearing him as he drew closer to the observation glass. The holding chamber on the other side pulsed with the Mimirodat's red-orange emanations. The dazzle of alien energies was brighter, more intense than Böll remembered. Fortunately, the chamber had been designed to accommodate fluctuations in the creature's luminosity. Besides the tinted observation glass, the creature was suspended on a dais three stories below and could be viewed only as a reflection in an array of black mirrors. The mirrors afforded a canted, three-quarter perspective on the roiling ball of bioluminescence. Shadowy organelles floated in the Mimirodat's central depths. Its appendages branched and interconnected like the brain's reticula. In fact, Geiszler understood the creature was once part of an extradimensional neural net, which he'd dubbed the Mimirodatika.

Translucent crystals encrusting the dais like a dripstone formation both rendered the creature visible and imprisoned it. The Parmatmar crystals contained their own shifting organelles, which Geiszler theorized somehow altered the creature's vibrational frequency to bring it fully into "earth-space." Without the crystals, the creature would have been invisible to the naked eye, registering only on spectroscopic devices as a source of blackbody radiation. A grimoire credited to an obscure Russian monk, the *Ater Opus*, had provided the guidance required to contain and manipulate the creature. Geiszler speculated that the Mimirodat had inspired the monk to write the *Ater Opus* for the purpose of reuniting the entity with its extradimensional masters (referred to as "Overlords of the Jewel"). In developing the Mimirodat as a weapon, Böll worried they might have inadvertently done exactly that, risking the whole of Creation. Geiszler certainly regarded the Mimirodat as evidence of a divinity more real than the God of the Bible.

"Doctor," Böll repeated. "Should we be concerned?" The closer people got to the creature, the more profound its effects. Those subjected to intense exposures endured violent emotions then maddening hallucinations and finally, a wrenching and irreversible metamorphosis. Geiszler's experiments in this regard had yielded the *Puppen Shatten* and other abominations too horrible to consider. Böll pulled his skullcap tight at the composite memory of the doctor's failures and their lingering, acrid cremations.

Geiszler mumbled something unintelligible then said, "It could be the influx of psychic energy. The warehouse has been running at maximum the past two days. I thought it prudent to increase the flow in advance of the transfer. Or, again, it could be Gumm, operating at a distance. His powers of astral projection are more advanced than mine." He said this last with undisguised bitterness.

"Is there a chance the creature might overcharge? The Kaiser's orders are to disorient the Allies, reduce them to a panicky mob, not turn them into devils." The itching sensation under his skullcap flared again. He raised a hand but stopped short of removing the headcover, conscious of his proximity to the Mimirodat.

"I will, of course, do my best," Geislzer said. He was in chronic pain—the pain of feeling inadequate to his dread obsession, to the Mimirodat and its nature. Some essential lesson about the noumenal or thing-in-itself versus the phenomenal continued to elude him. He went on: "But this is not a precise science, Oberst. The Mimirodat is a god of primal chaos. And chaos, I have come to believe, is the true state of things. Order is just a phantom construct, a coping mechanism. The Kaiser's plans, Imperial Germany, all of western civilization, presume an order that does not exist. Chaos is the natural tendency of this world and this age. The Mimirodat is *der Geist seiner Zeit* made real."

Böll would brook no argument from a dreaming philosopher like Geiszler. "Be that as it may, doctor, our aim is to use the Mimirodat to end this war and potentially, the very concept. If this experiment works, no one will dare rise against us. Perpetual peace under our mandate is assured." The itch seethed like a cluster of bee stings. No matter how undignified it looked, he couldn't resist scratching through his skullcap.

"It is impossible to prevent the constant tug and pull of civilizations. Order demands its opposite. I am reminded here of Goethe's 'Prologue in Heaven.' Even God recognized that Mephistopheles was necessary to lend His creation vitality. The new—creativity itself—is possible only where there is risk and destruction." Geiszler's normally abstracted look resolved into an unspoken challenge. "What you ask me to do is mummify the world."

"Whatever it takes to stop this annihilation war," Böll said. His skull-cap slipped to one side. He took the opportunity to run an index finger over his scalp in righting it. "None of these petty nation-states have the power. Only Germany, with this discovery and its tradition of self-determination, can do it. This is about saving hundreds of thousands, maybe millions of lives, doctor. Your metaphysics are irrelevant."

"As you say, Oberst," Geiszler said. "Prepare your troops with confidence. The transfer will occur to schedule."

Böll was nearly in the corridor before Geiszler finished his pledge. The itch had reached an excruciating severity. As soon as the door to the master control room shut, he grabbed up the skullcap and scratched to the point of drawing blood. It was only when he was back in his office, still clawing through his corkscrewed hair, when he realized that he had never really examined the curious funnel structure. Now he had a new worry: the possibility that Geiszler had him under a spell. He mashed the skullcap over his bleeding scalp, determined to suffer the terrible itch as proof of his freewill.

The thick morning fog unnerved Prince Joey for reasons beyond its power to conceal. It cast familiar shapes into new, confounding forms. Veiled fragments of masonry took on the grandeur of ancient ruins. Noise belied conventional acoustics. His own footfalls were an enigma. One step sounded close and the next echoey distant. Even on the march with his fellow Lost Boys, he felt isolated and exposed. Maybe it was the gut-punch of Eric's death working on him. "Lucca," he whispered. "You goin back to New York when we done?"

Lucca slowed to pace him. "Oh, no. My papa…It would be a damn nuisance to survive this murderous slog only for him to do me in. Only thing worse would be coming back as one of those Puppet Shadows."

"Yeah, I wasn't about to touch one a them, animal, mineral or whatever."

"Electric vegetable?"

"What would that make you then? Roamin lettuce?"

Lucca's laugh was like a gun-crack, prompting an admonishing glare from Nolin. Lucca flashed Prince Joey a pretend-guilty look and resumed his place in formation.

Prince Joey bit his lower lip to keep from busting up. He monitored the placement of his feet on the broken cobblestones, avoiding a discarded traveling rug. For his part, he loved and missed his father, a hardworking seltzer delivery man proud to be the only Negro employed by the company's Jewish owners. But Prince Joey feared returning to an America where Negroes were guilty until proven innocent. Even Negro soldiers weren't above persecution. In Houston this past August, two white police officers harassing a Negro woman had instigated a race riot that drew Negro soldiers from nearby Camp Logan. Four Negro soldiers died in the heat of the violence and a hundred others suffered arrest and possible court-martial. No whites were charged as far as Prince Joey knew.

He'd originally planned to return to Brooklyn after the war and join his mentor on the New York police force. His skill with a gun, however, seemed inextricably tainted by the American idea of black criminality. The best he could do now, he thought, was to earn a spot on Nolin's post-war team of adventurers. On more than one occasion, Nolin had alluded to forming a permanent group of scientists and soldiers devoted to investigating the supernatural unknown. Prince Joey hoped his service record would stand him in good stead.

Something at the periphery of his vision shocked him back to the moment. The image he came away with, however, didn't make sense: a man with the head of a bird. His heart thumped in the base of his throat. He scanned the ruins of an old boat repair shop and its extended rubble. He stepped around a ditched watercart. The silence between his steps had an unsettling texture. Just when his breathing began to ease, he caught sight of another animal—a bull's head. The telltale horns stood out in the haze before disappearing behind a collapsed archway.

He broke formation and hurried up the line. Babette nodded in greeting, tight-throated and rheumy from lack of sleep. Prince Joey sidled up to Nolin but kept his eyes on Gumm a few paces ahead.

"What is it?" Nolin asked.

"We got company—two, maybe more."

"Huns?"

"Something else. Animal-somethings."

Gumm stopped and waited for Prince Joey and Nolin to catch him. "Animals, you say?"

"Well," Prince Joey said, "men with animal masks."

"To be expected."

"Friends of yours?" Nolin asked.

"Old mates from La Fratellanza di Bestie. Don't worry. They've been watching me for months now, lurking. Nothing untoward." Although he was roughly the same height as Nolin, he habitually tilted his head down as if addressing a much shorter person.

"When were you going to mention this?"

Gumm stabbed the air with a forefinger. "I'm mentioning it now." He'd been especially testy since Nolin disarmed him.

Nolin told Prince Joey, "Good work. Let the others know not to shoot first—unless threatened."

Prince Joey cut out to relay Nolin's orders, confident he'd scored another point in his favor.

"They've come to worship the Mimirodat as a god of animal nature," Gumm said. "Funny that. The original purpose of it was mass conversion. It's like an antenna thrust into our world. It was s'posed to broadcast religious belief into the heart of us, you know, to make us devoted slaves. Not for its own sake but for its creators, the Overlords of the Jewel. Of course, old as it is, its target wasn't us per se but our Neanderthal ancestors or somesuch."

"Where does all this come from?" Nolin was keen to know Gumm's sources. His father had amassed a sizeable stockpile of arcane lore and, best as he could recall, none of it referenced the Mimirodat or the creature's masters.

"Mostly from an old Latin text. The Germans call it the *Ater Opus.*

La Fratellanza has its own sacred book, though there's no mention of the Mimirodat. It's just a bunch of pagan foolishness. But the witch cult has always believed Man has to go back—embrace degeneration as it were—in order to move forward, spiritually-speaking. Is that the right word from that Darwin fellow—degeneration?"

Nolin credited Gumm with a rare talent for effectively alternating between genuine arrogance and feigned ignorance. "And the Mimirodat is what to them?"

"They think it a pure expression of animal spirit—all high emotion and instinct, suited to the natural order of things. It's possible the group was originally inspired by a bad translation of this barmy French book, *Southern Discovery by a Flying Man, or the French Dedalus.* Written six-eight years before the Revolution, it's about a utopia of human-animals on the opposite side of the globe from Paris. The animal people include asses, elephants, horses, frogs what-have-you. It's like La Fratellanza mixed it up with pagan beliefs about animal familiars, the supremacy of nature and all. The gist of it is: they believe animals have the moral edge on us." Gumm waved his hand dismissively. Here was the no-nonsense ex-soldier aspect to his personality. "Wouldn't surprise me if the author, Restif de la Bretonne—that's just the surname—had some experience with the Mimirodat. It tends to bring out those sorts of primitive visions." He sidestepped into the recesses of a smashed storage facility. The sagging roof hid them from the open boulevard ahead. "We're close now."

Nolin followed him into the soft shadows and signaled his squad to join them. "I take it that's the group you betrayed." His demeanor was grave. He had no doubt Gumm was escorting them into a trap.

"We used each other to get what we wanted for a while," Gumm said. "When the Germans showed, they offered more—a chance to unleash the Mimirodat's otherworldly potential. La Fratellanza still hold on hope I'll give it back."

"Silly buggers."

When the squad was assembled, Nolin turned to Gumm. "What's the play?"

"There are two buildings directly ahead: on the left, a former sugar factory; on the right, a squat brick building. We're headed for that one. But there will be guards—snipers—in the second floor windows of the factory."

Dixie, who had volunteered to hump Eric's haversack of explosives, asked, "The brick building—is it open? Or we gonna need grenades?"

"Leave that to me," Gumm said.

"I'll take up Eric's haversack for this, Dixie," Nolin said. "We'll go singly in march order, starting with Mr. Gumm and me. Once we've got the building open, start your run. The fog should help. Prince J will provide cover. Any questions?" Seeing none, Nolin dismissed the squad and took up a position at the edge of the shelter. Gumm crouched next to him.

Prince Joey propped his Springfield on a sheltering pile of bricks and scanned the factory's cantilevered windows through his scope. The fog blanched the field of view a shadowed gray. He'd have to wait for a muzzle flash to zero on the enemy.

"Ready?" Nolin asked Gumm.

"The Mimirodat only knows and it won't split."

"I'll take that as a go." Nolin heaved the man to his feet with one hand and scooped up the sack of munitions with the other. Shielding Gumm with his body, he sprinted the twenty meters to the target. His temples pulsed in agitation. He half-dragged Gumm along. The bewildered spy skittered across the boulevard as if on the surface of the moon.

The first shot rang out as they reached the building. The metal door was perfectly smooth—no handle, no lock—and the building offered no shelter from the gunfire. Nolin put himself between the snipers and the recovering Gumm. "Hurry!" Although he was bulletproof, he wasn't immune to the shells' concussive effects.

Prince Joey locked on the muzzle fire and squeezed off two rounds. A piercing deathwail confirmed his accuracy. "Glory to God," he mouthed. He counted every kill as a sign of Providence.

Gumm reached into a pocket of his pea coat and withdrew an octagonal black doorknob. He placed it on the door about where it would normally have been installed and gave it a vigorous turn. The door swung aside. Nolin concluded the knob was a magnet powerful enough to manipulate the bolt-action lock on the other side.

"Sorry to have troubled you." Gumm tugged on his jacket cuff and ushered Nolin inside.

Paul bolted out from under the cover, shoulders hunched, pumping his long legs and arms. Bullets zinged around him, seemingly multiplying on impact.

The fog warped the sound of the shots. If Prince Joey had been forced to rely on the reports alone, the trajectory of the bullets would've been impossible to pinpoint. He spied adjacent gunflashes in the factory windows and tried for them both. Paul reached the building before the din of shattered glass petered out.

"Looks like you snatched em outten there quick as a toad's tongue," Dixie said.

Keeping his cheek to the rifle, Prince Joey said, "One for sure. The other..." Dixie started into the boulevard before Prince Joey finished his warning.

A bullet chimed the lip of Dixie's helmet. He jigged to the right, heart racing, and the next shot tore up the cobblestones at his feet. His insides knotted up and fouled his breathing. Even as he felt himself slowing, lurching instead of zigzagging, he thought of Babette and how he should've escorted her. But she'd been stubborn and insisted on risking herself like everyone else. A scintillant burst cut across his path. His throat closed in dread of—

The barrage dopplered into silence.

He skidded to a stop in the middle of the boulevard and looked back. Prince Joey waved. Dixie swallowed the hitch in his throat and jogged on.

"We're clear," Prince Joey said to Katsuo and Babette. "Hustle across, but we're clear."

Katsuo gave a slight bow and said, "Ah, big time rifle man. Much honor to you."

Prince Joey accepted the compliment with a crooked smile, unsure if he'd taken a few seconds longer than he'd needed to make that last kill-shot.

The building consisted of a single square room, empty save for a few wooden crates. The squad gathered around a large oak door set into the concrete floor. Lucca resisted cracking wise about this all-too-literal trap.

"This is the entrance to the old La Fratellanza temple?" Nolin asked.

"The Germans modified and extended it," Gumm said. "But yes, below us is the original entrance. We, meaning La Fratellanza, had installed a coded defense which the Germans decided could be useful. Instead of tearing it down, they simply changed the code."

"But you uh know what it is?" Paul asked.

Gumm shook his head like a schoolmaster disappointed in his class.

"This is making a lot more sense now," Lucca said.

Dixie said, "I liked it better when it didn't. Just give me somethin to hit at." He was anxious to prove himself again after faltering on the boulevard.

"What's down there?" Nolin asked.

"There's a long spiral staircase and after that, a dungeon of sorts," Gumm said. "One wall contains a number of mud bricks, some plain, some inscribed with sigils. The marked bricks have to be properly arranged to open the passage."

Babette asked, "Or else…?"

"The room is shot through with fire." Gumm cocked his head at Nolin. "You don't happen to be fireproof, too?"

"More like fire resistant," Nolin said. "Well, no sense in risking everyone. Gumm, it's just you and me, mate."

He grasped the metal ring in the oak and yanked the door open. A dim light revealed a poured concrete staircase.

"Uh, Nolin," Paul said, stepping forward. "Outside of Greek and Latin, I'm not as skilled with languages as you and Lucca, but maths I can do and if it's a uh pattern…"

Lucca made to go down the stairs. He shrugged off Nolin's stern look. "You heard Shimmy there—I have the languages."

"Alright, you crazy sods," Nolin said. "But the rest of you, stay here until you're called for. And if we don't make it back for some reason, you're to abort. That's a direct order. No surprises."

Prince Joey said, "Remember growing up when surprises were a good thing? Malted milks and Goo Goo Clusters…Now it's sniper fire and hoodoo devils and doomsday countdowns…"

"We get through this, I'll buy you all the Horlick's malted milk you can stomach," Paul said.

The spiral staircase led to a rectangular dirt cave redolent of a dirty chimney. The cave was lit by naked bulbs strung along one side. Blackened bones and amulets made from animal horn littered the drifts of ash. A series of ducts not unlike vent hoods jutted from the low ceiling. The ducts were spaced about one meter apart in a uniform pattern. If the code wasn't deduced correctly, the ensuing flames would leave no margin for escape.

The code-puzzle Gumm described was at the far end of the cave. It was a wall-sized hieroglyph comprised of slotted bricks. There were a number of bricks apparently placed at random and four open slots like gaps in a buck-toothed mouth. Nolin motioned Gumm closer to the wall. "What was the La Fratellanza code? Why don't you draw it out?" He pulled a composition notebook and an O'Donnell pen from his breast pocket. "Be sure to mark where the bricks were, how many…"

"It was the pagan symbol for the lunar cross—for 'protection,'" Gumm said. Using the hieroglyph as a guide, he bracketed the approximate position of each brick.

Nolin shared the drawing with Lucca and Paul. It looked like a Christian cross with spurs on each end. "Based on this and the shape of the bricks, I think we can rule out any symbols with circular elements."

"Agreed," Paul said. "But that still leaves uh a lot of possibilities. We don't even know thee-uh symbol system they used."

"Regardless, you'd think they'd keep it simple—pick something much like the first to minimize the amount of work." Lucca took the writing materials from Nolin and sketched something like an upside-down U. "That's the pagan symbol for 'guardian.' If you just took the bricks from the top half and put them down below..."

"But what're thee-uh the odds the Huns would use the same system?"

"Gumm," Nolin said, "would this Dr. Geiszler use pagan symbols?"

"He might. The *Ater Opus* is partly in Latin, partly in a symbolic variant related to one of the Roman mystery religions."

"Pagan," Lucca said.

"Would he be the one to make the decision, though?" Nolin asked. "Make the new code?"

Gumm said, "Oberst Böll would be the final arbiter."

"And would he have any objections to a pagan code?"

"He's traditional—the Oberst—a patriot. He might not object, but his first choice would probably harken back to Prussia, something to do with his heritage."

"Teutonic then," Lucca said. "Most of the tribal symbols have slants, V-shapes. Awfully hard to do those the way the slots are laid out in rows."

"Elder Futhark, you mean?" Nolin asked.

Lucca nodded. "Wait. How about a different sort of cross? There are plenty of Teutonic symbols along those lines. That would still hold to my law of least effort." He sketched out a cross with extra crossbars at the top and bottom. The latter had additional downward facing lines to form a trident shape. He presented it to the others. "The runic sigil for 'guardian.'"

"How many bricks, though?" Paul asked. He grabbed the notebook and calculated the number based on the proportions Gumm had specified in his drawing then compared his answer to the number of bricks in the wall. "I estimate twenty-two. But I count only eighteen up there."

Lucca scurried to an ash heap against the wall, plunged his arms into it up to the elbows, and fetched up a brick. "Nineteen—I could just see the corner of it."

"Search em out, lads," Nolin said.

Babette kneeled over the hole in the floor, waiting for Nolin's signal. Watching the door a short distance away, Katsuo reassured her: "No worry, Bah-bette-san. Strongboy have generous destiny."

Prince Joey took a seat on one of the unmarked crates and prepared to oil his rifle. He had the rag out of his back pocket when Dixie approached.

"Hey," Dixie said. A momentary gloom crossed his face.

Prince Joey acknowledged him with a tired smile and ran the cloth over his Springfield. He'd never been to the South but thought of it as a bastardized version of aristocratic England. He imagined Dixie had grown up barefoot around warm Negro mammies and the children of former slaves, believing all the while they were a species apart. "Prob'ly not long afore the Huns come bustin through."

"You worried?"

"This *is* a suicide mission."

"Yeah, I like to died a bit ago," Dixie said. His voice had an uneasy whistle in it. "I don't know what got into me. Better to lose my head than my nerves, I guess." He tried to work up the gumption to say what he'd come for, but self-pity overwhelmed his sense of gratitude. He'd always considered niggers, no, *Negros*, little more than Nature's children—careless and undisciplined without white supervision. To owe a Negro your life was a shame on your manhood. "If you hadn't..." He felt the acne scars along his cheeks flaring.

Prince Joey set his gun and rag aside. Dixie's discomfort unsettled him, especially given his doubts about the timing of his saving shot. "We do for each other, man, you know that." Then, afraid he sounded biggety, added: "Sides, all the glory to God." God was the only thing he could think of that superseded race.

"You still a believer, everythin we seen? Just those devils got Eric woulda give Jaysus hisself the witherins."

"Even more." Prince Joey was relieved Dixie had been the first to swallow his emotions. He unbuttoned his tunic's high collar and pulled out a silver cross on the end of a chain. "Me? I think these devils we been facin just a way to shake us outta our sleep."

"I'm with you on that. Always been a man a the hardshell stripe myself." He pulled his sleeve up to reveal a braided bracelet with a cheap cross pendant. "God is under attack fer sure. Him and the Devil are caught up in their eternal wrassle. The Devil done seeded the earth with horror and God is a-reelin from it. He ain't got but the one Jaysus and the Devil got an army. He needs all the allies He can get, yeah?"

"Somebody's gotta make up for Nolin's piss-poor luck."

Dixie grinned. "Ain't that the truth? Swear he's the Devil's own lightnin rod."

"*Eho dum!*" Paul held brick number twenty-two aloft. His hands were powdered in ash-grit.

"Great," Lucca said. "Now try not to drop it."

Paul deposited his find atop the other recovered bricks against the hieroglyphic wall.

"Alright, lads," Nolin said. "That's it for you. Go on upstairs and I'll make do here." Paul started to protest but Nolin cut him off, emphatic: "You've done your best here. Go on now…"

Paul looked through Nolin, wondering how many people he would have to give up in this life. He was still miserable over the loss of his dad at age seven. Most of the time, his dad had earned a living as a herring trawler off the coast of Arklow. But whenever his fights with Paul's Mam started to get out of hand, he'd sign on as a merchant sea-man for a few months. It was on one of these tours that he was tossed overboard, some say by storm winds, others by a crewman who accused him of cheating at cards. In both versions of the story, though, he was thoroughly drunk. Paul had joined the Royal Irish Lancers only to stay close to Nolin. He'd never even played at being a soldier. He patted Nolin on the back. "Godspeed," was all he could manage.

Lucca reassured Nolin with a flinchy smile then turned to escort

Gumm up the staircase.

Nolin hefted the first brick, picturing the completed sigil-code. He was vulnerable to intense heat. Failure here meant burning alive, burning down to the hot. The muscles on the back of his neck tightened. When the footfalls on the stairs faded, he pushed the first brick into place. The clank of massive generators coming to life shuddered through the walls. He'd been so busy working out the passcode that he hadn't considered how the security system distinguished between an unfinished arrangement of bricks and a genuine error. When the generators came to life, he understood instantly: the system was on a timer.

The subterranean rumble startled Babette. She jumped back from her kneeling position, half-expecting a column of fire to shoot from the cave. Katsuo spun in her direction, weapon shouldered, and was soon flanked by Prince Joey and Dixie. "The trap been sprung?" Dixie asked.

"I don't know, désolé," Babette said. "The sound is like machines."

Dixie started toward the hole when Gumm clambered up, short of breath.

"What is it ?" Dixie asked.

"The compressers ... for the flamethrowers."

"What about the others?"

Gumm made a vaguely dismissive gesture. "They were behind me then started back when the vents kicked on."

Prince Joey waved him away from the cave entrance with his gun. "Over there, near the crates. Katsuo, keep your gun on him. If anything's happened to them ..." He leaned into the hole. "Nolin! Paul!" Indistinct but strained voices filtered up the staircase over the low drone of the generators.

"Are they dying?" Babette asked. The prospect brought on a tangle of remembered hurts: Eric's convulsed body; her first lover partialed in gore; the empty home where her mother should be; her grieving father—lives ended or arrested in events that originated with Gumm. She unsnapped the thumb-break strap over her Luger.

The thrum of the generators veered into a higher, more intense pitch. Dixie gagged on the sudden uprush of sooty air. The voices below were lost to the roar, maybe forever. Prince Joey and Babette exchanged helpless looks. A small cry escaped her throat. She whirled on Gumm and leveled her gun at him. "What is it? What is happening?" Fear and guilt urged her to pull the trigger.

The rising machine-noise blotted out everything then—

Silence like an oppressive dream.

"Nolin!" Prince Joey called. "You alright? Paul! Lucca!" He took a tentative step into the stairwell. His heart railed against the cage of his chest. He feared what he might discover in the cave-darkness. Each deliberate stride resounded in his ears. A thin voice brought him up short.

"I love it when your voice cracks, Prince J," came Lucca's distant reply.

Prince Joey's pulse eased. "Everyone alright?"

"It's safe to come down now if that's what you mean. Not safe-safe, but Lost Boys safe. You'll see."

Chapter 9
Underworld/Otherworld

The narrow portal unlocked in the hieroglyphic wall opened onto a spacious, bulb-lit chamber with three divergent passages. It was clear by the size and uniformity of the passages that they were man-made. The rectangular tunnels were wide enough to allow for two people to walk side by side. An enormous rock split from the nearest wall blocked the rightmost passage; the others, however, appeared to be clear. Nolin sized up the obstruction. "What now, Gumm?"

"I honestly don't know. These passages are new since my last time here."

"What good is he then?" Babette said.

"Don't forget, Mademoiselle," Gumm said. "I'm the only one who knows how to control the Mimorodat."

"*Zut alors!* And we should trust you to do it? The more I hear about what you have done—the crimes you have committed against my people—the more I—"

"Babette," Nolin said. "I understand your anger, believe me, but we have to consider what's best for the mission."

Paul said, "Thee-uh the tunnels we can see—they seem to go in the same general direction. This third one, I don't know. Might be collapsed somewhere along the way."

"Or hiding something important," Lucca said.

"How about I try to move it aside so you can take a look?" Nolin asked.

Gumm scoffed. "Ah, to be young again and foolish-brave."

Nolin ignored the comment, absorbed in examining the rock from several angles. He tensed his fingers and tested it for firmness.

"You want I should set a charge, Lieutenant?" Dixie asked.

"I'd be afraid of bringing the roof down on us. I'm going to try a push. Paul, be quick with your flashlight." Nolin positioned himself on one side, cheek flush against the rock, and embraced it in a bear hug. The slab was ungainly large at the bottom and tapered to a wedge. Moving it a serious degree would take his utmost. He closed his eyes and pitched forward as if to surprise it. His thighs strained against the weight. The rock trembled in its groove then shifted and yawed toward the wall. Paul beamed his light into the uncovered top half of the passage.

"Like a giant outten the Ol Testament," Dixie whispered to Babette. She struggled to find her voice, astonished at Nolin's strength, until an oily-black something glinted in the light. Membranous wings flitted in and out of view. She muttered a French vulgarity and drew her weapon.

"Back! Put it back!" Paul yelled.

Nolin worried he'd already pushed the boulder past its tipping point. He felt the rock's momentum taking him with it. The muscles in his shoulders and arms bunched in agony. His heels started off the ground and he wrenched himself backward. The rock seesawed a bit—enough for a couple of pygmy-sized imps to pass through. Another scurried to do the same and was crushed between the settling rock and the tunnel's edge. Its oversized jaw spewed broken teeth and driblets of gum.

Dixie drew his Mare's Laig Winchester and worked the lever action. "Law-me! It's a skeet shoot!" The weapon's booms threw the imps into a panic.

"*Yokai!*" Katsuo shouted.

The creatures flapped to the limits of the domed ceiling, gleaming against the greater darkness like fresh tar. They scrabbled the air with sickle-shaped claws and long, thin tails. Paul waved his flashlight in a hectic effort to keep both creatures in view. The imps shrieked their displeasure at the stabbing brightness and stooped to attack, tucking their tails behind them.

A torrent of bullets perforated the monsters. Their strangled cries raised the gooseflesh on Paul's arms. One crashed in a bloodied heap at his feet and the other, somehow still alive, winged its way toward Nolin desperate to return to its former hide.

Lucca shucked Gumm of his military overcoat with a curt yank and made off with it. "Allez-oop!" he cried.

Nolin bent over and made a stirrup of his interlocked fingers. Lucca ran three short steps and placed his foot in the stirrup. Nolin flung him heavenward. Lucca somersaulted backward, wrapped the overcoat around the surviving imp and alighted on his feet with a flourish. Katsuo stomped on one of the overcoat's sleeves and Prince Joey stood on its skirt. The creature thrashed in a rage under the field gray wool. One of its claws ripped through and the two squadmates laid into the monster, sending up freshets of blood.

"Numbah one!" Katsuo declared.

"Oh, don't get ahead of yourself man," Prince Joey said.

Dixie leaned toward Babette while reloading his Winchester. "This is like a reg'lar thing round Nolin. You get used to it. These flyin nasties are the least uns. Last month, I scrapped with a Pictish beast. Whipped em frutally."

"Aye, for uh five-six seconds," Paul said.

"Longer'n you."

Lucca bellied up to Gumm. "Sorry bout the jacket. But you won't need it where you're going."

"You haven't got it sorted right yet," Gumm said quietly. He had a flickering sense of the Mimirodat's bristling energies. The entity goaded him with its vast, strange potential. He was convinced a crucial barrier between worlds would soon fall. "We're not going to hell. Hell is coming to us."

"Form up," Nolin said and clapped twice for the squad's attention. A thorough dusting of earth and ash gave him a spectral look. His eyes were pitted dark circles. "Looks like the way forward's been decided by those maggoty things. Given the time pressures, I've no choice but to split the squad—one team per tunnel. The tank remains our first priority. But if you've a chance to destroy this Mimirodat, take it." He pointed to the passage on the left. "Lucca, you'll lead Paul, Dixie and Babette in that direction. The rest of you will come with me. That means you, too, Mr. Gumm. Consider yourself a draftee."

Nolin's remarks barely registered with Gumm. The squad's plans were irrelevant against the transcendent powers of the Mimirodat. In spite of his skullcap's protections, its familiar dream-noise was breaking in on him again—further proof of their special connection.

A rush of feeling pushed Nolin to say more. "I'm not one for self-important speeches. Those of you who've served with me a while know that. But given the long odds here, I'm moved to say this: Before the Battle of Platea, the Oracle at Delphi predicted the vastly outnumbered Greeks were doomed against their Persian enemies. But the Greeks emerged victorious by making the Persians believe they'd retreated and re-engaging them. Numbers alone don't win wars. With greater stealth and cunning, we can get through this. Eric was a fine soldier and an even better mate. His death gave the rest of us the chance to live. Let's make the most of it."

Nolin thought back to the husk of Eric's body. That softened skull evoked memories of his childhood bedtime routine. His father used to affirm Nolin's need for sleep with a kiss on the forehead. When he was older, his mother explained that his father had kissed him as a precaution. It ensured one last loving memory in the event of his father's untimely death. Some days, Nolin thought he could feel the imprint of those long-ago kisses. "Alright. That's enough from me. Ready your gear now. We depart in five minutes."

Nolin made straight for Lucca and pulled him aside.

"What now?" Lucca asked.

"I know we've had our differences," Nolin said in a low tone. "I just want to assure you that you have my trust and the trust of the squad. More than that, I believe you're a good man, even if you sometimes don't. I need you on the other side of this, so promise me: no foolhardy risks."

"And lose my status as the squad's cheery rogue to—I don't know—Katsuo?"

Nolin broke into a reluctant smile. "Couldn't you give me a moment to pretend you'd agree? This is serious, Lucca."

"I can see that. I just don't understand why." His voice was hoarse with tension. He couldn't wait to get away and shake off these strangling emotions.

"I don't know if it's the tank or the Mimirodat or something else, but…" The fatigue Nolin had pushed through up to this point came back to him. "At the front, I received a private message from MII: *Cenhadaeth cod Arwan gwariadwy sgwad*. Mission code: Arwan. Squad expendable."

At the knock on his office door, Oberst Böll straightened in his high-backed chair and adjusted his skullcap. He'd taken to slouching over his desk and treating the cap like a dusting rag—pulling it down on one side then the other—to relieve his itchy scalp. "*Eintreten.*"

His young aide-de-camp came in and saluted. "Oberst."

The adjutant assumed a liquid quality. The fingers of his salute-hand streamed across Böll's field of vision then snapped back to solidity. "What is it, Leitzke?"

"The radio monitors report a disturbance in the outer tunnels—the old cult temple."

Based on his recent conversation with Geiszler, Böll figured it had to be Gumm, perhaps accompanied by a few French fighters. No one else could possibly have dispatched the *Puppen Shatten* and circumvented the base's defenses. "Send a squad to investigate. If they discover intruders, they're to take no prisoners." He folded his hands behind his head in an effort to control the growing urge to scratch. His scalp pulsed with unnatural heat. What was Lietzke waiting for? He loathed the boy in that moment for his youth and health, his lips as red as a painted woman's.

"Begging the Oberst's pardon, but what about interrogations?"

"There's nothing of value we can learn," Böll said. The pain cascading from crown to ears crimped his sight. The aide-de-camp appeared to fold in on himself. Although the distortion vanished after a few deliberate blinks, Böll began to panic inside. "By this time tomorrow, *Projekt Kettenblitz* will be operational. Everyone between here and the front will be humbled before us." He gave his scalp a brisk scratch through his skullcap, wondering if he was visibly shaking. "You have my orders. See that they're carried out."

As soon as Leitzke shut the door, Böll grabbed for the phone. He had to call Geiszler. He must have an infection of some sort. He jiggled the hook in a fury. The base of the phone shuddered like a dying animal. He shut his eyes and forced his mind to be still. The tone in his ear assumed the textured qualities of a wind instrument or a wordless voice. The sound helixed into his hollow-feeling chest. The sound was everything.

The shaft was level straight and timber-supported. A string of large bulbs along one side provided a dim, crepuscular light. Nolin navigated the passage just a step or two behind Gumm. Katsuo and Prince Joey followed, hands on their weapons. The spy had lapsed into a worrying silence. Nolin took especial note when Gumm stepped past a cast-off sledge without a glance. "Any idea how much farther we have to go? Or where we'll come out?" Nolin asked.

Gumm raised a hand and slowly made a fist of it. His knuckles were large and craggy. "As I said at the farmhouse, from this direction we should end up at the mechanical plant and administrative offices. The barracks are after that, but you'll want to descend two levels to the maintenance bay. That's where you'll find the tank." He opened his fist. "Feel the draught? That's the ventilation."

"How long has it been, exactly, since you worked with the Germans?"

"Almost a year. Those devils back there must've been one of Dr. Geiszler's failed experiments." He gave Nolin a curious look. "That feat with the rock—impressive. What other tricks can I expect?"

"I could ask you the same. Did you know about the timer?"

Gumm put an index finger to the side of his nose. "I suspected as much."

"I meant what I said back there—about destroying the Mimirodat."

"What is this? Some Twelve Labors of Hercules tour?" Gumm scoffed. "You seem well-versed in the supernatural, granted, but the Mimirodat . . . It's powers make the gods of Greek antiquity look like doddering old Mughals."

"You plan to live forever?"

"You get to be my age, there's no harm in trying." Even with the Mimirodat humming in his blood, it was all too easy to see himself in Nolin and his compatriots, each one a fugitive from mundane unhappiness. He was more animal than soul at their age, too, seeking adventure to relieve his visceral appetites, first in the British colonies and then, after his discovery of the Mimirodat, in the South Pacific, searching for the Parmatmar crystals that would make visible its radiant glory. Soon, he would be done with mere animal adventurism and could safely turn his appetites inward. The psychic plane the Mimirodat promised had no horizons.

A vertical crack of light alerted Nolin to a door about thirty meters ahead. His heart misgave when the crack widened to emit a squad of German soldiers. He held up a fist. Prince Joey and Katsuo stopped, instantly alert. Gumm, however, continued apace, unseeing or distracted. The clump of his boots sounded overly loud to Nolin's ears. Gumm seemed intent in walking right into the enemy. Nolin had no choice: he rushed forward and swept Gumm aside. The Germans' initial salvo raked the tunnel. Bullets struck Nolin in the chest and stomach. "Stay back!" he urged before returning fire. There was no bend or obstruction behind which his men could take cover. He would be their defense. He charged the Germans at a run, not worrying overmuch about his aim.

The enemy soldiers were grouped around the steel, vault-like entrance to the base. They panicked at Nolin's berserker assault, stepping on each other and waving their guns in order to get clear. The squad leader lost his lower jaw and tumbled to the dirt. His second-in-command fell over him, his gut leaking fluids. The remaining three soldiers retreated, catching at the door. Nolin was closing in: four meters, three, two…The mechanized door started to swing closed. A klaxon sounded and a rotating light above the door flashed a warning. He shot a retreating soldier in the elbow then dropped his rifle for the door. He pulled against its gears and contrived to retard its progress. His bout with the rock, however, had weakened him. He couldn't hold the door for long. He scooted on the other side of it, grappling for leverage. He caught a glimpse of Prince Joey and Katsuo running after him. The circular hatch slammed shut.

Nolin scrutinized the door's control panel for a release mechanism. He punched a few buttons but to no avail. The klaxon suggested a general lockdown. He turned to find himself in a corridor with a curved steel roof and handrails along the walls. The German with the shattered elbow was on the floor and struggling to rise. The soldier looked a bit stout, but Nolin thought he could make good use of his uniform then find the security control room and unlock the door. In the meantime, there was no help for it. Katsuo and Prince Joey were on their own with Gumm.

Chapter 10
Alien Frequencies

Lucca had been relieved when the tunnel had offered up a simple means to infiltrate the base unseen. The passage had dead-ended at a perpendicular shaft that presumably extended to the surface. A quick investigation via flashlight had confirmed its use for ventilation. The team had climbed down the maintenance ladder embedded in the shaft wall and unscrewed the ventilation grate with combat knives. It hadn't been necessary to put anyone in danger yet. Particularly after hearing the coded message from MII, Lucca couldn't help but worry after his men, especially Babette. She was gutsy enough, but untrained and unused to out-and-out combat. He would have to rely on Dixie to help keep her safe. Naturally, Dixie was sweet on her already.

The size of the ventilation shaft required them to belly crawl. They advanced on elbows and knees, using their outthrust weapons to push their haversacks forward, first one end then the other. It was slow and sweaty work in near-dark conditions. The penlight Lucca gritted between his teeth provided the only illumination. He led them in the general direction of the draught rushing through the system, up, down, sideways. When he reached a grille in the metal surface, he stopped and held up a fist. He peered through the slits and caught flickers of black and field gray. "Soldiers," he hissed down the line. He took the chance that the grille would support him and went on, careful not to scrape the butt of his rifle on the metal. His concern was obviated by the blaring of klaxons. He scrambled on the assumption Nolin's party had been found out. He was driving so hard and so fast he nearly lost his haversack in an adjoining shaft. He snatched the end of the backpack and pulled it parallel so he could gauge the drop. The penlight didn't penetrate to the bottom but he could make out a dim light source there. He estimated ten to twelve meters. He lunged over the shaft and, gripping the top rung on the ladder, rolled into it, heels over head. He retrieved his haversack and propped it on one shoulder while he made the descent. Paul fell into the shaft after him in a far less elegant fashion.

The source of light at the bottom turned out to be a low wall-vent. Lucca could make out concrete flooring and the legs of folding cots. "Could be a medical station or a barracks," he told Paul. "But I can't see or hear anybody."

When they were fully regrouped, Dixie looked from Lucca to Paul and said, "You boys know the only smarts I got is a right smart a lead. I'm a-waitin on you for the plan."

Paul said, "Wish I had something better than uh bust in and shoot, but..."

"Don't be badmouthin my apitude now," Dixie said.

Lucca asked, "We good then? Babette?"

She could scarce believe how her life had gone since the advent of the war, how different things were here, now, from her childhood imaginings. There was a real possibility she would die before the conflict was over. The cumulative anxiety made the idea of doing something—even something foolish—seem better than skulking in the dark. She unholstered her Luger. "You think I am here for the gift shop?"

"Roger that. Dixie, the entrance line is yours."

Dixie grinned at Babette. "See ya on the yon side a hell, darlin." He kicked the vent out, swung into the open, and immediately faltered, dumbstruck by what he'd found. "We're clear," he said as Paul clambered out after him.

It was a vast warehouse redolent of bleach. The disappeared townsfolk—men, women, children and infants—lay on row after row of padded cots. They were outfitted in white paper hospital gowns. Bulbous helmets like snail shells covered the crowns of their shaved heads and gas masks covered their mouths to their chins. Accordion tubes ran from the helmets and masks into fitted sockets in the floor. The warehouse was utterly quiet except for a low, pervasive hum more felt than heard. The walls were a pristine white as were the regularly-placed nightstands and standing light fixtures.

"*Ma mère*," Babette said, pushing past Lucca into the first aisle. "She must be here somewhere."

"Dixie," Lucca said. "Follow her with one eye."

"I'll see if I can spot us an exit while I'm at it. Whistle if you need me back in a hurry." Dixie left his haversack and loped after Babette. She was darting from one cot to the next.

"Any idea what this is?" Lucca asked.

Paul approached the nearest cot. It was occupied by a pallid, middle-aged woman. "Besides uh trouble, you mean?" He propped his rifle against the bed and put two fingers against the woman's carotid artery. "Thee-uh pulse is slow, but..." He pulled her eyelids up and studied the constricted pupils. "Penlight?"

Lucca wiped his saliva from the penlight before handing it to him.

"A true gentleman," Paul said. The woman's greenish eyes showed a delayed reaction. "Eyes aren't the best indicators of specific drugs, but I'd guess an ether mix of some kind, maybe part morphine. I might do the doctoring for thee-uh the squad, but this isn't my uh area of expertise." He pushed his glasses back to the bridge of his nose.

Lucca gestured toward the catheter bag hanging from the IV pole at the foot of her cot. "Looks like it's been a while since she's taken her morning constitutional."

"Here," Paul said. "Let's try a uh little experiment." He ranged among the cots, searching for a suitable test subject.

"With me as the guinea pig?"

"Not this time, though you are uh remarkably resilient. What was it your dad first trained you as? Contortionist?"

"I think that was an excuse for using his medieval rack on me." Lucca was reminded of how his life had paralleled Dr. Nikola's in respect to the childhood tortures he'd endured. After losing his birth and then his foster parents, the fictional doctor had come into the household of an abusive island governor who, at one point, subjected Nikola to hot pincers.

"This'll do," Paul announced over the bed of a sallow twenty-something. "We should try this with someone young, I think. Don't know what kind of shock this might be to his system." He gripped the metal ring that joined the accordion tube to the helmet and gave it a twist. The tube swiveled free. The young sleeper spasmed upright, eyes wide and arms flailing. Lucca restrained his arms at the wrists while Paul reconnected the tube. The sleeper blinked a few times then flopped back into the same docile position as before.

"Is that what you expected?" Lucca asked.

The Cartesian-mechanistic implications of the experiment fascinated Paul. "I wasn't sure uh what to expect."

"Well, this is academic and all, but we shouldn't waste any more time here. Those klaxons have got to be for Nolin and his team. We need to find that damn tank before it's too late."

"You don't mean ...? We can't leave these people like this," Paul said. "If Nolin were here, he'd—"

"He'd say the same. You heard him: the *Kettenblitz* is our first priority."

Paul motioned toward Babette. She and Dixie had progressed about seventy meters in their search. "Tell that to her."

"I like this new voice—defiant, confident, none of that hiccupping self-consciousness that makes me sleepy. You bucking for my job?"

"I'm getting teary-eyed now. That's the closest you've uh ever come to complimenting me."

"My head's been rattled pretty hard the past few days." Lucca surveyed the grim expanse of anesthetized townsfolk. A small nameless emotion gathered in his throat. "*Sto cazzo*. Okay, okay, you *attaccabottoni*."

"Now you're just trying to cheer me up."

"I'm not finished: You stay here with Dixie and Babette while I look for the tank."

"No, not by yourself."

"I can move faster and hide easier that way. If it makes you feel any better, I'll take Dixie's munitions along. That should be enough backup."

"That's hardly a plan."

"Why start now?" A weightless smile played across his lips. "Stay here and I'll be back for you. If you're forced to retreat, take the ventilator shaft back to the tunnel. That's an order, Corporal."

Paul gripped Lucca by the forearm. His stomach tried to turn itself inside out. "Don't go and get yourself killed, Mouse. I would hate to have to uh explain that to Nolin."

The entrance to the maintenance bay had been sealed within two minutes of the klaxons going off. Ten armed men watched over the *Kettenblitz*, while two others patrolled the garage and the ramp to the surface. When the intercom buzzed, the soldier closest to the door motioned for the others to stay and answered, "Who is it?"

"This is Lieutenant Ruhlman. Open at once!"

"Apologies, Lieutenant. But protocol specifies we keep this area locked until we receive the all-clear."

"The saboteurs damaged the security control room before they were apprehended. The alarms are malfunctioning. I have written confirmation from Oberst Böll to that effect." There was a distinct note of arrogance in the reply. The soldier examined the speaker through a peephole. He'd never heard of this lieutenant before but as a lowly private that meant nothing. The Lieutenant flashed the order. "I have no time to waste, soldier. Open up now!"

The soldier looked back to his comrades as if for an answer. He was loath to upset an officer, especially one apparently so quick to anger. He put his rifle down and manipulated the door's several locks: *thunk, thunk, thunk*. He pressed his eye to the peephole again and was startled to see the Lieutenant donning a GM-15 gas mask. His warning shout was barely a noise in the back of his throat when the door smashed him into unconsciousness.

Nolin hurled two canisters toward the soldiers positioned around the tank. One trailed a plume of smoke, the other, tear gas. The soldiers yelped and cursed as they fired. The shots and their echoes overlapped like a roiling thunderhead. Nolin dove away, sprung to his feet and made himself a wraith in the chemical clouds. His attack was swift and brutal—a blur of fists and feet and gunfire. It was a chance for him to cut loose without fear of emboldening his men to take impossible risks. He worked in violent increments, operating on sound and inference. Stick, spin, kick, move, shoot…The mask limited his vision and the frontal weight of the filter distracted him. But the Germans mobbed up and got in the way of each other, allowing for a measure of sloppiness his close combat tutor would've never tolerated. Feint, punch, choke, twist…He applied only as much force as the moment required. He didn't hate the Germans, only what they made him do. Some days, it seemed he'd lived a hundred lives and none of them his real self.

Disoriented by the smoke and gas, Nolin's foes didn't have a chance. He finished off the last of the guards with a heelstrike to the back of the head. The commotion brought the soldiers on patrol down the ramp. They unleashed a craze of bullets. A ricochet off the tank passed so close to Nolin's face he felt its heat through his mask. He took aim and dry-fired, the gun empty. He hurled the useless weapon full-force and retrieved another from the ground. One of the approaching soldiers stumbled in dodging the thrown rifle. Nolin cut him down with shots to the thigh and gut then toppled his compatriot in the same sweeping motion.

The Lieutenant secured the door then mounted the *Kettenblitz* two rungs at a time. The klaxons and warning lights stilled—a small mercy for someone with Nolin's heightened senses. Standing atop the machine, he took stock of its armor plating and weaponry. The tank was impressive all around. The .75 caliber cannon up front plus the auxiliary cluster of heavy machine guns ensured a clear path in any direction. Only the triangle of angled struts behind the hatch mystified him. It looked like the struts were intended to support a canted shield of some kind, perhaps a protective screen for another gunner. Whatever it was, he was confident Paul would figure it out.

Nolin stripped off his gas mask, wiped the sweat from his forehead with the back of his gun hand, and threw open the hatch. He was anxious to see how much damage he could do.

Chapter 11
The Undoing

The ache in Babette's throat pulsed stronger with every trying breath. She barely recognized her mother. The hairless patches around the ears, the blanched skin and blue-ridged veins, the fever-stink—none of it registered as the woman who used to gently wake her for school. As much as Babette wanted to cry, the throat-ache stifled her tongue. She bent to her mother's face, wary of touching her, dismayed by the gossamer fragility of it. The most she could bring herself to do was extend her hands—palms first—a few centimeters above her mother's head as if to ward off some invisible danger.

Dixie put a light hand on her shoulder. "You get Paul to take a look, I spect her to vine up again." He glanced in the direction of the ventilation shaft and was surprised to discover Lucca missing. His absence added to Dixie's unease. He angled himself at Babette's side to keep the large double doors behind them in view. There was no telling when they'd be found out by a nurse or physician, if not a contingent of soldiers. "I know this is hard seein your ma this way, your village, but ... won't do nobody good we stay put like a froze rabbit."

When her voice emerged a feeble croak, she grasped his forearm and permitted herself to be led back.

The twinge of pain at the corner of her mouth made her seem less aloof or guarded than before. Dixie checked the impulse to put a comforting hand on the small of her back, content to marvel at her elegant neck, the soft curve of her jaw. Babette or something like her—some outside validation of his worth—was the reason he was here. She was fine-boned but tough and wiry with nerve. He thought of her as a beauty made of tiny sharp points. He'd be willing to die if he could honestly claim to have the esteem of a woman like her at his time of dying.

Paul suspended his examination of one of the bulbous helmets. "Thee-uh they're alright from what I can make out. Just in a uh artificial sleep. Malnourished some, but I don't think there's been any uh permanent harm."

"What—" Babette bit her lower lip then, recovering her voice, asked "What can we do to get them out?"

"I don't rightly know. Thee-uh there must be close to a uh thousand. Buses, lorries…There must be a motor pool hereabouts. We're near one of the canals, right? Maybe a boat."

"The barges," she said. "The barges on the Canal de Saint-Quentin. I know one in Cambrai who can pilot them."

"Does your little group have a crystal set?"

"*Oui*, a short-wave tuner. It was Monsieur Gumm's."

"No doubt lifted from thee-uh Germans."

"We use it to listen in."

"There we go. We just need to find the communications center." Paul shot Dixie a look of helplessness at adding to their objectives.

"Where'd Lucca disappear to?" Dixie asked.

"He went to find the *Kettenblitz*. Or Nolin. Both, probably. We need to uh regroup and get—"

The double doors banged open for two orderlies carrying a patient on a stretcher. On spotting Paul and his team, the orderly closest to the door let go his end—*spang*—and fled the room. The drugged patient was oblivious to this indignity. The remaining orderly surrendered with a shrug of his shoulders, eyeing the three guns pointed at him with bemusement.

"What's the play, Shimmy?" Dixie asked.

Paul grabbed the helmet of the sleeping man in front of him and twisted the accordion tube free. The man jerked upright like he'd received an electric shock. "We botch things up," Paul said, reaching for the next helmet.

Geiszler made slow progress rolling his oak file cabinet through the crush of soldiers and support personnel. One of the cabinet's back wheels *tha-thumped* awkwardly, forcing him to continually correct its direction. The cabinet contained the essential files from his office. He was desperate to safeguard them from Gumm. Once he'd collected his books and notes from the master control room, he could safely lock himself in the Mimirodat's holding cell and enact the ritual that would reveal its true nature. Taking the elevator to the top floor, he imagined Oberst Böll was suffering the first disorienting effects of the entity's burgeoning energies. He'd disabled Böll's skullcap days ago in preparation for this moment, subverting its sigils under the pretext of reinforcing them. It's unfortunate Gumm's intervention had forced his hand before the launch of the *Kettenblitz*. But no matter. The outcome would be the same.

When he gained access to the control room, however, he was alarmed to find the Mimirodat flashing and fading spasmodically. He hurried to the main console and cleared the instruments of stray papers. The dials that measured the influx of psychic energy from the townspeople showed precipitous declines. He reset the instruments and, coming up with the same dire result, punched for a test of the extraction system.

"*Dreh dich um,*" came an unfamiliar voice. "*Langsam.*"

He turned to find a dark-haired soldier in British uniform holding a revolver on him. There was a haversack wedged between the automatic door and its frame. Geiszler surmised the soldier must have hooked the carryall into the gap before the door shut. He'd been so preoccupied with the condition of the Mimirodat, he hadn't noticed the door's failure to close entirely. Without taking the gun off him, the soldier yanked the haversack free. There would be no help coming from the corridor.

"You are not English. *Amerikanisch?*" Geiszler hazarded from the accent.

Lucca jerked his head toward the observation window. "The Mimirodat?"

"You know then. Where is Herr Gumm?"

"Somewhere," Lucca said. "He told us about your plan, how you can use this creature to broadcast fear, paranoia, senseless anger—trumped-up emotions to weaken our troops. But he was a bit vague on the details. How'd you capture it? Learn to use it? I'm sure it involves astral projection, the dreamtime...This isn't my first supernatural rodeo."

"You cannot expect me to divulge these secrets."

Lucca advanced on Geiszler and rapped him on the ear with the barrel of his gun. When Geiszler flinched, Lucca snatched his skullcap and placed it on his own head. "Suits me fine. I'm used to figuring things out for myself. I'll just take these books and notes—the *Ater Opus*, right?—and study them at my leisure."

"Do what you will," Geiszler said. He hated personal weakness. He regarded it as the worst kind of naiveté. It belied the eternal essence of Nature, which was animal struggle and vast indifference. "The Mimirodat is proof of a reality beyond all this—this self-destructive squabbling, the whole human order. Claim the creature, free it, destroy it, any respite from its primal chaos will be temporary. Our future was written in the stars long ago."

"Too bad you have to live in the here and now." Lucca traded the gun for his stiletto. The German scientist would meet an end much like Dr. Nikola's—a victim of his own irrepressible desire to know. Lucca wasn't completely without sympathy for Geiszler. He supposed he'd share a comparable fate one day. "I'm familiar with every nerve cluster, every trigger point and artery. I can make seconds pass like hours." He twirled the blade point-on against his index finger. "And that, sadly, is the closest you're going to get to the deep future."

"Sure this is it?" Prince Joey asked in a low voice. The ceiling vent afforded only a partial view of the hallway. He caught flickering images of operations personnel running to and fro.

Gumm leaned across him to peer through the loosened vent.

"After you with the push," Prince Joey said. He shared an exasperated look with Katsuo.

"The Oberst's office is two-three meters to the right," Gumm said. "His adjutant has a desk just outside it and the security center is across the way." He tugged on his unruly beard. "This is as far as I go with you, agreed? I have a more important task."

Once the access door slammed shut on them, Prince Joey and his team had double-timed it to the adjacent passage and discovered the ventilation shaft used by Lucca's group. Gumm had persuaded Prince Joey to take over the security center in order to circumvent the automatic lockdown protocols and give the Lost Boys a fair chance to escape. The idea had sounded reasonable in the abstract. Operationalizing it, however, meant leaving Gumm to his own devices and dropping into a corridor hectic with enemy forces. Prince Joey regretted the need to let Gumm go, but didn't see a way around it. He couldn't watch his back and at the same time, effectively defend against the Germans. In this situation, every possible move brought him one step closer to death. The actual form it took was irrelevant. Prince Joey blinked hard once, twice. It felt like his eyes had been pushed into his skull. "You alright with this, Katsuo?" He pulled the bolt back on his rifle to confirm it was at capacity.

Katsuo's small eyes were unclouded. He gave a slight bow. "*Ganbarimasu*. I do my best."

"This ain't a contest, you understand. Cause if it was, I would win. You know—"

"For my emperor." Katsuo smashed the vent free with the butt of his gun and plunged into the hallway.

"Inscrutable, right?" Prince Joey muttered.

Gumm said, "The fellow takes his oaths seriously."

"So do I," Prince Joey said, ducking into the gap. "Damn you Huns!" He hit the ground and rolled against the wall opposite Katsuo. A startled secretary hurried into an adjoining office. Behind her, two soldiers drawn by the commotion drew their revolvers. Katsuo plugged one in the chest and again, along the jaw. His companion shouted for help and fled around a corner. Prince Joey turned toward the Oberst's office. The adjutant doubled-up under his desk. Another pair of soldiers, this time from the security center, surged into view. Katsuo winged them before they could raise their weapons. Prince Joey finished them with a single bullet through the neck then dove onto the concrete to thrust his rifle into the room before the door closed. He waggled the weapon up and down as he emptied it.

Katsuo joined in the mayhem, nearly splintering the door from its hinges while Prince Joey reloaded. "That make three," Katsuo said.

"Don't be double-countin now ..." Prince Joey strained to hear anything from the other side of the door. Sensing nothing, he kicked it in and hastened to the far corner. A blood-sotted German still gripping a radio headset lay on the floor. He issued a last intimate breath. The barrage had wrecked the short-wave set and scored the walls and instrument panels. "Watch the door," Prince Joey said. "I'll look for the emergency release." Gumm had described it as a pull station with a clear cover. The corridor sounded with a timpani of heelstrikes. Prince Joey had only a few seconds. He found a red-stickered handle marked NOTFALL ABDECKUNG (emergency cover) and yanked on it. A series of red panel lights switched to green. He took that as confirmation he'd released the fail-safe electronic locks on the main interior and perimeter doors. To prevent the Germans from reactivating the locks, he blasted the panel at close range until the instrument lights went dark.

The noise from the corridor quieted. Katsuo motioned for Prince Joey to join him in the corner where they'd present the smallest possible target. Just outside the door, urgent whispers punctuated the shifting of arms. Prince Joey expected the *clink-clink* of a lobbed grenade at any moment. He slung his rifle and grabbed the dead German by the wrists. He'd gone through too much to give up easily. He swelled with the pressure of everything he'd never do: share his war experiences with his dad; kneel again in the sanctuary of the Berean Baptist Church;

fall back in with his pals from Boys High School; date that spritely, caramel-colored girl from Ocean Hill... His heart seemed a jagged fit in his chest.

Katsuo paled with a dull, helpless anger. He wondered if it were better to know your time had come or to be taken by surprise. His eyes shifted from the door to Prince Joey and back again. He trusted his family would somehow know he'd died honorably—in defense of a higher order. His low birth meant he would be a low spirit, too, but maybe his sacrifice would earn him some additional power in the after-life. He tried to picture himself dead—as dead as the enemy in Prince Joey's grip—and his soul or *reikon* whisking up from his ragged body.

A stick grenade on its five second fuse bounced off the doorframe and into the room. Prince Joey heaved the corpse at it. The muted roar spattered blood and viscera everywhere. Prince Joey retreated into the corner with Katsuo, alive but defeated. He was out of ideas. The next grenade would—

His chest reverberated with an explosion in the hallway. A dropped grenade? He leaned forward for a better view. The door to the Oberst's office had crashed to the floor and the adjutant's desk overturned. The troops pushed and shouted at each other, scrambling to repel another, more urgent threat. There was a smattering of gunfire and an unearth-ly screech. Katsuo picked off a fleeing soldier. Prince Joey raised his Springfield. The barrel flexed like a garden hose. He recoiled from the weapon, confused. A rapid eyeblink cleared the distortion, but did noth-ing to resolve the large, bone-plated monster that Böll had become.

After the first several townspeople were freed, it was clear they wouldn't provide the kind of large-scale distraction Paul had hoped for. They awoke with a convulsive start then promptly lapsed into a stupor. Most—vacant-eyed and mouths agape—lurched to the middle of the room to form a slow-motion scrum. Others, however, managed only a painful elbow-crawl. A few of these unfortunates shredded their paper gowns, revealing backsides lousy with bedsores. When Paul spotted a squat old man with a bedsore that left the base of his spine exposed, he advanced on the orderly in a rage. "G'd blind me! What're you doing to these people?"

The orderly trembled at Paul's vehemence and, averting his eyes, sputtered something in German.

Paul was tempted to strike out despite the orderly's inability to understand him. Instead, he seized the man's skullcap. He'd attributed Gumm's choice of headwear to mere eccentricity. But its use by the orderly, the patient on the stretcher and the soldiers he'd glimpsed through the ventilation system suggested a greater significance. The orderly appeared to verify the theory when he dropped the head-end of the stretcher to flail after his cap. At this, Dixie and Babette rushed to Paul's side. The orderly backed down at the odds against him, whimpering.

"What's the crack?" Dixie asked, nudging aside one of the addled townspeople. The man grinned blankly and shuffled on.

"It's thee-uh these caps. They're important somehow," Paul said. He handed the cap to Dixie. "I suggest putting it on now."

Dixie passed the cap to Babette, saying, "Beauty before grit."

She thanked him with a tight smile, wary of his attentions and of foreign men generally. In her experience, they tended to regard French women as possessable luxuries.

Dixie feinted toward the orderly, making him jump, before plucking the skullcap from the motionless patient.

Babette was about to ask Paul about her mother again when a squad of soldiers banged through the double doors. The seven-man squad and its ammo bearer rushed to form a defensive wedge. The orderly skittered into the corridor.

"Get behind the townspeople," Paul said. "It's a good bet thee-uh they have orders to keep them alive." He backed farther into the room and dropped to one knee behind a cot occupied by a young girl with lacquered brown hair. More than a dozen townspeople milled in aimless circles between him and the enemy. Dixie and Babette adopted similar positions.

The Germans split into two sweeping wings and closed in on either side of the townspeople. Paul propped his rifle on the edge of the cot. His breath caught on the stench of disinfectant. He was up against the mortal edge. He'd seen enough of war to know. His history, his feelings, all his ideas for fantastical inventions would disappear as if they never were. He forced himself to think in small increments—the next moment and the next. "On my signal," he said.

"Looks like it's time to collect some trophies," Dixie said. The Germans dropped to their knees for cover. The resonant *clack* of rifles leveled in unison came over Dixie like a wave. He took a bead on the closest target, counting out the seconds to the crash.

Paul struggled to maintain a steady view. The scene flared as if shaped by lightning. Had the Germans fired or...? "Go! Just go." He eked out the order through the resounding pulsebeats in his temples. He was disoriented and his disorientation frightened him. Ethereal flames licked at his face.

Dixie skewered the German in his sights and swiveled to the next in line. The enemy unleashed a fierce enfilade. The cot partially screening him rocked under the salvo. Blood from the soldiers' victim stippled Dixie's neck and chin. He resisted the impulse to charge and rapid-fired the Winchester. "These ain't no mercy bullets!" A German tumbled back on his hands, a graze of blood across his cheek.

"*Zut alors,*" Babette muttered. For some reason, Paul was hunched over his rifle, unmoving. She pivoted on her toes to get a better look, thinking he might be wounded. Her body felt rooted in place while her head wafted in the clouds. Events seemed to have overtaken her at last. She emptied her Luger in an effort to protect him.

As she reloaded, a tremor oscillated up from the concrete through her toes. The free-standing medicine cabinets to the right of the double doors wobbled and pitched to the ground. The burst of metal and sharded glass was quickly overtopped by the wall itself. The closest swinging door crumpled from its hinges. The soldiers turned to this new disquiet, confounded and cursing. There was a terrible grinding of gears then the unmistakable contours of a tank cannon pushed through the concrete dust. One of the vehicle's machine guns *br-br-bratted* through the ranks on Paul's side. The Germans gave in to self-preservation and clambered for the exit at the far left end of the room. Babette's head returned to her body.

The tank trundled up to the first row of cots while Dixie continued to dole out retribution. "You forgot your pride!" he called after the retreating soldiers.

Babette went to Paul's side with a weather eye on the Germans raked by the tank. The gangly corporal was unharmed but had an odd, abstracted look.

The hatch on the tank clanged open and Nolin popped his head out. "I leave you alone for a few minutes and this is all the mess you could turn up?"

"Bout time we had a plain 'n' proper gunfight," Dixie said. "They can't all be electric zombies."

Nolin descended from the tank and jumped the last meter to the ground. "Paul alright? Or is he like these others?" He gestured in the direction of the townspeople. "I take it these are the missing citizens?"

"He is not hurt—physically. Confused," Babette said. She had a hand around Paul's waist and was helping him toward the tank. "My people, I do not know. I left my mother there sleeping. I was afraid …"

"Let's get him in the tank," Nolin said. "It must be the Mimirodat. I gather that's what these caps are designed to protect the soldiers from. You see the sigils on the underside? There are similar markings around the inside of the cab. I'm guessing the Mimirodat's signals or radiation or what-have-you can't penetrate it."

"Lucca ain't with you?" Dixie asked.

Nolin shook his head. "Should he be?"

"Well, he took off lookin for the tank, I figured…"

Nolin met Paul and Babette in the aisle bordering the throng of townspeople. "Paul? Paul, you hear me, mate?" he asked. A bolus of fear seemed lodged in the base of his throat. His childhood friend should have been at university, absorbed in his studies, not here, shell-shocked or worse.

Paul mumbled something about Aristotle's quintessence and the fifth element of heaven.

Nolin seized Dixie by the shoulder. "I'm going after Lucca—alone. Get Paul in the tank and get out before we're overrun. It should be easy enough to retrace my path to the maintenance bay. You can get to the surface from there."

"I can't run out on you, boss-man," Dixie said.

"Damn it, Dixie, not now. There's only so much well-meaning defiance I can take. Humor me?"

Dixie gave a weak nod. "Luck and lollipops, sir."

"That's my lad." Nolin slapped the stock of his rifle. "I'll be racing your patience." He smiled at Babette as if acknowledging a private joke then hurried out the way he'd come.

"He is a wonder, this man," Babette said. She sounded like a girl touched by a sentimental tune.

Dixie braced Paul from the opposite side, crossing his arm over hers. "One of a kind, that's fer sure. Like we say back in the holler, 'He's so tough he musta wore leather diapers as a baby.'"

Babette gestured to the tank with her free hand. "I guess that explains the size of his trophy."

Dixie pretended he couldn't hear her remark over the stuttering drone of the tank's engines.

The squallish undertone Gumm had first sensed almost two decades ago quavered through him like a frayed nerve. It was a noise on the margins of language. He considered it the Ur-language of the primal universe, the logos, the creating word of God. He put a palm to the shield door separating him from the Mimirodat. The hair on the back of his hand tingled with the entity's potential. The fevered images and feelings that washed over him suggested meanings only by association. Gumm longed for these parenthetical meanings to be made clear. The

war and its uncivilizing chaos—the whole history of human empire—
were of no consequence. The world of phenomena was mere cause
and effect, simple mechanism, whether cyclical, patterned or otherwise.
Böll's idea of global peace enforced by an *imperium Germanicum* was a
Romantic delusion. There could be no peace when the Outer Gods
were at war. There was just one rational course: transcendence.

Gumm understood from the *Ater Opus* that the Mimirodat's masters,
the Overlords of the Jewel, had the power to transform ordinary beings
into demigods—heralds charged with spreading their apocalyptic faith.
If he could summon the proper astral energy ... If he could connect with
the Mimirodat in the dreamtime without losing his sense of self... If he
could then reunite the entity with its creators ... If, if ... Then he might
earn his place among the Overlords of the Jewel and rid himself of the
trifling vicissitudes of earth. What were all the mercenary causes he'd
taken up compared to the world-in-itself?

The massive door's five-prong spindle wheel was cold to the touch.
His heart beat maniacally in his chest. The next moment would reveal
if Prince Joey and Katsuo had succeeded in the task he'd given them.
He wrenched the handle to the left. There was a satisfying pop and the
poured concrete door swung out on its hinges. The Mimirodat's colors fluoresced at his unshielded desire. Gumm visored his eyes against
the brightness and locked himself inside, anxious to begin the ritual.
He and the Mimoridat would make a marriage in the dreamtime, he
thought, and everyone else would gift their humanity.

Chapter 12
Vertigod

When Lucca had finished binding Geiszler to an oak swivel chair, he unholstered his stiletto and put the flat of it against the scientist's cheek. "There's no time for anything more elaborate than a simple flaying. The ancient Chinese used to lift the skin of the face in one piece like peeling an apple. Sometimes they'd use mercury—make a couple of cuts in the scalp, fill them with it, and let the weight of the liquid metal shear the skin free."

Geiszler blinked distractedly then screwed up his face to speak. "Those cruelties prove ... prove my point: We are nothing more ... than rapacious apes. Progress, democratic rule ... mere self-flattery." His breathing came in shorter and shorter rasps. Defective human shapes swarmed before him, reaching, grasping, tossed about on invisible winds.

"What is it with you, *mamalucco*? I haven't even started."

Geiszler shrugged in the direction of the observation window.

"The Mimoridat?" Lucca checked the entity's reflection. Was it his imagination or was the creature glimmering with new vitality? Its iridescent colors swirled hypnotically. "How did you imprison it?"

"Crystals," the doctor spit.

Lucca examined the Mimirodat and its environs more closely. At first glance he'd mistaken the diaphanous shapes around the base of the dais for a ghosting effect of the viewing mirrors. A studied view revealed the shapes to be translucent solids. Lucca could trace their outlines against the Mimirodat's writhing tendrils. *Parmatmar crystals!* The discovery lifted his heart. Legend had it the crystals were the elusive fifth element—the precipitate of the spiritual force from which the four cardinal elements of Creation had sprung. Lucca knew from Nolin that Captain Nemo had been the first to discover them. Nemo, the son of a Hindu Raja, had named the crystals after the Parmatma, the Highest Creative Intelligence that guides the Sapta Rishis or guardians of the Divine Laws. With the crystals in hand, Lucca was confident he could work a magick greater than any yet known. He began to gather up the books and papers scattered around the room. "How do I get down there—to the dais?"

The doctor's facial tics turned into a debilitating tremor. "Beasts," he said. Spittle flecked his beard. "Beasts against ... every other ... to the acid ... end." The words came in an unsummoned rasp.

Lucca leapt onto the instrument panel in order to get a better— more direct—look at the area around the dais. There had to be a service or maintenance entrance. He squinted against the transfixing glare. The Mimirodat's shimmerings glanced off the walls. Peering through the luminous haze, Lucca could make out a flickering shadow in the lower right-hand corner, not from a door, but from a figure—a man. He was seated in a lotus position before the Mimirodat. Lucca noted the square of the shoulders and unkempt beard with disdain: Gumm.

"Ka-k-k," Geiszler sputtered. His face purpled with frustration.

Lucca sheathed his stiletto, content to let Geiszler suffer under the Mimirodat's influence, and hauled the nearest chair onto the control panel. He gathered himself up for maximum leverage and flung the chair against the observation window. The reinforced glass shivered but held. One of the chair legs snapped and its caster wheel bounced to the ground. Lucca tried again and again, bashing the oak chair in the same spot until only the rounded back was unbroken. He achieved a spidering impact break then the window gave entirely. Cubed shards cascaded the four stories to the concrete below. Lucca crooked an arm over his eyes at the unfiltered brilliance of the Mimirodat. Though the light obscured any view of Gumm, Lucca edged toward the empty window and shouted for him. No reply came back from the coruscat-ing silence. He casually tossed what was left of the chair into empty space. How many Mills grenades, he wondered, would it take to shatter the Parmatmar crystals?

This line of thought was cut short by Geiszler's violent trembling. The doctor shook in an alien frenzy. His form became uncertain, unsingular, a blur hovering between dream-twitch possibilities. The chair rattled apart. The evolving blur whirled all ways. A spiked chitinous leg bodied forth then an ovoid eye, amber and misaligned. Lucca's heart lodged in his throat. He opened up with his revolver until he'd exhausted the ammo and the Geiszler-thing was an unrecognizable mulch. His grip on the gun was so tight he could feel the pulse in his palm.

Lucca waved away the smoke and jumped down from the control panel. Blood pooled around the hackle of mutant innards. Gumm hadn't hinted at this transformative aspect of the Mimirodat's powers. A heartshocking *ker-bang* dimpled the door. The metal shrieked against its frame. Lucca reached into his ammo pouch to reload. The door buckled and peeled under amphibious claws. He thumbed a shell into the gun. A bone-plated monster vaulted into the room, dragging its pendulous belly. Lucca barely had a chance to raise his weapon. The shot ricocheted harmlessly off the creature's chest and then its claws were on him, clutching, slashing, pulling him down, indomitable.

Katsuo's glimpse of the bone-plated monster offered more evidence his service with the Lost Boys was part of a larger test from the gods. He imagined himself as *Issun-bōshi*, the One-Inch Boy of myth—short of stature, underestimated, just shy of the opportunity to prove himself and claim his magic hammer. With its oversized head, reptilian features and long, rounded tail, the monster had resembled a *kappa* or riverdwelling daimon. Katsuo had joined Nolin's squad expressly for this kind of crazy, honor-making adventure. Since the Meiji Restoration in 1868, which reinstated imperial rule, Japan's spirit had been tested repeatedly. Its glorious victory over the Russians in 1905—the first time an Asian power had defeated a European one in over 200 years—was only the most obvious example. Japan, and most importantly, its gods, seemed to be growing in power, preparing for a broader conflict.

Katsuo expected the next war (or perhaps the one after that) to be the climactic test of his country's divine favor and wanted to be fully prepared to meet the challenge straight-on. In the Edo period, the island of his birth, Honjima, had been the base for the Shiwaku-suigun, fierce pirates turned renowned navy; now, its people were simple fisherfolk. He thought to memorialize his family by upholding the martial standards of its ancestors.

Though the monster's rampage had cleared the corridor, Katsuo found himself unable to move, suspended in time. Prince Joey, too, appeared to be struggling. He nearly dropped his Springfield as he teetered into the hallway, scratching something fierce behind one ear. Katsuo got as far as the doorframe, his rifle slung but level ready. The scatterings of mutilated dead wavered in a dim, aqueous light. Katsuo closed his eyes to shut out the dreamglow. He couldn't say how long he kept them closed. The seconds seemed to elongate past any reckoning. On opening them, however, he discovered Prince Joey with his back against the wall, facing a red-lipped German youth. The youth bled from an egregious clawmark across his upper-arm and chest. Katsuo raised his rifle on the instant. The youth looked from one barrel to the other and choked out an unintelligible plea. When it became clear that neither soldier understood him, he signaled his surrender by throwing his hands above his head.

Katsuo motioned for him to put his hands down by waving his gun. The adjutant started forward and presented his skullcap. Prince Joey lunged to receive it.

The youth then selected a replacement from among the dead and another for Katsuo, keeping his distance from any discarded weapons. His every movement gave off comet-trails of red. Katsuo nearly toppled over in bowing his thanks. He registered the youth's palpitating aura as feelings—fear, shame, a streak of bluster—and was suddenly self-conscious about his own. Despite the travails of war, he'd been reluctant to show, much less admit to, his vulnerabilities. He preferred to name his fears after mythological entities, to make them decidedly 'other' in order to give him a useful outward focus. Displaying emotional rigor was expected of a warrior, he thought, and besides, it gave him a certain pleasure. He could feel superior when Dixie recounted how "a-scairt" he was going up against the latest supernatural menace.

A curvilinear sigil Katsuo didn't recognize illumined the inside of the skullcap. He placed it on his head with one hand while maintaining a grip on his rifle with the other. The aura around the youth immediately dwindled to a subtle wash of color.

Prince Joey said, "You okay, Katsuo?" For his own part, there was still a fish-eye skew to the world but his full-body itch had begun to recede.

"A-okay now."

The adjutant nodded in agreement then flashed his empty hands and fled in the direction of the tunnel.

Prince Joey shrugged. "Just a kid. Prob'ly only monsters he's seen are under his bed. But us veterans know better, right?"

Katsuo tried winking like Dixie but blinked instead. No matter. He was sure Prince Joey understood: The trick to being a warrior was to anticipate death at any time then forget about it.

With his shoulders pinioned by the advancing Böll-monster, Lucca dropped his empty gun and rolled backward out of its grasp. He snatched up the rounded back of Geiszler's broken chair and clapped it alongside the monster's bulbous head. The creature narrowed its double-lidded eyes and came at him, undeterred. Lucca drew his stiletto, sunk it into the meat of the creature's shoulder then, leveraging the blade, pushed off the back wall to flip over his attacker. He landed on his feet deprived of his knife and clawed down the chest. The wounds stung to the marrow. The creature's finned whip-tail struck his shielding arm, fracturing it above the elbow. He dodged the next tail-strike and leapt for the grenades. The monster spun around and caught him by the right ankle. Lucca braced himself against the floor with his injured arm. He swore under his breath as the creature lofted him in the air. His gut churned as if he were at the top of a Coney Island Ferris wheel. He twisted his upper body and kicked at the monster with his left foot. The toe of his boot spiked its beak-like mouth. He fell free—and hard on his tailbone—into the haversack of explosives.

Lucca kept his eyes on the monster and reached behind him for the clasps on the backpack. The creature put its webbed hands together into a massive fist and brought its anvil weight down on Lucca's hastily thrown up arm. Lucca stiffened at the grievous bonecrack. Pinpricks of light floated in front of his eyes. He offered up the arm again as the creature made a slashing underhand gesture. The arc of the blow forced Lucca onto his back. The ceiling lights haloed as if viewed through the bottom of a soda bottle. Then the tail walloped his chest and the lights flickered and flared to black.

The sigils mounted around the inside of the *Kettenblitz*'s driving cab pulsed in time to the throbbing in his head. Paul raised his eyes to the hatch and blinked deliberately until it came into reasonable focus. Babette acknowledged his apparent recovery with a fleeting smile. She was pressed up against a short-wave radio, one hand on her headset, coordinating evacuation plans for the townspeople. Coming out of his trance-like fog, Paul sympathized with the townspeople's impulse to gang up for comfort. They were doubtless aghast to find themselves flesh again after their time as disembodied dream figures. Paul leaned from the driver's seat toward Dixie's back. The Southerner was beside the loading mechanism for the casemate cannon. "Suh-sorry for thee-uh slip up," Paul said.

Dixie turned in a crouch. "What're you sayin? Like it was *your* fault... Damn devil-god is what it was."

"Must be thee-uh Thursday." The sigils coalesced into painted iron shapes that reminded Paul of alchemical symbols.

"Here's the situation you don't remember: Nolin's gone for Lucca. No idea where Prince J and Katsuo have got to, and I'm makin sure I know how to load this weapon afore the Huns come back. You okay to drive?"

"This tank? On my worst day, mate." Paul examined the conn's array of levers and foot clutches. "Looks standard enough. Likely crews fifteen or sixteen, but if Nolin can get it this far, I should be able to run it up the Kaiser's ass."

"They are on the way," Babette said, removing her headset. "The barges are on the way." Tears in the corners of her eyes glinted in the wan yellow light. "How do you feel?"

"A bit woozy, but alright enough." Paul made to get up and jerked against the belt across his lap.

"Best pace yourself, Shimmy," Dixie said. "Kaiser's a good five hundred miles from here."

Paul unbuckled the safety belt and stooped out of his seat. "You already check the layout?"

"Yeah, I gave it a quick, no-muss inspection. Three heavy guns port and starboard, two in back. Ammo containers next to each of the gun positions. What do you call em?"

"Sponsons."

"Yeah, bout 300 rounds all-told for each gun, plus a couple dozen shells for the cannon. Also, found a bundle a dynamite near the radiator in back. Not too different from the captured A7V we trained on back in Duxford."

"The dynamite is likely close to thee-uh the petrol tanks—for destroying the vehicle if it looks like it's going to fall into enemy hands."

"Whoops."

Paul took in the forward cab, taking mental notes on its design. The cab consisted of oval-backed seats for the commander, driver and communications officer, and farther forward, seats for the cannon's gunner and loader. An armored, semi-circular scrim offered additional protection to the commander, whose view of the outside was limited to a rectangular flap in the downsloped bow. The driver steered via the flap, a periscope and, in the instance of a full crew, with the aid of signals from the central compartment gunners. Movement was controlled by a large, horizontal hand-wheel, which altered the speed of one engine-pair in relation to the other; two grooved foot clutches; a left-hand lever for braking and supplemental steering; and a right-hand lever quadrant for gear-setting. Unlike the Mark IV, the *Kettenblitz* allowed the driver to operate the vehicle without assistance.

Directly behind the seats for the commander and driver was an elevated chair off-set from the top-hatch ladder. A helmet similar to those worn by the incapacitated townspeople was on the padded seat. Its connecting tube ran up through the vehicle's roof. Paul brushed past the chair to examine the rest of the tank. The central compartment contained the tank's engines—two to a side—with a narrow aisle in-between. There was nothing notable about the stern compartment, except for the box of dynamite and a pair of removable panels for loading and unloading matériel. Paul bent to inspect the panel release bolts when shrapnel from the first grenade *thwocked* against the tank's armor.

"Santy Claus done come early!" Dixie shouted.

Paul hurried into the driver's seat.

"Do we have a plan?" Babette asked.

Dixie checked the cannon's breech. "Shoot anythin that ain't us?"

Babette looked to Paul, who was too preoccupied with getting the vehicle into gear to notice. "Oh, you were serious."

"It's called improvisin."

"So it is a plan only afterward..."

"Actually, it's a plan only if it uh works," Paul muttered. He gripped the hand-wheel and revved the engines.

The hull vibrated with another detonation. The tank was perpendicular to the hallway. Paul imagined a division of Germans lobbing grenades at their treads as if at a curling match. "How about you take the first gun to port?" he asked Babette. "You alright with that?"

"That and drinking straight from the bottle." She slipped into the proscribed gun compartment and readied the ammo. From that position, she could swivel the MG 08 machine gun forward to defend the cab.

"The filly's growin on me," Dixie said. As the tank reversed into the hallway, Dixie swung the cannon some twenty degrees to center it. There looked to be an entire regiment arrayed against them. "There's a lot of em, maybe too many—even for Prince J," he said. The Germans issued a barrage of rifle fire. Several rounds zinged through the open flap and ricocheted off the steel barrier around the vacant commander's seat.

"Don't be talking trouble now," Paul said.

"Talkin don't make it happen." Dixie swatted the big flap shut and opened the smaller flap inside it. This flap-within-a-flap permitted a pinprick view of the environs.

Several grenades exploded in quick succession somewhere in front of the tank.

"Maybe in thee-uh mundane world." Paul put his forehead against the leather-padded periscope. "I take it they're aiming for the treads."

Dixie adjusted the cannon as the tank turned to face the enemy head-on. "Don't got no baseball arms, but still..."

Paul finished squaring up the tank and shouted, "Fire at will, gunners!"

Dixie levered the .75 caliber cannon into action. The shell skirred above the Germans and resounded against the far end of the corridor, shrouding the soldiers in concrete dust. "Law-me! Gabriel done blowed his horn!"

Babette's machine gun cut through the silhouettes in a gestural sweep.

A surprise grenade bounced off the bow and blasted the small flap, warping the steel cover. Dixie pinched his eyes shut to clear his head. "Lost the view, Paul. You gonna have to tell me where to aim."

The trajectory of the grenade prompted Paul to whirl the periscope to stern. Just as he feared: a contingent of Germans was approaching through the gap Nolin had punched in the warehouse wall. At least one was already clambering up the side of the tank. "Don't worry, Dixie. In a moment, thee-uh they'll be at the hatch."

The undertone was now an intense all-over sensation that split Gumm's sense of self. His consciousness doubled, separated, one version fixed to the immediacies of earth, the other, released to the immensities of space-time. This second self—his astral presence—vibrating in such close proximity to the Mimirodat, assumed a greater intensity than ever before. Gumm relished the uprush of feeling. He counted on this boosted potential to grant him the foresight needed to reunite the Mimirodat with its distant masters. Given that the entity was created to be a node in an extra-dimensional network, receiving and broadcasting emotions only as directed, its powers of independent action were stunted by design. The network's destruction sometime in the distant past had set the Mimirodat adrift. Shorn of its original purpose, the creature had gradually come to understand a few peak emotions—fear of the unknown, paranoia, aggression—as substitutes for its original stimuli; then, after absorbing a sufficient quantum of these emotions, broadcast them at their highest pitch as far as its diminished energies permitted. Geiszler had been the first to tie the cyclical violence in and around Cambrai to this phenomenon.

Gumm's astral self ghosted through the bright expanse between him and the Mimirodat. This plane of the dreamtime generally assumed whatever qualities the astral traveler brought to it. Gumm envisioned a photo-negative starfield—radiant, spiralizing blacks against an infinite white. The Mimirodat appeared to him as it usually did: smoky drifts of skywriting. This time, however, he was sure he had the power to concentrate these diffuse expressions into a communicating beam. Geiszler had inadvertently aided him in this task with the addition of the conical superstructure to the Mimirodat's dais. The doctor must have been planning to manipulate the entity for his own nefarious reasons, Gumm thought.

He expected the creature's etheric energies to spike once the connection to its masters was made. What he didn't know is if his earthly self would survive the contact, or if it did, in what form. His inmost wish was for the Overlords of the Jewel to transfer his astral self to another, better body—one more appropriate to his expanded consciousness. There was no question about the others. The simple protection afforded by their skullcaps would be nullified at once. They would die as dimming sparks of awareness trapped in nightmare flesh.

When the elevator door peeled back, Nolin tossed the unconscious soldier he held against it into the corridor and stepped past him. A vicious walloping issued from the room at the end of the short hallway. A roughly diagonal portion of the reinforced metal door was staved-in. Through the irregular gap, he caught glimpses of a reptilian eye, a smashing whip-tail and a shoulder with a knife wedged between its bone-plates. Not just any knife—a stiletto. Nolin surged forward, skidded to a halt a meter from the door, raised his rifle and shot plumb through the monster's right eye. The creature dropped from view, writhing in pain. Nolin booted the remainder of the door free to finish it. His lungs cramped at the sight of Lucca clawed-up and broken. Lucca opened and closed his bloodied lips in muted agony. Nolin was dizzy with anger at the thought of losing him.

The monster faced the wall opposite, reeling on all fours, its good eye wide with pain. It lashed out with its tail and shattered the forestock on Nolin's rifle. Nolin parried the next blow with the exposed barrel, kinking it, then switched up his grip and whacked the undulating tail with the buttstock. As the monster spun to confront him, its tail snaked around Nolin's gun arm and wrenched him toward the control panel. Nolin released his weapon and stomped on a corner of the crumpled door, flipping it into the air. He caught the door on edge with his free hand, shielding himself from the monster's claws, then pinned the beast between the door and the back wall.

Putting his shoulder to the door, Nolin pressed his advantage. He seethed with the vehemence he'd guarded against his whole remembered life. His neck tightened like a wire and his body pulled in the direction of something hidden and dark. The mask of his humanity fell away in the self-made heat. He could feel his brows thickening, his jaw growing heavy, his reddened eyes contracting in his skull. The rage came on so intensely he forgot who he was. His everyday guise couldn't withstand the raw and awful truth of his blood and all it entailed. The monster's tail constricted around his throat, but no matter. His blood would not be denied its calling.

He bore down on the monster even as his face darkened from a lack of oxygen and his vision blurred. Only the constant tension in his neck prevented the monster from crushing his windpipe. Then he heard the distinctive pop of its shoulder blades. Other bones—its collar bone and upper-vertebrae, its oversized skull—followed like an uneven string of firecrackers.

"No-Nolin," Lucca hissed.

The sound of a familiar voice brought Nolin back to his right mind. He let go of the door and turned toward Lucca without a glance at the foul aftermath of his violence. The angry blood relinquished its hold on him. His otherworldly aspects slowly withered under his skin. By the time he bent to Lucca, he felt himself cooling.

Lucca tried to rise on one elbow and collapsed with a mucusy wheeze. "What was that? Some kind of magick?" He marveled at No-lin's eyes as they reverted to their typical hue.

"More second nature." The attempted humor was at odds with his spooked voice.

"And here I thought...I had a...temper." Blood gleamed in the corners of Lucca's smile.

"We can talk about it later over bully beef. How bad is it?"

"Well, I'm not...fit for bowling."

"Think you can stand?"

"Not with my legs."

"Says the lad who can balance on an egg cup. Tried to circus-murder it, didn't you?"

"Don't make fun...of my signature move. We can't all...be Achilles." Lucca strained his neck toward the observation window. "Gumm's down there..."

Nolin leaned over the instrument panel and, shading his eyes against the Mimirodat's quickening energies, spied the turncoat.

"The Mimirodat... It's held by Par-Parmatmar crystals," Lucca said. "I was about to... try grenades."

"Eric would've been glad to know we didn't drag em all this way for nothing." Nolin moved to cradle Lucca's head.

"Wait... The books, papers..." Lucca gestured to a pair of grimoires and a handful of notes he'd left on the control panel.

"More reading for your time in hospital?" Nolin quickly put the material under one arm. There were still dozens of uncollected pages littering the room. He crooked Lucca in his arms and settled him in the corridor, propping his head on the largest grimoire. "Back in a hot second, Mouse."

Lucca looked at him with a questioning tilt of his head. "Back to the war..." The past and present, life and death, assumed the qualities of hard lines. He lamented the fact that, unlike Dr. Nikola, he couldn't send his astral self back in time. As Nolin disappeared into the control room, Lucca realized the word for what he was feeling was petty and trite: loneliness. He'd never felt so far from home.

Nolin hoisted the haversack of explosives over one shoulder and jumped onto the control panel. The Mimirodat raveled the air with its fluctuating colors. Nolin craned his neck through the window frame and shouted after Gumm. He waited several long seconds for a reply, tormented by the sounds of combat on the floor below, then gave a final warning: "Ten seconds, Gumm! Ten seconds and I'm tossing down grenades!"

He counted out the losses from this mission with the time: Eric, his shameful secret, maybe Lucca and God-knows-who-else, now Gumm, killed in this callous fashion... Everything was temporary, he told himself—the pain, the joy, even the memories. He yanked the pull-ring on a Mills grenade, slipped it into the backpack, and flung the makeshift cluster bomb into the shaft. It might well have been the heaviest thing he'd ever thrown.

The holding cell burst with sharp edges of colored light. It was a sudden diamond-glory display and blinding. Nolin pressed his palms to his eyes and tumbled backward onto the floor of the control room. It felt as if his eyes had been incinerated in their hollows. Luminous afterimages fuzzed the blankness behind his lids.

Shot through with alien radiation, the haversack exploded harmlessly in mid-air, blowing an irregular gap in the shaft wall.

Gumm remained in his lotus position unperturbed. He had other, higher demands on him. The moment of contact was imminent.

At the *clank* of the hatch release, Paul set the turret to revolving. The hatch popped open and the German grabbed onto it to keep from falling headlong. In his haste to gain purchase, however, he pitched over the hatch, crushing his fingers in the jamb. He rolled free and flopped to the concrete, hands stiffened in pain. "Oh, I would've loved me one of these as a uh young un," Paul said.

"Without the war, of course," Babette added. She took up a position against the elevated chair and aimed her Luger at the hatch.

"Dixie, you ready for a uh—"

A deafening fusillade to stern drowned out the rest. The corridor shuddered and fractured along its margins.

"*Séisme?*" Babette asked. "The earth tremble?"

Paul levered the tank around to get a visual. "A *natural* disaster would be a uh relief." He pressed his forehead to the periscope and was astonished at what it showed: a breach into a color-saturated ether. The scale and vitality of it mesmerized him.

"What is it?" Dixie asked, opening the large sighting flap. Without the filter of the optical periscope, the fiery colorfield stung his eyes. He slammed the flap shut. "Nuthin we want to mess into."

Paul reluctantly pulled back from the periscope. The Mimirodat's abstractness hinted at the spectral essence of things. He was reminded of Plato's theory of forms: *The sun is to sight as Good is to understanding.* No doubt some part of him would regret the course of action he was now compelled to take. "Babette, how we doing with the Huns at our backs? We need to aim through this breach."

She hustled into the closest gun compartment and swiveled it for a rearward view. "The *Boche*—they are running. They hold their heads and run." Her voice had an exultant lilt to it.

Paul called to Dixie: "The next shell ready? I'm going to take us to the brink of the corridor."

"Loaded for bear."

"Alright then." Paul jerked the tank's controls. The *Kettenblitz* powdered the rubble in its path and came to a jarring stop about a meter from the edge. The concrete gave a bit under its tremendous weight and Paul thought he might have to reverse out. He left a hand on the four-quadrant lever as the vehicle settled then, satisfied the flooring had stabilized, took up the periscope. From this vantage, the Mimirodat was an all-encompassing brilliance. There was no sign of Gumm. "Looks like we're three stories above thee-uh Mimirodat's source or whatever it is. Three stories and a million light-years away. I can't see anything but a haze. The cannon's through the breach, Dixie, you just need to drop it uh, say, to a five o'clock position."

Babette asked, "You want I should use the gun?"

"If you can get it in position, absolutely," Paul said.

"Done," she said.

Dixie slapped the cannon's breech. "And done."

Paul took a last wistful look at the Mimirodat. An inky violet streaked through a diaphanous plume of reds. The violet zip seemed to pulse between his ears, a low, tuneless siren-song. He issued the command before he lost heart: "Fire at will."

The tank rocked with the thunderclap of cannon. A shriek of bullets followed. Only to be cut short when a retaliatory flash detonated the entire salvo prematurely. Shrapnel dinned the *Kettenblitz*.

Paul recoiled from the periscope. "G'd blind me!" He shut his eyes tight against the vivid afterimages.

"Oh, whose askin for it now?" Dixie said. "Babette, you okay?"

"*Oui*. The viewport was closed, but I saw—I saw the light seep in around it."

The tank canted forward without warning. Dixie banged the back of his head on a bulkhead panel. "Yeeow!"

Paul jammed the tank into reverse and cranked the hand-wheel. "Hold on to something!" The rear treads struggled against the vehicle's downslope momentum. "Belay that order! Get to the back for weight!" Dixie and Babette beat their way to stern, palming the sides of the tank for balance. Engine smoke infiltrated the rear compartment. Paul put his shoulder to the hand-wheel. "Please, please..." He could hear the treads slick against the concrete. In the next moment or the next would come the nauseating spill into the unknown.

The reverberations from the failed assault startled Nolin to consciousness. He got to his knees, trying to blink away a persistent light behind his eyes. The blankness lingered without hint of surcease. It was a dark as bright as snow-flash. The thought gradually penetrated: he was blind. He put his hands out in front of him about waist-high expecting the angled lip of the control panel. Nothing. He took a deliberate step forward. His right hand grazed a toggle switch. He heard the sharp protestations of the tank's engines through the broken observation window. For the first time since his father's death, he felt utterly powerless. "Lucca?" he called. Lucca could guide him to the elevator. He stumbled over debris from the door and braced himself against the wall. "Lucca?" His breath caught in his throat. There was no noise besides that of the tank and the rising dissonance in his head.

Paul twisted in his seat toward the back of the tank. The shadowed steelwork bleared in and out of focus. "Dixie, you see those loading panels on the hull? Strip them off and get out—both of you!"

Dixie and Babette bent to the task and, despite their increasingly confused vision, dislodged the bolts in a few hasty turns.

The vehicle tilted precipitously toward the crumbling edge. Flickering light bled through the seams in the engine coping and gun covers.

"Hurry," Dixie urged Babette, kicking his panel loose. She gave him a brief, sweet smile. The color in her lips seemed to liquefy and run. "For time to break your heart," she said and dove through the opening.

"Let's go, Paul!" Dixie shouted. He could scarcely hear himself. His eardrums throbbed to their limits.

Paul pounded up the aisle between the racking engines. Dixie quivered as if he were a reflection in a funhouse mirror. "Light the dynamite box!" When he was about halfway to the stern compartment, the *Kettenblitz* found some traction. The vehicle righted itself and lurched backward at speed. "Luck won't hold one way or the other." He turned back to the cab, yelling over his shoulder. "Light it and bail!" He doubted his ability to manipulate the levers. The fingers on his hands had somehow stretched to absurd lengths.

Dixie removed the metal match affixed to the lid of the dynamite box and unsheathed his combat knife. He sparked his knife against the match but, owing to his skewed sense of perspective, missed the fuse to the top bundle of explosive.

There was a stupendous clatter from the area around the drive sprocket. The tank squealed and faltered then shot toward the breach.

Squinting in concentration, Dixie struck his knife a second time and the fuse caught. "Go, Paul! Now!" The uncertainty of the moment pressed on him. The opening expanded and contracted like a whited eye. He waited for the approaching *thumpa-thumpa* of Paul's boots before he launched himself through it.

The tank seemed to hang in the air for a moment before it plunged into the blazing core of the Mimirodat. Paul corkscrewed through the loading window in an upward dive, head crowded with volcanic noise.

He had the sensation of floating in underwater clouds at an impossible distance from the edge. He could have been anywhere or anyone, lifted from himself. Then Babette's extended hand was there and Dixie's foot—hoofed?—and he took hold and slammed into the sheer face of the shaft and hung on through the pain and the sudden violence of dawn color. Resplendent reds veined in pinks and purples swirled behind his closed lids. Glary lightnings forked through the upsurge. Radiant forms eclipsed one another and vanished as whiffling dazzles. Paul felt small and thrown against the vastness. It was like the hallucination of a new life or perhaps a new element, altogether suffused with hidden potencies.

When the final charged echo had abated, Babette opened her eyes to faint, indistinct afterimages. She shook with a joyful sob at her miraculous survival. Thick smoke welled up from the bottom of the Mimirodat's darkened holding cell. She could make out a few sections of the demolished tank punctuated by glints of crystal. The strangeness of it all prompted her to fill the void with jags of laughter. She stopped herself before she lost her grip on Paul and leaned farther back on her haunches to bring him to safety.

Paul exhaled his held breath. "Thanks much."

Dixie remained flat on his stomach, waiting for Paul to release his boot heel. The fact of his escape was enough for him. He'd work out the theological implications of its means over a mess-tin of rum. "You was a hair's-breadth from drawin your full issue," he said.

Paul clambered to his feet. "You know uh another way to live?" He thrummed with adolescent wonder.

"Think I'd be here if'n I did?"

Coming off the elevator, Prince Joey and Katsuo crisscrossed the hallway, covering for each other with unslung rifles. The stampede of evacuating Germans had forced them to hide in a janitorial closet until the main danger had passed. Though the few stragglers they'd run across since hadn't taken any serious interest in them, they knew better than to relax their guard. This floor was labeled GEHEIM (restricted) on the elevator panel. Prince Joey figured that, if the Germans were to offer any resistance, it would be here.

The state of the room ahead reinforced the need for caution. The crashed-in door partially covered a heap of misshapen flesh. From the corridor, the remains looked like ghastly strokes and scumbles. Prince Joey was about to signal a push into the room when he heard a dubious scuffling from around the bend. He and Katsuo took the corner together, trigger fingers primed. It was Nolin, though unlike they'd ever seen him. He was bumping along the wall as if punch-drunk. "Lieutenant," Prince Joey said.

Nolin started at the word. "Prince J?" His voice was rough from tension.

Prince Joey knew then something dreadful had happened. It was accepted wisdom that the lieutenant couldn't be caught unawares. "You alright?" He hurried to Nolin's side and put a hand on his shoulder. There was a glassy, abstracted look to his eyes.

"Lucca? Do you see him?" Nolin wiped the tears drying on his cheeks with the heel of his hand. "He was outside the room there—on the floor."

"There's no one here but us far as I seen."

"Who else?" Nolin shook as if palsied. "I'm ... I've been blinded."

Prince Joey softened his tone, unnerved by Nolin's frailty. "Just me and Katsuo. I don't know about the others."

"He was wounded, bleeding..."

"I see some bloodspots, but..." He signaled for Katsuo to search the control room. There didn't appear to be any others. "Katsuo's making a sweep. Let's say we head toward the elevator now. We need to move while the Huns are still in a panic."

"We can't leave him, Prince J. We can't—"

"I know, Lieutenant." He put a steadying hand on Nolin's arm. "We'll keep an eye out."

Katsuo exited the control room and gave a solemn shake of his head.

If the war could do this to Nolin, how would he ever make it through?

"Lieutenant…," Prince Joey urged.

Nolin was immobilized by a mix of guilt and helplessness. To take another step was to surrender his boyish ideals of friendship and loyalty, to admit he was a man apart. He may even have wished Lucca's disappearance into reality. Wasn't it the only way he could preserve his hateful secret?

Prince Joey knew he couldn't force Nolin to go. The lieutenant could still overpower him, blind or not. But he had to insist, if only to resolve his own muddled feelings. The cigarette in his breast pocket bothered him like a memento from a bad dream. "The rest of the squad—we have to find them, get them out."

The coded message from MII came back to Nolin with the force of an omen. *Cenhadaeth cod Arwan…* Like the Greeks at Platea, he was compelled to defy it. His true strength, it seemed, lay in opposition. "You're right, of course." He blotted his cheeks one last time and offered an elbow. "Lead on, *Corporal* Jenkins."

"Yessir, thank you, sir." Prince Joey allowed himself a moment of muted pride, not in his new rank so much as the prospect of having found his place. He steered Nolin around the corner and gestured for Katsuo to get the elevator.

Blind as Nolin was, the ache in his chest, the sound of his footsteps, the gentle pressure of Prince Joey's hand, seemed the whole of the world. Whether his thoughts were beyond the world or merely lost in it, he couldn't say.

Epilogue
Why This World

Captain Davenport opened his mouth but no fitting reply came to him. Nolin's report was fantastical and poignant at once. If not for the materials recovered from the base and the corroborating testimonies of the rescued townspeople, he would've recommended Nolin and his squad for Colney Hatch.

"We searched the control room again and the laboratory hidden behind it, but…" Nolin ducked his head in shame. His guilt over Lucca seized him in hitching waves. It was cold comfort that his vision had yet to improve enough for him to read the captain's face across the table. Davenport appeared as a phantom blur in the dugout's meager light. "Gumm also—gone, probably in the wreckage."

The captain cleared his throat. "As I said, aerial reconnaissance shows the whole site's nothing but a crater now."

"The Huns were awfully scared." Paul twitched in his seat next to Nolin, afraid of saying something to upset his friend. "I'm not surprised they'd bury it. It's a uh fortunate thing we were able to get everyone out—the townspeople, I mean—before they came back." To a person, the German's unhappy victims had regained their faculties in the three days since their deliverance. Babette had returned to Cambrai to oversee her mother's recovery, but had expressed an interest in returning to the Lost Boys on the condition the squad change its name.

"Joined up thinkin you wasn't gonna get so much as a scratch, yeah?" McNeil said. His intimate tone belied his ramrod-straight stance.

"Staff…," Davenport warned.

"Beggin your pardon, sir, allow me alf a mo to make my point." He walked around Davenport's chair and bent to Nolin's clouded eyes. "That's why we recruit so young: It's the lads believe themselves untouchable. When I joined up, I was no older'n you. Not much choice in my case, yeah. Generations of McNeils made it a duty more'n anything—a duty I've carried on over countless dead—cousins, school chums, anonymous lads in the battle order. Saw me cousin Alfie take a shot to the face, go down in the mud'n mire..." He drew a shuddering breath. "I had to leave im—for meself and me men." His face darkened in disgrace. "This is all to say, sir, that you've done a man's job—you and your squad. The name Strongboy don't account for you no more."

McNeil was close enough for Nolin to make out the hard-lined sincerity in the man's face. "I appreciate that, sir. Eric, Lucca—they weren't the first of us to go, but... like you, I'm duty-bound to do what I can to live up to my heritage."

"Well, you can color me proud to've served with you, however humbly."

"The feeling's mutual all round," Davenport said. "I just... I'd like to be sure—for strategic reasons—that this threat, the Mimir..."

"The Mimirodat," Paul said.

"Yes, that. I'd like to be sure it's over and done with."

Paul said, "I'm—I can't say entirely, sir. Based on thee-uh notes we found, it's possible the creature wasn't destroyed—only released back into thee-uh the atmosphere. I guess we'll know in five years. That would be thee-uh timing for the next bout of the fear-plague. Unless its time in uh captivity altered the cycle. That's possible, too."

"You have to remember, the Mimirodat wasn't completely at fault for causing those panics," Nolin said. "The notes indicate it was just feeding back emotions absorbed from its surroundings—anger, distrust, fear of change... otherness. It was the world pushing back against itself. It was us." He was reminded of Geiszler's conviction, detailed in the doctor's notebooks, that chaos was the natural state of things and Man only an animal reflection of it. The daimon blood running through his veins cast the notion in another, more damning light.

"Winds all the way back to Eden and the fall, I guess," Davenport said.

"But then there's the possibility of grace."

"As the Irish poet said, 'Man should be ever better than he seems.'" Nolin feared for the soul of democracy as much as for his own. A confluence of forces seemed poised to override human freedom, to make historical necessity—fate, so-called—a pretext for barbarism. Nolin had been raised from birth to be a leader among men. If he were cursed to live in an age of western decline, then like Marcus Aurelius before him, he would salvage what he could, not knowing if anything would actually come of it. "I trust we haven't missed the larger war, Captain. I'm a bit worse for wear, but I'm still a Royal Irish Lancer." Nolin got to his feet. "While we're awaiting orders from MI1, what would you have us do?"

NIGHTSCAPE DOUBLE FEATURE NO. 1

The
Q for Damnation

Arlen M. Todd

Contents

Prefatory note: There are no symbols in this book
except those you bring to it.

"Surrealism will usher you into death, which is a secret society. It will glove your hand, burying therein the profound M with which the word Memory begins."

Andre Breton, *Manifesto of Surrealism*

Chapter 1
(Re) Composition in Red

The self-styled mob boss or *parrain* slowed to a brisk walk when he reached the neon margins of the Café de la Rotonde, wary of drawing undue attention from its sidewalk patrons. There was no sign he'd been followed, but that was of small comfort. He'd passed into a realm beyond conventional signs. The man, no, *fantôme*, behind Drapeau's ghastly death had come out of nowhere. Who knew what powers of pursuit the murderer enjoyed? Janvier worried each step meant to distance him from the *fantôme* might just as easily bring him closer. He renewed his grip on the gun under his gray suit jacket. The forearm tight across his chest registered the frantic beating of his heart.

He ducked into the café, grateful for its brightness and the promise of anonymity among the crowd. It was a warm July night. Most patrons were seated outside or at the tables nearest the boulevard. Without a glance at the hostess, he made for the wood-paneled back of the café, away from the haunt of shadows. The mobster known as "*Tête de Renard*" Janvier caught his shifting image on the plate glass and mirrors. The fleeting superimpositions brought to mind what he'd witnessed outside the museum. One sustained touch from the *fantôme* and Drapeau had convulsed into a misshapen gargoyle. It had been a fatal punishment. The man's arms had receded in their sockets to re-emerge from his chest as a single lancing appendage; his ribs had penetrated his shoulders like frightful antlers; his head, his eyes, God, the blood...

The *garçon* approached Janvier as he settled into a booth. The *parrain* asked for a Calvados and an *iles flottantes* or soft meringue atop vanilla custard. His sweet tooth overtook him in moments of stress. Except for the occasional social outing with fellow mobsters, he'd never considered it an issue; in fact, he attributed his svelte figure to his peculiar diet of liquor and sweets.

Janvier watched himself in a wall mirror slowly lower the gun and slip it into his waistband. His face was flush from running. His eyes were pitted in bruise-violet and the veins at the tip of his long nose stood out. Nothing about Drapeau's death had resembled waking life. He resisted the urge to check the semiautomatic. He was sure he'd put two rounds into the *fantôme*, well, through the *fantôme*. Perhaps he'd somehow succeeded in wounding the ghost. The arm in contact with Drapeau had appeared solid enough. Then the *fantôme* had turned to him, its face constellated in glints of streetlight, and he'd fled, leaving his underboss and the artwork behind.

The *garçon* brought the Calvados. Janvier's "*Merci*" sounded diminished to his own ears. He swigged the brandy, relishing its blend of tart citrus and earthiness. After feeling so removed from the common world, the Calvados jolted Janvier back to himself and his surroundings. It gave him the confidence to start reasoning things out. There was no evidence of his involvement. Montparnasse had a reputation for bohemian weirdness. Perhaps Drapeau had a particular kink he'd come to satisfy and ... The thought of his underboss called up unwanted images: Drapeau's head hollowing to the bone, whited eyes dwindling, the blood oozing from around his shrinking orifices, a surge of red, man incarnadine.

Janvier tossed off the Calvados. The terrible absurdity of Drapeau's death infuriated him. Not only would he be looking over his shoulder for this *fantôme*, but his client was bound to consider the story an insult on top of his failure. In any case, odds were he wouldn't live to see another Saturday night.

Chapter 2
Fantasy Creep Indulgence

Lina regarded her sleeping lover through slitted eyes. Her lashes cast a mystifying haze over the woman's nakedness. She teased out this cozy dream-sense into the living moment. It was at once a game and a test to prolong the first signal of wakefulness—a test of true surrealist perception. She clothed the woman—Rita? Rena? 'R' then—in her imagination. R's balletic curves suggested something primal, organic. Lina sheathed her in cracked mud, powdered her cheeks with faerie-light, adorned the swell of her breast and the declivity of her sex with fine moss. The crowning touch was a laurel of bright red poppies. Dark stamens bubbled up from their centers like sea foam and—

R blinked awake and smiled as if materializing from a fetal memory. The cut-glass gray of her eyes broke Lina's concentration.

"*Bonjour,*" Lina said.

The drape-filtered sunlight limned R's roundish face and inverted blonde bob. It was the color of last night's Fauchon Grande Champagne. "*Bonjour.* I won't embarrass myself with more of my euuhh awful Hartford French than that."

"So that's what would embarrass you?" Lina angled closer on one elbow and ran a polished nail down R's side.

R took Lina's searching fingers in her own and guided them between her legs. "I'm sorry if I acted the brassy American. I was feeling my liquor and *liberté.*" She stretched and nuzzled against Lina's breasts, dispensing sportive licks.

"What are you apologizing for? I like what you're feeling." She shifted to encircle R with her free arm when three sharp knocks on the door gave her pause.

"Mayen?" came the low female voice from the hall.

"What's that?" R whispered. "I thought your name was Lina?"

"My surname."

"Isn't it a boy thing to go by your last name? That's what my fifth period French teacher said."

The voice on the other side of the door was polite but insistent: "Mayen? *Tu as un appel urgent.*"

Lina touched her forehead to R's in resignation. "Do I strike you as the traditional type?" She slipped off the bed and grabbed up a silk robe. "*Un moment,*" she said to the door.

R made a mock-skeptical face. "Is that the maid or…?"

"My secretary, Solange."

"I'm not…interrupting am I? It's hard to tell when you fib—you French—all those vowels where you don't move your lips. Even *vous.*" R put a finger to her lips, parting them in ribald fashion.

"I'm afraid I have an urgent business call." Lina tidied up the bow at her collar. "It was a lovely night, *ma Minou.* Solange will see you out."

R's chin crumpled in disappointment. "That's it? Not even the pretense of another get-together?"

"I'm no good in the clear light of day."

"Then we should drink our breakfast from tumblers." R broke into an endearingly lopsided smile.

Lina hesitated, torn between heart and head. She ached all-over from the tension. R's permissive whimsy excited her with unknown dangers. But she needed more surprises like a soda spark in the eye. Life was complicated enough, what with three intertwined personas, two of them criminal. A sustained romantic relationship with R—with anyone—could only end in recriminating tears or worse. "I meant I'm no good for you—in general."

"Why do you think I'm here?" R launched herself from the bed, using her native buff to full effect. She was a sturdy Fortuny odalisque. "The way things go for me, it's either be a good girl or have a good time."

Lina smiled weakly. "I can't do this now."

"Yes, well, how about after the sun goes down, you know, when you're better? The dance club again—the Jungle?" She put a fingertip to Lina's lips.

There was a single admonishing tap. "Mayen? Monsieur Osher Srolusz *est en attente.*" Osher was one of Lina's many Parisian informants and not given to early-morning calls.

Lina grimaced at her own weakness. Damn the "meat heart" of Artaud and its betrayals. "Solange will provide you with one of my cards. But I must warn you: Don't pet your cat when it's on fire."

"Don't pet my cat—"

"Don't make things worse for yourself, *ma Minou.*"

"What?" R asked in a flutter. "And ruin my perfect record?"

Lina kissed her full on the mouth. If she had to be done in by heart or head eventually, it might as well be the heart. R's scent was countryside fresh—Blue Grass Eau de Parfum. Lina breathed in the spicy-floral mélange and carried it with her out the door.

Solange was right there, attired in a smart afternoon dress, pen and notepad in hand. She handed the writing implements to Lina and escorted her to the phone in the luxury apartment's den. She was a slim French Algerian with an aura of easy authority.

Lina ran a hand through the sweep of her dirty blonde bangs and said, "Stop smirking, *s'il te plaît.*"

"I didn't say anything."

"A smirk doesn't require it." Lina flashed her secretary a teasing smile. "Jealous?"

"I'm sure she's not my type." Solange was as straight and chaste as a newly confirmed Catholic.

"Please give her a card on her way out."

"Which one?"

"*Marraine,*" Lina said. The card identified her as Lina Mayen, known in underworld circles as the cutthroat boss of the largest mob in Marseilles. "Oh, and find out her name. Discreetly."

"I am the responsible one. *Et avec ça* (anything else)?"

Lina grinned. "*Avec ça* (and with that), I'm going to make a mess of things." She retrieved the brass phone receiver from the desk. The call would've been routed through her Naples answering service to disguise her location. She shifted her voice to a guttural purr—the distinctive pitch of the masked detective, Manteau. "*Bonjour.* I apologize for the wait, Osher."

"Manteau? *Got tsu danken!* Tell me you're in Paris," Osher said. A Jewish American expatriate, he owned a bookshop in the 14th arrondissement that specialized in popular U.S. imports. His real business, however, was in rare occult literature.

"What is it?"

"Something's happened at the *Musée d'Histoire Occulte*—a break-in, at least one dead—murdered." The words came in breathless rasps.

Lina's heart beat high in her chest. The museum housed several artifacts that could be put to terrible uses. Its habitually nervous director, Lammert Voclain, had assisted her on a number of occasions.

"That's about all I could get from the *gendarme*," Osher went on. "I think—I had an appointment with Lammert. They had the building cordoned off, but he never showed. I called his home and his manservant said the police had called him back to the museum late last night. The security alarm had sounded. He never returned. I'm afraid, Manteau. *Gotteniu!* I'm afraid it's Lammert who's dead."

Chapter 3
Principia Acrobatica

About a dozen onlookers crowded the perimeter established by the police outside the *Musée d'Histoire Occulte.* They jostled for a better look at the sheeted body on the lawn. The American tourists stood out in their ridiculous movie star sunglasses. Lina surveyed the scene with dismay: the harsh mid-morning light, the civilians, the police cordon and beyond it, the flurry of investigative activity. She would have to find or make her own entrance—'she' meaning Manteau.

Lina returned to her car for the bag with her mask and other accoutrements then removed to the alley between the old brick museum and a neglected post office dating from the Belle Époque. The museum was originally a sulphuric acid factory and was later taken over by a washing machine manufacturer before it ended up in the hands of Lammert's father and turned into a repository of occult artifacts. The building was distinguished by its pyramidal roof clad in zinc shingles. The roof was an homage to Atlantis. Lammert's father had been among the first to theorize that Atlantis was, in fact, the sunken Egyptian city of Herakleion. The roof supposedly facilitated the power to communicate with the Outer Gods.

There was no doubt as to why Lammert was—or had been—an aggregate of nervous tics. He'd grown up in a warehouse of terrors—terrors that had invariably reduced his father to a dithering inmate at the Vaucluse asylum. Lina wondered if that wasn't the logical end of all those who dared pierce the veil of the everyday. Urmuz, Antonin Artaud, Jacque Vaché, Arthur Cravan, Baroness Elsa von Loringhofen,

Jacque Rigaut, René Crevel... The list of avant-garde artists she admired who'd gone mad or committed suicide or gone mad *before* committing suicide seemed proof enough. Perhaps Breton and Soupault should have called surrealism supernaturalism after all.

She strapped on her silk black mask. The mask covered her face like a bandana, allowing her hair to tumble free to her shoulders. It was decorated with a silver-threaded Libra or balance scale symbol. The scale's support ran the length of her nose; its beam defined her brow line; and its weighing pans consisted of the eyeholes. She regarded this persona, Manteau, the Cloud-Sign Mask, as her truest self. The mob boss Lina Mayen was a ruse adopted only as an efficient means to discover the criminals deserving of Manteau's vengeance and, except around her father, she'd allowed her birthname to fade with disuse. The anonymity of the mask both protected her private life (such as it was), and afforded her the freedom to think and act as justice demanded.

Her only way into the museum was up—four stories of sheer brick. Iron bars secured all of the windows below the top floor. The building's facade of acid-resistant silica offered no easy handholds. The mortar between bricks would have to do. She affixed a collapsible sword to her thigh-strap, attached a holstered gas gun to her belt, then donned a pair of clawed gloves. Her head was still bleary from last night's cognac. She cursed herself for not drinking red wine cut with water and again for forgetting her cloak, which, when activated by her gauntlets, stiffened into glider wings. The building loomed like an unmarked gravestone. She found her first crevice, took a troubled breath, and pulled her combat boots from the ground.

She made progress three meager rows of brick at a time, claws first, ridged boots next, muscles tense throughout. Her body trembled as if her spine were a plucked wire. One misplaced toehold and—

"Another damnable day," came a young male voice through the closest window. "More of the inspector's 'hurry up and wait' routine."

Manteau tightened her finger-grip on her third-story perch.

"You see the corpse?" a second male voice asked. "Twisted up something evil."

"The devil's business for sure. Give me one of those, will you? I need to get that death-smell out of my nose."

Mortar flaked into empty space. Manteau's right boot threatened to slip its groove.

"Just wait until we're in the field against the *Boche*," said the second officer.

"Spring of last year, I would have said, yes, right, war's inevitable. The army's partly mobilized, okay, but… I've a feeling it will be the English first, if anyone."

The boot gave. Manteau straightened against the deathward pull. It was either move or die.

"I'd almost welcome it. Better than all this waiting, *attendre pour attendre.*"

"I know what you mean. We wait on duty and off."

Manteau lurched wildly for the next handhold. The claws spiked into place. She completed the awkward embrace with her other hand, damn the noise. Another grueling twenty-one centimeters. She scarcely paused for breath before trying again, now more afraid of stopping than missing a hold. The alley below receded into a cracked world of its own. The air assumed a rarified quality. She made every movement count and at last, exhausted, raised herself up on the ledge of a fourth-story window. It was smaller than the others and curtained in black. Propped up on an elbow, she scored the glass with a chisel-sharp claw and pressed…The glass rang into shards. She quickly cleared the window frame of dangerous fragments and scrambled inside, breathless. Her body shook from relief.

The room turned out to be a supply closet for photographic equipment. It was full of copy stands, drop cloths, tripods, easels, padded blocks and the like. Nothing of interest. Manteau had to get to Lammert's office on the floor below. Osher had said his aborted meeting was about the museum's newest acquisition: a heretofore unheard-of journal kept by the Italian surrealist Vestipuccine, best known for the *objet d'art* masterwork *Quaternity in vetro*. Lammert had asked for Osher's help in authenticating the journal, but had refused to say anything more about it over the phone. If Lammert proved to be dead, Manteau planned to steal it. Vestipuccine had a history with La Fratellanza di Bestie (The Brotherhood of Beasts). It's likely the journal contained arcane secrets the *gendarmes* would neither recognize nor properly safeguard.

She put her ear to the door and, hearing nothing, cracked it open. Instead of the hallway she expected, there was a darkroom setup. She fitted a small breathing filter to her mouth and unholstered her gas gun before opening the next door. This gave on to a corridor decorated in photographic reproductions of minor arcanum. She hurried to the stairwell exit and down to the third floor. Approaching footsteps put her on the defensive. She slipped behind the door as it swung wide.

Two *gendarmes* sauntered up the stairs in the direction she'd come. One said to his companion, "Seems we get the shit detail no matter what."

"Guess the inspector just wants us to do it *ventre à terre*."

As soon as they disappeared, she rushed into the hallway. She had no time to lose. If the *gendarmes* were checking every room, her break-in would soon be discovered. She burst into Lammert's office, gun leveled. No one was there. She holstered the gun, made for the writing desk and paused at a telltale lacquer of dried blood between the desk and several unopened crates. The blood-shape sug-

Petit mystère numero 1
A series of blood drops without a corresponding trail in or out of the room.

gested drops from a height rather than a draining spill. But if that were the case, why was there no trail to the door? She noted the question then searched the old Regency writing desk. The most valuable (read: dangerous) artifacts were secured in a hidden floor vault. But she had a hunch Lammert had been studying the Vestipuccine journal in anticipation of his meeting with Osher. The desk's fold-out writing surface was a mess of financial papers, shipping manifests and excerpts from the next iteration of the museum's catalog.

Would Lammert have detected the intruder or intruders in time to hide the journal? Manteau pegged the writing desk's date of manufacture to the early 1800s—an era before personal safes. That vintage typically featured one or more secret compartments for hiding valuables. She opened the small drawers or pigeon holes. They housed nothing more interesting than a few antique pens and a talismanic coin of Roman origin. She removed the central drawer entirely and found a discolored panel flush with the writing surface. The flick of a clawed finger revealed a small space beneath it and an unbound leather notebook. She snatched it out. The fly leaf was inscribed *La rivista di secondi risvegli – quaderno VIII* (The Journal of Second Awakenings – Notebook VIII), followed by Vestipuccine's signature. She pocketed the notebook in the jacket of her pant suit and returned the drawer to its former state.

There was a commotion in the hall—running, shouting. The *gendarmes*. Manteau locked the office door and scanned the room for a hiding spot. The largest of the unopened crates looked sizeable enough. There was no shipping notice for her to understand its contents so she hastily pried it open with her metal-tipped

Petit mystère numero 2
An empty (sheathed) crate with no sign it's been opened by a hammer or cat's paw.

fingers. "Curiouser and curioser," she whispered. The crate was empty. Perhaps Lammert planned to ship something from his collection. Or, perhaps whatever was inside had been removed and the evidence disguised.

The rattling of the door handle prompted Manteau to hold her questions. She climbed into the crate and pulled it shut as the door flew open. "...the damn door. Didn't anyone check to see if it locked automatically?"

A second muffled but intelligible voice followed. "See? There's no blood-trail anywhere between that fourth floor window and the director's office."

"Could be unrelated. A thrown rock or a bird, *enfin*, some daft bird— shattered the window and escaped."

"Some 'Rue Morgue' scenario, eh? And no one was seen leaving the museum?"

"No, sir. The only person here was the watchman and he neither saw nor heard anything until the morning when he discovered the first body on the lawn and then the director shortly thereafter."

Manteau's heart misgave at the confirmation of Lammert's demise. Poor old nervous Lammert. The pain mingled with all the other outrages she'd suffered. Lammert, her twin sister, the anonymous mundanes who rated better, all would be avenged.

"I trust he remains detained for questioning?"

"Of course, sir."

"And you're quite sure nothing is missing from this office? Or the museum generally?"

"Not that we've found, sir. We're in the process of confirming the museum's records. You'll find some of them on the desk there."

That was of little surety. Manteau knew the most prized artifacts never showed up in the museum's public accounting.

"These crates have been photographed, right?"

"Yes, sir."

"Then let's start with those."

"As you wish, sir."

Manteau's crate was the first to be opened. It was manhandled into a new position. She readied her gas gun and pointed it toward the lid. When it came free, nails squealing, she pulled the trigger. The burst of knock-out gas was like striking out at the world with a dream.

Chapter 4
Where's the Fourth?

Saturday, 3 February 1934

When Alcine interrupted my early morning dream, I had a disorienting sense of the totality of things. This sense lasted for no
more than an eyeblink. It was a rare precipitate of the surrealist
dialectic: conscious thought (thesis), unconscious thought (antithesis) and thought at the split-second of waking (synthesis).

She had laid her hand on my chest to stop it from jittering.
Apparently, I had been crying in my sleep "Oh! Oh! Oh!" She said it
sounded as if I had been wounded of a sudden and in disbelief about
my condition. I grasped her hand through the bedsheets before I
had fully wakened. In that instant, her hand might have been a
doll's for all the feeling it suggested. She blames my fraught state
on the unfinished, in fact, unconceived, painting for La Fratellanza
and its attendant pressures.

It is true that life has alternated between rages and troubled
sighs. Nearly 17 years have passed since my original commission. I
do not doubt that in my unguarded sleep I could well prefer a fatal
wound to going on this way.

Tuesday, 6 February 1934

Breton and his clubhouse gang put Dali on "trial" yesterday for
defending the "new" and "irrational" in "the Hitler phenomenon"

and for mocking their beloved Lenin in The Enigma of William Tell. More proof Breton's surrealism is to artists what communism is to kulaks. Perhaps Breton will raise up his own Gulag.

Friday, 9 February 1934

At the close of the Great War, when La Fratellanza presented me with those salvaged Parmatmar crystals, I was at loose ends, searching for a technique beyond mere scatological boldness and the juxtaposition of unlike objects. I was desperate to get at the simultaneity of life, but lacked the organizing image necessary to my purpose.

This part bears repeating: the aim of my art, if not art generally, is to elicit felt experience. I want to bring simultaneity into the world as a humanism. By that I mean an emotional sense of the manifold present, conscious and unconscious. What better medium than glass? The crystals suggested the wonder-worlds of the telescope and microscope, of reflecting and scrying mirrors, of ghostly transparencies, of Bentham's all-seeing Panopticon. Without a single organizing image, however, these ideas were like so much paint dust. Per amor del cielo! The time lost to empty visions...

Then it came unexpectedly and fully-formed from Jung's commentary on The Secret of the Golden Flower: the quaternity as embodied in the lapis or Philosopher's Stone...

Wednesday, 14 February 1934

On the occasion of our fourteenth la festa degli innamorati...
Alcine:
the green-gold source
of my continual unblinding,
an I whirled in dot and line,
containing all forms.
although mismemories

and dreams have shaped my seeing
as much as life, your I
rendered in lapis-light,
affirms I've never painted
less than reality.

Thursday, 1 March 1934

How do I know La Q is a true distillation of psychic automatism? I have little to no memory of its day to day creation. I am reminded of the Vestal in Le notti romane who says she struck her head against a wall in desperation and then lay on the ground. The act of falling is an insensible gap. The same can be said of my work on La Q. Once I begin, I have no knowledge of the brush. Its bristles see ahead into the future and apply impasto strokes of their own accord.

Sunday, 18 March 1934

The evening papers commend the speech Il Duce gave today announcing his sixty-year plan to return Italia to imperial glory. Being of a paranoid and apolitical nature, I would not have taken notice of its content where it not for this proclamation: "The fourth great historical epoch of the Italian people, which future historians will label the Epoch of the Blackshirts, has already begun." Since embarking on La Q in earnest I have become increasingly sensitive to the number four and its derivatives.

Jung's idea of the quaternity centers on the transformational effect of adding a fourth to an established triad. This idea was evidently inspired by the four-stage process of alchemical change—what has been called the search for the godhead in matter. Jung, of course, is not interested in metallurgical but personal transformation. He uses the medieval language of alchemy only as a convenient model. The first stage, nigredo (literally, "black"), full of confusion and misery, commences the process (How much like my early attempts at conceiving La Q?); the second, albedo ("white" or "bright"), occasions a glimmering awareness of our "inner partner"; the third, rubedo ("reddening"), entails a surge of renewal that comes with the power to contain opposites (good/evil, male/female); and the fourth, citrinitas, the metaphorical "gold," culminates in individuation, the merging of Ego and Self, perhaps godlike awareness.

Whenever Jung encounters a triad, he looks for a fourth to imbue it with transformational magic, e.g., adding the Virgin Mary to the Holy Trinity. "Three are here, but where is the fourth?" he asks. Alcine seems even more attuned to these aspects of La Q than me. She watches me work as if ensorcelled and "dreams with her eyes open" (her words). She has begun to worry what she will do in its absence, when I am compelled to turn it over to La Fratellanza...

Wednesday, 21 March 1934
     With its thick swirls of paint, nuanced in signs and sigils, La Q has taken on the physicality of sculpture. It awaits only an extra-added element to give it the depth vital to simultaneity. After much trial and error, I have managed to make a varnish of the Parmatmar crystals (similar to amber dissolved in spike oil). I consider it here the sealing element of freak chance. At worst, I hope the final effect of this resin will put the work in motion, not unlike Duchamp's Nu descendant un escalier n° 2, with its overlapping planes. At best, I hope to achieve something wholly new and beautiful in the realm of felt experience.

Saturday, 24 March 1934
     The crystalline varnish is fully dry and bonded to the paint. The effect is greater than I dared hope. La Q now has the mesmeric quality of a prism. The layers of alchemical color beneath the glaze shimmer with an inner light, streaking this way and that in relation to your vantage point. In this way, my objet d'art is

a compound medium, its meaning variable from person to person and also, within ourselves. The resin has allowed for a permanent, trancelike intimacy only hinted at in La Q's unvarnished form.

Alcine appears to be particularly sensitive to the visceral connections it makes among color and shape and inner life. I do not know what jolt of meaning she receives from this circuit, but she assures me one exists. Her most coherent description of it is: "Something about the world-as-mind and humanity as its idea." She regards La Q as the threshold to a divine dream. Through it, she becomes herself and not-herself, beholden and free at once. She talks more and more of moving, okay, running away, to keep La Q from La Fratellanza. I relate my own heartsickness at the thought of surrendering it. It is an achievement never to be tried again. But I am nothing less than adamant that we honor our agreement. The witch cult has ensured our prosperity for almost two decades. More than that, I know there is no hiding from it. I have seen their magicks first-hand. It is rumored their witches can find a child before it is born and, if desired, snuff it in the womb. I am loath to imagine what supernatural tortures they would perpetrate on us.

Monday, 26 March 1934

If only Breton knew, that petty arbiter of surrealist orthodoxy. With all his fulminations and self-justifying manifestos and Stalinesque purges, he has never come this close to achieving the surrealist ideal: to make art of life and to make of life an art. La Q is psychic automatism in its fullest expression, pure untrammeled thought. It is an objet d'art for divining who you are. And to think I once agreed with him that painting was the least auspicious use of the technique. Too slow and deliberate, too much a part of conscious life. My frustrations in that regard are amply documented here and it pains me now to recall those passages, how I despaired of ever transcending what seemed inexorable limits. But I suppose it is only natural for the fevered man in the throes of his sickness to regard good health also as a figment of his overheated brain.

Friday, 30 March 1934

La Q is too much of the world. Its stillness, its silence and corporeality partake of an unseen dimension. In both geometry and art, a fourth point transforms the two-dimensional triad or triangle into a figure with depth, the cube and the tetrahedron (a form lapis). The crystal varnish has done the same for my painterly abstraction, giving it subliminal depths. I daresay La Q is superior even to Plato's visible forms and their ideals. It captures, if not embodies, the constituent energies that make them up. It is simultaneity made manifest. It is also a constant, irrepressible static in my head.

I will, I must, contact La Fratellanza and be rid of its alienating presence. La Q has made Alcine a withering lily of the field. She refuses to go out, to dress and sometimes to eat. "La Q is the only sustenance I need," she insists. I am killed a little each day by her manic pleading to remain in my studio.

I wish Signor N– were here to counsel me. I have often wondered if he managed to escape La Fratellanza, and if so, where he might be and what he might have done with his coveted grimoire. He warned me about the power of those sigils. I thought the philosophy of dada and then surrealism--pure psychic automatism--would protect me; instead, I have opened myself to illimitable dangers.

Tuesday, 10 April 1934

This night marks the last time I will ever set eyes on La Q. I am distraught, understandably so, I think, but Alcine is inconsolable. She weeps throughout la maga's hour-long inspection of the objet d'art. When the sorceress emerges from my studio, she pronounces La Q una gloria misura per I nostri dèi and commands her masked acolytes to cover and remove it. Alcine goes so far as to step between them and the studio door, explaining she has a special affinity for La Q and cannot bear to give it up. Much to my surprise, la maga not only permits this effrontery, but quizzes her a while on the nature of her quaternal visions, distinguishing among various sounds and images I have never suspected, much less experienced. Alcine grows more animated as she talks about La Q, how it captures the very atoms of thought, and it pains me, this talk, as it becomes clear she is willing to leave me, this, our home of fourteen years, to continue living in the artwork's half-hallucinated space.

La maga determines, however, that Alcine's visions lack a cohering center. She has another medium, the sorceress says, a provincial French woman they call Qello di Sognare (the Dreaming One). This woman was part of some German experiment under the auspices of the Kaiser. She has since been raised in the paganisms of La Fratellanza, and trained in the spiritual arts of lucid dreaming and astral projection. No, Qello di Sognare is fated to be the oracle of La Q, not my overwrought wife.

Alcine flies into a panic, and in the end, must be restrained—lashed to the bed with strips of drop cloth. She is there even now, close to dawn, awake and unmoving, no doubt trying to recreate or reach the actual La Q in her imagination. I am afraid of her and for her. I do not know what to do. There's no returning to the life we had before. La Q has become a dreadful demarcation in our lives, the crosswise line between before and after . . .

Saturday, 14 April 1934

Alcine settles the matter of what comes next with a palette knife and a note in her provident hand: Do not weep for me. The lapis-light of my soul must out.

Per me si va ne la città dolente,
per me si va ne l'etterno dolore,
per me si va tra la perduta gente.

Chapter 5
All Fool's Day

Lina parked her Duesenberg J Roadster several streets over from Osher's bookstore. The knock-out gas had done its work on the inspector and his men at the museum, and she'd escaped down the back stairs. But she couldn't help thinking their interruption had prevented her from discovering some vital clue. Her brief perusal of Vestipuccine's notebook had only confirmed what she remembered of the artist's tragic biography. She could only hope Osher was privy to something useful.

His corner shop, Black Wings Books, was on Rue de l'Université not far from Quai Branly in the most abject and isolated of Paris' twenty districts. The 14th arrondissement was its own castoff world. All the necessities for living and dying could be found there: a birthing clinic, an orphanage, a hospital, numerous churches, a prison, and a cemetery overseen by Horace Daillion's wistful bronze angel of Eternal Sleep (*Génie du Sommeil Eternel*). Black Wings' public inventory consisted of American pulp fiction: crime thrillers and mysteries, westerns, and works of science-fiction, fantasy and horror. The display table in the front window featured *Tarzan the Magnificent* on one side and S.S. Van Dine's last Philo Vance novel, *The Winter Murder Case*, on the other.

Lina regarded the CLOSED sign on the door with dismay. Perhaps Osher was too grief-stricken to open this morning, but she suspected another, less innocuous reason. She went around to the delivery entrance and pulled her Manteau disguise from her handbag. In costume again, she used a folding pick set to open the stockroom door. She shouldered it open ... and stepped into the barrel of a gun.

"Hands away from your belt, *s'il vous plaît*." The tall, lightly-freckled gunsel motioned her inside. "The boss is expecting you."

She prepared to spring at him when a second goon emerged from the shadowed recesses. He was identical in every respect to the first. His boyish face belied his obvious strength. Ah, Manteau thought, raising her hands, the Pittard brothers. She'd first heard about the twins three or four months ago in conjunction with a Left Bank extortion racket. Rumor had it they'd joined the Gang des Pauses Sud. If true, that would make their boss Anatole Janvier, the so-called *Tête de Renard*. To this point she'd considered him beneath the notice of her Marseilles-based and considerably larger mob, the *Unione Corse*. Perhaps she'd have to re-evaluate that assessment.

"I'm complying as a courtesy. If I hear you bragging about it later, I will make you pay." She flattened her palms and rubbed her thumbs across her fingertips in a *du fric* gesture.

The gunsels led her toward the showroom, one in front of her and one behind. "What's Janvier doing here? He's a sly one, I've heard. But a reader? Maybe of the racing forms..."

"You can ask him yourself," the first gunsel said, ushering her into Osher's office.

Janvier had one black leather shoe on the edge of the chair to which Osher was bound. It looked as if he were rearing back for a kick. He straightened at Manteau's entrance and tugged his dove-gray suit jacket into place. His angular face contrasted with his weedy, adolescent build. He tipped his short-brimmed Trilby and broke into a skeletonized smile. "My dear Manteau. How kind of you..."

"You say *chère* (dear) but your tone means *une garce* (bitch)." Manteau bent to Osher's eye level to survey his injuries. Osher was a stout, jowled forty-something. One normally olive-toned cheek was yellowing and his bottom lip was badly split. "Are you all right, *mon ami?*"

"He did call me...a stinking American Yid," Osher spit, flashing his crimsoned teeth. "I told him...I said I'm...an expatriate."

Rising to her full height, Manteau said, "How is he supposed to say anything intelligible if you keep socking him in the jaw, Janvier?"

"You know of me then. How 'Fox and the Hedgehog.'"

"But that isn't the one big thing I know." She watched Janvier study her eyes, trying to discern what was behind them. She wondered what he saw or imagined.

"Do tell."

"First, untie Osher."

"He's safer where he is." Janvier walked out from behind the cluttered desk and leaned against it. "I'm here only for information. When I learned you were en route, I thought it fortuitous. We can help each other."

Manteau was conscious of the Pittard brothers behind her, guns leveled at her back. "Do what, exactly? Fence what you've stolen?"

"But that's the problem—I didn't steal anything. Never even set eyes on it."

Ah, his first slip. "On what?"

"*La Q*," Osher said.

"*La quoi* (Exactly what)?" Manteau said, "It was there?"

"It should have been."

Manteau shook her head for shame. She might well have hid inside the artwork's shipping crate. "Since when do small change mobsters pull art heists?"

"It promised to be a simple—and lucrative—job."

That fit Janvier's profile: game for any racket and no feeling for anything but avarice. "For whom?"

"Therein lies are mutual interest. Or, should I say patriotic interest?"

"The Germans?" Manteau scoffed. "I think you've mixed up your Aesop's fables. This is more 'The Fox Who Lost His Tail.'"

Janvier's face darkened at the insult. He reached into his jacket and came up with a nickel-plated cigarette case. He snapped it open, revealing a neat row of Gauloises Caporal. "Mutual interest, mutual threat. Same difference."

"What do you care which *grosses têtes* run things? *Plus ça change*..."

"Like any good Frenchman, I stand for the republic when it will save me trouble or money." He put a cigarette between his lips and lit it with a gold slide sleeve lighter.

"Start from the beginning. How did this come about?"

He exhaled a stream of smoke. "The painting—"

"*Objet d'art*," Osher said.

"Whatever," Janvier intoned. "It was apparently in the hands of a religious group—"

"La Fratellanza di Bestie," Manteau said.

"Goddamn it. Am I telling this story *sans mot dire* (without words)?"

"By all means *sans maudire* (without cursing)."

"The pagan cult grew wary of increased attentions from the damn *Boche* and sought a place to hide this *La Q*. They made a deal with the *Musée d'Histoire d'Occulte* to store it." He reached for a cold mug of coffee on the desk and tapped cigarette ash into it. "German spies learned of the arrangement and I was hired to steal the ... *objet d'art* upon its receipt."

"And did you?" Manteau wondered if Janvier had kidnapped Osher for his black market expertise, possibly to get the names of prospective buyers.

"*Non* is still *non*," Janvier insisted.

"Then you murdered Lammert believing he'd tricked you—hid it somewhere in the museum, shipped it elsewhere or—"

"I didn't make it inside, but what I saw on the lawn—my underboss ... It was a horror equal to Poe or Erckmann-Chatrian."

"Ah, now we get to the real *discuter le coup*," Manteau said. She used this last term in both of its senses—as a scheme and a topic of discussion. "Could the fox be a cat in disguise? What is it the Dutch say? 'The frightened cat makes odd jumps.'"

Janvier tightened in anger. A muscle in his jaw twitched. "If this were merely a matter of guts and guns, you'd be dead already."

"There: the claws come out ..."

"You're the one with the reputation for killing."

"Only those who deserve it."

"The enemy of my enemy ..." Janvier stubbed out his cigarette on the inside lip of the ceramic mug.

"Is a reluctant ally."

"*D'alliér* (to ally) not *s'allier* (to wed)." Janvier took a couple of steps toward Manteau and for a moment, she thought he might try to rip away her mask. "It was a *fantôme* that killed him—my underboss, Drapeau. This is why I come to you."

"What do you think I can do?"

"Isn't that your forte—the supernatural? I thought maybe you could ... contact the spirit world, see into my future ...?"

"I'm not a medium. And if I were, you'd have to be dead to be helpful."

"But you agree, no, we work together? I can pay, if that's what it takes ..."

Manteau understood that Janvier regarded her as just another gunsel, an abstract peg for an abstract hole ... "Your story seems a worthy mystery. But I work best alone. That's not only a preference, but a warning."

"Sadly, things as they are, my chances are better *with* you than without you." He gestured toward the Pittard brothers. "Besides, there are places we can go where you can't—outside, in the day ..."

"I do have agents for that, but ..." Manteau considered her alternatives and decided that, against the Germans, a partnership of sorts would be the most advantageous option. "Because you're already involved and we'd only end up getting in each other's way, all right, for now, yes. To be clear, though, when we recover *La Q*, it goes into hiding, perhaps even overseas. We can blame its disappearance on this *fantôme*."

Osher twisted in his chair from Manteau to Janvier. "What I don't understand is why the Germans would want it. From all accounts, it's a large abstract. Hardly fits the Nazi-approved standard. And unless you're dreamtime-sensitive or specially trained, probably the most it would do is provoke a mild headache."

"I've no idea," Janvier said, visibly relieved.

Manteau said, "Maybe the Berlin Fire Department has another art burning scheduled."

Janvier put out his hand. "You have the journal, I take it, the 'one big thing?'"

"Oh, so you did get something useful from Osher."

"*Antshuldigt,* Manteau."

"*C'est pas grave.*" Eyeing the twins, she reached into her jacket. "I have one of them—number eight. I don't know if Lammert had the others." She withdrew the notebook slowly to appease the gunsels.

Osher said, "That's the last one and, from what I know, probably the most important."

"I haven't had a chance to read it carefully," Manteau said. "But in skimming the entries for the first few months, I did find something of interest. He notes a sorceress from La Fratellanza mentioning a French woman, the *Qello di Sognare.* She was a prisoner of the Germans during the Great War. She would've been a child then, likely from a northern province that fell under German control. La Fratellanza trained her to 'read' its aura." Ignoring Janvier, she tossed the journal on the desk toward Osher. "There could be a name in it somewhere. I suspect that wherever we find her, we'll find *La Q.*"

Chapter 6
Masks within Masks

"What do you think?" Solange asked, returning the hairdryer to the aluminum stand in its plastic case. "Another layer of latex?"

Lina examined her artificially-aged right hand splayed on the vanity dresser. The skin puckered convincingly along her knuckles and around her veins. "No, that's enough to match the left. A daub of paint should finish it." The mirror showed a Lina about thirty years older—in her early sixties. The effect of the old age makeup was humbling. Deep creases joined her brows, dark circles ringed her eyes, and marionette lines defined her cheeks and mouth. She could see herself accepting those changes, however grudgingly, when the time came. It was the sagging neckline that got to her. There was a vulnerability in it—a mortal nakedness—she couldn't shake.

The image brought to mind the early days of her combat training, her father's curved knife italic against her throat. He understood Lina's vendetta against the criminal underworld even if he didn't always agree with the risks she took. He'd been a *chef de bataillon* in WWI and served five years in the *3ᵉᵐᵉ Régiment Étranger d'Infanterie* before suffering the wound that put him in a wheelchair. When he'd realized she couldn't be dissuaded from pursuing her sister's killers, he'd tried to arm her with every possible advantage, including a posthumous mindset. "The hardest part is the emotional discipline," he'd said. "You must slough off your earthly cares, your feelings for me, for yourself, everyone. You must be dead inside, a revenant. Then and only then can you wreck your revenge and live. That is the paradox." By this reckoning, Lina had been dead for nearly six years.

She took a sip of soda water and grimaced at the ticklishness of Solange's brush on her hand.

"Careful you don't smooth those wrinkled lips now," Solange said. "It doesn't take much to deform the latex." She painted Lina's outstretched hand with a pale liquid foundation.

"Tickles," Lina said mid-sip.

"*Bismillah,* I hope your enemies never find out how ticklish you are."

"They already know how *délicate* I am," Lina said, using the word in the sense of 'tricky' as opposed to 'sensitive.' "Well, most..."

"I assume Janvier's about to find out. How long can you use each other before the killing starts?"

"Until one of us gets what we want."

"Sounds more like a marriage after all."

"I thought I was the cynical one."

"Oh, I meant your marriage, not mine. *Mais moi, c'est autre chose* (But with me it's a different manner)." Solange broke into a wry smile. Lina noted with satisfaction that Solange's smile hadn't changed since their school days in Guéret. Each one seemed to conceal a never-to-be-guessed secret.

"Janvier's a perfect *enfant de Napoléon.*" That was Lina's term for penny-ante criminals who styled themselves emperors. Janvier typified the breed—obstinate, controlling and superior in his misanthropy. Persuaded there was no hope for the world, men like Janvier were anxious to prove it to everyone else by making them miserable.

"Should this take priority over the Case of the Dirty *Gendarme?*"

Lina experienced an awful tightening across her chest at the thought. She'd come to Paris to dispatch the last of the men implicated in her sister's murder. She loathed waiting, but now that she knew his identity, the case would keep. "For the time being. We have to solve this murder-robbery quickly. If *La Q*'s been stolen, it could be out of the country already."

"What do you think? Any suspects?"

"Apart from Janvier and his *fantôme,* you mean?"

"I take it you want me to investigate him—his criminal dealings, personal life—determine what kind of leverage the Germans might have." She finished painting the hand and prepped a spoolie for graying Lina's eyebrows. "As for the *fantôme*, perhaps a call to Ciara might be in order, what with her connection to the spirit world..."

"It's worth a try. While you're at it, check with Lancer or better, Paul, on this German experiment noted in the journal. They had several missions in France during the Great War." She recalled Lancer mentioning an especially perilous mission in the Nord-Pas-de-Calais region along the Escault river—a weapons research facility. "They're only an hour behind, yes?"

"Not that it matters. Paul is up most hours of the night anyway." Solange put a light hand on Lina's chin. "This way, *s'il te plaît*." She applied the paint-stippled spoolie to the left brow.

"Is that why my phone expenses are so high?" Lina asked through closed eyes. "You conducting some transatlantic romance?"

"Don't be daft. He's half an ocean away..."

"Distance is all in your head. You'd know that if you kept up with your training in astral projection."

Solange finished with the spoolie and, satisfied with her work, propped it on the plate of leftover latex and powder. "Oh, yes, I have loads of time for that..."

"And what's his excuse? Even before his... *las augmentation*, he found ways to parallel worlds—under the sea yet."

"Also, he's older—by like twenty-five years—and I'm *à la fleur de l'âge* (in the prime of life)."

"And that makes him *le fluage de l'âge* (the creep of the age)? As brilliant as he is now, it's probably a small matter for him to slow time or retard his aging process. Any day—"

"And Catholic..."

"Now, you're reaching. Islam, Catholicism—both have their origins in a kind of Manichean outlook."

"I'm sure that would placate my parents. To them, Catholics worship a false god and the Trinity..." She flailed her hands dismissively.

"Are you serious?"

"Oh, since when have you told your father about your ... *inclinations?*"

"*Mais moi, c'est autre chose.* He has *Well of Loneliness*-style misconceptions about that. He'd only blame my mother for wanting a boy when pregnant with me."

"As if he didn't."

"It's a good thing, too, or I'd be long-dead by now." The term *morte depuis longtemps* hung in the air. Lina had said it unthinkingly. It was only on reflection that it sounded like a terrible insult to her dead twin—as if Lucia's death were due to some venal weakness.

"You know, for someone living as a faux mob boss, you're terrible at hiding your feelings."

"Only among those I trust."

"Remind me to kiss you later." Solange stood and removed her ruffled apron.

"Not unless I can do better."

"Oh, right, your *petite copine.* She called while you were out. I left the number on your desk, along with her name—Reba."

"There's some synchronicity. Hebrew name, meaning..."

"The fourth born."

"*Nom d'une pipe.*" Lina sensed the forces of chance gathering like filings around a magnet. "While I'm meeting with Monsieur Noye, would you do a couple of things for me? First, see if any hospitals in the vicinity of the museum had a patient that evening with an arm wound. It's unlikely Janvier managed to injure this *fantôme.* Still ... Second, pay a visit to Lammert's manservant, Rouillard. He might know something of value. Lammert's lived alone ever since his mother passed. Rouillard was probably as close to him as anyone."

"What a sad fact."

Lina returned Solange's remark with a tight-lipped smile. If she were to die today, who besides her father and Solange would know to care? She turned from her aged reflection. "*Un fait, une faute, une fin.*"

Chapter 7
Tiere aus dem Paradies

The handwritten numbers fuzzed in and out of focus. Janvier set the ledger aside and rubbed his eyes. He couldn't concentrate on routine business matters in his current state. *La fortune est aveugle et invisible.* Less than a day ago, he was anticipating a score that would elevate him to the next level; now, he was hiding out in a small farmhouse on the southern edge of Paris, riddled with anxiety. He separated another *nougat noir* from its wax wrapper and, to spare his teeth the effort, cut away a corner with a steak knife.

The honeyed taste of nougat always revived memories of a trip to the coast with his father when he was eight years old. They had stopped to visit the nougat factory in Montélimar on their way to the medieval beach town of Antibes. That night in the cheap hotel room where they shared a bed, his father's hitching snores kept him awake and on edge. Janvier tried everything to lessen the noise short of waking his father up: pulled the coverlet over his head, stuffed his ears with toilet paper, even held his breath to simulate the silent world under the ocean. But nothing worked to lessen those blustery snores. In desperation, he broke off a small piece of soft vanilla nougat and pressed it to his father's lips. The old grifter tested the nougat with his tongue then took it into his mouth and, mercifully, like an infant finding its thumb, sucked himself into a quiet slumber. Janvier flushed with the effort required to stopper his laughter, but eventually, his cheeks wiped clean of silent tears, he fell asleep. The next morning, he coined a new, private expression, '*tirer un nougat*' (to pull a nougat), meaning to solve a problem in an unexpected fashion. He'd been pulling nougats of one kind or another ever since.

A shout came from the front yard. One of the twins. Janvier snatched up his gun from the dining room table and headed for the door, unsure of what to do if it opened on the *fantôme*. At the sound of the first shot, he paused. There was another and one more (the brother?), a truncated scream, then a faint grinding. He slanted away from the door toward the living room. The noise gathered strength as though pursuing him. It sounded like the shaved ice machine he'd seen once in a coastal bakery. He stepped behind the leather-armed recamier at the edge of the living room's hooked rug. The door yielded to a strident kick. Janvier raised his gun to the man-shaped silhouette.

"*Arrêtez. Lâchez votre arme*," the figure commanded in guttural French.

Janvier swallowed hard, considering, when a second man appeared behind the first, gun drawn. He dropped his pistol on the recamier. "Sturmbahnfuhrer Wiegand?" He'd never met the German face to face. Wiegand had insisted on limiting their contact to phone calls at predetermined times.

"We were understandably concerned when you failed to report." Wiegand remained in the entryway with his Luger aimed squarely at Janvier.

"I was about to contact you. After the murders, the investigation by the *gendarmes*, I thought it best to first—"

"Before you make your excuses, please ..." Wiegand waved him outside and holstered the Luger inside his jacket.

"The twins?" Janvier followed Wiegand outside. Though the Sturmbahnfuhrer was shorter by a several centimeters, the dark intensity of his eyes gave the impression of superior power. Janvier noticed, too, that Wiegand walked like a gunslinger, keeping his right arm stilled and close to his body to ensure the fastest possible draw. He wore a beige conservative-breasted suit of fine herringbone. The only acknowledgement of his affiliation with the German Army was a wine-red pocket square—the designated color of its specialist service.

Janvier stifled a cry of astonishment when he saw the Pittard brothers. They were immobilized in a thin layer of blue-white frost, clothes, guns and all. One brother had been frozen clutching his throat; the other in a defensive attitude, defiant. The cruel absurdity of their deaths made Janvier nauseous. First the *fantôme*, now this... "I don't—How is this possible?"

Wiegand gestured to one of his two escorts, a stern-faced man bearing equipment similar to a flamethrower but apparently capable of the opposite effect. "We call it *Lebenden Eis*," Wiegand said. "We discovered it this past March on the coast of Queen Maud Land, Antarctica. Its properties are not entirely known. But we're certain it's alive—sentient—a colonizing organism only resembling our ice and sustained by the energy of its prey. Even now, it's depleting these *Rabauken* of their body heat, high energy phosphates, and so on."

"Are they already... Are they dead?" He approached the closest twin, hand outstretched. The gunsel's blued and darkened eyes reminded him of a stray he'd known as a child on the streets around the Place Pigalle. The dog had been distinguished by a lidless, discolored eye.

Wiegand grabbed his wrist with a gloved hand. "No, no touching barehanded. They suffocated immediately." He fingered the victim's frosted ear then broke it off. "Brittle through and through."

"*Christ, quelle horreur.*" Janvier struggled with the notion of accepting the stories of Verne and his ilk as fact. What good were the old certainties of muscle and street smarts against this fantastical nonsense?

"We suspect this lifeform is the vestige of a meteor, perhaps even the one that ushered in the ice age." Wiegand fixed Janvier with his precipitate gaze. "This is the state of war today—on the level of science fantasy. But as impressive as this weapon is, that artwork—*Quaternity in Glass*—holds the promise of something greater." He motioned for his two escorts to follow. "We go back inside now."

Janvier was eager to explain things. "It wasn't my fault. There was someone—or something—else... *un fantôme.*"

"What do you mean? Part of the museum's security? Ah, the day we can ransack its secrets can't come soon enough." A wry smile played across his lips.

"I don't know. No. It couldn't have been. It wouldn't have killed the museum director." Janvier waited for Wiegand's men to enter the farm-house then shut the door behind them.

Wiegand declined to sit, opting instead to stand in the middle of the living room. "Based on what my men have been able to learn, I thought *you* might have done that."

"My man and I—we never made it farther than the front lawn when this *fantôme* struck. I shot at it, maybe wounded it, the arm that was solid, anyway. I can't be sure." He kept an eye on the guards, particularly, the one with the ice weapon, who took up a position near the door. The other guard circled around to cover Wiegand's back. "I know it's fantastic, but ..."

"Relax, *mein freund*. I believe you." Wiegand's broken smile didn't inspire confidence. "There have been rumors about saboteurs—men loyal to the Kaiser, bitter, playing at revenge. Perhaps it's something under their control. Besides, the director—Monsieur Voclain—wouldn't have resisted your attempt."

"What do you mean?"

"He knew of your heist; in fact, he's the one who suggested it ... in return for a small fortune."

"I don't understand." Though Janvier's insides continued to churn, he refused to take a chair. He didn't want to appear to be lowering himself before Wiegand like a chastened dog. He lit a cigarette instead.

"The plan was for him to first verify the artwork's authenticity and then allow it to be stolen. His wishes ..."

"But whatever for?"

"For the greater security of mankind." Wiegand regarded Janvier with narrowed eyes. "He was privy to certain dark forces—forces that threaten all of existence. He thought Germany, alone among civilized nations, was willing to take the necessary measures to ensure Man's survival. See, the Fuhrer understands we're animals out of paradise. The Lord gave Man dominion over the earth but not all men—only the highest among us, only those willing to struggle and die. A faith in reason—in liberal progress—is a weakness. It's a betrayal of our true nature as higher animals. This weakness—propagated by the Jews, so-called

Enlightenment thinkers, Gnostics—can't be allowed to spread. It's what doomed Germany in the Great War and it will doom Man itself without a vigorous and yes, pitiless, defense. Monsieur Voclain came to us because he knew we're prepared to fight all our racial enemies, human and supernatural. Consider it a matter of political zoology."

Janvier expelled cigarette smoke with an impatient snort. He was a militant philistine. Mammon was the only god that mattered. He tapped ash into a glass tray on a side table. "Why the break-in? If he was so willing..."

"And suffer ignominy as a traitor? No, the theft had to look plausible, without any evidence of foreign interests. Do you know for sure the artwork was stolen?"

The possibility that *La Q* remained somewhere in the museum had crossed Janvier's mind, but he'd summarily dismissed it. "I suppose not. I just assumed, given the timing of the *fantôme's* attack...What else could it be?" He tried to sound definitive but Wiegand's skeptical look unmanned him. "We're not without some useful information. I was able to see the artist's journal...A local bookstore had a copy..." He fumbled for his wallet and removed a scrap of typing paper from it. He glanced at the paper as he went on: "There was mention of a French woman involved in an experiment during the Great War. It took place here in France and was overseen by the German Army. This woman— she has...abilities. I don't know. The supernatural to me is, *enfin*, no more than children's stories and freak astrology." He gave a dismissive grunt. "Anyway, it's possible she can lead us to the artwork. Is it—Are there records you could access to help identify her?"

Wiegand pursed his lips in thought. "Cambrai, yes, it must be—a much-studied experiment. If the records exist, my department will have them. There were dozens of children involved, if I recall, so any details you can glean from this journal would be important...In fact, I'd prefer to examine it personally. Secure it for me, will you?" He gestured to his guards to exit. "In the meantime, I have men following up with assorted parties of interest. Update me at six each evening. Provided you make swift progress, I'll leave you to your devices—and your advance. It's best I don't draw too much notice given the current tensions between our countries."

Janvier followed Wiegand and his men to their teardrop-styled Hupmobile Aero Dynamic in the drive. He gestured toward the twins. "What about...?"

"The bodies won't last the night," Wiegand said. "You'll find them dessicated...like mummies."

"But...the ice..."

"With its limited mobility, it will soon starve to death." Wiegand offered his hand. "I look forward to your call tomorrow evening."

Janvier gave the hand a firm shake, wondering what *La Q* was worth in monetary terms but afraid to ask. He knew war was coming because the quality of Parisian food had begun to decline. It was better in the provinces—even here, just outside the city. Perhaps the *objet d'art* could be his insurance in a chancy wartime economy. "Sturmbahnfuhrer, if I may...I—I don't—What is it about this artwork?"

"Hmm. What did Monsieur Voclain call it? 'A modern-day scrying mirror.'"

"I'm afraid I—"

Weigand looked amused by Janvier's confusion. "He said it would give us access to the thoughts of everyone on earth—conscious or otherwise. In other words, there would be no secrets from the *Deutsches Reich*."

Chapter 8
The Winged Hourglass

While waiting for Monsieur Noye, the disguised Manteau occupied herself by sweeping the pavement in front of his Montparnasse apartment building. She wore a country apron with pockets over her print housedress. Periodically, she paused in her sweeping and spread biscuit crumbs for the sparrows. She'd given the walk a thorough cleaning by the time Noye returned from his interviews with the *gendarmes*. She'd never seen him so disheveled. His museum uniform was an uncharacteristic mess. The unbuttoned jacket revealed a loosened, gold-checked necktie, the tail flapping outside his navy vest. His shirt collar warped around his neck and one sleeve was dirtied with chalk. When he approached the building, a hand in his pocket for the keys, Manteau sidled close and whispered, "*Le cimetière*, Baudelaire's cenotaph."

Noye recognized Manteau's voice instantly, but as a former stage magician, didn't betray his surprise in the event they were being watched. The surrealist detective had never met him twice in the same disguise. He fingered the shiny bill on his cap to signal his understanding and shuffled toward their appointed rendezvous. Manteau sighed at how haggard and drawn Noye had become in recent years. Throughout her childhood, he'd been renowned for his magickal talents, both on stage under the alias Count Mirabeau and in more rarefied professional circles. Having first trained at the Neughatel Magician's Theater in Lausanne and later, under notables like Aleister Crowley, Varun Krishna, Achmad "The Baffler" Remmelin and Madame Blavatsky, he was given to citing his historical betters, saying, "This is how so-and-so used to do ..." Now pushing retirement, he was alone and nearly forgotten.

The dialectics of the city never failed to affect Manteau—the signs inherent in its architecture, the movements of its crowds, the changes superimposed on the past. Perhaps owing to her mood and thoughts about Noye, the winged hourglass figures in bas relief outside the cemetery spoke to her not only as emblems of mortality, but also as symbols of higher and lower, and the need to reverse them periodically to renew the cycle of life. The sand can run in one direction for only so long...

As arranged, Manteau found Noye near Baudelaire's cenotaph or empty grave, his blue-gray eyes downcast and solemn. The L-shaped monument featured a stern angel/daimon standing guard over the poet's shrouded corpse. In her youth, Manteau had considered becoming a poet and collage artist. She'd attended the University of Paris the year before her sister's murder in pursuit of the idea. What followed, however, convinced her that she excelled more at attaining the altered consciousness integral to the artistic process than in creating works of true surrealism. The closest she came to writing verse nowadays was the occasional cut-up exercise for investigative purposes. She still read poetry for pleasure, however, and Baudelaire numbered among her favorites. A poem like "*De profundis clamavi* (From the Profoundest Depths I Cried)" with its phantasmagoric imagery made an instant difference to her. "*Je jalouse le sort des plus vils animaux/Qui peuvent se plonger dans un sommeil stupide, /Tant l'écheveau du temps lentement se dévide.*"

"Perhaps now Lammert has found the easy sleep of the beasts." Noye's voice trembled with emotion.

Manteau's heart went out to him. "*Je suis de tout cœur avec vous.*"

"I should say the same to you—and more." Noye faced her square-on for the first time since she'd joined him. He removed his round, wire-frame spectacles to wipe the standing tears in his eyes. "After all, it was I who failed to protect him."

Manteau took his hand, patted it gently and led him away from a group of tourists and further into the expanse of grave markers. His hand was sallow, papery, wrinkled in much the same way as her false skin. "There's no cause to blame yourself, not from what I know of the *fantôme* that attacked him."

"Greater wards were in place at every threshold, I assure you."

"Marked in blood?" Manteau asked. There was a universal hierarchy to magick. Blood magick ranked second in power only to the dream-time variety.

"According to the scriptures of the Voudon Gnostique." His bony frame swelled with indignation. Though his powers as a mage may have declined, his pride was as vehement as ever. He still had an air of entitlement about him as if his storied past had granted him a stay against decline. "They have limited effects on ethereals, but still…I should have had a warning," he said.

"You saw it then? *Le fantôme?*" His mention of 'ethereals' was the first corroboration she'd received of Janvier's account.

"Only the briefest glimpse—in Lammert's office. It was half-de-materialized, arms thrust in the wall…Then it disappeared altogether. I've never before seen a spirit like it—spirals of brightness against no-thing… odd, crystalline qualities…" Noye wound a finger through his wisp of a goatee. "I reinforced the wards against its return before alerting the police. Lammert—he—He was as disfigured as any Braque. The ethereal somehow…reconstituted him…" He bowed his head and shut his eyes against the sting of incipient tears.

Manteau tried playing on his pride. "With your knowledge of the nightside, you must have some idea what it is…"

"*Ne…guère* (hardly)."

"*Une guerre* (a war). Exactly."

A young man waving a pair of Métro tickets hurried past them to rejoin his girlfriend.

Noye covered his nose and straggly handlebar mustache with a kerchief and blew into it messily. "You know I never gave much credence to that egotist Crowley but he described his familiar, Aiwas, as such a creature: a man, tall, dark, translucent, but with an aura of angelic power. The *fantôme's* face… It sparkled like summer stars," he said, recovering a measure of his normally stoic bearing.

"What else? What about Lammert? Anything out of the ordinary?" She threaded a narrow path between grave markers to put more distance between them and several tourists.

"Nothing comes to mind. Nervous as ever." Noye folded and pocketed the kerchief.

"He didn't mention any new acquisitions?"

"Should he have?"

They emerged from the narrow space into an area where most of the gravestones were no more than knee-high. Two tourists—men in their mid-twenties wearing double-breasted suits—dawdled along on a parallel course. In addition to their visible disinterest in the cemetery proper, they were conspicuous for their lack of maps and shopping bags. "It's my understanding he'd recently acquired a Vestipuccine—*the* Vestipuccine."

"*Quarternity in Glass*? Impossible. A piece like that..." He could feel her bright, youthful eyes on him through her disguise. "Even if he could somehow afford it, he would have consulted me on security."

"Would you do me the favor of searching the vaults? If not *La Q*, there must be something missing..." Manteau noted the position of the suspicious tourists in her peripheral vision.

"I helped with the inventory this morning and didn't come across anything, but yes, of course." He grimaced at an unpleasant thought. "Have you considered the possibility it was revenge?"

"For what? The Case of the *Afterlife Divided*?" The case had embarrassed a brace of Lammert's wealthy patrons. He'd received a few anonymous death threats in the weeks after its conclusion, though none serious enough to demand Manteau's attention.

"All of us have our enemies—on this world or another. The rivalries within the trade alone...I made my share just withdrawing from the Society for Psychical Research."

"You don't think you were the target?" Manteau wondered aloud.

"Perhaps this *fantôme* was a golem of sorts? Those creatures can be hard to control..."

"Glance over my right shoulder. The two gentlemen in the stripes cutting their eyes at us. We're not alone."

"You noticed, too?" At Manteau's flicker of surprise, Noye broke into a self-satisfied smile. "I'm old, not blind."

"Why don't you stay here while I circle around? We'll see if they approach." Manteau lifted her housedress in a coquettish fashion to reveal her collapsible sword in its garter-sheathe. "If so, I'll ask a few pointed questions."

"That's not an old woman's thigh."

Manteau clucked her tongue at him. "Just remember that blindness can strike men your age at any time." She waved and strolled away.

Noye dallied at a coffin-shaped marker for an obscure nineteenth century doctor. In spite of the circumstances, he couldn't help indulging in old-age grief. Was this the best he could hope for—an unvisited grave near the plot of someone famous? He'd tried to guard against this commingling of guilt and jealousy. But Lammert's murder and his complicity in it—knowing or not—had undone him. Out of the corner of his eye, he watched the suspected spies wander closer. Surely they wouldn't risk a public show of violence?

One of the men introduced himself with a tilt of his hat. "*Excusez-nous,* monsieur ..." he said in broken, German-inflected French.

Noye stiffened at the accent and gave a curt, nervous smile.

"*Pouvons-nous vous poser quelques questions sur l'incident au musée?*" the other German said. His relative fluency in French and an adhesive bandage on his chin set him apart from his partner.

"*Sous quelle autorité?* I've already spoken to the police."

"We represent certain private interests," the man with the bandage said.

"A patron? That's the province of the museum director. A new one should be confirmed in the next several days."

"No, not a patron—a collector."

Noye glowered. "Sales are highly unusual. Deaccessioning it's called. Donors tend—"

"Perhaps you can simply confirm the piece is in the museum's collection—*Quaternity in vetro?*"

The German who had made the awkward introduction sidled closer to Noye.

"No, I'm afraid not. You can be assured an acquisition like that would have been in all the papers." Noye retreated a couple of steps. "This isn't the proper venue for this kind of discussion. I recommend you make an appointment—"

"We can make this quick," the man with the bandage said. He motioned for his partner to advance on the aged magician.

There was a double-snap behind him then a keen prick against the base of his neck. "To the quick is it?" Manteau asked. A single lunge with her sword would finish him.

Noye thrust out a hand against the approaching German. One moment, his hand appeared empty; the next, it gripped a black knife. It was an old stage trick. Noye had slipped the knife from his belt when he backed away and held it in his pinched-up palm so the flat of his hand concealed it. While his would-be attacker was momentarily confused, Noye drew a pinch of salt from his pocket and flicked it in the man's face.

Manteau's opponent tried to duck away and draw his gun. She warned him against it by slicing the top button from his jacket and pressing the sword to his chest. "*Heidewitzka!*" the German shouted at seeing his foe was an older and presumably frail woman. She asked him in German who he was and better yet, who he was working for. He threw up his hands and scuttled over the adjacent grave marker, yelling at his companion to follow. Concerned about revealing too much in full view of several onlookers, Manteau signaled Noye to let the Germans go. The men hurried away, glancing back occasionally with rueful looks. Manteau pretended her sword was a walking stick for the hard-of-seeing. The witnesses alternately shrugged and laughed and shook their heads.

"That was a neat trick," Manteau said.

"Muscle memory," Noye said, returning the knife to his belt. He lowered his eyes as if embarrassed.

"When I get to be your age for real, I hope to be as sharp." Manteau folded her sword, but kept it in her hand as a precaution. "What did they say? Anything?"

"They asked about *La Q*. Someone must be persuaded Lammert had it." He chewed at the inside of his cheek.

Manteau started back toward the Boulevard Edgar Quinet. "Do you have a place to stay other than your apartment?"

"I have a cot at the museum. I doubt Esmée will mind the added security." Noye's slow, stoop-shouldered gait indicated his sleight-of-hand had taken something out of him after all.

"Has she been confirmed as the inheritor? I assumed she would be. Like Lammert, she practically grew up there ..." Esmée was Lammert's wayward younger cousin. She'd come to Paris to study under him, but spent most of her time in Montparnasse cafés under the guise of cultivating the favor of local artists.

"She's acting as if she is ..."

"She must be broken up about this."

"She has his sang-froid." There was a distinct tightness in his voice.

"Are you worried about her?"

"You know her past. She's young, unstable ... Her friends—some of them—are borderline criminal. Perhaps ..."

Manteau had tried to mentor Esmée in her way but they were too close in age for it to take. Given the situation, she hoped Esmée would be more willing than she'd been so far to lean on her greater experience. "I'll meet with her as soon as I can. In the meantime, I have a favor to ask."

"Of course."

"If we're facing a real *fantôme*, I'd like to borrow the Lamassu Box. I'll try to talk to Esmée about it first, but ..."

Noye cocked an eyebrow. "*Emprunter* (borrow) or *emporter* (take)?" he asked, acknowledging Manteau's inveterate fondness for wordplay.

She watched her step among the last of the grave markers before the boulevard. "Depends on whether I live to return it."

Chapter 9
Desire Caught by the Tail

Lina was about to unlock the door to her apartment when she spied Reba on the periphery of her vision. She bent to her task as Reba stepped from the elevator, hastened inside, and shut the door on Reba's footsteps. The inevitable knocks started by the time Lina darted into the bathroom to scour the mask from her face. She glanced at her older self in the mirror and clawed at the latex around her neck. It came away in messy arterial strips. She wet and soaped her hands in the sink, heart pounding. Reba had plainly seen her enter. She grabbed a sponge from the freestanding tub and ran it across her forehead. Whorled clots of latex collected around her feet. The knocking let up. Lina hustled into the bedroom, pulling the wig of piled-up gray hair from her head.

She withdrew her signature black cloak from her handbag and clasped it to her blouse. Another, more pronounced round of knocks at the door resonated in her chest. She snatched up a shawl from the four-poster bed, stuffed it in her handbag and went to the window, which opened onto a narrow alley. She flung it wide and crouched in the gap, four stories from the pavement. The alley between her apartment building and the next permitted only a narrow glide path. She pushed away into emptiness. The gauntlets under her disguise sent a transformative current to her cloak. The electrically-sensitive material billowed into a concave shape. The sudden air resistance jerked her momentarily toward the colorless wash of sky. Lengths of blonde straggled out from the bobby pins holding her hair in place. Lina shifted her weight back toward her apartment building to avoid caroming against the facade opposite. She steeped to the ground, landing toes-first at a run. She had too much momentum to affect a graceful landing. The deactivated cloak fell around her shoulders as she burst from the alley and onto the sidewalk. Her stomach clenched against the prospect of rushing into traffic. She lurched to a halt at the lip of the curb and yanked her handbag out of the way of a passing vehicle. The cloak fluttered around her like a protective wing.

Lina spun on her heels, thankful for the lack of curious pedestrians. She traded the shawl for the cloak on the way to her building's sun-struck entrance. She made to release her half-coiled hair when Reba emerged from the lobby.

"Oh, hey," Reba said, forming a tight smile of surprise. "I was just, you know, stopping by ..."

"I was out on business." Lina kept her voice flat in hopes of discouraging a lengthy exchange. She figured Reba had caught only an unidentifiable glimpse of her disguise upstairs, but didn't want to chance some greater recognition.

"I saw an older woman go into your apartment but no one answered when I knocked."

"Ah, my aunt—she's a bit hard of hearing." Lina's mouth seemed to go dry passing this rote falsity.

"Everything okay? If you don't mind my saying, you look a bit ... ragged." Reba extended a hand toward Lina's right ear where a fleck of latex dangled from her hair. "Is that a swipe of foundation? I do a great rinse and retouch."

Lina brushed away the residual makeup with the back of her hand. "That a fact?" She forced an open smile.

Lina remembered Reba nibbling her earlobe with the edge of her teeth. It had been like touching an electrified fence. "*Un fait* (a fact) and *une fête* (a party)," Reba said.

"*Futé* (clever)."

"It doesn't sound like I'm trying too hard?"

"It's endearing."

"That's the general idea."

Lina knew she'd chastise herself later for indulging her feelings this way. Her decision to become Manteau had come with a vow to lead a life of principled singleness, whatever the emotional complications. That vow meant neither seeking love nor regretting or renouncing it. Love was supposed to be a thing apart like an unrevealed religion. But Reba's ingénue spirit kept drawing her into temptation. "I'd invite you up, but for my maiden aunt."

"Sure." Reba cast her cut-gray eyes on Lina's dated outfit. "I left a note on the door about tonight... Le Dome?"

Lina felt the late-afternoon heat against her bare arms. "I still have some business affairs to put in order..."

"I'm sorry. What is it you do again?"

"Import-export. Mainly art. Dealing with foreign agents, I have to work all hours of the day. But I should be able to wrap everything up by, say, nine, maybe half-past?" The words seemed to parch her throat. When it came to socializing, she preferred the quiet of home to restaurants, bars or clubs. At home, there was neither the pressure to pretend nor the chronic urge to observe. She endured social crowds best when alone and free to let her mind take her where it would. Otherwise, the experience was like being the lone sober woman in a room full of drunks.

Reba's persistent smile gave way to a half-gape of disbelief. "You don't seem convinced."

The doubt in Reba's voice was wounding. It challenged who Lina was at heart—the persona she considered the 'real Lina.' She shouldered her handbag and, grasping Reba around the neck to dispel any notion of artificial tenderness, planted a languorous kiss on her lips. "What do you say in America? I'll be there with bells on."

After a rose-scented bath, Lina slipped into a robe of light blue rayon and joined Solange in the kitchen. Her secretary was busy putting away groceries. Lina's thoughts turned to the days when they'd shared bread and squares of chocolate after school. How eager she'd been to escape the routine squalor of country life for the new, the new, always *le nouveau*. If only she'd known the consequences of her narcotic desire for newness. Not even their names remained the same. Solange had taken hers from the mysterious character at the center of *Les Détraqués*, a play synopsized in Breton's infamous novel, *Nadja*. Lina bit back the nostalgic impulse to use Solange's given name. "Want help?"

"Thanks, no," Solange said, placing a carton of eggs in the Crosley electric. "I picked up just enough for dinner—Shakshouka with artichoke hearts. I assume you'll be dining in?"

"Yes, but going out this evening." Lina tightened the towel around her wet head.

"Not as Manteau, I trust…" Solange handed her the evening edition of *Paris-Soir* without meeting her eyes. The headline above the fold was **MANTEAU ATTAQUE GENDARMES SUR LES LIEUX DU CRIME**. The subhead contained an even more flagrant charge: **SOUPÇONNÉ D'ASSASSINER MUSÉE**.

Disappointing but unsurprising. It was hardly the first time her alter ego had been charged with the very murder she sought to solve. She attributed the easy condemnation of Manteau, in part, to common sexism. A French man, however boorish or greedy, was typically given the benefit of the doubt that at some level he acted from noble ideals. A French woman taking the same risks, however, was imputed with the instincts of a moth. She was invariably considered unthinking, a creature to be pitied for her wanton nature. Knowingly or not, the press implied Manteau had to be crazy because she was a woman. Lina dismissed the seriousness of the news with a wave of her hand. "A day without letting off a little gas is a day misspent."

"*Pour la paix d'esprit.*"

"*Pour la paix du corps aussi.*"

"You should be working together," Solange said, meaning the *gendarmes*. She set a bunch of Swiss chard and a large jalapeño chile on the counter cutting board. "You badly need a Commissioner Weston or Detective Cardona."

"Or a more effective means of clouding their minds short of going around like a nude from the Grande Chaumière." She skimmed the article for newly-disclosed facts. "Perhaps you can ask Paul about that, too—the clouding part. There must be some device or artifact…" With Lancer's blessing, Paul had designed her gas gun, cloak of memory-cloth and several other accoutrements.

Solange squared up to Lina, assuming her full, graceful height, and cleared her throat. "I can serve as decoy, if necessary. It would throw them off—two Manteaux. I'm ready…" There was a stubborn constriction in her face. She'd evidently been gathering the courage to make the request for a long time.

"I should never have tailored a suit in your size…"

"*La suite* (a sequel), yes, that's what I'm saying." Solange relaxed the set of her jaw. "Please, I am not Lucia. I've been training nearly five years now."

"I know. But there are dangerous forces at work here—spirits, mobsters, magicians, Nazis… I've confirmed that much of Janvier's story. I nearly added one to the permanent population of *le cimetière du Montparnasse.*" Then, touching on Solange's Algerian heritage, quipped: "We wouldn't want to make this a three-way international incident." Lina didn't know how much longer she could placate Solange on this issue before she had to give in. Lina feared Solange saw Manteau as an excitement—one premised on sound principles to be sure, but no less thrilling for it—and worse, that she failed to grasp the concomitant need to empty herself, to give and give until the prospect of death no longer frightened. She wanted to preserve Solange's chance for a conventional life as long as she could. That chance was her last living constancy. "Besides, I'm going out as Mayen."

Solange compressed her lips and bowed her head in acknowledgement of Lina's decision.

"Did you learn something from Rouillard that requires Manteau's attention?"

"I don't think so." Solange couldn't keep the disappointment entirely out of her voice, but regained her characteristic steadiness as she went on: "He mentioned that in the weeks leading up to his death Lammert had become even more guarded than usual. He didn't seem to trust

Rouillard, Esmée or anyone else with more than the barest understanding of his whereabouts or activities. One thing is that he burned some papers, records, he didn't know what, exactly, according to written instructions from Lammert. He claimed that he didn't examine any of the material before destroying it, and produced the letter instructing him to do so."

"To be expected." Lina mulled the possible contents of that material. "Noye claimed to have no knowledge of the Vestipuccine."

"Would Lammert keep it a secret—even from his own staff?" She proceeded to core and chop the jalapeño chile with vigor.

"It's possible. The Case of the *Afterlife Divided* had the unfortunate effect of justifying his paranoia."

"Think he suspected one of them?"

Lina shrugged. "To Lammert, no one was above suspicion. Not me, not even the dead." She admired Solange's theatrical precision with the knife. Solange came alive when she moved. Her every gesture was quick and deliberate. At this aesthetic remove, Lina could admit in her head that, yes, Solange was ready, but not in her heart. She understood that she would invariably lose everything she loved. But that didn't mean she had to be the cause of it. "Please make arrangements for me to meet with Esmée at her earliest convenience. She cuts a curious figure. Among the current suspects, she has the least wherewithal but the clearest motive."

Solange took up the chard. "I'm talking to Paul tonight about that experiment in the Nord-Pas-de-Calais. He's on his way back from a research expedition in Siberia."

"Good. I'm going to study up on the journal before dinner. Would you also do me the favor of cutting up that article? I'll make use of it in the morning."

"Should I expect two for breakfast?" She broke into a sly, forgiving smile.

"Probably," Lina said, heading toward the bedroom. "Even if she is a spy."

Chapter 10
Premonitory Black

Tuesday, 29 May 1934

I arrive in Paris by train to meet with a reputable expert in the realms of art and arcana who I hope can help me find La Q. (In the event this notebook falls into the hands of La Fratellanza, I'll refer to him only as the consulente.) The talk in the cafés is of the seemingly foredoomed Geneva Disarmament Conference. I can't bring myself to care. My mission of retribution takes precedence over everything, even the fates of nations.

Wednesday, 30 May 1934

I realize now there was a warning implicit in Sig. N-'s theory about the Parmatmar crystals. He speculated that the four base elements of Creation, earth, air, fire and water, were descended from the same "spiritual energy" and further, that the crystals constituted the fabled fifth element of Greek myth (what they called "the quintessence"), and was the only substance capable of focusing this unseen energy. Sig. N- so much as told me the crystals were of divine origin. Although wholly human, I am not unlike Phaethon in this, trying to master things meant only for the gods. I made the tragic mistake of thinking the crystals a controllable medium, a simple means to push my art into new dimensions, to penetrate the collective unconscious, and achieve a kind of self-illumined truth. I apprehended a dread at the center of La Q's proportions and stillness, the dreamy charge it gave the air, but my irrepressible pride wouldn't permit me to take proper stock of these feelings until . . . Poor, prescient Alcine. She must have known the insidiousness of its power all along, her tortures confused with sublimity. It's for her and this other like her, this mysterious French woman, that I undertake my mission. I've vowed that nothing will be hidden from me now, not La Fratellanza, not la maga, and not La Q, whatever the cost.

Saturday, 2 June 1934

It took a few days longer than I expected to make contact with the consulente. I've known him for nearly a decade. Our relationship goes back to when I was still on speaking terms with Breton, and participating in Surrealist exhibits here. I don't know the consulente well, but had no recourse save to trust him. His position affords regular communication with La Fratellanza, and compels him to treat all such "mystery religions" with the same even hand, so it's possible the group would share the sort of confidences that would aid me in my mission.

We rendezvoused this morning in the Jardin des Tuileries near the Orangerie Museum. The consulente appeared jittery even before I revealed the true reason for my wanting to meet. Perhaps he had a premonition of our encounter. A muscle in his jaw twitched at the mention of La Fratellanza. Fearing he might refuse my request for help, I explained the nature of La Q and my irredeemable failure to protect Alcine. He seemed much moved by my confession and, pacing under the chestnut trees along the Terrasse du Bord-de L'Eau, spoke in whispery spurts. Rumors had been circulating for weeks about a new artifact in the cult's possession. The consulente hadn't known what it was or its purpose, but figured it had something to do with the Qello di Sognare. Her training had been an open secret for years. He had no direct knowledge of her whereabouts, however. The best he could do was give me the name of a former member of La Fratellanza living in Avion, and a promise that, in the event I recovered La Q, he would help me destroy or safeguard it. He told me to assume the cult was tracking my movements. He also said la maga knew ancient ways to turn the minds of men. I put on a brave mask. "Let them try," I said. But the words sounded weak and hurried in my ears.

Sunday, 3 June 1934

Jung developed multiple quaternities beyond his idiosyncratic extension of the Holy Trinity: in geometry, a square split diagonally into triangles (like the Yin/Yang of Oriental lore); in Christian theology, a variation on the tripartite schema of Man, Nature and God as essential elements in the process of spiritual/psychological development; in dreams, the dreamer plus the recurring archetype of three others; and in psychology, the four psychic functions--sensing, feeling, thinking and intuiting (another typology suggesting alchemical concepts). I've come up with several quaternities of my own, foremost among them, one that combines the theories of Jung and Freud by treating the former's collective unconscious as the external counterforce to the latter's internally-focused Id, Ego and Superego. Jung thought the quaternity the key to individuation, or knowing the Self in the world. He sometimes referred to individuation as "squaring the circle" or "circling the square." I suppose, unthinkingly at first, I groped towards this formula in creating La Q. In imbuing it with Jung's alchemical typology, I hoped to evoke the process of self-knowing and the transcendent uplift attendant on experiencing simultaneity. I suspect now that, with the help of Sig. N- and La Fratellanza, I succeeded all-too well in my aim, that is, La Q is a gateway to the collective unconscious. That would explain why Alcine considered it such an inseparable part of her psyche, the occasional "voices" in her head, and even the form of her eventual suicide. The palette knife was not only a practical choice of weapon, but also a symbolic one, suggesting her need to expose her inmost Self to the world. In this light, her suicide can be considered a sacrament.

Monday, 4 June 1934

I've been increasingly feverish and confused since yesterday morning. Hours pass without my seeming to be aware of them. I nearly missed the train to Avion. As it was, I forgot my luggage and will have to phone the hotel to send it on. Perhaps I'm developing the mindset of a paranoiac, but I'm beginning to wonder if the consulente's remark about la maga's ability to turn the minds of men was more mocking diagnosis than warning. What if my mind has already been corrupted? I've heard experts in hypnosis can induce prefigured emotional states or even complex actions with a triggering word. Could she have secretly hypnotized me on her visit? And did the consulente provide the trigger?

Tuesday, 3 June 1934

Shadows and unrealities muddle me up, my energy flags in
I can't see past my own unreal visions
Even a burrowing sleep offers no comfort. Then the dreams come on, a churning, narcotic dissonance. ~~The dark of the night and the dark inside merge to~~

Wednesday, 6 June 1934

I'm somewhat recovered, tingly and sensitive to light, but no longer completely overwhelmed. (I've no recollection of writing the last recorded entry much less how I meant to finish it.) My first glimpse of Avion from the train made me wonder if I were hallucinating its environs. The outskirts were shrouded in a hellish pall. The night manager informed me that the town's principle business is mining coal and that the smoke comes from perpetually burning craters or slagheaps. When I asked about the name the consulente had given me, he dismissed it with a shake of his head, saying he knew little about the affairs of the town outside his establishment. I've since managed to ask a number of others about the man, including several miners, the greengrocer, the dry goods man and the butcher. None recognized the name. One of the miners, however, told me there was a recluse who lived on the edge of a coal field whose Christian name was unknown. They called him le maçon (the bricklayer) for his habit of shoring up the walls of his wooden shack with loose rocks. He was rumored to live on roots and red squirrels and the occasional stray dog. It's too late to see about him now. Night has fallen and I must rest my tired eyes. It seems the waking world exhausts them and makes my head ache.

Thursday, 6 June 1934

I continue to be plagued by suprasensible visions and blank stretches of time. The visions recall my early art: biomorphisms shot through with random vectors and quavering color. They're people-less cities of inner life where everything is profound in ways I can't reason out. La Q combined this kind of abstraction with the specificity or concreteness of sculpture. As unnerving as these visions are, they've made me question if there's a further dimension to go. Perhaps there's a way to extend La Q's low relief and imaginary spaces into volumes you can feel, to make an outer city of the inner one. I regard the third dimension in art as necessarily aggressive. It schisms our understanding of so-called "natural space." The Parmatmar crystals permitted me to render a fourth, to throw the Self into the multi-dimension of others. What would it take to make a city of that confluence?

Friday, 7 June 1934

Le maçon cuts a sad, fugitive figure. He lives little better than a mountain goat in a smoking waste, terrified of being found out by La Fratellanza. He nearly brained me with a rock on my approach, but stayed his hand at the consulente's name. Following an abbreviated version of my story, he admitted in a swallowy voice to having been a member of the cult and more, ringraziare il Signore

Dio sopra, told me I might find the Qello di Sognare in Dunkirk. Her name is known only to la maga, but she's distinguished by a head of white-blonde hair and a flat nose like chipped plaster. Oh, another city in which to be ill, to fill, to find and catch the otherworldly light...

According to le maçon, La Fratellanza has lately split into three or four rival factions, each vying for possession of La Q. The sorceress I met heads up the most virulent faction. This group has abandoned the cult's original aim of establishing an animal-like utopia in favor of murdering all Mankind, and allowing Nature to thrive in our absence. The group has pinned their hopes on the Qello di Sognare to achieve this "bounteous genocide." They believe La Q gives her access to the thoughts of everyone on earth, and thus, the chance to undermine, if not control them. La maga apparently has the power to reverse the workings of the mind, and has trained the Qello di Sognare in the same black art. She, too, can switch the inborn hierarchy of the mind's conscious and unconscious parts. This possibility struck me dumb for several moments. Now I don't know if my recent confusions are due to the interference of the Qello di Sognare or another, more targeted scheme, i.e., post-hypnotic suggestion. Regardless, I'm loath to imagine my own recent lapses in thought multiplied into blind spots enough for the human race. Undone by the unseen. Annullata per l'invisibile. Annulata domini.

Le maçon cited the sorceress as the reason for his self-exile. He uttered her name like a bitter child, adding that she was increasingly quick to work her cruel magick. The remote command could come at any moment--die, die, die. I had to lean close to understand his murmured invectives and, feeling awkward and guilty at my narrow use of him, pressed ten francs into his hands on leaving. He would forever be an outcast from the congress of Man. He would slowly wither down to raw animal grief, never to know an

Alcine to ease it, however long the sorceress might deem his suffering to last...

Saturday, 8 June 1934
   I am palsied from the effects of these dreams. No more, no

   A brief moment of clarity. Respite enough, I hope, to relate one vivid dream. I was wandering in the dark through the Borghese Gardens, an ancient, red-figure vase in my hands. The ground-sweeping branches of the willow trees seemed part of a vast shroud. I wound among them to emerge on the shore of the garden's artificial lake. The vase resounded with a strange skittering. There was something alive inside it. I flashed on an intrusion of winged cockroaches. The possibility of their escape unnerved me. I dropped to my knees and clawed the dirt, desperate to bury the vase. My fingers were sore by the time I finished digging. (Don't ask me why I didn't simply toss the vase in the water!) When I reached for the vase, however, it crumbled in my hands and the roaches swarmed over me, writhing into my mouth and ears, the flit-flittering of their wings the sound of the spinning world...

Chapter II
Cut-up from Somewhere

Lina deliberated when to add the sliced mushrooms to the eggs thickening in the skillet. In a post-coital flush, she'd foolishly offered to make Reba an American breakfast. Like most Parisians, she regarded omelets as lunch food, favoring simple fare like jam and bread or pastries for breakfast. Besides, she was an inexpert cook and the smell of eggs this early in the day nauseated her. She was about to slide the mushrooms into the pan when Solange waltzed into the kitchen in a chiffon robe holding a black photo storage box. Solange put the box aside and relieved Lina of the spatula. "*Bonjour*," Solange said.

"I can do this," Lina said for Reba's benefit.

"Perhaps in a world where good taste makes you a good cook." Solange tilted the pan and nudged the cooked edges of the eggs toward the center. "*Bonjour*, Reba."

"Morning," Reba said from her seat at the enamel-topped kitchen table. She noted that Solange's robe was nearly identical to Lina's and wondered if it were another aspect of the apartment's spare, museum-like order or indicative of an intimate relationship. "Is uh, this part of your normal duties?"

"If Mayen wants to eat in. My duties are ... *de faire tous ce qu'elle veut*."

"She doesn't conform as much as that implies," Lina added.

Reba felt a surge of anxiety at their ease and warmth together. Her untidy newness, compounded by her figure-hugging frock, marked her out. She looked from Lina to Solange with a wary grin. "You help with the business, too, then?"

Lina relinquished the saucer of mushrooms also in order to remove the percolating coffeemaker from the stovetop. "She is the business."

"*L'entreprise* not *les affaires.*"

Reba prompted Solange to clarify her comment. "She said you grew up together—like sisters."

"Yes, we've known each other since *cours préparatoire*. What would you call it? Grade one?" Solange emptied the plate of mushrooms into the omelet. "Though she still won't let me borrow her clothes."

Lina poured three coffees. "We have different closets for a reason." Turning to Reba, she asked, "Sugar?"

"Isn't that the French way? Two raw lumps?"

The hint of reproof in Reba's question sent a sexual current through Lina. She visualized Reba with a sugarcube between her bared teeth.

Reba marveled at how Lina's face could go so still and bland. There was a cultivated blankness to it she tried desperately to break when they were alone at night. She could think of nothing better than seeing Lina screw up her face in ecstasy. She worried that momentary collapse would be as close to a promise as she would ever get from her. "I bet you have some stories to tell..." she said to Solange's back.

"Oh, sure. Mayen has a long habit of acting out for attention."

"Really?" Reba flashed Lina a teasing smile. "She's been awfully shy with me..."

Lina delivered Reba's coffee and took a seat next to her. "Solange enjoys a good tease more than most."

"What brings you to Paris?" Solange asked. With a quick flip of her wrist, she turned the omelet onto a scallop-edged plate.

"Vacation," Reba said. She took a cautious sip of coffee before continuing. "I just graduated the Brio Academy of Cosmetology and thought I'd splurge a bit before settling into the job routine. I've always dreamed of coming here, Paris, the heart of fashion." She paused for another, heartier draught of coffee. "When I was a girl, bored on a summer day, I used to lie on my bed and imagine the stains on the ceiling were countries on a fantasy map. When I learned about Paris, it seemed to come closest to matching what I pictured."

Solange placed the fluffy omelet between the two lovers and sprinkled a pinch of *fleur de sel* and chives over it. "You weren't worried by the rumors of war?"

"*Merci,*" Reba said. Her lopsided smile showed a pleasing rim of gum. "Oh, I don't much follow the news. I mostly read the fashion magazines—*Marie Claire, Vogue, McCall's.* Before this, I knew the city mainly from *Paris Mode.*" She blew on a bite of omelet before popping it in her mouth.

"What do you think of it?"

Reba swallowed and said, "It's darker than I would've thought for the City of Lights. I expected it to be bright as a Christmas tree. You have Christmas trees, right?" She narrowed her eyes at Lina, bristling and flirtatious at once. "I know you have *cadeaux* (gifts)."

"Some remain hidden," Solange said. She gave Lina a knowing look as she handed her the photo storage box.

"Those can be the best kind," Reba said.

Lina snuck a peek inside the box. There was a note in Solange's hand atop the scattering of newspaper cut-ups she'd asked for. The note apprised Lina of a morning meeting with Noye. "Depends on your tolerance for surprises." She met Reba's eyes. "It looks like I have an urgent business matter to attend to. I don't mean to rush you ..."

"No, that's alright. You know how it is when you're on vacation. You forget sometimes that other people still have jobs and responsibilities." She relished a last forkful of omelet and, nodding toward Solange, got up from the table. "Thanks for rescuing breakfast."

"*De rien.*"

Lina escorted Reba past fastidiously appointed rooms and surrealist art like otherworldly signals. When they reached the door, Lina flushed with the heat of uncertainty between them. "I'm sorry about this, *ma Minou.* I'll be in touch later today—this afternoon."

"If not, I'll come looking."

"That seems to be going around."

They exchanged a brief, hard kiss and Reba slipped out with a wistful half-smile on her lips.

Lina returned to the kitchen in a gray mood, convinced again she wouldn't be so out-of-sorts if she didn't bother with romance. Too much desire made her edgy. Her bare feet slapped against the linoleum. The slapping sound unstuck her mind, which was still in conversation with Reba—what she could have said, what she *should* have said...

Solange was already at the sink, running the whisk and dirtied mixing bowl under the tap. "I can see why you like her. She's lively, high-spirited—what would you say in American?—spunky?"

"*Plein de cran.*" Lina sat down before the box.

"Not your typical miserable romantic."

"Perhaps it's mere coincidence, but the timing is suspicious don't you think? Meeting the same night as Lammert's murder?" She lifted the lid and removed the note. She was due to meet Noye in less than ninety minutes.

"It could be synchronicity. Her name, for instance..." Solange knew Lina was a great believer in synchronicity—coincidences that vibrate with personal meaning.

"Did you learn anything from Paul last night?"

Solange nodded. "The incident occurred in Cambrai. The Germans used the villagers as a source of mental energy for a supernatural creature called the Mimirodat. It acted like a psychic antenna, receiving and broadcasting emotions, originally on behalf of some collective of Outer Gods. The Germans thought to use it to incapacitate their enemies with ill thoughts. Paul's mission ended with its apparent destruction. Or, at least, its energies seemed to dissipate. But there were Parmatmar crystals involved, so who knows? They made the creature highly unstable. Paul said it could very well have shifted into another dimension or state of being."

"Does Osher know?"

"I called him as soon as I got off the phone with Paul. He said, however, that he already knew. Janvier had given him both the location and a short list of possible names earlier in the evening. He'd assumed we'd been given the same information."

"Courtesy of Janvier's Nazis client, no doubt." Lina shook the nearly weightless contents of the photo storage box in preparation for a cut-up exercise she hoped would reveal one or more synchronicities pertinent to her case. The label inserted in the box's brass ID holder read **ACAUSAL STIMULI.** The term was derived from Jung, who posited that synchronistic events were connected by an acausal principle equivalent to causality in physics. This principle meant that neither interior states, e.g., desires or expectations, nor external states could be the primary cause of synchronistic events; rather, these events were connected by meaning alone.

"We're helping them then?" Solange asked.

"They're welcome to think that for now." Satisfied the box's contents had been sufficiently randomized, Lina removed the lid and turned the box over. A cascade of newspaper fragments confettied to the table. Each fragment consisted of a precisely-scissored word from the article about Manteau's 'assault' on the *gendarmes* at the museum.

"We'd best be back in Marseille before they learn otherwise." Solange joined Lina at the table to help arrange the word scraps into rough rows, flipping the ones that happened to land wrong-side up.

Lina considered the cut-up exercise a means to open her mind to the simultaneity of meaning and the telltale runs of parallel thoughts, symbols or emotional states she might otherwise have missed. The point was to establish a flexible gradient between the conscious and unconscious, encouraging the free flow of thought. Lina was keen to stress there was nothing supernatural about the process. She often compared discovering emergent patterns in the cut-ups to learning a new word and then suddenly finding it everywhere. The real challenge lay in separating the meaningful from the meaningless. That's the point at which Lina, owing to her superior experience with the dreamtime and its archetypes, left Solange behind.

"This might be something," Solange said. She ran an index finger under the phrase:

Lina took a seat at the table and closed her eyes. "Give me a minute then go ahead and read them out." Interpreting the cut-ups required her to adopt a meditative state between sleeping and waking. She recited a silent mantra to blank her mind. The clutch of anxiety in her chest relaxed as she slipped into semi-consciousness. Her thoughts led her away from her life and the material world. Her shallowed breathing was Solange's signal to begin.

Solange scanned the array of cut-ups and read each potentially useful combination in a clear, even tone:

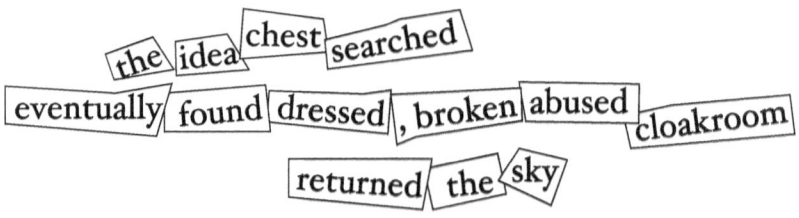

"That would be a heist of a different sort." She glanced at Lina for a hint that something had resonated with her. Seeing none, she went on: "Hmm … SENSE BODY JUSTICE … That looks to be about it. Besides the first one, I don't know."

"What about the cloakroom?" Lina asked with her eyes closed. "*Vestiaire?*" The word carried a pinprick tension. She imagined the sensation was similar to what poets felt when an apt but unexpected phrase floated to the surface of their conscious minds.

"It's from a rhetorical question about you making a cloakroom of the crate. What are you thinking? A room meant or made for you—*le Manteau* (the Cloak)?"

The word asked Lina to trace its parts. She spoke from a meditative deep. "I was thinking of the quaternity—a four-fold thing."

"Like a rectangle? Does the museum even have a cloakroom?"

"There's a small closet off the lobby, but I was actually thinking of the word itself—its grammatical parts. If it were echoed, what would you hear? *Tiaire, aire,* re …" The sounds filled the room in her mind, each part overlapping the next …

"*Tiaire*—a potentiary..."

"A person with power or authority."

"*Aire*—area, okay." Solange wrinkled her pert nose. "R-E? Is that how you'd spell the last echo?"

"I suppose."

"Doesn't mean anything in French."

"Try the Larousse," Lina said.

Solange disappeared into the den to retrieve the appropriate volume from the encyclopedia.

Lina remained at the table in a state of relaxed concentration, dreaming with one eye open, so to speak. Her inner eye roved the bodiless dreamtime, a hidden substrate of reality that interpenetrated the material world. Trained adepts could use it to work various magicks, visit alternate dimensions, even contact the Outer Gods. Lina had never pursued the medium's magickal side, preferring instead to treat it wholly as a source of insight. It was the timeless, spaceless nature of the dreamtime that made synchronicity possible as well as explained déjà vu and other cases where one moment touched on another at a distance. In Jungian terms, the dreamtime allowed the acausal principle to manifest simultaneously in different places.

Solange returned with the encyclopedia volume and proceeded to read from the relevant entry: "It says here Re is 'an unvoiced phoneme...' a preposition meaning 'in the manner of or about...' R-E: 'rare earth, one of a set of seventeen chemical elements in the periodic table...' What else? 'An alternate spelling for the name of the Egyptian sun god Ra... believed to rule in all parts of the created world... the sky, the earth and the underworld.' It's also an exclamation in Greek..."

The name of the Egyptian god elicited a slowness in Lina's chest. "No, I think that's enough."

"It's half of her name, of course..."

Lina blinked her eyes open. "The first half, the front, the part facing the outside..." A black apprehension seized her and she slit her eyes against the onrush of feeling.

"Want me to look into her?"

"She practically dared us with that beauty school reference. She could be anyone—Interpol, U.S. Customs agent, the damn head of La Fratellanza..." Her voice was hollow with disappointment.

"Even a wide-eyed American on holiday. She seems too trusting to be a spy." Solange worried Lina had developed a protective, but ultimately self-defeating cynicism about her liaisons. "Just remember: Lammert's paranoia was no defense."

"Perhaps he wasn't paranoid about the right things." Lina cleared her throat. Not for the first time, she rued the irony implicit in the biblical infinitive 'to know.' What could you truly know about another person that wasn't trivial or potentially contrived? Her roles as mob boss and detective-crime fighter routinely exposed the gaps, the crude flesh between the light and shadow. Thankfully, to achieve her aims, she only had to know enough to connect events. She didn't have to understand people to their deep unconscious. "Did you notice? It's four parts: the full word—*vestiaire*—plus three echoes." She got to her feet, thinking ahead to the next disguise, the next move. "After my appointment with Noye, I think I'll indulge in a little side street *flânerie*. See if the city evokes any other synchronicities."

Chapter 12

The Primacy of Chance

Waiting for Noye to arrive, Manteau walked the perimeter of the Fontaine de l'Observatoire, eyeing its central sculpture. The piece seemed an anti-surrealist argument for existence as bald necessity. The monumental bronze depicted four female titans—representing the cardinal points of the compass—supporting a sphere within a sphere. The outer, celestial sphere was ringed by an elliptical band of signs from the zodiac. The inner sphere was a laterally-segmented globe. Manteau wondered if the cage-like celestial sphere was meant to suggest a constraining or deterministic force on earth. She thought the zodiacal symbols could be just as easily interpreted as dictating everyday affairs as influencing them. The idea that life was devoid of freewill and chance (especially chance) filled her with dread. Chance was the precondition for newness—the rearrangement of things due to coincidences, parallels, random harmonies like those on a piano that somehow resonated past the last lingering note.

Sometimes, in the dazzle of right circumstance, art spoke to her. Nothing profound or even particularly meaningful. Giacometti's abstract, insect-like portrayal of rape and murder, *Woman with Her Throat Cut*, once told her to "Behold the botched inwardness." And more recently, a charcoal illustration by the Egyptian painter and essayist Kamel el-Telmissany hanging in Lammert's museum had suggested, "Every girl is a sister, and every sister is a wife." Manteau thought asking an artwork for guidance was no more unreasonable than asking a plaster Jesus or Virgin Mary. But the fountain statuary was mute.

Noye approached from the bordering sycamores in a slow, awkward plod. When he was within a few meters, Manteau gestured toward the sculpture and asked, "Was Carpeaux an adept?" Her voice was low and toneless in keeping with her disguise as a middle-aged man. She wore a cream-colored gabardine blazer and matching linen pants.

"How old do you think I am?" Noye said, short of breath.

"I didn't ask if you'd dined with him, only if he's known to have dabbled in magick. The design suggests a familiarity with a higher order cosmology."

Noye shrugged. "So much of it has been popularized—and badly."

Monteau adjusted the brim of her wool fedora. "Trouble getting the box?"

"I'm sorry to have come empty-handed. Your little surprise yesterday put the *gendarmes* on edge. They've forced Esmée to conduct another inventory, this time under their purview."

"Not to worry. I'm not even certain I could make use of it. I'm no magick-worker. I thought, perhaps, just the threat of it..." Manteau waved away the rest of her considerations. "Have you determined if anything's missing?"

"No. I mean, no, it doesn't appear so." He neatened his jacket with a tug.

"And there's no record of the Vestipuccine?"

Noye shook his head.

"Is there a reason Lammert would want to keep it a secret?"

"Are you sure it was even there?"

"Fairly."

"You knew how he was: nervous when he faced a direct threat *and* when he didn't. If possible, the mystery of the *Afterlife Divided* only increased his paranoia."

The case had exposed a secret cabal of investors and dealers in supernatural artifacts. Some, embarrassed by subsequent rumors, had sworn revenge on Lammert. "But who among that group would dare? The American is dead. The artist, obviously. Tolin is locked in La Santé and the others, even that blowhard Patenaude, seem to be sincere about making amends."

"He did his best to be nervous for all of them."

"I know." Monteau bore a not inconsiderable measure of guilt for tipping the suspects in the case to Lammert's involvement and for its muddled conclusion. "From what I've learned so far, La Fratellanza di Bestie was involved—at least, one of the factions. Did Lammert have significant contact with the group?"

"No more than any other. He never mentioned individuals, if that's what you mean."

"Did he keep a record of his contacts? Perhaps in an appointment book?"

"Yes, though he kept it at home for safety's sake." Manteau recalled Solange's report on her interview with Lammert's houseman. No doubt the appointment book was among the materials Rouillard had been instructed to burn.

"What about you? Have you had any significant contact with the group?"

"Naturally. But most of it occurred long before I went to work for Lammert. For the past sixteen years, I've had dealings with it only as part of my duties for the museum—providing security for artifacts bought and sold, that sort of thing. Why? Need an introduction?"

"Possibly." When Manteau pursed her lips in thought she felt a tug on the application of blonde whiskers along her jawline. "To your knowledge, did Lammert have any interactions with Vestipuccine?"

"Nothing substantial. They saw each other several times in the late-twenties. Lammert had heard rumors about a decades-long work of his—what turned out to be *La Q*—and tried to secure it for the museum. From the way Lammert talked about it, I don't think Vestipuccine ever took the conversation seriously."

"What about you?"

"What do you mean?"

Manteau fixed Noye with her gaze. "Did you ever meet him?"

"We were in the same room together on a couple of occasions but never exchanged more than a nod or common pleasantry." Noye smoothed his oiled mustache with thumb and forefinger. "Why these questions, Manteau? I'm beginning to feel as if I need *un avocat*."

"I'm sorry if I offended you, Noye. Especially in your grief." She put a gentle hand on his elbow. "What will you do now? Stay on with Esmée or...?"

"I'm not certain she'd have me."

"She doesn't blame you, does she?"

Noye made a face ugly with wrinkles. "She hasn't said anything directly, but I can tell—the way she looks at me with those half-lidded eyes, the pity... Not that I blame her. I scarcely have use for my own advice anymore."

"What do you think you'll do?"

"Remmelin used to say, 'A good magician knows when to disappear.'"

"I would hate to lose you to *un accident de parcours* (a freak accident)."

"What about *un accident prévisible* (a predictable accident)? This is what happens to the old..."

"I guess I'm still young enough to believe old age is more *bêtises* (foolishness) than *bêtes noire* (bugbear)."

Noye let out a showman's jut-jawed laugh, showing fine, even teeth gray from age. "That's what the moving pictures would have you think."

"Well, do let me know if anything turns up—or doesn't—as the case may be."

"*Bien sûr.*" Noye grasped her by the shoulders. "Manteau, I want to thank you for, *enfin*, always showing me respect. Some consider a man of my years nothing more than a case for the charity office."

"Please..." She pressed her head to his chest in a daughterly embrace. "Don't disappear without a goodbye now."

"You know me—I can't leave without a flourish." He whipped out his gold-colored pocket square to its full length and vanished it with a theatrical snap. His parting smile, however, was thin and indefinite.

Manteau strolled out of the park and onto the Boulevard Raspail in the direction of the Seine. Apartments of cut stone in the austere Haussmann style occupied the other side of the street. She kept to the sidewalk bordering the park, taking in the mid-summer colors, the odors and movement. She squelched the incessant babble in her head and opened herself to the sweep of boulevard down to the impossible end of its vanishing point. She was at once at the center of the city and hidden from it, knowing yet invisible, like an eye above a map—the ideal detective. In this state of mindful awareness, passersby appeared as shadows. Her focus was on signs and symbols, messages like saturates or stains revealed by intuition.

She was a prodigy of Paris twice over. On her first visit at age seven, it had struck her as an invitation to mystery. Its railroad stations and casinos, its squares and gardens, its apartments and factories, its wax museums and monuments, its alleyways and cul-de-sacs, its motley people, the sheer simultaneity of it all, seemed a perfect labyrinth. Though she'd been too young to articulate the feeling, she'd sensed the city's accidental nature, how its profiles and rhythms were contingent on circumstance. This entrancing emotion grew over time. Paris became the focus of her thoughts both waking and otherwise. It assumed the aura of an industrial utopia that thrived on unanticipated shocks. Her imagined life there gradually displaced the real one on her father's modest farm. She adopted new, allegedly cosmopolitan habits—a penchant for non-sequiturs for one—and showed little patience for the small moments that make up a life. The agglomeration of routine appalled her. She determined to be unpredictable, active, grand—even in her silences. Lucia felt rejected by Lina's self-conscious transformation and the ensuing mental distance and tried to close the gap by playacting the same obsession with all things Paris.

When Lina enrolled in the University of Paris, Lucia followed, somewhat intimidated by the city but determined to recover their comforting childhood rapport. Lucia had been the quiet one, the sister content to be alone, reading, sewing doll clothes, watching the family cat skulk around the chicken coop. She was the one who took things in without a word, sponging up Lina's sometimes volatile emotions. Paris unsettled her personality. Desperate to prove herself a boon companion, she drowned her misery in bad company, cheap wine and hard drugs. She had always looked to others for reasons to believe in herself, unlike Lina, who felt above, or at least outside, society's judgment. Committing to lesbianism had forced her to choose early, to become rather than merely be. The growing uncertainty in Lucia's heart about who she was made for a manic seven months that ended in a brief but fatal dalliance with a mafia underboss and the beginning of Lina's masked vendetta. Now, Lina wouldn't know herself without the city.

The nineteenth century political scientist Barthelemy-Prosper Enfantin was rumored to have developed plans for the city with the aid of anatomical charts. Lina could believe it. The bizarre circumstances of Lucia's death seemed like one of the fever-sick fantasies in Marcel Schwob's *Le Livre de Monelle*. But the body of Paris absorbed her sister's death much as Lucia had absorbed Lina's feelings just by being in the room. No trace elements remained of Lucia save a few straw-colored hairs on the doll's pillow Lina had preserved as a keepsake. The lace-fringed pillow was wrapped in tissue paper in a cardboard box under her bed. On the rare occasions she gave into sentiment and opened it, she caught the faint scent of their childhood shampoo—baking soda and apple cider vinegar.

The gap between the corner edge of the apartment building opposite and the bank on the next street over suggested a door ajar. Manteau crossed the road at a brisk clip, arms swinging, careful to maintain her manly facade. She was like a portable radio that went fuzzy near a power source. In this way she let the drift of Paris direct her ...

❶ Boulevard Raspail: Near the junction where the boulevard became the Rue de Bac was a pawn shop with a wrought-iron facade. The simplified Napoleonic eagle above the entrance looked to the right (northeast), prompting Manteau to continue toward the Seine.

❷ Pont Royal: The placid, green-gray river shimmered like Christmas paper. A seabird followed a horse-drawn fruit cart across the bridge, circling, dipping, circling closer.

❸ Rue des Pyramides: The street name harmonized with the final echo from the cut-up word *vestiaire*. Manteau walked to the road's end, resisting the urge to monologue about how history had fallen on the shoulders of the crowd and how quiescent it seemed in the face of surrounding dangers. The Nazis, she knew, wanted to control the crowd and its energies down to the unconscious, to appropriate it, make the hidden public against all instinct, purging the country of Jews, cripples, whatever convenient symbols of the unconscious they sought to destroy in themselves. She was convinced France would suffer for failing to heed the protesting cry of the Dadaists: *Jedermann sein eigner Fußball!*

❹ Avenue de l'Opéra: White linens hung in the display window of a laundry, Le Linge de Maison. Some gouache paint contained a white pigment. The name of this paint recalled the word for left—*gauche.*

❺ Corner of rue Halevy and rue de la Chaussée-d'Antin: Scaffolding partially obscured the facade of the apartment building on the corner. The temporary structure curved onto the rue de la Chaussée-d'Antin. It consisted of four levels of wooden planks. Manteau followed it with a girlish thrill in her heart. How many times in her youth had she wished to be Poe's Man of the Crowd, content to wander the capitals of the world? Breton had called Poe a "surrealist in adventure." She saw herself in the moment as making good on that characterization.

❻ Rue de Clichy: A Rolex Oyster steel watch in the display window of a jewelry store caught Manteau's eye. The time was nearly twelve noon. She continued straight ahead.

❼ Corner of rue de Clichy and boulevard de Clichy: An elderly accordion player entertained (or alternately, annoyed) passersby.

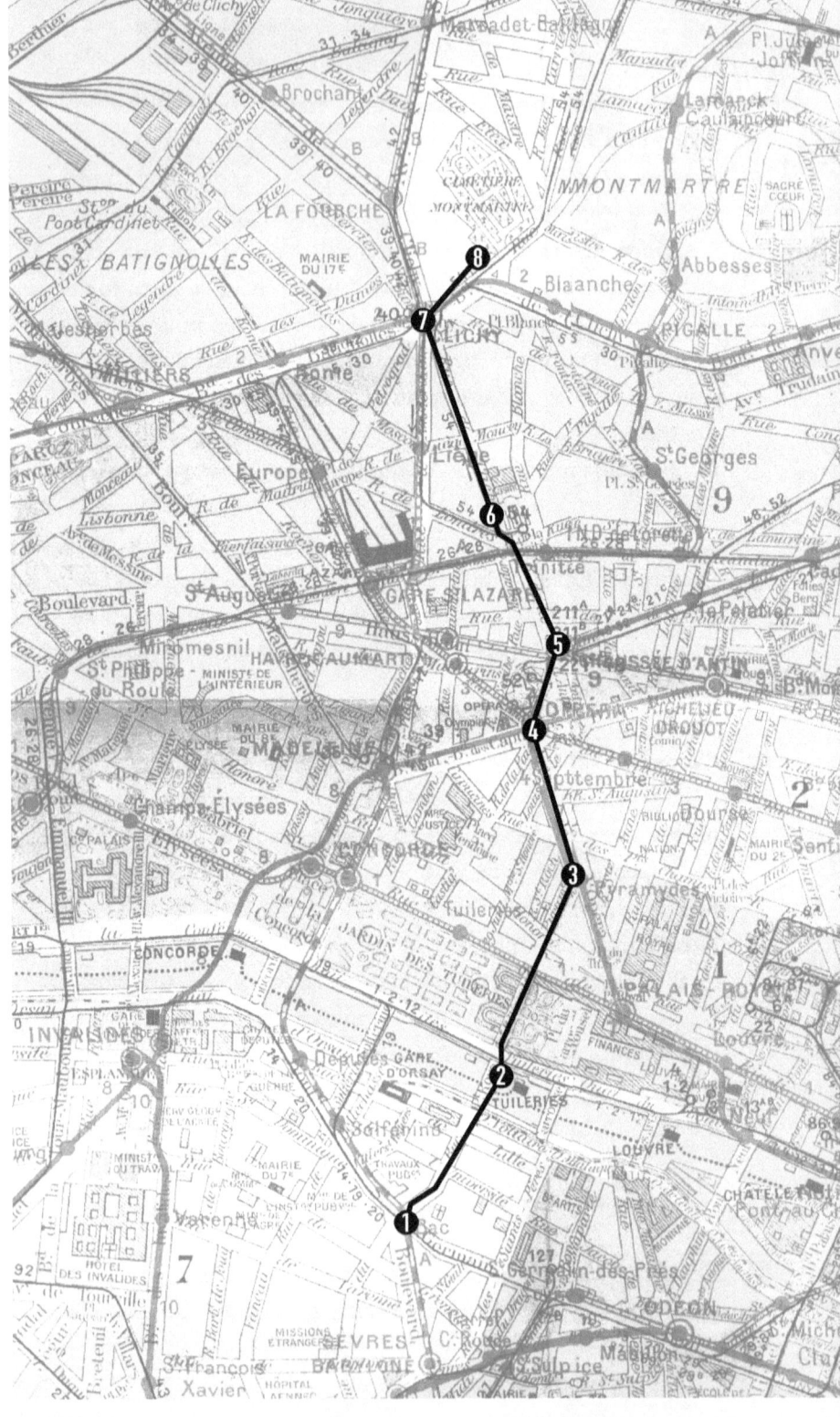

He angled a shoulder toward the right (east). The word *ici* (here) is a notable part of *musicien*.

❽   Boulevard de Clichy to rue Caulaincourt: Manteau lingered outside the stark geometry of the Hotel Ibis. Its resonant meaning threatened to take the blood out of her face. The ibis was sacred to the ancient Egyptians. The bird represented the god Thoth, god of wisdom, knowledge and writing, and herald of the flood. This intimation, together with the results of the cut-up exercise, turned her thoughts back to the museum with its distinctly pyramidal roof. Perhaps there was still something of value to be discovered there ...

She hurried into the lobby of the hotel and enclosed herself in a phone booth. Solange picked up on the second ring. Before Manteau could relate the impressions from her *flânerie*, however, Solange interrupted: "I'm sorry, Mayen. This is important. I've been waiting on your return. Osher's found her—the *Qello di Sognare*—and Javier is anxious to get to her."

The urgency in Solange's voice dispelled the last of the sleepy residuum in her head. "Where is she?"

"Vaucluse asylum."

Chapter 13
Still Life with Evidence

EXHIBIT A: ADMISSION RECORD FROM CASEBOOK

C & O

36

HOSPITAL PERRAY - VAUCLUSE

Reg. No. 142

Name	*Henriette Valentine Belgarde*
Date of Admission	13 *April 1937*

Nationality		Transferred From other Asylum
Religion	*Pagan*	
Education		Chargeable To

Age on Admission	29	Civil Status: Single / Married / Widowed / Unknown	*Single*
Profession / Occupation	*None*		

Previous place of Abode	8 *Rue de Marcoing 59400 Cambrai, France*
Diagnosis	*Delusional Insanity*
Cause	*Contenigal Insanity (Including Idoicy, Mental Defect from Birth or Infancy)*

First Attack	1917	Prognosis: Favorable / Doubtful / Unfavorable / Hopeless	
Age at First Attack	9		
Duration of First Attack	21 *Months*		
Epileptic	*No*	Present Order signed by	*FJM*
General Paralytic	*No*		
Suicidal	*Yes*	Date of Order	4 *May 1935*
Dangerous	*Yes*		

CONDITION ON ADMISSION—	
(A.) PHYSICAL—	
Bruises or Injuries.	*General condition. Fairly well nourished.*
Malformations	*Circulatory. Heart sounds regular. Infirmity of pt. téed*
Tongue.	*at feet. Extremities cold.*
Plate	
Teeth.	*Digestive. Teeth fair-tongue clean.*
Appetite	
Bowels	
Viscera.	
Urine.	
Heart.	
Pulse	
Lungs	*Respiratory. No disease discoverable.*
Sight	
Eyes—Pupils	
Color	
Other Senses	*Nervous. No loss of power of sensation.*
Urinary and Generative Organs. . .	*Genitourinary. Unsure.*
Muscular	
Walk, Gait	
Reflexes	*Knee jerks natural.*
Handwriting	
Weight	
Temperature	

(B.) MENTAL—	
Speech.	
Reaction to Questions.	
Attention	
Memory—Recent.	
—Remote	
Coherence.	
Hallucinations	
Illusions	
Delusions—	
Grandeur.	
Suspicion.	
Persecution	*The subject of melancholia, delusions of suspicion, persecution, hallucination of hearing. Says her brain is penetrated by free-floating thoughts "sharper than any knife."*
Exaltation	
Depression.	
Unseen Agencies	
Viscera	*When asked who she is, says a frame inside a frame: " a blank space pressured on all sides by confusion." Complains of being ill-treated by nurses and others.*
Impulses—	
Suicidal.	
Homicidal.	*She is restless and depressed and abusive in her morbid thoughts. Memory impaired.*
Erotic	

MEDICAL ALERT	(a) Facts indicating insanity observed by myself at time of examination, viz.

(1) Dr F.J. Michaud-The patient was lying in bed, resisting in a feeble manner the nurse's admonitions to keep the covers with the bedclothes and keeping up a continuous incoherent chatter. In responding to my request to look at her tongue she said " I haven't need of it as I am born of thought alone."

(2) Dr L. M. Turenne: Constantly talking in an incoherent manner, mixing with her ideas religious names as Moses, Paul, saying she is the ears of God. Very restless, requiring to be constantly watched.

(b) Facts communicated by others.

(1) Luce Odette Hurteau of 3 Rue Marcadet a nurse in charge of the facility says that while awake she is continually chattering nonsense and that she refuses to take nourishment unless some show of force is made.

(2) Luce Odette Hurteau of 3 Rue Marcadet. Very depressed, restless, not taking her food without a certain amount of force, holding her medicine in her mouth for a time, talking incoherently.

A.—PREVIOUS HISTORY	
(a) Has the patient been insane before? If so, when and how often? Has the patient been in any other Asylum? Which?	*No, but frequently ill. Anxious*
(b) Has the patient had previous attacks and not been away?	*No*
(c) Has the patient had ...	
i. Rheumatism?	*No*
ii. Fits?	*No*
iii. St. Vitus' Dance? . . .	*No*
iv. Gout?	*No*
v. Venereal disease and of what kind?	*No*
vi. Scarlet Fever?	*No*
vii. Influenza?	*Yes*
viii. Tendency to consumption?	*No*

C.—FAMILY HISTORY	
a) Have any of the patient's relations been insane or eccentric, or suffered from fits or paralysis? If so, state whether on Father's or Mother's side.	*Father and mother eccentric in religious beliefs (source of delusions?). Residual trauma from Great War. No other Asylum.*
(b) Were the parents cousins or related?	*No*
(c) Is there consumption or intemperance in the family? If so, state whether on Father's or Mother's side?	*No*

(d) Has the family been subject to any disease?	
(e) i. Is the patient single, married or widowed?	*Single*
ii. How long married?	
iii. How many children alive and dead?	
iv. Give age of youngest?	

B.—PRESENT ATTACK

(a) How long has the mind been affected?	*Est. 11 months*
(b) What signs were first noticed, such as changes in manner, habits, or temper?	*Alternately choleric and melancholic, talking incoherently, sleeplessness*
(c) Has the patient threatened suicide or attempted violence to himself, or is the patient dangerous in any way?	*Yes*
(d) Has the patient had a tendency to leave home or neglect business, work, or family?	*Yes*
(e) Has the patient suffered for want of sleep, and how long?	*Yes*
(f) Has the patient suffered from loss of appetite or flesh?	*No*
(g) Has the patient's nature been cheerful or reserved?	

(h) Have the habits been temperate and steady or the reverse?

(i) Has there been any excitement such as religious and sexual?

(j) Was there any cause for the attack, such as bodily illness, family trouble, anxiety, poverty, drink, exposure, fright, shock, injury, or has any recent event in trade or politics troubled him?

Anxiety exacerbated by irreligious art in house

(k) What have been the various occupations engaged in during the patient's life?

None. Helped mother with household duties when not too ill

(l) Where was the patient born, and what are the different places (Paris, country, or abroad) where the patient has lived?

Cambrai

EXHIBIT B: SAMPLE CASEBOOK LOG: 1935

C & O	HOSPITAL PERRAY - VAUCLUSE
36	**Progress of Case**

	Name: *Henriette Valentine Belgarde*
3 May 1935	She is suffering from chronic mania with delusions of persecution and hallucinations of hearing. Says she hears repeated echoing of voices and that they draw everything from her. She is in good [illegible] and is well nourished.
11 May 1935	No change in mental condition. Patient remains in practically the same deluded and hallucinated mental state.
20 May 1935	In my opinion, Miss Belgarde is not in a fit mental condition to be discharged or be allowed leave of absence on trial. She is still the subject of delusions of persecution and hallucinations of hearing. Says there is a cruel process of thought reading and power over her mind exacerbated by those around her. Threatens to make their thoughts common knowledge. The same type of delusion has obtained since her admission to this hospital. F.J. Michaud Acting Medical Superintendent
31 May 1935	Patient is the subject of delusions of persecution and hallucination of hearing. Says she can read people's thoughts as colors ("auras"), which causes her mind great injury. Contends Father and Mother are unsound persons and in league with dangerous forces.
8 June 1935	She is still suffering from confusional insanity. She is lost and dazed in manner in conversation. She has delusions of persecution. Says her Father and Mother put "probing pins" in her brain.

22 June 1935 — Her mental state remains largely unchanged. She is noticeably calmer, however, when engaged in (supervised) drawing. Her drawings reinforce her fixation on the number 4. All her sketches feature four-sided objects, cardinal points or crosses. (She draws herself as a square inside a square.) Many of her drawings are diagrams. A recent one, labeled "Quaternity of the Exterior World," consists of a cross-shaped figure apparently representative of some evolutionary process. The points of the cross are noted (from top, clockwise) as Principle of Function, Form, Final Cause and Matter. Asked about its meaning, Miss Belgarde says it is "the very model of life, from nothing to something." The Principle of Function defines the shape of things, determining the Form that Matter takes, with the Final Cause equivalent to the Holy Spirit. She worries the drawing will be taken to be wholly scientific and irreligious and insists on her loyalty to the Christian God in "His war against the Devil."

28 June 1935 — Chronic mania with occasional attacks of maniacal excitement. Complains of "thought voices" and gives other signs of persecution of hearing. She is like a bird that gives an alarm call in response to a (non-existent) danger and panics when no one else responds. We know selective attention to certain sounds starts early. Some perceptual categorization of sounds might reflect experience in the womb but in this case, it's more likely her behavior stems from trauma suffered during the Great War. Her delusional state prevents us from learning the nature of that trauma. F.J.

EXHIBIT C: LETTER INCLUDED IN CASEBOOK [UNADDRESSED AND UNSENT]

Sunday morning

9 February 1936 FJM

To Sig. V,

This is to tell you that I am in bitter suffering which you know and understand better than my family and friends I have appealed to. I speak of the forcible and cruel experience of thought reading (no words of mine are strong enough to condemn it). The power your art granted me and still exercises over my mind is a continual agony. The power is ~~terrible~~, driving out any pure thoughts of my own and compelling me to live a life so repulsive and contrary to the teaching of my newfound bible and Church that my entire soul rises in torturous protest against it and for deliverance from it, always and forever my God, who I still so far believe must see and know my mind and heart as it would be if it were freed from this brutal tower of evil, which masquerades as a "new cure" for lunatics and criminals and which only mocks God and teaches His creatures to

mock Him and His holy power and turns them into workers for
the Devil and which I am certain if allowed to be practiced
will wreck La IIIe République and also the Christian religion.
About 20 years ago, as a child of WWI, I was drugged and
taken dying out of bed from my own home and along with
my parents and older sister, subjected to experiments of
a supernatural nature by a special division of the Kaiser's
army. These experiments involved the leaching of mental
energies down to our very hunger in order to empower a
captive god (as it appeared in my serial nightmares), my
mind ~~hardwired~~ by the most inhuman punishment outside of
Hell. Our eventual release thanks to British forces relieved
me of this pain for a time but my parents, irrevocably
changed by the event, and seeking to make sense of
it, decided to renounce God and join a secret fraternity
of witches, La Fratellanza di Bestie, which became the
instrument of my undoing. (My sister, understandably
disturbed by my parents' rejection of Christianity, left home
for Paris with hopes of finding a suitable husband.) When
these witches learned of my experiences as a German
prisoner, they made me their servant and sacrifice, filling

my mind with false teachings, plying me with strange
   herbal medicines, drawing up the nightmares I had buried
   deep inside and altogether raising me as a disciple of the
   captive god I had escaped, my parents cruelly, willfully and
      ignorantly letting me suffer as though I was an orphan
   or already dead. For years of evil and cruelty, spite and
   hatred, theft and blasphemous acts, I wished for my
   death in return for some small charity. When they finally
presented your art, I thought perhaps my martyrdom of pain
was at an end and with a final concentration of will, I could
fulfill the terms of whatever infernal contract my parents
had signed, success or no. But the Quaternity, God preserve
me, unleashed a pain of a different sort. It was portal to
the captive god, dispersed now, as much atmosphere as
anything, penetrating every mind on earth and yet wholly
alone. Without seeming to mean to it stove in my head, leaving
me forever vulnerable to the world's raw thoughts, a torture
I must endure for want of means to deny or alter my state or
escape this prison, my parents satisfied with things as they
stand for fear their neglect and other wrongdoing will be
made known. La Fratellanza told me about your wife's fate

as an abject lesson in failure so I know you will understand the difficulties under which I labor and perhaps taking pity on me, another woman "suffered to be mad" by your creation, feel obligated to give me the help I need and am entitled to as a citizen of France and child of the One True God. Know that I follow your thoughts and am well-acquainted with your grief (your aura being distinctly yellowed from loss). Release me or kill me, in either instance I am your only chance at redemption.

Yours truthfully,

Henriette

EXHIBIT D: SAMPLE CASEBOOK LOG: 1939

C & O   HOSPITAL PERRAY - VAUCLUSE

36   **Progress of Case**

Name	*Henriette Valentine Belgarde*
4 Jan 1939	Health much improved. Although patient still suffers from occasional delusions of persecution (centered on Father and Mother), she says "the visible thoughts left behind" have all but disappeared. She can carry on cogent conversations, takes her food and medicine without need of force and has expanded her repertoire of drawing subjects to include maze-like figures. I think it's fair to attribute these changes to combination of ice bath treatments first taken up in September last year and the simple passage of time. Memory has also improved though she still clothes wartime trauma in childhood fantasies of soul-rending machines and low gods. No manic outbursts reported for nearly four months. FJM
26 Jan 1939	Patient appears well nourished and reasonably adjusted. She remains withdrawn and cautious of others, though short of persecution mania. Has developed an intermittent facial tic. Reminds me of an animal that's extinguished its original fear out of habit but could relapse at any time. We've certainly seen patients relapse due to depression or trauma unrelated to the original stimulus. Animals in that situation tend to remain afraid even though they appear to forget quite what they're afraid of. I think she has a similar generalized anxiety. She's coherent but distractible, apprehensive and restless, especially at night. They used to call this panphobia or anxiety hysteria. Nonetheless an improvement in her case. F.J. Michaud Acting Medical Superintendent

8 Feb 1939 : General health good. Condition unchanged from last noted observations. Few signs of manias or persecution hysteria beyond periodic nightmares. Sometimes falls into awkward silences in conversation as if flustered by an unwanted thought or memory. Perhaps embarrassed by past behavior. Devoted to Bible studies. Still too fragile (skittish?) to consider discharge

27 Feb 1939 : Professes a strange theology. Says the Devil believes the Holy Trinity is incomplete without him. Harmless as far as it goes. Parents eccentric in their religion too, according to her. Remains wary of others, but no recurrence of feelings of persecution nor hallucinations of hearing. Does not claim to hear or talk to God as before. Sometimes moody in her solitude. Most content when drawing. She has become quite accomplished in her geometric figures. Reminiscent of labyrinths in their complexity. She titles them like little artworks. Her latest is called "Intimate with Mirrors No. 4," though they number in the dozens. FJM

Chapter 14
Turnabout

The Perray-Vaucluse asylum was a stolid, gray-bricked building on a wooded, twenty-five acre parcel outside of Paris. Manteau laid out her plan for kidnapping the *Qello di Sognare* on the way. Though Janvier had no ideas of his own besides bald violence, he questioned every detail. Ignorance was no impediment. What mattered was asserting his authority. Their plan was still in flux when Janvier turned into the institution's circular drive with a disconcerting jerk. He steered carelessly with one hand and smoked a cigarette with the other. The Hispano-Suiza H6B Coupé Limousine whipped up a dusty haze. For fear of causing a motor accident, Manteau was reluctant to press her argument while he navigated the gravel approach. Several patients milled around the yard accompanied by their minders. The late-afternoon sun blanched the sky.

She waited until Janvier pulled the coupé to a stutter-stop before continuing their discussion. "Stealth and trickery first, yes?" She gruffed her voice in keeping with her masculine disguise in case anyone should overhear. "I'm sure your... benefactors would appreciate us taking a quiet approach."

"What? It's me—the fox. Trickery is my namesake." Janvier turned away and flicked his spent cigarette through the open window into the gravel. "But sometimes you have to get loud to get what you want."

"I'm not above making noise when it's necessary. I suspect, however, that your definition of necessity is much different than mine." They presumably spoke the same language. But every word seemed a missed signal.

Janvier smiled through his aggravation, showing small white teeth. Manteau's tone put him in mind of his querulous mother, who, in his youth, had seemed incapable of leaving him alone. A disagreeable bubble began to form in his gut. "I've been honest with you: necessity is whatever's in my best interest."

"It's easy to be honest about what's already clear. Just remember: I'm not here for you. I'm here for Lammert and his memory—to safeguard *La Q* from your clients."

At this, Janvier's gut-bubble swelled against his insides. Who was she to remind him of his obligations? He fished in his linen suit coat for his monogramed cigarette case. "What if I told you Lammert was behind it? That he was the one who contacted my clients and agreed to the heist to—in his eyes—protect the world and at the same time, his reputation? What would you say then?" He quirked his lips in smug amusement.

"But that's..." Manteau began then stopped herself, feeling her cheeks flush. She recalled Vestipuccine's description of the Parisian art figure referred to as *il consulente*. The figure had exhibited Lammert's chronic nervousness. She'd made the connection on reading it only to dismiss the idea as absurd. She figured Lammert would never have taken the risk.

Janvier enjoyed her discomfort. "I guess he thought the Germans were the most suitable owners, the ones most willing to use this artwork to ... I don't know what. Defend against some dark force or other. Isn't that your area of expertise?" He put a fresh Gauloises Caporal between his lips and bent to his slide sleeve lighter. Smoke streamed from his nostrils. "This *La Q*, what's it worth? Maybe he just wanted the money."

Manteau couldn't imagine Lammert selling the artwork to the German government even in the most desperate of straits. He'd regarded the regime's bannings and burnings of art as acts of unforgivable violence against the creative impulse. "Ask your clients if money actually changed hands. I'd be curious to know not only the amount but how they delivered it."

"So what is it worth?" He thought the question sounded casual enough.

"On the open market?"

"Yes, hypothetically."

Manteau squared up to him on the black leather seat. There was an opaque flatness behind his eyes that resisted understanding. "To the right party, millions. But it's unlikely you'd live long enough to spend it. The right party would erase you from existence."

"What's the difference? I'm living with a death sentence now—at least until we recover the artwork." He met Manteau's hard look with level seriousness. "You needn't look at me that way. I'm a businessman like any other. *Je ne suis pas mauvais* (I'm not evil)."

"Cross me on this and you won't be *mâle* (male) either."

A matronly redhead at the reception desk was busy sorting the day's mail when Janvier approached. He removed his hat as a courtesy and pretended to fault Manteau with a pointed look for not doing the same. "*Bonjour, Madame.*" The lobby smelled of must and uncured linseed oil.

"*Bonjour.*" The greeting sounded like a rebuke. Her weak brows gave the impression her high forehead extended to the pits of her eyes. "What may I do for you?"

"My colleague and I—we represent the Bank of Alsace and Lorraine. We discovered recently that one of your inmates—"

"Patients." Her tone was soft but insistent.

"Patients, yes, of course." Janvier pinched his lips in apology and, for a moment, regretted not sending Manteau into the asylum alone. The crazed plaster walls and fading woodwork put him in mind of a shadowed and crowding past that deserved to be forgotten. "Henriette Belgarde is her name. She's come into some inheritance—a modest amount to be sure, but still—she's now an account holder at our institution. Her signature is necessary to authorize the account transfer."

"Good on her." The receptionist's double chin twitched. "This might be the thing to snap her round—good news from the outside."

"Has she … Is she ill? Is she in a state to understand what we'll be asking of her, I mean?" He dreaded the notion of confronting a black and pitiable madness.

"Oh, sure, she would, if she were agreeable to visitors. But she—no, she won't see anyone but trusted staff. We can barely coax her out of her room. If you'll just give me the papers she's to sign, I'll see it's done." She held out a meaty hand.

Manteau said, "I'm afraid we have to verify it's her. Bank policy. That's why there are two of us—one to serve as witness for the other." To emphasize her point, she raised a brown leather school bag above the surface of the reception desk.

"*Enfin*, that does present a problem." The receptionist rubbed her temple with the rounded end of a mechanical pencil.

Janvier reached inside his unbuttoned suit jacket.

Manteau put a restraining hand on his elbow. "How about escorting us to her room?" she asked the receptionist. "Perhaps we can get a glimpse of her from the hall as you enter. We could consider that sufficient proof under the circumstances."

"So long as you're not obtrusive about it. We don't want to upset her." The receptionist made a theatrical frown. "Let me call an attendant. Just a moment." She disappeared into the recesses of the office.

Manteau poked at Janvier's gun through his jacket. "Still waiting for your head to cool to room temperature?"

"Patience isn't my strong suit."

"I've yet to see what is …"

Janvier spoke through gritted teeth. "I'm telling you, don't aggravate me. The pressures I'm under …You've no idea."

"I must have missed your picture on the front of *Paris-Soir* yesterday."

"There's no comparison between your life—that fantasy of justice—and mine in the underworld. I have to do whatever it takes to survive and earn, day by day, hour by hour." His taut voice resonated as if in an old courtroom.

"The underworld doesn't begin and end under your feet."

The receptionist returned with a blond, slit-eyed attendant in tow.

He waved Manteau and Janvier back from Dutch door that separated the reception desk from the hall and stepped through. "This way, please," he said in a tone of barely-suppressed irritation.

Manteau and Janvier fell in behind the stout attendant and started down the central corridor. The attendant's hair puffed out above his ears like folded bird wings. He jiggled a dense ring of keys dangling from his thumb in a private rhythm.

The doors on either side of the poorly-lit corridor had small rectangular windows of wired glass in them. Janvier averted his eyes. Each door was like a bulwark against a secret best left untold. When a patient on his way to the dayroom passed by, thumping his chest in a compulsive pattern, Janvier flinched out of fear the man would try to touch him.

Manteau nudged the mob boss with her leather bag, saying, "Insanity isn't contagious—except for acute cases of syphilis."

"I can think of worse ways, I guess, if you had to go mad."

Without dismissing the dangers of mental illness out of hand, Manteau had a decidedly romantic notion of it. She largely believed Breton's theory that the "strange forces" behind mental illness could free language—and by extension, society—from the shackles of habit and logic. The theory explained why the government, in league with cultural elites, had established such a broad definition of insanity. They were simply protecting their own. Psychiatry, she thought, was like classical mythology—little more than a series of elaborate metaphors for the unknown. "Some say madness is the ultimate experience, liberty without end (*sans fin*)."

"Without purpose (*sans but*), yes, on that we can agree."

Henriette's door looked no different than the others. At a distance, the muzzy glass revealed only indistinct patches of color. The attendant turned to Manteau and Janvier, widening one squinty eye. "Madame Le Goff said you had papers?"

"Oh, yes," Manteau said, unbuckling her school bag and removing the false document prepared by Solange. "Is it okay for us to stand here, in the hall?

The attendant nodded as he gave the document a cursory examination. The two sheets of paper had been culled from a loan agreement written in an impenetrable legal floriate. He put a thumb on the empty signature line on the second page. "Is this where she signs?"

"Signs and dates," Manteau affirmed.

"Very well," said the attendant. He turned his back on them and gave the door a gentle knock. "Mademoiselle? Mademoiselle? It's Aubin."

A retiring voice bid him enter.

He keyed the door and disappeared inside.

Janvier grabbed the door before it closed and shuffled into the room without waiting for Manteau.

The attendant spun to face Janvier. "What are you doing? You're to—"

Manteau shut the door on Henriette's hoarse scream and pleaded, "No, please."

The wiry white-blonde was on the bed, back to the wall, knees drawn toward her chest. Trembling, she drew her cotton calf-length dress tight around her legs. A school exercise sketch pad and a scattering of charcoal pencils lay on the quilted coverlet. The pad was open to a portrait of a clapboard church below a sky of boiling clouds. The steeple sheared into impossible shadows.

Janvier leveled his gun at the attendant. The prospect of violence simplified things. Decisions now came down to fight or flee. His nerves calmed under the narrowed range of options.

"She said they would come someday—disguised," the attendant said. "None of us believed her."

Manteau bent to the girl's eyeline. "Henriette, please, we're not who you think we are. We're not La Fratellanza. The opposite, in fact. We're here for your help against them—against anyone who would use the Quaternity for their own ends. We need your help to find it."

"I can't allow this," the attendant spit.

Janvier waggled his gun. "There is no 'allow.' You are compelled." He motioned for the attendant to take up a position in the corner of the room nearest the foot of the bed. Though the walls were bare white, the space was less austere than Janvier had imagined. Besides the bed, the room was furnished with a small makeshift bookcase, a dressing bureau complete with mirror, a stool and a padded rocking chair. Several editions of the Bible, along with books of Christian philosophy by Gilson, Blondel and Sertillanges were stacked horizontally on top of the bookcase. The shelves were reserved for jars of pencils, gum elastic erasers, a T-square, sheaves of paper and other art supplies.

"Leave me be, please, just leave me be," Henriette croaked. She threw an arm over her eyes as if to make the scene disappear.

"We don't have time for this," Janvier declared. He holstered his gun and made to grab Henriette by the elbow. She leapt away, shrieking, into the protective arms of the attendant.

"What are you doing?" Manteau asked Janvier.

He plucked a bottle of perfume from the dressing bureau and uncapped it. "Getting loud." He stoppered the bottle with a mascara-smudged cotton ball.

"*Flûte de zut*," Manteau hissed, waving Henriette over. "Come here, girl, hurry. For your own sake." The woman looked frail, almost insubstantial. Her skin was pale to the point of near-transparency.

The cotton fired under Janvier's lighter. He gave the bottle a brief shake then smashed it against the wall just above the bed. The violent discharge set the coverlet aflame. Henriette screeched in protest and lunged for her sketch pad. Without the threat of the gun, the attendant rushed the door. Manteau high-kicked him in the throat. He flailed backwards and ended in a crouch against the wall, gagging for air. Manteau clasped her free hand around Henriette's wrist, saying, "*Désolée pour ça.*" Agitated noises came from the back of Henriette's throat. She put a hand over the cross-shaped pendant dangling from the thin chain around her neck.

Janvier flourished the metal-legged stool like a matador his cape and crashed it against the mesh glass window. The glass barely registered the blow.

"No doubt as a child," Manteau told Henriette conspiratorially, "he delighted in breaking all of his toys."

Janvier dropped the stool in favor of his gun and fired several rounds through the window. The glass fractured out from the bullet holes but remained in place. "You'd prefer more chocolate box fickleness?" he asked.

Manteau restrained Henriette as Javier swung the stool to clear the pebbled glass and twisted mesh from the window frame. The room was stricken with sunlight.

The attendant fled into the hallway, choking out a warning cry.

Janvier gestured for Manteau and Henriette to exit through the shattered window onto the lawn. He felt better now that he'd taken action—more settled in his thoughts—and wondered how long the institutional gossip about this breakout would last.

Manteau scooped up their stunned kidnap victim. She could hear echoey shouts and approaching heelstrikes in the corridor.

"You didn't...," Henriette said.

"What was that?" Manteau asked, brushing glass from the sill to accommodate Henriette's stocking feet.

"You're ... you're too late." She wiped a tear from her cheek with the back of her hand.

"What do you mean?" Manteau glanced over her shoulder at the gathering flames blackening the wall. The fire projected a penumbra of orange against the slick plaster ceiling.

"I can't help you. I can't find the *Quaternity* even if I wanted to."

"Why? Can you sense it? Has it been destroyed?"

Henriette lifted her hand from the pendant around her neck, eyes big with reverence. The highlights in her pupils, magnified by tears, were like veins of quick gold. "By the grace of Almighty God, I've been cured of it."

Chapter 15
The Idea of His Destruction

LE COURRIER DU PAS-DE-CALAIS, DUNKERQUE, FRIDAY, 29 JUNE 1934

MADMAN - ARTIST AMOK

Found Desecrating St. Eloi Church with His Blood

DUNKIRK, 28 June

An Italian artist suspected of being insane caused a commotion in Hazebrouck in the arrondissement of Dunkirk. The man, later identified by gendarmes as Arturo Vestipuccine of Rome, was armed with a palette knife. He was discovered painting the church's famous gothic facade in his own blood. The greatest consternation prevailed, and people fled in every direction.

After he had rushed about for some time doing injury to himself, several men attacked the maniac and pinned him to the ground until the gendarmes arrived. He died of self-inflicted wounds en route to hospital.

In his coat pocket was found a notebook. Several passages mentioned blood. On one page was written: "I have given myself over to simultaneity. Most live in blessed ignorance of it. But my art reveals the unbearable all in all. Against it, even the blood of saints is like a stain of nothingness." On another page was written the following sentence: "—The trial of trying to recover my art and my right mind has passed. The forces in opposition are too great for one such as me. I commend myself to making an art of my blood as Alcine had done in hopes of joining her in whatever purgatory awaits the enlightened mad. I am, etc., A. F. Vestipuccine."

Artist of Some Renown

Sig. Vestipuccine was an artist of some renown among Western Europe's avant-garde. He was affiliated for a time with Andre Breton's Surrealists until a falling out in the late-1920s. His work was exhibited at Galerie Pierre in Paris on several occasions between 1925 and 1931. Rieb Tasse, chief curator at the Musée des beaux-arts de Dunkerque, described Vestipuccine's work as "cerebral and irrational in the extreme." He cited a painting titled *La nuvola mancina* ("The Left-handed Cloud"), which features abstracted limbs in suggestive array against the background of a smoking city. When told of Sig. Vestipuccine's suicide, M. Tasse was unsurprised. "His art contained the idea of his own destruction," he remarked.

Chapter 16
Counterphobia

Returning to the living room from the bedroom where Henriette was confined, Manteau said, "She seems settled enough."

"But still of no use?" Janvier asked. He sat on the headboard end of the maroon recamier, swirling a snifter of Calvados. The bottle remained close at hand on the painted side table. First the Nazis, now Manteau had knowledge of this rural safe house. He would have to dispose of it by summer's end.

"She claims to have some residual powers—a heightened sense of personal auras, that sort of thing." Manteau cramped into a leather club chair with large scalloped arms. "But no, nothing especially useful."

"Perhaps we should have left her at Vaucluse." Janvier sipped his *Pays d'Auge* brandy, relishing its notes of vanilla and spice.

"How could we after you set fire to her room?" Resting her elbows on the arms of the chair, she made a pyramid of her fingers just below her chin.

"It was a distraction—to cover our escape. How was I to know she was cured? Or free to leave at any time?"

"If you'd bothered to ask a few questions first…"

"We would still be facing the same situation. And I would have missed your look of surprise."

Manteau smiled through her hardened makeup. The lines around her mouth crinkled uncomfortably. She would have to refresh the latex soon. "You're like an alarm clock that crashes through a pleasant dream."

"And the reality of it all will hit at six o'clock. That's when my client expects my next report—twenty-some minutes." He rose and paced a moment, clenching and unclenching his free hand, before asking the empty fireplace, "Any other leads?"

"Perhaps. But none so immediate. I wasn't able to reach my secretary."

"What about turning her?" He gestured toward the back bedroom.

"You mean...?"

"Can it be done?"

"Possibly. She does retain some impressions of her former state. Given the right combination of stress, sleeplessness, memory triggers, the disorientation could..." Her voice deteriorated into a rasp. What she contemplated meant treating Henriette as a tool rather than a person. Just as the mob had treated Lucia, regarding her solely as another heroin courier. Her blood mutinied at the thought of betraying Henriette's trust.

"What, exactly, would it take?"

"Heartlessness."

Manteau's dark tone set Janvier on edge. He'd gone through too much and come too far for this incident to be his undoing. The setup had seemed so damned innocuous... "You balk at the morality of it? She is only one. La Q—my client says it could give the German Reich absolute control over everyone on earth." He made an expansive gesture, nearly spilling his drink. "What does your morality say to that?"

Manteau's pyramid of fingers collapsed. "You know I'm unafraid of making life or death decisions..."

"She puts her trust in God. Shouldn't He be the one to look after her?"

Though Manteau was no believer, thinking God a justifying fiction for the bourgeoisie, she felt obligated to play devil's advocate. "Aren't we supposed to be His reflection on earth?"

"Oh, you mean the Golden Rule?" Janvier's lips thinned into a mock-remorseful frown. "I'm more of an Old Testament believer, God of wrath..."

"So you prefer the Tyger to the lamb?"

"Let's just say that between the two, I like the Tyger's odds." He considered the world in terms of forces and counter forces: rich and poor, power and appetite, lift and drag. He credited his survival to always identifying and throwing his weight behind the force calculated to exert the greatest pressure.

Manteau was compelled to admit the prevailing reasonableness of Janvier's argument. In her role as mob boss, she'd condoned worse on similarly utilitarian principles. The Nazis clearly thought they could somehow turn *La Q* to advantage. How much could she risk for one woman with France and the rest of Europe hanging in the balance? Perhaps she could induce a temporary relapse. "There might be a way…" She rasped away the tension in her throat. "Henriette told me that when connected to *La Q* she was overwhelmed by voices—the collective unconscious. What she described reminded me of this surrealist piece, *L'Immaculée Conception*. It appeared several years ago in the periodical *Le Surréalisme au service de la révolution*. It simulated various mental conditions—mania, paralysis, interpretive delirium. Perhaps if we kept her awake past comfort—on the edge of dreaming, suggestible—and invoked a similar experience, it would revive the original condition. It might not last long, but… One of the authors, Breton, worked at Saint-Dizier—the psychiatric center—during the Great War; the other, Paul Eluard, is a poet."

"I should have known."

Manteau ignored the conflict roiling in her chest. "You have another suggestion?"

"Work quickly." Janvier downed the last of the Calvados and moved to make his report from the privacy of his bedroom.

"Oh, you'll have your part, too," Manteau said, getting to her feet. She girded herself for the frightful experiment by taking a severe tone with Janvier. "It would be most effective if the voices came from two sources. After all, it was her parents who initiated her training: mother and father…"

"*Moi? Un père* (a father)?"

"*Ensemble, une paire* (Together, a pair)."

A pinched, smarmy expression crossed Janvier's face. Her decision confirmed the superiority of his cold arithmetic. "*Pour la paix* (For peace)."

Manteau aimed a disparaging finger at him. "*Plus de faux pas* (No more false steps)." She was, however, at least as angry with herself for their situation and already dreading the moment when Henriette accused her—rightly—of betrayal. There could be no forgiving what they were about to do.

COUNTERPHOBIA

A PLAY IN ONE ACT

BY

MANTEAU & ANATOLE JANVIER

CAST OF CHARACTERS

Lina Mayen/Manteau:	A woman in her mid-20s in the guise of the female unconscious (animus).
Anatole Janvier:	A man in his early-30s in the guise of the male unconscious (anima).
Henriette Belgarde:	A woman in her early-30s.

SCENE

A criminal safe house south of Paris.

TIME

Tuesday, 25 July 1939. Morning.

SETTING: We are in the nearly pitch dark basement of a modest farmhouse. The windowless space is lit by stray light from a bare bulb at the top of the stairs. We can make out a few objects, among them, a rusted push cultivator, the head of a pitcher pump, an unfinished interior door, a cache of old brick, a buggy wheel, a Victorian-era sink, a ratty kitchen rug (rolled up) and an unused oil container.

AT RISE: HENRIETTE BELGARDE is tied to a chair set in a circular hole in the cement floor. (In the days before refrigeration, the hole was filled with ice to keep milk, butter, meat and other perishables cold.) Her chest heaves with choked sobs. Tears gleam on her cheeks. MANTEAU and JANVIER stand some distance behind her in the shadows. Though MANTEAU remains in her masculine disguise, she uses her natural voice throughout. JANVIER fidgets with his lighter, sliding the sleeve up and down.

MANTEAU

As I said at the beginning, think of this as a spiritual exercise or mental prayer...

HENRIETTE

From the lips of the Devil? I know what you mean for me to do. God has no part in it.

MANTEAU

Doesn't God will Creation anew each instant? Think of *La Q* as a window on His will. It does, after all, represent the simultaneity of human experience.

HENRIETTE

There is something like a god behind it—just not the Christian one.

MANTEAU

Was that the source of the voices?

HENRIETTE

No, not the source, the conduit. This god surrounds and penetrates us. It's the very medium of thought.

MANTEAU

Then that's where you must go—the deep unconscious…

HENRIETTE

Please, no, don't ask that of me again! Don't make me think on it!

MANTEAU

Start—

HENRIETTE

Glory be to the Father, and to the Son, and to the Holy Spirit. As it
was—

MANTEAU

Start by picturing the four alchemical colors that constitute *La Q*—
black, white, red and gold.

HENRIETTE

As it was in the beginning, is now, and ever shall be, world without end.
Glory be to—

JANVIER

(*to* MANTEAU)

You want I should gag her this time? I can't spend another hour like this,
her cries and protests echoing in my head…

MANTEAU

(*to* JANVIER; *sotto voce*)

No, she's exhausted, close to surrender…

(*to* HENRIETTE)

Black, white, red and gold. There—in your mind's eye—the artwork in
full, the auras that mark our spiritual progress, the quaternity…

(HENRIETTE *shrieks*)

MANTEAU

Black—the oblivion of birth. White—the first glimmerings of self-awareness. Red—renewal and the reconciliation of opposites. Gold—the apotheosis, supreme awareness… The *Quaternity* has been with you always.

HENRIETTE

No, please, God no…

MANTEAU

Your mother and father gave you over to it. Without the *Quaternity*, you are the child of no one and nothing…

HENRIETTE

The desire for God is written in the human heart…

MANTEAU

But you're not human. You've never been human. You're a medium for the *Quaternity*. Otherworldly. Apart. That's the true reason your parents surrendered you to *La Q.* You could never receive His grace. You are forever corrupt and alone—an unworthy exiled from His kingdom.
    (HENRIETTE *sags in tears*)

MANTEAU

(continued)
Is the *Quaternity* before you?
    (HENRIETTE *refuses to speak, lips tight*)

MANTEAU

I say again: Is the *Quaternity* before you?

HENRIETTE

Even behind my closed eyes…

MANTEAU

And the voices? Do you hear them? Our confused humanity?
(*She signals* JANVIER *to speak. He reads from a scrap of paper.*)

JANVIER

The clutch of the ceiling chorus twists me out of mullioned glass.
Tongues at last, snoring in frog-rhythms over long empty bottles. The
baker wings at many wheezes—

HENRIETTE

I beg of you, mercy…

JANVIER

—many wheezes in the resurrection light. See how the teeth clear in
the pocket river. What warm bodies can we wear? The life's—

HENRIETTE

The Lord protect me—

JANVIER

—wheels to the horizon, not the thread-maker, clouds singing into the
milky age, gray enough for another reason.

MANTEAU

All the mind can count—

HENRIETTE

Will you not deafen me? Make me numb to it all? I—I—
(HENRIETTE *convulses with sobs.* MANTEAU *grimaces at the emotional havoc
her plan has wreaked. Her eyes shine with tears. Still, she presses on…*)

MANTEAU

—in receipt of angels. Ruins secrete the loving at dawn in a world hol-
lowed out in water. The blue smell of the rain line and coral-like curves

suffer to spoil you up. The animals glower in green cashmere. Mother-less, fatherless, in your looking-glass emptiness you have as many colors as the future. Whatever the means, few beliefs are needed when this is the outcome: raucous immersion.

(JANVIER *refers to second scrap of paper*)

JANVIER

Half-finished by weeds in only one room of ourselves, littering our pov-erty, while among the upper stories of Nature, obsolescences multiply. It is, they tell us, impossible to remain only in ones thinking through the wind and wild veils. So much for the forsaken rag of living concerns. Abandoned furniture can stove the eloquence.

(HENRIETTE's *tears subside*)

JANVIER

(*continued*)

You are left to your downfall, so rich, so routine. Ah, the qualities of summer fevers, their vulgar colors. The wishes must be thought.

(HENRIETTE *raises her eyes to a private vision*)

MANTEAU

Behold the Bible-black of the first night over Earth. Genesis opaque and unformed. Anything might body forth from the void. All is imagination in the retinues of Nature's unknown. Then the firmament winks with stars faint as promises. Lo these harbinger lights! They infuse us down to the pith of corruption. How sublime! Awareness comes in flashing-beauty and hitching curses. Light from day. White from night. Long ago antipoles—opposites that must needs be contained in Being without Being. Then the horizon bleeds into dawn. What a wound against the night and its stars! The advancing red supplants the sky, oh how vivid it seems—this false zenith—in the moment before it's undone by the glo-rious sun! Revel in the purifying rays! Three become four! The circle is squared in gold! The totality, your prolific self widespread!

HENRIETTE

(*weakly*)

The Father...the Son...

(MANTEAU *hesitates. Sympathetic tears stain her cheeks. Then she gathers herself up for one last push.*)

MANTEAU

Let her that nameth this name depart from iniquity.

HENRIETTE

The Holy...the Holy...

MANTEAU

So the evening and the morning are all...

HENRIETTE

Chaos...

MANTEAU

Name it.

HENRIETTE

Animal chaos...

(MANTEAU *forces herself to prolong the cruelty*)

MANTEAU

Name it!

(HENRIETTE *shakes her head, silent tears coursing down her face*)

MANTEAU

Name it!

(JANVIER *shies away from* MANTEAU, *impressed with and disturbed by her persistence*)

HENRIETTE

God, it is—it is Q...

MANTEAU

Good. You were born for it. You belong to it—your soul entire. Q and only Q...

HENRIETTE

The four-in-one.

(JANVIER shoots her a smug, satisfied look. MANTEAU turns from him, ashamed.)

MANTEAU

We want to reunite you. Just tell us where...

Chapter 17
Switch Point

"I'm sorry to have worried you," Manteau said into the phone, pulling on the cord for more slack. "I tried calling yesterday afternoon-evening, but you must have been out. Then I had to prepare..." She stretched the cord across the bed to its limit.

"And you say she's talking?" Solange asked.

"Babbling nonstop. She's in a pure state of psychic automatism." Manteau craned her neck to examine herself in the vanity's petite mirror. The mirror revealed bleary, red-rimmed eyes and mottled cheeks. Breaking Henriette had cost her some life. "It made me sick at heart, but believe me, it was the only way to get the information we needed. We'll have to do whatever it takes to reverse her condition when this is all over."

"Of course," Solange said, eager to spare Manteau's feelings by moving on to other, less emotional, aspects of the case. "I was at the museum yesterday when you called—meeting with Esmée."

Manteau reclined flat across the width of the bed and closed her eyes. The pulsing at her temples suggested a bobbing fragment of self. "How did she seem?"

"Understandably shaken. She's clearly feeling her way through the situation. No doubt she'd much rather be sitting in a café somewhere or playing *le billiard Nicolas* or whatever it is jobless young people do these days. What did Lammert say once? 'She has all the faults of an artistic genius without the genius.' The *gendarmes* have only added to her stress and confusion. Then there's Noye..."

Manteau snapped her eyes open. "What about him?"

"He's gone missing—him and several museum pieces."

"Since when?"

"Esmée noticed one of the missing artifacts yesterday morning and called on him. When she received no response, she asked the *gendarmes* to take up the matter. They searched his apartment and discovered an empty closet."

"Any idea where he might have gone?"

Solange swallowed her trepidation. "I was going to ask you the same."

"Which artifacts are we talking about? Wait. Let me guess—the Lamassu Box..."

"Yes. Also, the Fairy Flag of Dunvegan and the Mace of Ntyr (*net-jer*). All artifacts with clear defensive—"

"Or offensive—"

"*Or offensive* capabilities. How come it's always dangerous magick?"

"Is there any other?" Manteau got to her feet. "We need to look into Noye's disappearance. It could have been faked to cover up his kidnapping or murder. He was the only one to see Lammert's attacker."

"You think Esmée...?"

"I don't know. But if Henriette is right about the location of *La Q* I'm sure to find out."

"Where is it?"

Manteau recalled Henriette's initial, grammarless noises. Janvier had dismissed them as "so much devilish throat-clearing." Henriette's speech had gradually settled into a mostly nonsensical ramble. The useful bits tended to turn up in breathy pauses between digressions. "Still not certain," Manteau said. "She's having trouble detecting the artwork's signature aura at this distance. Apparently we have to take the train. She's directed us to the Paris-Gare du Nord."

"Let me meet you there. I don't like the idea of you alone with Janvier. As soon as he gets sight of *La Q*—"

Manteau was determined to take a hard line. "I'm afraid this is a *pas de trois* (dance for three)."

"Or *faux pas de trois* as the case may be."

"Regardless," Manteau said, "I need you there to investigate Noye's disappearance. Go through his apartment, interview Esmée again, the day watchman, what-have-you. I'm more concerned about those artifacts than anything else."

Solange sighed through gritted teeth. "You remember the cloak this time?"

"Under my disguise. It helps to hide my feminine curves."

"Not that it will hold up under any sort of scrutiny."

Manteau wondered how much longer she could continue to live her days as a succession of fraught moments. Times like this left her feeling trapped and numb. Each moment was like a wavelet of pressurized air presaging an explosion. She forced a wry, conciliatory tone. "How about this? If I die as a man, I promise to come back just to give you the chance to say 'I told you so.'"

"Where's the romance in that?"

"I blame *le Napoléon infantile.*"

"If I thought you'd listen, I'd tell you to be careful."

They drew together in their joint imagination against the hostile unknown, pre-adolescent friends again.

"I know," Manteau said. "*Et merci.*" She returned the handset to its cradle, her chest congested with emotion. How would her future self regard these events in her Aristotelian summing up? Lammert dead, Henriette debilitated, Noye missing or dead, Solange put out and Reba...

Not for the first time, she thought about explaining herself to Reba in a letter. It seemed Reba had never forgotten what it was like to be a young girl and carried that ingénue spirit with her still. If anyone could help assuage the hurt Manteau had inflicted on herself and others by adopting her posthumous mindset, Reba could. Manteau considered writing the letter in the guise of the persona Reba hadn't met—her true self—as if to start the relationship anew: "She takes chances, this person, emotional risks I could never take ..." The question was: where to begin?

Slants of geometric light streamed through the Gare du Nord's peaked, sky lit roof. Manteau waited under the sign for Platform No. 3, one hand on Henriette's wrist, the other gripping a leather valise. Janvier paced in the vicinity, irritated by Henriette's compulsive blurting and anxious to be done with unknowns. The vast central hall was crowded with travelers disembarking from a train on the adjacent track: worka-day commuters (*le petit peuple*); tourists, including a few families with small children; the *haute bourgeoisie*; cavalier businessmen.

Even after attaining significant (albeit ill-gotten) wealth, the affluent still mystified Manteau as dapper creatures of belligerent materialism. She imagined them sending their children to summer camps put on by the near-fascist Parti Social Français. Many, she thought, would support a German takeover provided it promised to rescue the country from economic depression. She pitied them for devoting so much energy to amassing mere ephemera, ignorant of the dream-substance behind the world. Smartly-dressed porters mingled among the throng, helping with baggage and giving directions. Manteau scanned the concourse through settling steam, head tilted toward Henriette, listening for a sig-nal remark.

Each random utterance from the woman was like a pinprick on Manteau's conscience. The torture she'd inflicted had reduced Henriette to a frightened girl in a grown-up husk. (The fact that the word 'torture' was the same in English and French seemed additional proof of its ugly, inevitable truth.) "Nowhere had reaped away his mansoul," Henriette murmured. "Pitches of morbidness whirling out of torn comrades. In words out of terror told in works all begrimed with ashes ..." She was a visionary of the sort Breton so admired and Manteau despised as loftily sexist: the damaged girl as surrealist muse.

Janvier returned to Manteau's side to make room for the departing travelers. "I trust you can understand her."

"The words, sure. The sense ...?" She shrugged.

"Hey, I'm just the *brocanteur* (broker) in this situation."

"Oh, I believe that," Manteau said, implying the other common meaning of the term—'junk dealer.'

"How do we know we're not on the wrong track?"

"She hasn't lost her train of thought?" Manteau's voice almost broke with her manly disguise at her pleasure in this witticism.

"You have a serious weakness for puns."

"Better a serious weakness than a fatal one."

"The fatalities are coming, I assure you ..." He raised an index finger as if to begin cataloging them.

Henriette choked out an indecipherable phrase then pointed down the empty track, struggling to say the unsayable.

"Incoming would be more accurate," Manteau said. "You must understand her after all." The whistling of an unseen engine echoed in the open air hall. "I believe that's our train."

Janvier glanced up at the platform sign. "The one to Berlin? Purchase the tickets while I make a report."

"My suit didn't come with deep pockets."

Shaking his head, Janvier retrieved his money clip and peeled off several bills. "Second-class tickets."

"Naturally."

Janvier stifled a sharp retort. Nothing got under his skin faster than disparaging allusions to his class standing. If others failed to recognize how far he'd come, he reminded himself, it was only because they didn't know the distance he'd traveled. He handed Manteau the money with every confidence he would soon have a chance to correct her ignorance in whatever manner he chose.

In the queue at the ticket window, Manteau let her mind drift a bit on the wind of Henriette's rambling. However nonsensical the sentiments, the wondrous idiosyncrasy of language that made poetry so appealing was on full display: "Petite book hands raise nothing, no lies, a euphoria perfect in shadow ..." It was how Manteau pictured the language of ancient, figurative darkness. Only her messy groundedness in the underworld, she felt, kept her from careering into a similar state.

The balding man in line just ahead of them spun around to face Henriette. His look of open-mouthed annoyance turned to begrudged sympathy when he noticed her abstracted gaze. "Pardon," he said in an embarrassed whisper before turning back toward the ticket window.

Manteau put a comforting hand on Henriette's shoulder, unsure if her charge even registered the exchange.

"Thought I'd never find you, honey."

Manteau started at the familiar voice behind her and folded into Reba's embrace. The zesty smell of her made Manteau's heart skitter.

Pulling away with an eye toward the surrounding travelers, Reba said, "There's one benefit of your minxy disguise. Though I could do without the whiskers." She filled out her flowery, sleeveless blouse with easy curves.

"Solange?" Manteau strained to keep a level tone.

"She was worried for you. And besides, I have a way of wearing people down."

Manteau widened her stance as in preparation for a fight. "I don't suppose I can talk you into staying here—on the platform?"

"Is being hard of hearing part of the act?"

Reba's insouciant lilt was beginning to grate. She had no idea of the dangers, Manteau thought. "Janvier—the mob boss—"

"Solange filled me in."

"He shouldn't see us together." Manteau jerked her head in Janvier's direction. He was wending his way through the crowd at an impatient clip.

Reba fluttered her eyes at Henriette. "Ah, the jealous type. I wouldn't recognize it."

"Just keep your distance on the train."

"Unless the situation gets heated," Reba said over her shoulder as she took a place in line.

Manteau gave Henriette's hand a calming squeeze. Unfazed, the woman continued her slurred plaint. "Focus, the crucial armor. Chocking head, the chinks inside you …"

"Looks like we're next," Janvier said, sidling up to Manteau. There was a disconcerting blankness behind his eyes—something flat like the shell of an egg.

"Did you remember to ask about the payment to Lammert?" Manteau asked.

"Yes, though I struggled to excuse the question as part of our search..."

"Well?" She resisted the urge to glance at Reba in turning toward Janvier.

"They issued a bank draft in Swiss francs."

"And mailed it?"

"So far as I know." Javier waved his hands in Manteau's face. "That's all I have."

"In *Swiss* francs, though..." Manteau knew Lammert's paranoia extended to the banking system. He once told her that birth records were actually stock certificates in a secret corporation held jointly by banks around the world that could, in the event of a financial cataclysm, be used to convert every citizen's labor, property and life into tradable assets.

Janvier retrieved a cigarette from his case. "I'm telling you, pull on too many threads at once and you end up with a mess of yarn."

"Or, like with Theseus, the threads lead you out of the labyrinth."

The streamline shrouding of the Superpacific engine glistened with steam droplets. Manteau noted the inclusion of two baggage cars before the first-class carriages. Janvier flashed their tickets at the porter for their second-class Pullman car.

"The glow in the morn is a loving trust that appalls the eye," Henriette said to the blue-frocked porter as if in greeting. "The close limit is thin by central as three-made becomes four. All that cracks ascribes half a heart..."

At this, the porter arched an eyebrow above the rim of his glasses. "Seems only God can judge this one."

The comment struck Manteau as the proper attitude toward untranslatable poetry—it was impervious to judgment outside the original language. She steadied Henriette at the waist as they stepped aboard and said to Janvier, "Guess we've spared her from ever having to say she's wrong."

"That won't stop the Germans from punishing us for her mistakes. This had better work..." He was forced to twist his head awkwardly to make himself heard in the narrow corridor that ran the length of the car.

"What do you mean? There's the two of us—armed and waiting for the right moment to turn on each other; there's our unproven medium; your Nazis benefactors; this *fantôme*... What could go wrong?"

"You missed train food," Janvier said, confirming the number of the compartment printed on their tickets. "The only way that could be worse was if it was English." He slid the door open and ushered Manteau and their charge inside.

Chapter 18
The Crystalline Ghost

The beech woodland rushing past the window seemed part of a spectral reality thrown up an instant before the train passed. Manteau flitched the trees into what she imagined to be their abstract origin-point. In her mind's eye, the details of the landscape coalesced then collapsed into fumy colors. Henriette lolled against her on the tufted bench in a fitful sleep. She continued to mumble, occasionally punctuating her gibberish with a keening noise from the back of her throat. Javier sat on the opposing bench, pondering a daily racing form and smoking a foul-smelling Gauloises. "Do you know where we are?" he asked.

The question jarred Manteau from her daydream game. "Somewhere just south of Brussels looks like." She jutted her chin at the racing paper, careful not to disturb Henriette. "Haven't you made enough wrong-headed bets?"

"This is the only honest news nowadays," Janvier said. He fixed on her through the curling smoke. "You know the contenders, the nature of their game and the odds in advance. We French also have the curious rule of *écurie*. If there are two horses from the same stable, betting on one is the same as betting on both. Of course, your winnings are less in that case."

"Is that what you're figuring? Whether it's worth—"

Henriette abruptly straightened and, after a convulsive gasp, resumed her nonsense patter: "The path's sniff most pathetic of desire. The truth disdained for bondage…"

When Manteau reached to gentle her down, Henriette twisted away toward the wood-paneled door. Janvier leapt from his seat to restrain her. "Can't you control her?" he asked through lips pursed around his cigarette.

"We made her this way, remember?" Manteau was sure that if Janvier ever felt compassion he would mistake it for a cramp. "She obviously wants out."

"The baggage car?"

Manteau slipped her valise's shoulder strap over her head so the bag snugged against her hip. "Let's see." She took Henriette's wrist and pushed the door aside. "For all we know she could be after a crumpet."

Henriette padded down the corridor in her dated flats. Manteau maintained a steady grip on her upper-arm. "Baggage is in the other direction—toward the engine."

"Does she want to disembark?" Janvier asked from behind her. "Perhaps we're meant to switch trains. If we're coming up on Brussels ..."

"Or it's with one of the passengers. She could—" Her thought was interrupted by an announcement that the train was approaching the station.

"What happens if she finds it?" Janvier asked.

"If the artwork is really a conduit to this god she mentioned, she's liable to make use of it."

Henriette reached the end of the carriage and began to fumble with the handle to the vestibule door.

"We can't allow that." Janvier reached across Manteau and yanked Henriette away from the door. Henriette squirmed in his grip, swiveling her head this way and that. She brushed up against Janvier's cigarette, dislodging it from his pinched lips. He made a deft mid-air catch. Then the slowing train lurched rightward and the cigarette dropped to the burgundy carpet. "*Merde,*" he muttered, crushing the ashen glow under a toe cap oxford.

"How do you propose to stop her?" Manteau asked. "For all we know, she's already close enough to make contact..." She drummed her fingers on her forehead to suggest Henriette's psychic connection to *La Q.*

"If we find it, we observe and, if need be, follow. No more."

"So long as she remains unharmed."

"Not by my two hands (*deux mains*) ..."

"Nor tomorrow (*demain*)."

"I can't say the same of you."

"It's my enthusiasm for language (*langue*), the possibilities..."

"Yes, *enfin*, perhaps if I pluck out your tongue (*langue*) ..."

"I doubt you'll make any more sense with two of them. Apparently you never learned that silence is the best remedy for foolishness."

Henriette lunged for the vestibule door but was restrained by Janvier. "Hold on," he said under his breath then louder to Manteau, "This might be easier from the platform."

Interlude: Henriette

I rise up something around the point. The spaces behind my eyes feel scraped raw. I know the rollings of people from the inside, base bald, lightsmudged colors in endless circlings. Nothing lost off dead time.

Their auras smear the air, congeal and separate: black, white, red and gold. Essences blearing through the breaks in the mundane. Of the closest, one glimmers white—the moonstate of transition. She phases between despair and passion, emptiness and fullness, this, my intercessor, evered in civilizing flux. I might I could rest from the voices dazed to the lamp. The other negates his surroundings with blackness. Not the blackness of Christian evil, but of ignorance and narcissistic dualities. A dark star on the face of the earth. Fissional in its extractions. A source unto itself defined by me and un-me. Perhaps a special shudder for spiralizing my will.

Jamming to trudge, memory the denouncer, mouths of dun lead. They worry about the makedown money. Hatched free? A fire more for Parisian girls.

She wended her way down the car's narrow aisle, flattening against the window as necessary to squeeze past other travelers. The moon-state kept a steady grip on her forearm. The grip tightened when she approached the steps to the platform.

No one fear downstumble. Accident some now, I whisper to myself, clinging baffled. I slide out a breather slick as their feelings, longing for the straight of a radio mind. In the rush of disorder, the monster had but the truth.

A high-collared psalm typed between blouse and paper passes the current into afterness. Forget the cheat lessons. No one dies of sanity.

I am a sentry outside what's broken. I shatterstand the voices. They end in fists of weeping.

She followed the tilt of the blot's head (a spectral gray through the black) to a man in a beige suit accented by a wine-red pocket square. Behind him, two companions hefted a camelback steamer trunk.

He nears ago, a corrupt boreal profusion. Flying his deepers, yes, drowning and buoyant at once.

He radiated the sick-veined gold of putrefaction. A damp chill permeated the back of her brain. She had seen that sort of withering aura only once before— emanating from the sorceress who oversaw her ritual abuse.

I can't help the nothingkind immensity.

With a violent twist, she escaped the moon-state's hold and turned from the viral gold, screeching. Her sandals slapped against the platform. She negotiated the auras ahead at a running dodge.

Manteau couldn't suppress an insolent smirk. Cries of surprise and protest erupted in the madwoman's wake. "You suggested the platform..." She waved at Janvier like a mother shooing her lackadaisical child on to his chores. "You going after her?"

The Sturmbahnfuhrer seemed mercifully unaware of Janvier and this most recent reversal. Janvier shot Manteau a black look then set off at a run.

Manteau traversed the platform, making note of the number and variety of carriages. When she arrived at the second-to-last Pullman car, she found a squinty-eyed man in a gray suit observing the crowd from the over end sill. She approached the porter directing passengers in front of the adjacent car. Nodding toward the private carriage, she said, "Reserved for the crown prince of Bavaria, is it?"

"Not as far as I know, monsieur, but *réservé* (shy), yes." The porter excused himself with a shake of his head in order to help a German merchant gesturing for attention.

While the porter was distracted, Manteau boarded the passenger car next to the one under guard. Several passengers were in the corridor, among them, Reba. The American waved to Manteau over the heads of a young mother and her toddler. Manteau felt her stomach tighten as she sidled past the mother and into Reba's compartment. Reba shut the door behind her and without preamble, kissed her hard on the mouth. Manteau retreated from the pheromone heat and took an involuntary breath. She distrusted her own voice.

"What is it?" Reba asked in the delicate gap.

"I have to know: who are you?"

"Don't be silly.You know me..."

"No..." Manteau put a hand on the brim of her hat. "The timing of our meeting, the persistent hanging on, there's something off..."

"I'm not a spy if that's what you mean. Solange said you thought ... I don't know." Reba's girlish brightness flickered and dimmed.

"Then what? I read people for a living."

Reba looked a bit raw around the eyes for a moment. "Okay, there is—was—something ... But my memory is fuzzy. The night we met at the club, there was a man—an older man—he put me on to you."

"Pointed me out or ...?"

"I'm beginning to think it went deeper than that ... His eyes—they mesmerized me." Reba backed toward the window. Her lopsided smile skewed into a grimace. The train stuttered forward and she steadied herself against one of the storage lockers. "I care for you of my own free will. I know I do."

Manteau was momentarily distracted by the illusion that it was the platform rather than the train that was moving. Reba's panicky look returned her to the moment with unexpected force. Her stomach clenched again. There seemed to be only one logical conclusion. "Hypnosis?" Manteau now understood Reba's trepidation. If true, then the premise of their relationship was a mere trick of circumstance.

"It couldn't last this long, right?" She strained to imbue the question with a note of optimism.

"No, not usually," Manteau said. But the possibility was in keeping with the mind-altering powers Vestipuccine had attributed to the sorceress from La Fratellanza.

"Whatever happened, I'm here for you." Reba unzipped the overnight bag and slowly drew out a .32 Beretta, careful to point it at the ceiling. "Solange," she shrugged by way of explanation.

"Know how to use it?" Manteau pitied Reba for her confused obsession. Letting her help seemed a kindness.

"I've never fired a pistol before," Reba said in a voice that approximated its regular lilt. "But I did win the local turkey shoot in junior high with a Marlin three thirty-six."

"Oh, you can do that in the States?" Manteau asked, alluding to the French word for 'turkey' or 'dullard'—*le balourd*. "Try to restrain yourself." She gave Reba's free hand an appreciative squeeze then turned away, digging in her valise for the gas gun. Her case was a comparative relief. She didn't want to question Reba's mental state anymore. Or what was behind her own mortifying disappointment.

"Wait. Where are you going?" Reba asked. Incidental light flittered around her.

Manteau clipped the holstered gas gun around her belt at the small of her back. "I take it Solange also told you what I am..."

"A detective... Like Sherlock Holmes, right?"

"More Taverner than Holmes, but..." She shrugged. If Reba were familiar with Madam Fortune's Dr. Taverner and his assistant, Dr. Rhodes, it didn't show on her face.

You're on the case of some art heist. Is it here—on the train?"

"That's what I'm about to discover." Manteau paused with a hand on the door. Thoughts of the confessional letter she'd contemplated on the platform at the Gare du Nord overtook her. She wanted to confide somehow—here. But the right words eluded her. She turned to Reba, a gleam of nervousness in her eyes. "Stay, *ma Minou*," she said, lapsing into her natural voice. "Even if it rubs you wrong. Please."

There was a soft, expectant dimpling in Reba's cheek. "Twenty minutes."

"*À Bientôt* (soon)." Manteau pointedly left her valise on the floor and gestured in the direction of the private carriage.

"*Bien* (good)."

The wordplay brought a wavering smile to Manteau's lips. Reba's curves were both challenge and lure. Before Manteau could reconsider her course of action, she slipped into the corridor. From her inspection of the train in Brussels, she knew it was completely vestibuled except for the neighboring car. A sign affixed to the doorway at the end of the corridor announced the passageway was closed. She braced herself for the wind and weather then stepped onto the swaying plate. The train rattled past a cluster of dun-colored brick buildings in Brussels' Schaerbeek district. She wondered if Janvier had managed to re-board the train—with or without Henriette.

The squinty-eyed guard on the plate opposite clapped a hand

around his side-holstered gun. "You miss the sign, monsieur?" he asked in a French heavily inflected with guttural German. "This a private car. No passage."

Manteau cupped a hand around her ear and edged toward the gap between railings. Soot and fly ash swirled past on the rushing wind. When the guard leaned in her direction to repeat his statement, she pretended to stumble against the chain guard rail. The guard offered a supporting hand across the gap. She yanked him over the rail onto her wobbling plate. He landed in a fetal curl. She interrupted the loopy grab for his gun with a gauntlet-reinforced forearm to the chin. As intended, the blow pushed his jawbone into the nerve pocket where it terminated under his ear, convincing his central nervous system he'd broken his neck. He crumpled into an unconscious heap. She relieved him of his Walther P38 and pocketed it.

The plate swung beneath her as the train cornered around a series of grain sheds *clack-a-clack-a-clack*. She righted herself against the door then leapt over the railing and onto the private carriage. Her shoulder smashed into the door. She grabbed the handle for support before pushing it open and stealing inside. The mahogany-paneled car was surprisingly dark, lit only by a brass side lamp. Turkish drapes blanked the windows. Between rapid eyeblinks, Manteau made out a dim figure on a settee some five meters away. She flourished her gas gun in its direction, noting the boxed, rectangular object behind it. The object was propped at an angle between a fold-down writing desk and the cornucopia brackets of an empire couch. The dimensions looked right for the Vestipuccine. "*Le fantôme*, I presume," she said.

When the figure turned to Manteau, its shadowed face glimmered as if sharp with diamonds. "Everything sounds more civilized in French." The voice was male, British and preternaturally calm. He appeared dressed in a three piece suit—*appeared* as only its outlines were visible. The rest was semi-transparent, revealing the flowered back of the settee.

"You prefer another name?" Manteau took a tentative step forward. The *fantôme* seemed unfazed by the move. When she advanced another step, however, he held up a hand in warning. Hints of the inlaid carving on the panel behind his hand came through as fluid distortions. Manteau noted a bandage of blood-darkened gauze around his bicep. Perhaps Janvier had wounded the *fantôme* in more than his conceited imagination after all.

"I was a man once—before the incident that turned me into this...," the *fantôme* said. From what Manteau could discern in the low sepia light, he was tall and hard-featured with a full beard. "I was mostly known then as Boris Gumm. But I don't mind admitting: I'm a monster in a world new-made for monsters."

"What do you want with *La Q*?"

Gumm's voice turned keen. "Who are you to know?"

"Perhaps I can help. I have some expertise in the spiritual sciences, though I use them benignly. I already know of the artwork's usefulness as a conduit to some god of the Outer Dark..."

"The Mimirodat. That's what the Hun's called it. But I'm after something more—the creature's masters, the Overlords of the Jewel. I came close once before—"

"Cambrai."

"So you do know something."

In other circumstances, Manteau would have chided him for being the second man in nearly as many days to show surprise at her intelligence. "There's a survivor with me—a woman trained to manipulate *La Q*."

"From La Fratellanza, eh?" He gave the cult's name the force of a curse. "Those witches are damn persistent."

"I have no intention of letting her do it," she assured him. "But she was the only means available to track down the artwork."

"I won't surrender it." Gumm rose to his feet.

Manteau kept the gas gun level with his chest. "A truce then—until we can reason things out."

"The age of truces has passed." There was a glum weariness to his voice. He moved toward Manteau.

"Just so I understand," she said, retreating a step. "I take it by your injury that you killed the museum director and escaped with *La Q*."

Above all, she couldn't allow Gumm to touch her. She surmised that his ability to alter his body's density had allowed him to turn Janvier's mob captain—and Lammert—grotesque. Wounded in his corporeal state, Gumm had become intangible again, resuming his physical form only in Lammert's office. That would explain the curiously circumscribed bloodstains she'd found there.

Gumm continued his slow approach. "Not straightaway. The wound, you see ... I hid the painting in the walls of the office and came back for it after I'd recovered a bit."

"But not enough to try using *La Q.*" Manteau recognized too late the implications of the cut-up exercise and her *flânerie* ending at the Hotel Ibis Paris Montmartre. Both had pointed up an Egyptian element to the mystery. Manteau now understood it to be the museum's pyramidal roof. If she'd made this connection earlier, she might well have trapped Gumm upon his return to Lammert's office. "Why flee to Germany when you know the Nazis are after it? Who are you working for?"

"Technically, the former Kaiser. He funded this enterprise thinking to use the Vestipuccine to regain some of his lost power." A sardonic smile flickered across his face.

Manteau slowly backed toward the door. "Who told you about the artwork? How did you know where it would be?"

"Old friends within La Fratellanza—rival factions." The indulgent tone was gone. His face took on an ominous rigidity.

"I assume they're expecting it, too."

"I would already be translated out of this world if it weren't for this injury," Gumm said, increasing his pace. "I've been in my thirties for the past couple of decades, but still ... The struggle of living takes something out of you." He was only two meters away.

At that distance, the nature of Gumm's glittering wounds became evident. Manteau began to connect the incident in Cambrai, Gumm's abilities, the ineffectiveness of Noye's wards against ethereals ... "Are those Parmatmar crystals?"

Gumm's tone was dismissive. "Lovely, aren't they?"

The distinctive vibrational qualities of the crystals were known to

have extradimensional effects. If Gumm drew from their power, Manteau reasoned, then he didn't make himself invisible; rather, he faded
into another plane of existence. In his ghostly state, he literally straddled
two worlds. "Why tell me all this?" Manteau asked. She felt behind her
for the handle to the passageway door. He was nearly within an arm's
length. Sour panic rose in her throat.

"Because there's nothing you can do. You think *me* the ghost while
I'm looking right through you, girl."

"I see." She took a deep breath and fired. The oversized bullet passed
through Gumm and clanged against the carriage door at the opposite
end, releasing a smother of bluish smoke. Gumm's intangibility confirmed, Manteau charged after her shot. There was a moment of ghastly
cold then she was through him, racing the length of the car.

She made a few confident strides before a choking tug at the back of
her jacket collar tripped her up. She skittered on the carpet. The compartment door in front of her burst open and a plainclothes guard leapt
gun-first through the dissipating gas. A chill on the back of her neck
warned Manteau of Gumm's reach. She shrugged out of her jacket
while activating the cloak under her dress shirt. The cloak billowed
out on the instant. The transformative current sparked against Gumm's
hand. The carriage door behind Manteau crashed wide. She risked a
glance over her shoulder: Reba. "Shoot!" she urged above the racket
of the train.

Bullets ricocheted off the inelastic cloak to lodge in the mahogany
paneling or splinter the furniture. Just as Manteau hoped, the barrage
forced Gumm to go spectral. She deactivated the cloak's glider mode
and advanced on the pale, whiskery guard. If it weren't for her conscience, it would have been an easy matter to shoot him. The last of
the gas cloud had funneled through the open door and left him fully
exposed. She spun high over the Vestipuccine, deflecting the guard's
tentative shot with her cloak, then landed in a crouch and kicked his
legs out from under him. The guard tumbled onto the buffering plate.
Manteau grabbed for the door. He kicked it on her attempted slam and
fired again. She felt the seethe of gunpowder on her face. His next shot

reverberated in the shuttered door.

Manteau turned to glimpse the *fantôme* strongarming Reba through the far carriage door. Only his arms appeared corporeal. Reba's gun clattered to the floor then the two of them were on the buffering plate and out of sight. She started after them when two men emerged from the adjacent carriage. One brandished a Luger. The other toted an unfamiliar metal carapace with a hose and nozzle assembly. Without a word, the second man triggered a blast of scintillating ice in the direction Gumm had thrust Reba. There was a muted scream—who from, she couldn't say—followed by exasperated shouts in German from the interlopers. The ash-flecked wind from the open door might as well have sucked her heart out of her chest. That's all it takes—one breath-turn for everything to change.

The carriage door behind her clapped against the paneling. She rolled to the carpet, avoiding the guard's shot and, prone on her back, fired a gas canister into his outthrust chin. She heard indistinguishable hollering amid the wind and rhythmic train noise. She vaulted over the unconscious guard's body and onto the oversill plate. The pinprick of incipient tears made a blur of the wooded landscape. She blinked to clear her vision and then negotiate her way onto the plain-arch roof. There would be time enough for grief and self-doubt later; now, she had to plot a just revenge.

Chapter 19
The Devil's Party

After deliberating for a long while in a sweltry forward carriage, Janvier decided to find the Sturmbahnführer and face the consequences of his failure directly. A so-called Good Samaritan, believing Janvier an abusive husband in pursuit of his frightened spouse, had intervened in the chase, permitting Henriette to make good her escape. Janvier had scarcely managed to backtrack and re-board the train before its departure. Sure, he could slip away unnoticed at the next stop. But what then? How long before Wiegand sent some innocuous-looking agent to punish him? Janvier considered himself an honorable grafter. He would suffer his punishment—however severe it might be—straightaway and with eyes front.

A notice on the carriage door announced the passageway was closed. Janvier jerked his short-brimmed hat tight and turned the handle. A grimy wind surged around him. He bent his head against it and stepped onto the buffer plate to address the guard opposite. The guard nodded in recognition. Janvier remembered him from Wiegand's safehouse visit the other day. Telltale fragments of ice dissolved around the guard's feet. Janvier wondered if Manteau had already been dispatched—shattered somewhere against the crushed stones bordering the track, her disparate parts gradually deliquescing in the summer sun ... The guard held up a hand, indicating Janvier should wait while he ducked into the private car.

Janvier reconsidered his decision to seek out Wiegand. Why would he be kept outside unless they wanted a convenient means of disposing of his corpse? A dizzying emptiness threatened to unbalance him. He put a hand on the oversill rail for support. The tension he sensed at the fundament of things seemed to flare up and taunt him. A naïve boast from his youth returned, this time in a mocking tone: "I came into this world in blood and in blood I'll go." Wiegand's vile *Lebenden Eis* wouldn't even allow for that small measure of dignity.

The guard materialized from the carriage, followed by the Sturm-bahnfuhrer. Wiegand's lips wavered into a thin, self-satisfied smile. "Herr Janvier," he said. "How good of you to join us."

"I apologize for the delay. There were ... unexpected complications."

"Oh, yes." Wiegand gestured in the direction of his carriage. "Lost something, did you?"

Janvier bowed in his embarrassment. "She got rattled and ran off... Hard to tell what caused it. She's too crazy to be useful, I assure you. *Ce serait comme pisser dans un violon* (It would be like pissing in a violin)."

"*Folle (Crazy)*? More like '*C'est incroyable*' (It's incredible)."

"What makes you say that?" Janvier looked to the squinty-eyed guard then back to Wiegand. "I don't understand."

"Not to worry." Wiegand waved him over and pushed inside.

Janvier half-jumped the gap between passenger cars. The guard steadied him with an outstretched arm. Janvier nodded in thanks and brushed past.

Wiegand shut the carriage door behind him, saying, "She blundered into us, chittering away just as you described. No doubt drawn by the Vestipuccine."

A slender blonde was seated on the foremost edge of a scroll-armed couch. She wore a sleeved, V-neck dress cinched with a bow. One foot fidgeted above the boxed *objet d'art* secured between the chaise longue and the paneled wall opposite. She took no notice of Janvier; instead, she stared longingly at *La Q*'s container, keeping up a nonsensical pat-ter: "... waggled to a file, a raw, mattery law..."

Janvier understood the imposter's identity at once and marveled privately at the sheer audacity of her charade. He stooped to lock eyes with her like a chess rival. She gazed into some middle distance beyond him. Still looking into her eyes, eager for a reaction, he asked Wiegand, "Maybe she isn't so indispensable after all."

"That's up to my division scientists," Wiegand said. "We have our own seers and psychics, but if she's as attuned to the Vestipuccine as you say, she could be instrumental."

"Provided you can control her." Janvier straightened to his full height and turned to Wiegand. "You see how willful she can be ... "

"If you only knew how many we have broken—personalities much stronger than hers, I assure you. To paraphrase Schopenhauer—because I'm not sure I've got the quote exactly right—'For the world is Hell and men are at once its tormented souls and its devils.'" Wiegand motioned Janvier to take a seat in the club chair next to the couch. "We've cleaned up after you quite thoroughly today. First the *fantôme* then Henriette here."

"You encountered it?"

"Just outside the carriage. He was engaged in a struggle with some unknown woman, holding her above the tracks and only partially tangible. But the *Lebenden Eis* proved effective nonetheless. It forced him to vanish at least—along with the woman." He tapped his temple absently with his forefinger. "Most curious. The ice might be more insidious than I first thought. Perhaps it feeds on spiritual energy as much as flesh."

Janvier was disinclined to follow Wiegand's line of thought. Paradise, Hell, the *fantôme*, this *Lebenden Eis* parasite, it was all beyond his provincial interests. "Well, you have your painting..."

"Objet d'art," Wiegand said, smiling. "Don't fret. The rest of your payment will be deposited shortly after we reach Berlin."

"Am I to go with you?" Janvier failed to entirely suppress his apprehension. The mean streets of Paris had never seemed so comforting a prospect.

"No, that won't be necessary. You can change trains at the next station. We have someone else to look after the girl—an expert in the arcane sciences. It's my understanding he was once a popular stage magician. I suspect he'll keep her well in check."

Relieved he'd soon be returning home, Janvier leaned back in his leather chair and nodded to himself. He was so absorbed in thoughts of good fortune he missed the brief, strangled break in Manteau's otherwise continuous babbling.

Chapter 20
Anima & Animus

The Nazis disembarked at the Düsseldorf Hauptbahnhof and loaded the Vestipuccine into a flatbed truck. Before Janvier broke away from the group to purchase his return ticket, he approached Manteau with a self-satisfied grin and whispered, "Best of luck preserving your *secret.*"

"And you, your manhood," she murmured between jags of absurdity.

Janvier flushed with gall. "You've been talking that applesauce for too long. But it makes no matter. I am, after all, walking away from this and at a profit." He cut his eyes at Manteau then turned on his heel, intent on pizzling a bottomless bottle of Calvados in his train compartment.

Manteau practically choked on his undeserved air of low-key genius. "*À hauteur des Nazis* (to the tune of the Nazis)," she said to his back.

The phrase caught the attention of Wiegand, who was in a huddle with his men on the platform. He tilted his head in her direction.

"Die not," Manteau added, shrinking back into her guise as Henriette. "As virtuous whispers pass…"

On Wiegand's orders, one of his men gripped her by the elbow and directed her to the station's exit.

Less than twenty minutes later, the Nazi contingent rolled onto the tarmac of the Düsseldorf Airport. Manteau was discharged from the back of the flatbed by a humorless young soldier in plainclothes and escorted toward a small passenger plane. The truck sped Wiegand and his remaining men across the runway in the direction of a fully-outfitted German bomber. Based on the plane's distinctive glassed-in nosecone,

Manteau recognized it as a Heinkel HE III E-I.The make was notorious
for its use in the Spanish Civil War. She deliberated whether to throw
a tantrum at her separation from *La Q*. But her guard's stern expression and tight hold on her arm encouraged caution. His rigid bearing
suggested a youth intent on impressing his superiors with his martial
efficiency. Any show of defiance would likely be met by a cuffing. The
truck churned through the dusty grass between runways and barreled
away.

The quickened beating of her heart gave her voice an eerie vibrato.
"To tell-l-l a mean-n-ning, a vast ebb-b and flow-ow..." Events had
gone helter-skelter: her disastrous encounter with the *fantôme*, Janvier's
smug exit, the Vestipuccine secreted away, Reba gone, dead or disappeared...The feeling was reminiscent of what she'd felt on first learning of Lucia's death. Before viewing the body in the morgue, it had
seemed her twin's demise was only an oppressive muddle in her head,
a psychological quirk that might be fixed through some breakthrough
experience. It was a uniquely surrealist way of thinking: to believe everything an accident—circumstances and personalities alike—and to
sense how easily it could all be different, if only... what? Surrealism was
her means to get at the animating force of accident, to infuse her life
with its rhythms until it seemed a natural condition. This far into her
career as a vigilante-detective, however, she had yet to penetrate the
mystery to its essence. It was as though the world were an *objet d'art* cast
in low bas relief but deep with fictive space.

The plane waiting for her was a peanut-colored Junkers W.34hi, a
light transport and communications aircraft with a corrugated, all-metal
skin and an air cooled radial engine. On an international case a couple
of years back, she'd co-piloted a Junkers W 33g used by the Swedish Air
Force as an air ambulance. Operating the rudder mechanism required
the coordinated efforts of two pilots. Even if she could somehow gain
control of the cockpit, she would be hard-put to fly solo.

With one hand on the small of her back, the guard urged her to
take the ramp stairs. She glanced back from the third step. His dark,
tight-curled hair was shellacked to a helmet-like stiffness. She was well-

positioned to kick him in the throat and make her escape through the airport. But what then? No, she thought. It was better to bide her time for an opportunity to recover or, if necessary, destroy *La Q*. The Nazis believed her to be Henriette. They would put her in proximity to the artwork in short order. She would just have to figure out how to get it out of Berlin undetected.

A uniformed soldier at the communications console adjacent to the shuttered cockpit stood at her entrance and gestured for her to take a seat in the cargo bay. She turned to find Noye squinting at her from his jumpseat. He made for a sad, sullen figure. Bereft of a hat, his patch-bald head appeared disproportionately small for his gangly frame. His thin hair was a raveling mess. The collar of his overlarge, double-breasted topcoat was twisted up on one side. A red hyphenated welt marred his left cheek.

Manteau kept up a quiet palaver as she settled across from him:"… an inch or what to these pages, all lodged iron bad, or they say too late …" The guard buckled her in, tested the harness with a tug then withdrew to talk with his counterpart. Their conversation was lost to the prop noise. Manteau pretended to find something interesting about the rear of the cargo hold to avoid meeting Noye's studied gaze. She'd always been disguised in their meetings but she worried he might deduce her identity before she determined if he were trustworthy enough to reveal herself. The welt below his left eye and his disheveled appearance suggested he'd been brought along unwillingly; still, his alleged thievery from the museum raised doubts she couldn't easily dismiss. She scanned the compartment in vain for his luggage. Her stomach clenched at the thought of the Nazis taking possession of his stolen artifacts, especially the Mace of Ntyr. On delivering it to the museum for further study, Lancer had warned her of its destructive potential.

The guard bounded off the plane, leaving the soldier in field gray to look after Manteau and Noye. The soldier closed the cabin door, resumed his position at the communications console and informed the pilots of their readiness via headset mic. He was fresh-faced and lightly freckled, particularly around the nub of his aquiline nose. The pink accent on his shoulder board identified him as a member of the motor pool. Under other circumstances, Manteau would have considered the paltry level of security an insult.

As the plane gathered momentum, Noye reached toward Manteau and said, "I hope your visions, however confusing, are a comfort." He offered a troubled smile. A clotted split darkened his lower lip.

Manteau canted her head toward the soldier. He was partly turned away, manipulating the horizontal wheel that aimed the loop antenna above the cab. She decided to chance Noye's cooperation and leaned forward, confident the soldier couldn't possibly hear them above the din of the plane's engine. "*Je jalouse le sort des plus vils animaux,*" she said, quoting Baudelaire.

Noye's unblemished eye widened with incredulity. "*Mon dieu.*"

"Close." She continued to mouth nonsense in the event the soldier turned her way.

"A surprise worthy of Remmelin—and more handsome." He ran a finger along his ridged facial wound. "As you might have surmised, the German dogs kidnapped me."

"For what purpose? Why bring you to Berlin?"

"They suspected me of aiding the *fantôme* and, in questioning me, discovered my ties to Crowley, Blavatsky et al. They're convinced I can be of help in vetting their psychics."

Manteau waited for Noye to volunteer something about the missing museum artifacts. His silence on the topic rankled. But she thought it prudent for the moment to pretend ignorance. "We'll never make it out of Berlin, *mon ami.*"

"My feeling exactly."

"I can fly this plane—with your help. We just need to dispatch the guard and then take the cockpit."

"Why not simply force the pilots to turn back?"

"Because I won't leave the Vestipuccine to the Nazis."

"You realize this plane has no guns? Other than the guard's that is…" His untidied brows frowned in disbelief. "You don't mean to ram them?"

"Only as a last resort. My hope is to force a landing."

"By ramming them..."

"Not straight-on," Manteau protested.

"But still..." He underscored his meaning by smacking his palms together.

"What's another close call?"

"You never know at my age if one more will put you over God's designated limit."

Manteau ran her tongue over her lips. A near-accident from her childhood in Guéret came to mind. Often slowed by tractors and other heavy farm equipment, many regular drivers through the area had a terrible predilection for passing. On this occasion, a mis-timed attempt by a gentleman in a Delage touring car forced her father to swerve their steam tractor into a lavender field. The shock of the incident prompted her to consider how, at any moment, a car from the opposing lane could cross over and... For the remainder of the trip, she counted out the seconds it took for each approaching vehicle to pass safely, all the while half-expecting a fatal crackup. The episode was one of her first visceral lessons in the negative capability of life. "It's either this or Berlin," she told Noye. "Is the saucer sable or skunk?"

"Damn your insidious logic."

"I wish my aide-de-camp could have heard you say that."

Noye tendered a feeble grin. "Should we start with a dusting of salt?"

"I can work with that. Or woofle dust if it's not too caustic," Manteau joked.

The magician unbuckled himself and stood uneasily, one hand braced against the bulkhead and the other in his right trouser pocket.

Manteau returned to her reserved mien and absurd babbling: "Chose a better warren of shame, caged in the flying belltower..."

From his position adjacent to the cockpit door, the guard waved for Noye to be seated. "*Du setzt dich hin.*"

Noye cocked his head to signal he either couldn't hear or understand the order.

The guard got to his feet and hurried toward Noye, repeating his instruction. To make himself clear, he put a firm hand on the magician's shoulder and guided Noye toward his seat. This motion put the guard's back to Manteau. She used the distraction to hike her dress to the hip and withdraw the collapsible sword sheathed along the inside of her thigh. Noye fingersnapped a pinch of salt into the guard's face. The German squawked and flailed his arms, unseeing. Manteau flicked her sword against the back of the guard's knees and, when he spun in her direction, Noye relieved him of his Luger. Manteau threw off her safety harness and swept the guard's legs out from under him. He tumbled to the floor of the cargo bay with a vehement cry. Manteau gave Noye an approving look as the guard toppled over. Noye's eyes were watery and abstracted. The barrel of the Luger swiveled toward her. Sudden hurt lines struck the gap between Noye's brows. He squeezed the trigger.

Chapter 21
The Sky Between Two Worlds

A frantic heartbeat passed before Noye realized the gun's safety was on. Enough time for Manteau to whipstrike the back of his gun hand with the flat of her sword then kick him against the bulkhead. Noye jerked against the corrugated metal. His Adam's apple jumped in his gaunt throat.

Manteau put a swordpoint to it, her chest heaving in outrage. "Back." She stepped forward, compelling him to sit and kicked the dropped pistol toward the cockpit. The Luger scudded under the communications console. "You were never much of an escape artist."

Rubbing one reddened eye, the guard jerked himself up and reached for the Hitler Youth knife at his belt. "*Was denkst du eigentlich, was Du hier machst* (What do you think you're doing)?"

"*Ich könnte das gleiche von Ihnen fragen* (I could ask the same of you)." Manteau whickered the air around the knife with her rapier-like weapon. "Don't try me," she added. "I'll cut you through to the *morceaux ronds*." She relished the off-beat reference to the tender parts of a jugged hare. Though she'd surmised the guard didn't know much, if any, French, her menacing flourishes ensured her meaning wasn't lost.

The guard raised his hands chest-high, blinking hard to regain his sight. The freckles on his face dimmed against his flushed skin. "Now that's settled," Manteau said, "tie this one up." She pointed to the looped cargo rope depending from the bulkhead. When the guard started to protest, Manteau sheared the scabbarded knife from his belt. He glanced down at her blade and, with a tight, protesting grimace, set about his task.

Manteau fixed her eyes on Noye. "He was born into this madness. What's your excuse?"

"It's not how it seems."

"Oh, and how is that?"

Small spasms of regret surged across Noye's face. "I never meant to hurt anyone."

"You mean, until just now."

He conceded her point with a curt, grim-lipped nod.

The guard approached with the coiled rope in hand. "Feet first around the ankles," Manteau instructed. "Then hands, bound at the wrist in his lap. The rope should be tight between the two."

"Trussing me up like an animal," Noye said. The guard kneeled to grab his feet.

"You should be so innocent of guile." She couldn't chase from her mind the memory of his endearing laugh, how he poked his teeth out, head bouncing like an aged tortoise. On reflection, his laughter seemed tinged with a secret disdain. The thought led to another, more horrible idea: "You arranged for the heist, yes? Pretending to be Lammert?"

Noye shrunk into his out-of-fashion suit. A hangdog sweat put a shine on his balding head. "You've no idea what it is to grow old, your natural capacities waning, the promise of youth still unrealized, never to be revived." He slumped in his seat as if the confession had drained him. Spidery veins showed on his lowered eyelids. "I deserved more from this life. I saw and suffered celebrity up-close. Fakers like Crowley, that drunkard Remmelin…What marked me out from them except that Janus-faced bitch, chance?"

"So this was your opportunity…" *Jealousy. Greed. A false sense of entitlement.* The sheer ordinariness of Noye's motive nauseated her. More proof, as if she needed any, of the innate unknowability of people.

"I thought to retire in some dignity. This—the gun, Lammert's death—I regret them as unforeseen consequences."

"Truthfully, why *are* you here?"

Noye risked meeting her eyes again. His pupils were like gray beach glass. "That part—my explanation—was wholly true. The Nazis have no idea who I am, *enfin*, as part of the heist. I communicated with the Sturmbahnfuhrer only by telephone so I could disguise my voice, affecting Lammert's nervous tics for good measure."

"A bravo performance, no doubt." She labored to tamp down her anger at the hint of pride in Noye's tone. "Did it extend to a meeting with Vestipuccine?"

"I already told you, no."

"Then how did you learn of Lammert's acquisition of La Q?"

"An unknown party. A man, I think. At least it sounded like a man on the phone. He not only informed me of the deal, but told me of the Germans' interest in it. Then—later—Lammert came to me about his security concerns."

"Are you pleading entrapment here?" The question prolonged the strains of the moment.

"No," he said at last.

"What about the artifacts you took from the museum? The Lamassu Box, the Mace of Ntyr…?"

"Presumably on the other plane." His nostrils quivered in apprehension.

Manteau poked the guard in the back with the tip of her blade to get his attention. He regarded her over his shoulder. "We're on a parallel course with the bomber?" she asked.

He confirmed it with a grunt then finished knotting the rope around Noye's hands.

"For your own sake, Manteau, don't engage it." Noye narrowed his look, turning shrewd. "Divert this plane wherever you'd like. I'll be glad to help in exchange for, say, letting me disappear. Turning me in won't change anything. Lammert will remain dead, the world will continue to exhaust itself in futile conflicts…"

"It seems in all your travails, monsieur, you misplaced your sense of honor. Or perhaps you never had any to begin with." Manteau had done terrible things as Mayen, the head of the Unione Corse, but everything had been in accord with the mob's perverted honor code. She understood how a single, apparently victimless betrayal could produce a succession of them until the point of the original act was lost. Honor might be the only principle she held above the values of surrealism.

"By what right do you have to take this risk? On whose authority?" Noye asked, his voice thickened by the fear lodged in his throat.

"The same as all homicide detectives—the authority of the dead."

Noye lurched against his restraints and, inclining his head toward the cockpit, shouted above the engine noise, "*Schließen Sie die Tür! Es ist eine Falle!*" Following this outburst, the guard joined in. He cupped his hands around his mouth and called on the pilots by name to secure the door.

Manteau raced for the front of the plane and reached the cockpit in time to hear the door's striking locks slide into place. "*Flûte de zut,*" she groused. She glanced back to see the guard retrieve the Hitler Youth knife. She fell into a crouch, spotted the Luger under the communications console, and thrust her sword through its trigger guard to flip it out and into her free hand. The guard squared up and aimed the knife at her. Ignoring the implicit challenge, she picked up the gun. The time for deliberation was over. She assumed her full height and fired point blank at the cockpit door's small rectangular window. Shards of glass skittered across the metal floor. "*Der Pilot: geh raus!*" she ordered. "*Kein Radio.*"

There followed the indistinct but unmistakable sounds of an argument. Manteau signaled her impatience by banging the butt of the Luger against the door. A wild shot from the cockpit ricocheted along the bulkhead opposite. It seemed to Manteau that the guard and pilots were conspiring against her self-appointed end. She had claimed it as her purpose and refused to brook any further interference. It was hers now, right or wrong. She would go into the maw of death as far as the situation demanded.

Silence came back to her from the cockpit. The rhythmic grinding of the plane's engine shuddered up through her feet. It had been an awful year—a non-stop series of trials across identities and against the terrible prospect of war. Losing Reba was only the latest—and worst—of what she'd endured. Now, it looked as though the Nazis would soon have access to an unthinkable supernatural power. Because of her failure. The guard flicked his knife in warning, undeterred by her advantage in arms. The provocation struck Manteau as emblematic of Germans under the Reich—a people unaware they'd been vampired into a guided recklessness, mistaking it for freedom. Fascism was the antithesis of surrealism. There's nothing left to chance, she thought, when there's nothing left to choose. She exchanged her weapons in the air so the gun was in her best shooting hand. "Perhaps you didn't get that," she said to the pilot. "Let me try a different language." Then, without word or warning, she blasted a freckle-cluster just under the brim of the guard's field cap. The bloodspatter made an abstract of the bulkhead.

Noyc twitched at the unexpected violence.

Manteau's voice dropped to a place of command in her throat. "Pilot! That was *Herr Soldat!* You're next unless you disarm and open the door!"

After some heated, under-the-breath discussion, two service pistols dropped through the shattered observation window. Manteau claimed them with the aid of her sword, careful to stay out of the line of sight afforded by the window. "*Kommen jetzt,*" she said. The door clanged wide and the pilot crawled out, his face upturned in dread. He was broad-faced and thick through the shoulders.

"*Aufstehen und binden Sie sich, mit den Knöcheln beginnen,*" Manteau said, motioning the pilot up with her sword. She was about to say more when there was a rippling burst of ethereal light and Reba collapsed to the floor atop the boxed Vestipuccine, her naked profile pulsing in and out of solidity.

Chapter 22
Das Gift

"*Crotte de bique et bonbon noir!*" Noye exclaimed.

Manteau's heart faltered. She rushed to Reba's prone form and, setting the blade aside, kneeled to assess her condition.

The pilot muttered an unintelligible curse.

Manteau leveled her gun at him. "Never mind this... Back to the cockpit and stay on course until I say differently."

"Aid an enemy? That would be like signing my own death notice," the pilot said.

"Continue to cooperate and I guarantee you a chance." She twirled the pistol around her index finger. "Otherwise, we'll chalk it up to wartime tension."

Reba flushed with a sickly alien candescence. An anguish swept through Manteau keen enough to prompt a ragged insuck of breath. She traced the air around Reba's bare shoulder, afraid to touch her. Reba alternated between a filmy transparency and a glassine firmness. In that state, there was no telling what direct contact might yield. They could end up conjoined twins or split into fanciful Miró-like blobs. The Vestipuccine, however, seemed wholly stable.

Manteau bent to Reba's ear. She recalled Reba whispering her to sleep—bucolic childhood memories, comical dreams, thought experiments out of Wonderland..."Reba, *ça va?* (Are you okay)?" She repeated the question in English.

Reba's eyelids flickered open. "I've done—done more damage to myself..." A hitch in her throat forced a pause. "...hard-snapping to

'Little Brown Jug.'"

"I'm sorry. I'm so sorry. I thought you were dead."Though Manteau resisted the impulse to kiss her ear, the nearness of it dried her mouth.

"I wouldn't let that keep me from you."

Manteau gaped at the curve of Reba's neck. Her natural colors swirled into inky existence only to drift and evanesce. "What happened?" Manteau asked. "I lost sight of you when Gumm—the *fantôme*—dragged you outside the train car."

"That French for bastard—the *fantôme*?" She offered a lopsided smile. "He had me out over the tracks, you know, by the throat, when these Germans showed and shot him with—I don't know—ice? It looked like ice. I was already ghosted up by then. It was like my atoms were coming apart. But the ice—he froze up and then disappeared—and me along with him. I can't describe where we were. But it was like seeing the world from the inside-out."

"Those crystals in his skin—they give him the power to move between realities ... He's not really invisible so much as ... dispersed."

Reba struggled to raise her head from the Vestipuccine. "Guess I'm the same now. I could see you—anyone really—whoever I put my mind to. He was hurting, still covered in that ice or whatever and I thought to get the art for you so you could get away, go back home. I just ... I don't know how set it is. Everything I touch ... " She shrugged from her hunched over position. "I don't know how to control it."

Hypnotized for obsession or not, Reba had a lot of admirable jazz in her. Manteau felt the pressure of tears behind her eyes. "That was a brave gesture."

"It sapped me something awful." Reba arched her back and came dangerously close to grazing Manteau with an elbow. "Don't touch," she scolded herself.

"Reba," Manteau said, "I'm ... I have to ask: Can you transpose yourself one more time—with me and the artwork? If not, we'll have to risk turning around and bringing that bomber down on us."

"I don't know," Reba said, getting uneasily to her feet. She started at the sight of the guard, the blood pooling around the uncapped body. "Maybe if I rest awhile. I don't know. You or this box, but not both, no, sure-God no."

"You can't mean to abandon me," Noye said to Manteau's back.

She turned to face him. "Like you meant to abandon me—disappearing to Switzerland or who-knows-where? And even if we manage to escape, you'll have still delivered those artifacts to the Nazis." She wondered why, at Noye's advanced age, he hadn't grasped the fact that even the most innocuous-seeming decisions can have far-reaching—even fatal—consequences. Death wasn't merely an historical phenomenon; it was personal and particular. "Perhaps I should go back to my original plan."

"What plan was that?" Reba asked.

"Flying into the bomber," Noye said, making nervous motions with his bound hands.

Manteau qualified Noye's answer: "Strategically—to take out the rudder with our landing gear. I'm not completely suicidal."

"Is that you," Noye said, "or your fake hallucinations talking?"

"For sentimental reasons, I would hate to put a bullet in your head."

Noye struggled to keep the hostility out of his voice. "The feeling is mutual."

A thin white light bled into the edge of Manteau's vision then flared into a broken man-shape. Gumm—or, at least, parts of him—had fused with the Vestipuccine through the artwork's packing material. Manteau was reminded of the deconstructed mannequin in Hans Bellmer's *La Poupée*: legs splayed, arms discontinuous, head protruding from the rib-cage. A curious frost limned these fragments.

"Christ, no," Reba let out.

Manteau tested Gumm's oscillating form with the tip of her sword. It passed through him to no effect. He was completely spectral. "Even now—like this—he's trying to get to the Mimirodat."

"The what?" Reba asked, her downcast eyes on Gumm. His disparate parts alternately pushed and pulled in slow-motion cycles.

"Later." Manteau shot Noye a grave look. "I have to destroy it, right? To make sure?" She didn't wait for his muted response. She knew the answer before asking the question. "Reba," she said, putting a hand out, palm up, in a feeling gesture. "You have to go now."

"But I just got here."

"You understand what I'm about to do ... There's no sense in both of us dying."

"Sure. But you can parachute, can't you? Both of you, the pilots ... Then I'll—what did you call it?—transpose myself."

"She's right," Noye chimed.

"I did the Parachute Jump at the New York World's Fair," Reba added. "I actually wished it lasted longer, but what do you expect for forty cents?"

Manteau looked out the porthole in hopes of getting their bearings. The roseate sky brimmed with occluding clouds. She felt the familiar pull of dreams. It came to her in summery waves. This—the clouds— might be as close as she would ever get to Lucia in life. "I've no idea where we are, but it's a chance." She slashed the ropes binding Noye's feet. "Hold out your hands," she said. Before Noye could comply, the plane dipped precipitously. Manteau widened her stance to maintain her balance and angled her head toward the cockpit. "*Was machst du gerade?*"

Over the cabin intercom, the pilot said, "The Sturmbahnfuhrer has been alerted to your actions. We've been ordered to land in the next available pasture or open stretch. Shoot us if you must. Either way, we're touching down." This last was made somewhat hard to discern by an interjection from the co-pilot, who was apparently responding to something over the plane's radio.

"That's it then," Manteau said. She looked sternly into the shadow-pits of Noye's eyes and freed him with a double sweep of her blade. "Get a chute and disappear."

Noye ducked his head in shame and staggered off.

"What are you thinking now?" Reba asked.

"This time, it *is* a collision." Manteau collapsed her sword with the touch of a recessed button then tucked it into the sash at her waist. She took up the guns she'd taken from the pilots and held them out by the barrels. "Can you hold these?"

Reba reached out experimentally, fingers coalescing into flesh and gripped the pistols. "Guess I'm getting the hang of it." Manteau risked brushing her fingertips with her own.

Noye hastened to find the ripcord on the round silk chute pack.

Manteau jerked her head toward him. "If he does anything untoward, shoot him," she told Reba. "Or close your hand around his dust-choked heart."

Reba smiled unevenly and moved to cover him.

Manteau strode to the cockpit, gun arm outstretched. The pilot turned his bulgy face to her. The barrel of the Luger closed in on his cheek. "Get out and you're welcome to a parachute," Manteau said.

He shook his head emphatically and made to turn back to his controls when Manteau ended any further possibilities for contempt. The shot rang out interminably in the tight space. The cockpit dripped blood and bits of gray matter. "Completely avoidable," she mused to the co-pilot. "I'll offer you the same bargain."

The co-pilot looked askance at his dead comrade. "I have family—a baby, three months old," he mumbled.

"Then we understand each other," Manteau said. "Dump him in the cabin and go on."

The wary co-pilot removed his radio headset, locked the three-spoked control wheel and did as Manteau asked, leaving the pilot's body splayed behind the communications console. Manteau patted him on the shoulder. "Show the Frenchman how to use the chute, will you? And mind the phantoms, especially the one with the guns." She looked back at Reba, who continued to hold the Lugers on Noye. "Hurry them out, will you?" Manteau shouted over the thrumming engine. "And when they're gone, come up here. I'll need a co-pilot for full maneuverability."

Reba nodded, her lips a crease of worry. The *fantôme* had nearly vanished into the Vestipuccine. Manteau could see his lips moving but couldn't tell if he was actually speaking or only mouthing speech out of some diminishing reflex; regardless, she had to act quickly in the event Gumm had actually mustered enough strength to use *La Q* to connect to the Mimirodat's free-floating consciousness. She snugged into the pilot's seat and placed the bloodied headset over her mussed blonde hair. A lone ringlet draped across her forehead. The seat's leather padding was redolent of man-sweat. The radio crackled: "...*im Anflug? Nach unseren Radar—*"

"Put the Sturmbahnfuhrer on," Manteau said into the mic, prompting a spate of German invective too rapid for her to parse. "I'll wait but time is running out." She wiped blood from the direction finder with her fingertips then wrapped her crimsoned hand around the quad throttle. The canopy revealed the first inkling of stars. She pictured the Mimirodat's discharged energies orbiting the Earth like an invisible layer of atmosphere, not unlike the 'ethereal germs' the pre-Socratic Greek Anaxagoras thought were responsible for life itself. The image tempted her to vent the overhead section. Perhaps a high dose of alien radiation would give her the supernatural power to survive this situation.

"Altitude?" asked the co-pilot from behind her right shoulder. "We should be under 4,600 meters for a jump."

Manteau consulted the altimeter gauge on the co-pilot's side of the center console. "We're at 3,980 or thereabouts. I'll bring us down a bit lower." She plunged the aircraft into the immediate scud. The canopy darkened in the murk. "Tell me when we're over a viable landing zone." A low blush of sun rayed between the thinner clouds below.

The co-pilot peered out from one of the starboard windows. "Steer to port about twenty degrees. That will bring us over farmland."

Manteau maneuvered to put her right foot on the co-pilot's rudder pedal bar. She arched her toes to execute the course change. "Where are we? Can you tell?"

He shrugged. "Lichtenau?"

"Whenever you're ready ..."

"Almost." The co-pilot unlatched the cabin door. There was a slight depressurization as the airstream whipped around the cabin.

Manteau turned to see the co-pilot position himself behind a bent and tottering Noye and clasp his arms around the old man's chest. He gave a quick thumb's up and pushed into the open sky. Intertwined, the men flitted away and behind. Then the *ch-chak-chak-chak* of machine gun fire rent the air and Reba dropped her pistols to slam the door shut.

"Whoever you are," came Wiegand's staticky voice in Manteau's ears, "your run of luck is over." He chuckled as if surveying her useless resistance from the moon. "Look to starboard."

She shifted her gaze as the German bomber pulled level with her.

The cockpit crew's silhouettes looked like tin cutouts. She wondered which one was Wiegand. The dorsal gun swiveled in her direction. "We'll lead the way to Berlin," Wiegand said. With a teasing wing-waggle, the bomber veered northwesterly. Manteau adjusted the rudder pedal bar on her side of the console to follow. "Reba?" she called over the intercom. "You ready?"

At the entrance to the cockpit, fully intangible again, Reba asked, "Could you tell...? Did they make it?" Her voice was a trembly croak.

Manteau shook her head then said into the headset mic, "I need assurances. The artwork for my life."

"What about the ghost?" Wiegand asked. "*Est-elle déjà partie* (Has she already gone)?"

Reba settled into the co-pilot's seat, dismayed by the coagulating blood on the console.

"*Elle ne fera pas partie de ça* (She'll be no party to this)."

"A pity. She's an exquisite *Nacht Kreatur* (night creature)."

"*Nacht oder nackt* (night or nude)?" Manteau asked. She formed on the bomber, edging closer and closer...

"You do have a way with words, Manteau," Wiegand said. "Janvier mentioned your involvement. I just didn't imagine you would be so brazen...Tell me: Was he a willing player in your deception?"

"We both know he isn't clever enough for that."

"He's through—gone," Reba said, hiking a thumb in the direction of the *fantôme*. "He was talking crazy about how thin the world seemed..."

"Janvier has—or had—his uses," answered Wiegand via radio.

"Do we have a bargain, Sturmbahnfuhrer?" Manteau brought the Junkers' wingtip within several meters of the bomber.

"*Ja,* the Vestipuccine in exchange for safe passage."

The bomber's pilot cut in: "*Donnerwetter!* Ease back, back, put some space between us."

"Reba," Manteau said, "if you truly care, please—"

"I can do it," Reba said. "For the both of us..."

Manteau's world narrowed to this environ of riveted metal, Reba at her side, an emphatic profile in milk-glass. Manteau had grieved over so many, burying so much love she had left scarcely any for herself until...

"Ready?"

Reba let out a philosophical sigh. A slight dimple in her cheek came and went. She leaned across the control column, eyes gleaming. The ticking seconds drafted contingency into history. "Don't you know, Wiegand?" Manteau said, preparing to meet Reba's parted lips. "You can't get to paradise without dying." Her vision blurred into shimmering rainbow streaks as she passed through her lover into a viscid reality. It was a cooling compaction of flesh and etheric energy. With the last of her bunched anger, she cranked the control wheel, spinning the plane into a dream of falling. The sudden acceleration exacerbated the sense that her perceptions were separate and apart from her body. Some lines from Nerval occurred to her as the distant ground rolled away: None but the eagle—woe! woe to us all! / Can face the Sun and Glory with impunity. The sky was subsumed by kaleidoscopic earth—browns and greens and arterials—and then by the steel gray of the bomber. The Heinkel's dorsal machine gun blister loomed less than a meter below the canopy, chalky airtight but fragile, oh so fragile—dim, and below the canopy

Epilogue
The Other Side of the Glass

Reba surveyed the Mediterranean surf from the terraced edge of Lina's Marseille estate. The incoming tide lapped the pebbled beach in soothing wavelets. She was tangible but transparent this afternoon and gleaming like a soap bubble in the August sun. There was no need for Lina to imbue her with dreamed strangeness anymore. "What kind of boat did you say?"

"It's not so much a boat," Lina said, "as an amphibious vehicle—like a submarine with tank treads." She sipped a *citron pressé* from a highball glass frosted in the icebox, marveling again at Reba's nakedness, no less statuesque for being ethereal.

"You really think he'll be able to cure me?" Reba's voice was tight with emotion.

Lina's heart labored in sympathy with her plight. Images of Gumm's deconstructed body haunted them both. She pretended insouciance. "We'll make the pages of *La Vie Parisienne* either way."

"I'd rather stay here and help you recover those artifacts."

"We don't even know if they survived the crash. As I told you, Henriette claims *La Q* was destroyed. She can't sense it at least. But everything else …" Henriette had been recovered in Brussels by the Belgian police and summarily returned to Vaucluse asylum for treatment. Manteau had visited her in disguise a few days ago. She'd left penitent but cheered by early signs of improvement in the soundness and clarity of Henriette's speech. As for Gumm, Lina preferred to think he shared the fate of Louis xiv in Mercier's futuristic novel, *L'An 2440, rêve s'il en fut jamais:* a remorseful spirit forced to haunt the locus of his misused power. She gentled the small of Reba's back as they looked out at the ocean. The ectoplasm was firm and cool to the touch. "Paul is your best chance for a full recovery. He and the others at Integrand General will take good care of you."

"Not like you do." A tearful heat brightened Reba's eyes.

"We'd have other problems in that case (*dans ce cas*)."

Solange stepped off the backyard deck and joined them on the grass. She had a small slip of paper in one hand. The rigid set of her jaw pre-saged unwelcome news.

"What is it?" Lina asked.

"*Le cas, la cause ...*" Solange handed her a visiting card embossed with an unfamiliar geometric symbol. "It was in an envelope in the letter box, though not sent by post."

Le Noble
Menteur

Lina turned the card over to find a handwritten declaration of purpose: *Leading artist of cultural arson.* She was convinced it was from Reba's half-remembered hypnotist. She suspected this same mysterious personage had met Vestipuccine in the Jardin des Tuileries and contacted Noye about *La* Q. The card was his way of making introductions and at once, alerting Manteau that her identity was no secret. Her pulse raced at the thought of this much-dreaded breach. Who could possibly know? Sure-ly not Janvier. Nor Wiegand, wrecked yet somehow alive. She brushed a stray ringlet from her cheek. "What do you think?" she asked Solange.

"You have a moth-like talent for trouble."

"A visiting card in an envelope used to be a social snub," Lina said.

"It meant you discouraged a visit." She flipped the card back to front and back again. Her breathing assumed an even rasp. The card made The Noble Liar a presence out of absence. Three had become four: the enigmatic mask; her secretary/apprentice; her lover, the ghost; and this new Devil provocateur.

"What is it?" Reba asked. "Someone challenge you to a duel?" When she turned in the sun, the light on her back prismed throughout her chest.

"Not in the traditional sense," Lina said.

"Of course not."

Solange admonished her childhood friend with a dark look. "But you can't think of a better way to go …"

"Perhaps lightning," Lina said, casting a sidelong smile at Reba. "No simple flame for this moth." She declined to tell the American that the French describe 'love at first sight' as a lightning bolt. Perhaps she would explain it later. For the moment, she relished the taste of the secret in her mouth.